Landing

Also by Emma Donoghue

Emma Donoghue

Landing

HARCOURT, INC.

Orlando   Austin   New York   San Diego   Toronto   London

www.HarcourtBooks.com

Portions of "Home Base" were previously published in *No Margins,* edited
by Nairne Holtz and Catherine Lake, Insomniac Press, Toronto, 2006.

Library of Congress Cataloging-in-Publication Data
Donoghue, Emma, 1969–
Landing/Emma Donoghue.
p. cm.
1. Long-distance relationships—Fiction. 2. Lesbians—Fiction.
3. Flight attendants—Fiction. 4. Women archivists—Fiction.
5. Dublin (Ireland)—Fiction. 6. Ontario—Fiction. I. Title.
PR6054.O547L36 2007
823'.914—dc22 2006025375
ISBN 978-0-15-101297-8

Text set in Adobe Garamond
Designed by Linda Lockowitz

Printed in the United States of America
First edition

K J I H G F E D C B A

For Chris,
worth any journey.

Contents

Note

Ireland, Ontario, occupies the same spot on the map as the real Dublin, Ontario, but is in all other respects fictional. Likewise, the Irish airline for which one of my protagonists works is entirely imaginary.

Landing

New Year's Eve

DISORIENTATION (from French, *désorienter*,
to turn from the east).
(1) Loss of one's sense of position or direction.
(2) Mental confusion.

Later on, Jude Turner would look back on December thirty-first as the last morning her life had been firm, graspable, all in one piece.

She'd been sleeping naked and dreamless. She woke at six, as always, in the house in Ireland, Ontario, where she'd been born; she didn't own an alarm clock. In her old robe she gave her narrow face the briefest of glances in the mirror as she splashed it with cold water, damped down her hair, reached for her black rectangular glasses. The third and eighth stairs groaned under her feet, and the stove was almost out; she wedged logs into the bed of flushed ash. She drank her coffee black from a blue mug she'd made in second grade.

As Jude drew on her second cigarette it was beginning to get light. She watched the backyard through a portcullis of two-foot icicles: Were those fresh raccoon tracks? Soon she'd shovel the driveway, then the Petersons' next door. The neighbour on the other side was Bub, a cryptic turkey plucker with a huge mustache. Usually her mother would be down by now, hair in curlers, but since Boxing Day, Rachel Turner had been away at her sister's in England. The silence trickled like oil into Jude's ears.

She'd walk the three blocks to the museum by seven so she could get some real work done before anyone called, or dropped by to donate a mangy fur tippet, because this afternoon was the post-mortem on the feeble results of the Christmas fundraising campaign. At twenty-five, Jude—the curator—was the age of most of the board members' grandchildren.

The phone started up with a shrill jangle, and though she was inclined not to answer it, she did. It was the accent she recognized, more than the voice.

"Louise! Merry Christmas. Why are you whispering?" Jude broke in on her aunt's gabbled monologue. "Not herself, how?"

"I just don't think—" Louise interrupted herself in a louder voice: "I'm only on the phone, Rachel, I'll be right in."

As she stubbed out her cigarette, Jude tried to picture the house in England—a town called Luton—though she'd never seen it. "Put Mom on the line, would you?"

Instead of answering, her aunt called out, "Could you stick the kettle on?" Then, hissed into the phone, "Just a tick."

Waiting, Jude felt irritation bloom behind her eyes. Her aunt had always liked her gin; could she possibly be drunk at, what—she checked the grandfather clock and added five hours—11:30 in the morning?

Louise came back on the line, in the exaggerated style of a community theatre production: "Your mother's making tea."

"What's up, is she sick?"

"She'd never complain, and I haven't told her I'm ringing you," her aunt whispered, "but if you ask me, you should pop over and bring her home."

Pop over, as if Luton were a couple of kilometres down the road. Jude couldn't keep her voice from cracking like a whip. "Could I please speak to my mother?"

"The yellow pot, " Louise shouted, "the other's for herbal. And a couple of those Atkins gingernuts." Then, quieter, "Jude, dear, I must go, I've tai chi at noon—just take my word for it, would you please, she needs her daughter—"

The line went dead. Jude stared at the black Bakelite receiver, then dropped it back in the cradle.

She looked up the number in the stained address book on the counter, but after four rings she got the message, in Louise's guarded tones: "You have reached 3688492..."

"Me again, Jude," she told the machine. "I—listen, I really don't get what's wrong. I'd appreciate it if Mom could call me back right away." Rachel must be well enough to use the phone if she was walking around making tea, surely?

Jude cooked some oatmeal, just to kill a few minutes. After two spoonfuls her appetite disappeared.

This was ridiculous. Sixty-six, lean, and sharp, Jude's mother never went to the doctor except for flu shots. Not a keen traveler, but a perfectly competent one. Louise was six years her elder, or was it seven? If there was something seriously wrong with Rachel—pain or fever, bleeding or a lump—surely Louise would have said? It struck Jude now that her aunt had sounded evasive, paranoid, almost. Could these be the first signs of senility?

Jude tried the Luton number again and got the machine. This time she didn't leave a message, because she knew she'd sound too fierce. Surely the two sisters wouldn't have gone out a minute after making a pot of tea?

Her stomach was a nest of snakes. *Pop over,* as easy as that. The Atlantic stretched out in her mind, a wide gray horror.

It wasn't as if she were phobic, exactly. She'd just never felt the need or inclination to get on an airplane. It was one of those things that people wrongly assumed to be compulsory, like cell phones or gym memberships. Jude had got through her first quarter century just fine without air travel. In February, for instance, when much of the population of Ontario headed like shuddering swallows to Mexico or Cuba, she preferred to go snowshoeing in the Pinery. Two years ago, to get to her cousin's wedding in Vancouver, she'd taken a week each way and slept in the back of her Mustang. And the summer her friends from high school had been touring Europe, Jude had been up north planting trees to pay for her first motorbike. Surely it was her business if she preferred to stay on the ground?

Your mother's not herself. What was that supposed to mean?

Neither of them had called back. This whole thing, Jude told herself, would no doubt turn out to be nothing more than an inconvenient and expensive fantasy of her aunt's. But in her firm, slightly childish script that hadn't changed since grade school, she started writing out a CLOSED DUE TO FAMILY EMERGENCY notice to tape on the door of the one-room museum.

Rizla took the afternoon off from the garage to drive her to the airport in his new orange pickup. He was in a full-length shearling coat of Ben Turner's; Jude had found it in a dry-cleaners' bag in the basement, years after her father had decamped to Florida, and it gave her a shiver of pleasant spite to see Rizla wear it slung over a White Snake T-shirt stained with motor oil.

White specks spiraled into the windshield; the country roads were thickly coated with snow. Jude took a drag on the cigarette they were sharing. "So, how come when I called, it said 'This number has been disconnected'?"

"Just a temporary misunderstanding with those dumb-asses at the phone company," he said out of the side of his mouth.

"Uh-huh." After a second, she asked, "What are your payments on the truck?"

"Isn't she a beaut?"

"She is, she's a big gorgeous tangerine. What are your payments?"

Rizla kept his eyes on the road. "Leasing's better value in the long run."

"But if you can't cover your phone bill—"

"Shit, if you're planning to grill me on my budget all the way to Detroit, you can ride in the back."

"Okay, okay." Jude passed him the cigarette. "Why wouldn't either of them have called me back? I left three messages," she muttered, aware of repeating herself.

"Maybe your mom's got something unmentionable," he suggested. "She is British, after all."

"Like what? Bloody stools?"

"Syphilis. Pubic lice."

She flicked his ear, and Rizla yelped in pain. She took the cigarette back, and smoked it down to the filter.

"I bet the old gals are just getting on each other's tits," he said after a minute. "My sisters used to rip each other's hair out, literally."

"All your sisters?"

"Mostly the middle ones." Rizla came fifth in a Mohawk-Dutch family of eleven. An only child, Jude had always been fascinated by the Vandeloos.

"But if that's all it is, why wouldn't she just send Mom to a hotel? Why drag me halfway 'round the world with some line about 'She needs her daughter'?"

"England's hardly halfway, more like a quarter," said Rizla, scratching his armpit with the complacent air of a guy who'd been to Bangkok. "Hey, is it really Ma Turner's health you're freaking out about, or having to finally get on a plane?"

Jude lit another cigarette. "Why do you call her that?"

"Why shouldn't I? When she brings her little Honda in for a tune-up, she always sort of squints at me, called me 'Richard.'"

"It is your name."

He snorted at that.

When he wrenched his black ponytail out of his collar she noticed, for the first time, some streaks of gray. "It's mostly the flying," she admitted. "I'm nauseous already."

"Have a couple whiskeys, nothing to it. Actually, it's fun to see you lose your rag, for once. Everyone thinks you're so mature,"

Rizla added with a smirk. He put on a quavery voice: "'That Turner girl that set up our museum, she's got her feet on the ground all right.'"

The image struck Jude as heavy, mud-locked. She changed the subject to hockey. While Rizla raved about his Leafs' chances of making it to the play-offs, her mind was working over every word Louise had said on the phone.

Dropping her off, he pointed up at the sign that said KISS 'N FLY, and pursed his lips like a gargoyle. She gave his ponytail a tug instead, and climbed out into the freezing air.

The Detroit airport was worse than a mall: fluorescent lights, announcements, stray children, suitcases mummified in plastic wrap. Jude lined up at one desk after another until she was put on standby to London Heathrow with some Irish carrier she'd never heard of. Thank god she'd gotten around to applying for a passport last year because of the new U.S. border regulations. Then there was a commotion about her paying with cash. (She'd emptied her account this morning.) "You can't turn me away just because I don't have a credit card," she argued.

She inched through security in her socks, and had to buy a padded envelope to send her Swiss Army knife home rather than have it confiscated. *Let the flight be full;* then she could call Luton with a clear conscience and say she'd done her best. But at the gate, the woman in the green uniform and boxy little hat called out a list of names that included Jude Turner.

I'm off to England, she told herself, trying to rouse some enthusiasm, but all she could think of were those royal guards on the postcards, with bearskin straps cutting into their chins. As she shuffled down the tube that led to the plane, her tongue was glued to the roof of her mouth. Mountains cloaked in fog, wings bursting into flame, suicide bombers... *Your fears are total clichés,* she told herself. *Come on, how truly likely is any of that?*

Travel Sickness

TRAVEL (originally the same word
as TRAVAIL), to go on a journey.

TRAVAIL (from Medieval Latin,
trepalium, a three-staked instrument
of torture), to work, tire, suffer.

Jude was ten thousand metres above the earth, with her eyes jammed shut. She was trying to ignore the tang of puke from the waxed paper bag the old man on her left had just squashed into the seat pocket. He must have been too embarrassed to ask one of the cabin crew to take it away; maybe he was hungover from starting New Year early.

After the long, screeching takeoff—*it's all right, it's all right,* Jude had mouthed to herself, hunched against the tug of gravity— she'd thought the worst must be over. But the sensation of imprisonment only tightened as the hours dragged by. Every overhead locker was crammed, every inch of floor was littered with baggage, and three rows ahead, a woman's tote had spilled into the aisle: What quantities of garbage people hauled around the world with them! Jude prayed for the night to be over and herself safe at London Heathrow, where—according to the screen over her head—it was 4:29 on January first. Back home it was still last year; that was kind of funny, or would have been if she could have found anything funny right now. Did time zones only work on the ground, or above it as well? What time was it up here in the black void, where the plane seemed to be hanging quite motionless?

Last May, Jude had spent a day and a night looking after a baby, and the experience had taught her that time was a human invention. Of course the planet had a pulse—light and dark, winter and summer—but humans, in their elaborate arrangements, had long left earth time behind. At two months, Lia slept and woke according to her miniature body's dictates, and as Jude yawned over the aromatic little head at four in the morning she'd come to the conclusion that night and day, hours and weeks were all fictions. (Hadn't the French revolutionaries tried to implement a ten-day week, she remembered now? That couldn't have been popular.) And what a hoo-ha people made at New Year's Eve parties, shrieking "Don't go out for a smoke now, it's three minutes to, you'll miss it!" As if there were any real *it* to miss.

Jude arched in her seat to stretch her back. In the movies, airplanes looked so spacious, but this had to be how pigs were brought to the abattoir. She was only five foot six, but there was barely room for her knees; how did tall guys cope? To her right, across the aisle, sat a nun whose body spilled over the armrest, engrossed in something called *The Poisonwood Bible*. To Jude's left was the puker, his head tilted back, pale eyelids down. His briefcase was digging into her ankle; overdue for retirement, a minor executive for a multinational? Poor guy, but Jude wished him anywhere in the world but limp and acrid in the seat beside her.

Compassionless, worn out, rigid as a crowbar: What a way to see in the New Year! Jude was trying to remember the last time she'd gone this long without a cigarette, except in her sleep. On her fifteenth birthday she'd bummed her first off some girl with braids whose name escaped her now. She could feel the slim packet in her shirt pocket now, tantalizing the skin below her collarbone. Jude's palms were damp. She tried crossing her legs but there wasn't room, so she crossed her ankles instead.

Not herself—what could Louise have meant by that? Rachel Turner was always herself, sick or well. She scorned a fuss, and she was generally easy to live with. (Jude's friend Anneka thought the very idea of sharing a house with one's mother was peculiar; she claimed she got on much better with her own back in Stockholm now that their communication was limited to Web cam.) Jude started a list of all the illnesses Rachel could possibly have developed in the six days since she'd left Ontario, crossing off the ones that would prevent her from walking around making tea. Then she told herself to stop it. She couldn't stand people who worked themselves into frenzies.

Jude wrenched the in-flight magazine out of its plastic sheath: *Irish Eyes*, it was called. (Back home, she was halfway through *The Scarlet Letter*, but in her state of dislocation she'd left it by her bed, she remembered now.) The editorial was all about "rebranding as a low-cost, low-fares airline to meet the challenges of today's competitive climate." She scanned articles on body language, "Survival Strategies for Road Warriors," Cajun cookery. She was briefly distracted by the advertisements; she speculated about the kind of person who'd buy a CD of the sound of surf on pebbles, or a Personal Inflatable Oxygen Bubble for escaping from a burning hotel.

Fatigue swam in Jude's eyes. She shut them and took some slow, deep breaths. She pretended she was in the old Meetinghouse at Coldstream that she drove to every Sunday. *Wait. Center down. Way will open.* Or, as she used to paraphrase it when she was eleven and restless, *Shut up and listen!* But listen to whom or what, exactly? Quakers were better at questions than answers. Damn, she should have called the Petersons; who'd drive them to Meeting?

The window was a small egg of darkness. Really, there was nothing to worry about, Jude told herself, this was only a big steel coach in the sky. Just a vast, humming, groaning Greyhound bus with nothing but air under its wheels. Infinite black air outside the windows and very little inside. Jude heaved a long breath. "The bums in steerage only get about a fifth the oxygen the pilots do, I saw it on MTV," Rizla had told her on the highway. "That's what causes migraines and clots and Sudden Infant Syndromes and shit."

Jude's skin was crawling, her head hammering. She'd had a whiskey instead of the stuffed chicken breast, but it hadn't helped. She would have bartered a finger for a cigarette. Stiff-necked, she stared around her in the dim cabin. Passengers slept propped up like puppets, thin green blankets tucked under their chins; how did they manage it? Jude began letting down her seat back, but as soon as she felt it make contact with a knee, she released the button and was jerked upright again. Now it felt as if she were being folded forward. She thought of the bed in that Edgar Allan Poe story she'd read Rizla one insomniac night: the bed that waited till you were asleep before it closed up like a mouth.

That sick bag was really beginning to stink. Her seatmate was sleeping open-mouthed, helpless as a baby. Jude thought of pulling the bag out of his seat pocket, to dispose of it herself, but she feared it might be soggy; she didn't have her friend Gwen's ease with bodily functions. (Gwen liked to horrify new acquaintances with a story about having to remove, by hand, a ninety-five-year-old Sunset resident's impacted stool.)

A flight attendant went by like a gazelle, a South Asian woman in a green tailored suit of startling brightness, but Jude failed to catch her eye. The man in front let down his seat back, and the plastic tray slipped off its latch and smashed onto Jude's knee. She bit into the soft inside of her lips.

The plane heaved slightly, and Jude decided that one of its engines had fallen out; they were about to plummet, spin, and smash into the icy Atlantic. A weight landed on her shoulder. Jude blinked into thinning white hair. The old guy's head was on her shoulder, heavy as a bowling ball. She couldn't think how to get rid of it, short of a violent shake. Across the aisle, the nun got up, stretching, and gave her a little smile. Jude felt absurdly embarrassed. The nun walked off, as if there were somewhere to go.

Five minutes on, Jude decided that was it; the guy's time was up. Canadian politeness only went so far. She wriggled her shoulder. She tried tilting her body into the aisle, but the man slid with her; his head nestled into the crook of her arm like a lover's. At which point she took hold of the cuff of his gray suit with her free hand and gave it a shake. His hand shifted limply.

"Excuse me?" Jude's words were almost soundless; she hadn't spoken in hours. She cleared her throat. He didn't stir. "Sir? Could you please wake up?"

And then she knew something was wrong, because her heart was banging like a gong. He had to be ill. Because no adult, not even a worn-out *road warrior,* could snooze in that position, face slithering into a stranger's lap.

Bile rose in her throat. She searched the arm of her seat for that little icon you could press to call for help. A light sparked on overhead, the beam hitting her in the eye. The nun came back but put on her headphones before Jude could speak to her; the sound of merry violins leaked from her ears.

At last a flight attendant hurried up the aisle with a basket; she was the South Asian one Jude had noticed before. "Excuse me?" said Jude, putting her free hand out; it brushed the woman's hip.

She turned with a smile. "Here you go." With tongs, she dropped a white scalding thing into Jude's hand. Jude yelped and shook it off.

The woman was staring at her now. "Sorry, didn't you want a hot towel?" Angry? No, more like amused. Her eyes were an odd, tawny shade; her accent seemed British.

"No, I'm sorry, I just—" Jude looked with helpless revulsion at the man slumped against her. "I think this gentleman may possibly not be feeling well," she said, absurdly formal.

The woman's face changed. She set her basket of towels on her hip, bent, and leaned in. Her snaky black braid was long enough to sit on. Six inches from Jude's eyes, the shiny rectangle on the green lapel said síle o'shaughnessy, purser. That didn't seem like an Indian name. And wasn't a purser some kind of manager on a cruise ship? She wore expensive perfume; a gold choker swayed away from her throat. Her stockinged knee was touching Jude's, now. "Sir?" she said. "Sir?"

"He seemed okay at dinner," said Jude stupidly.

The woman held the man's wrist for a few seconds, her face unreadable. Then she straightened up, pressing her fingers into the arch of her back, as if tired.

"Miss! Towels, over here, please!" a passenger called.

"On my way," she said mildly. Then, to Jude, "Sit tight, I'll be back."

Jude's eyes locked onto hers. *Sit tight?*

But Síle O'Shaughnessy appeared again a minute later, leading a graying woman whose glasses hung on her blouse. They consulted in murmurs. Then she bent into Jude's row again, her jade skirt stretched at the thigh; she took the old guy by the shoulders, gently pushing him upright. Freed of his weight, Jude squeezed out. Not wanting to be in the way, she stumbled down the aisle to stand outside the washroom.

When she came back a few minutes later the old guy was lying the other way, a small white pillow between his head and the little porthole. What, no oxygen tanks, no CPR in the aisle, no infibrillator or whatever that machine was called? So it had to be that he was all right, just in a really deep sleep.

Feeling relieved but foolish for having made a fuss, Jude strapped herself back into her seat. Beyond the old man's flat profile was a gaudy sunrise; where had that come from? The skies of southwestern Ontario had nothing on this: malachite, and raspberry, and flame.

Then all at once she got it. She laid one surreptitious fingertip on the back of the man's hand. It was as cold as an apple. Now that was something else Jude had never done before in her life. Seen a dead person. Sat beside a dead man, in fact, ten thousand metres up in the air.

Her hand was shaking. She tucked it under her other arm. It just couldn't be that someone had died in the seat beside her and she hadn't noticed.

How could she not have noticed? Jude searched her memory for any words she'd exchanged with him when they'd boarded, back in Detroit. A minimal "Hi," at most. She should have introduced herself, at least. She'd been too wound up in her own petty anxieties. Had that been the guy's last conversation? Or maybe he'd spoken to one of the crew. He'd had the chicken, she suddenly recalled; it had looked so pallid and humid, she'd left the foil on hers and just nibbled the roll. "Chicken, please," had that been his last line? People were always claiming they wanted to pop off in their sleep, but they didn't know what they were asking. To have not a moment's preparation, to drop as mutely as a suitcase from this world into the next... *You know not the day nor the hour,* wasn't that the Gospel line?

"All right there?" The purser had come back to stand beside Jude, fiddling with the catch of her gold watch. Her arched eyebrows went up. "There's a seat at the back, if you'd like..."

"That's okay." Jude kept her eyes on her lap, embarrassed by the secret they shared: death, slumped in the next seat.

"Sure we'll be landing soon enough." Síle O'Shaughnessy dipped down till her head was beside Jude's. "At the gate there'll be an official with a couple of questions, if you wouldn't mind."

Why should Jude mind? Oh, questions for *her.* She nodded, speechless.

She could hear the woman's brisk voice all the way down the plane. "Any newspapers, headsets, plastic cups?"

In another quarter of an hour the cabin was full of yellow light. At they started their descent, Jude felt the pressure build up in her ears again; it was like being underwater. Where her fear had been there was only a numbness.

Landing, landing, coming back to earth with a bang. She'd thought it would be smooth, but the engines roared and the wheels clawed at the tarmac, and if it weren't for her belt she'd have been thrown out of her seat.

The nun pulled off her headphones and rubbed her papery lids. "I didn't get a wink," she remarked to Jude, "did you?"

Jude shook her head.

"Well, that's the price of taking the red-eye. Somebody's got a quiet conscience."

"Excuse me?"

"Your friend," said the nun, nodding over Jude's shoulder at the stranger who seemed to be sleeping like a newborn, his face soaked in light.

Sic Transit

On earth we are like travelers staying at a hotel.

—St. Jean-Baptiste-Marie Vianney

Síle watched an enormous brown case bound with a pink scarf make its jerky progress around the carousel. Then a globe-shaped parcel in snowflake wrapping paper went past again. Her mind was a yo-yo. She shivered, and buttoned her uniform coat to the throat. Smelling a cigarette, she whipped around, jabbing her finger at the sign on the wall: "Can you not read?"

The girl took a long suck of smoke before dropping it on the floor and extinguishing it with her boot. "Cut me some slack, could you?" she muttered.

Síle gave her a second glance. "Oh, sorry, pet, I didn't know you with your hood up."

The Canadian had clean blue eyes in an angular face. Soft brown hair that couldn't be more than two inches long. Very worn blue jeans, and not the kind sold expensively pre-aged. "Who was he?" the girl asked in a low voice.

Síle hesitated, then told her, "The manifest gives the name, that's all: George L. Jackson. He's in the mortuary; his next of kin should be getting the phone call about now. He wasn't wearing a wedding ring," she added, "but then his generation of men often don't."

A silence. "I can't decide which would be worse," said the Canadian, "for him to turn out to have this big devoted family, or—"

"—to have been a bachelor with only a couple of indifferent nephews?"

She nodded.

Jude Turner, Síle dredged up the name from the line on the form that said *Witness.* "I've just been put through the wringer by the manager of cabin services," she confided, on impulse.

"What could you have done?" Jude Turner asked huskily. "He was stone cold by the time I called you over."

Síle nodded. "The doctor confirmed it. But the airline's policy is *always defibrillate.* It was a judgment call: I decided that hauling the poor bastard into the aisle to shock him would do nothing but start a general panic."

"What about me," the girl asked, after a second, "didn't you worry I'd panic?"

"You didn't look the type."

Jude Turner flushed slightly, and turned her gaze to the carousel, where bags were beginning to form precarious piles.

"Nineteen years flying the friendly skies," Síle explained, "you get the knack of sizing people up. Canadian, yeah?"

A small grin. "Most Brits can't hear the difference between our accent and an American one."

"The huge maple leaf on the back of your jacket was a bit of a giveaway."

The flush reached the girl's cheekbones this time.

Síle only felt slightly bad about teasing her. "And I'm Irish, actually, not a Brit."

"Right. I meant, you know, from these islands," her hand making an apologetic circle. She stared at the flattened cigarette by her toe—probably wishing she'd had a few more puffs, Síle thought.

The crowd parted like water as three of her colleagues walked through smartly, wheeling their green carry-ons; one of them gave her a little wave.

"How come you have to stand round here with the herd?" asked the girl.

"Oh, it's entirely my own fault: I bought a trampoline."

Jude Turner ducked through a gap between two carts, and came back with a small black backpack. "A trampoline?"

"Mm, one of those cute little ones; you just get up on it and bounce, and the calories drip off you." The girl started to laugh, and Síle joined in through a sudden wave of fatigue. "I know, it sounds like an utter nonsense now I describe it. I spent $179 on the fucker in Detroit, and I still have to haul it through UK customs before I fly on to Dublin."

"Is that it?"

Síle's eyes narrowed. "Was it that big? Christ, the thing's five feet wide! I'll need a trolley—"

But Jude had already headed toward the line of gleaming carts.

"You're a star," Síle said when the girl got back. Between them they heaved the huge parcel upright on the trolley. Now was the moment to nod good-bye. "Listen," she asked instead, "are you in one piece? I couldn't be sorrier about all this," flicking her eyes upward to indicate the sky, the flight, the night.

"Actually, it was my first time."

As the virgin said to the bishop, Síle thought automatically. "Your first time seeing..."

The narrow head shook furiously. "I didn't see him die; I must have been reading the magazine or longing for a smoke. No, I just mean it was my first time flying."

"Ah, you creature! What a thing to happen to you."

Tears were striping Jude's jaw, dropping onto her jacket, onto the streaky floor of the baggage hall. She averted her face.

"Well, I made a right hames of that," said Síle lightly, taking hold of her arm above the elbow. "You'll have to let me buy you a coffee on the other side. How many more bags are you waiting for?"

Another speechless shake of the head.

In the Rive Gauche Airport Brasserie—after the Canadian had shot outside for a cigarette—Síle rattled on. "Síle's pronounced like *Sheila*, yeah. And is it Jude as in *Jude the Obscure*?"

"Good guess! Most people assume it's from the Beatles song," said the girl, her voice still a little ragged, "but actually my mom was reading Hardy's novel during labour."

"I like androgynous names, they disconcert people." Under the table, Síle slid her feet out of her new navy heels and stretched them.

"Listen, you're really kind, but you're probably in a rush to get on your plane to Dublin—" Knuckles against the damp eyelids, like a child.

"Ah, I've got three-quarters of an hour." Síle was about to add something flippant about breakfast being her sole priority. Instead she leaned forward and said, "Don't bother your head being embarrassed. You'd be surprised how many people have burst into tears on me, over the years."

An attempt at a smile.

"They've also patted my arse, told me they had cancer, tried to punch me, and thrown up a lot of peanuts—back in the days when we were let serve peanuts. Though I never mind the kids throwing up; it's in their nature, and it doesn't smell as bad."

"Really?"

"Less brandy," Síle explained.

"Have you got any yourself? Kids, I mean."

"No. The real perk of this job is, I get to play with other people's and then hand them back." *Hmm,* she thought belatedly, *was that a way of finding out whether I'm straight?*

Jude ate a very small piece of *pain au raisin*. "Thanks for the coffee, it's great."

"Well, that's a classic bit of Canadian politeness."

A blink.

"It's absolute dishwater," said Síle. "I only come here for the pastries."

Jude rallied. "Well, first of all, I really needed some coffee; I don't think I've been up all night since a slumber party when I was nine."

"Fair point. And second of all?"

"It's better than the kind I brew in an old pot with a strainer that lets grit through."

Síle grimaced. "I've become a shocking coffee snob," she explained. "At home in Dublin, there's this one Italian café on the docks I have to trek to whenever I have a day off."

"So you were happier before, when you didn't know any better?"

"Well—I suppose," she conceded. "You don't reheat yours in the microwave, at least?"

"I haven't got a microwave."

Síle stared. "You must be the last holdout in the Western world."

When Jude grinned, the curve of her cheek was as chaste as a white tulip. *She didn't have a second bag,* Síle registered belatedly, *she was only hanging round the baggage carousel to talk to me.* She looked down at her pastry, swallowed a buttery mouthful.

"I don't even have a cell phone," said Jude, nodding at the pewter-tinted device sticking out of Síle's handbag.

"Oh, this is far more than a mobile; I call it my gizmo." She picked it up fondly. It was a sample from a friend in the business; it gave her a shallow thrill that this model wasn't on the market yet. *You have 7 messages,* but she snapped the little screen shut. "It says the temperature out there is minus two."

"Nice."

"Are you being sarcastic?"

"No, that's mild for January, by my standards," Jude assured her.

"Jaysus."

"What else does it do?"

"You name it. It's my little bottled genie: takes pictures, plays music, surfs, voice recognition, ten languages..."

"Bet it won't know what *poutine* is."

"Spell it," said Síle. "Sounds a bit like *putain;* doesn't that mean whore?"

Jude spelled it out.

NOT KNOWN, said the tiny screen. She frowned. "What language is it?"

"Canadian. It means fries with cheese curds and gravy."

"Ugh!"

A brief silence. Jude wiped away the ring her coffee glass had left on the table. "If I'd noticed, a bit earlier—"

"Don't torture yourself." Síle put her hand over the girl's very white one, lightly, like a butterfly landing. With the three gold rings, the Keralan bangles, the watch, hers suddenly looked like the hand of a sinister older woman. *You're taking advantage,* she told herself, and moved it away.

"The only funerals I've been to have been closed-casket," Jude told her.

"I've seen lots of dead people...of course, I'm twice your age," said Síle with deliberate exaggeration, to punish herself for the moment with the hand. "Three uncles and an aunt, my grandparents—just on my dad's side, not the Indian ones—my art teacher...not my mother, I was only three at the time."

The girl's chiseled eyebrows shot up.

"Diabetes," Síle told her.

"I'm sorry."

Síle smiled.

"Do you remember her?"

"Well, I do and I don't. I get images, but I know some of them must be based on photos."

"How weird!"

"These women I know in New York," said Síle, "they play a dinner party game called dead exes, and the winner is the one who's slept with the most dead people."

"That sounds like necrophilia."

"It does a bit." She slugged her cooling coffee, then wished she hadn't. "When Da visits his old village, in Roscommon, so many of his relations are dead, it's like Oisín come home."

"It's like what?"

"Oisín," Síle repeated. "Son of Fionn Mac Cumhaill, leader of a band of heroes called the Fianna?"

"Ah, Finn McCool, the guy the pubs are named after."

Síle nodded. "So Niamh of the Golden Hair trots by on her magic white horse, lures Oisín west across the sea to Tir-na-nOg—that's the Land of Youth," she supplied.

"Like Never-Never Land?"

She made a face. "They're not children—but they never grow old, so yeah, sort of. Well, life there is fantastic; every day they hunt and every night they sing. But after three weeks our lad happens to see a shamrock and gets homesick. He tells the lovely Niamh, 'I have to go back to Ireland, just for a day.' She's not happy; she says, 'Go if you must, but stay on the white horse and don't let your foot so much as touch the ground.'"

"Ah," said Jude, nodding, "the magical pull of the native soil."

The girl was quick; Síle grinned at her. "Well, Oisín passes some puny fellas in the road trying to roll a big boulder out of the way. He asks them where the Fianna are hunting, and they squint up at him and say the Fianna have all been dead for three hundred years. Now Oisín doesn't believe this mad story. But he thinks he'll help them with the stone, so he leans out of the saddle and gives it one great shove."

"He falls off?"

Síle nodded. "Finds himself in the mud, a shriveled husk, more than three centuries old, and he knows he'll never see Niamh of the Golden Hair again."

Jude shook her head. After a few seconds, she said, "Bet she regretted lending him the horse."

Síle burst out laughing. "That's right. Keep 'em tied to the bedpost, I say!" This came out far too sexily, so she turned back to her *pain au chocolat.* Another of those odd silences. She knew she should check her watch, but she didn't want to end the conversation.

"So…what do you reckon happened to him?"

The girl didn't mean Oisín. Síle shrugged. "In-flight deaths are surprisingly common, though that was my first; they think it's the stress of travel." One long-haul airline had recently added a corpse cupboard to its Airbuses, though she didn't mention that. "A friend of mine from college, he went climbing in the Macgillycuddy Reeks with his son, dropped dead over his egg sandwich. Apparently the altitude can hit the fittest people the hardest."

"You mean…last night, it could have been the *altitude?*"

"No, no," said Síle, exasperated, "that was just an example of going quick and quiet. The cabins are pressurized, you know; it's just like being on the ground."

"It doesn't feel like it."

"Ah, you'll get used to flying, now you've taken the plunge. Suddenly shedding gravity—" Síle's hand mimed a sharp ascent— "it's better than a roller coaster."

"I throw up on roller coasters."

"Now *that's* a revolting image."

"I mean, afterwards," Jude corrected herself. "This one time Rizla—my ex—dragged me onto a huge one in Sudbury, I was nauseous for days."

"So is she a Luddite like you?"

The girl blinked. "Actually, it's a he. I mean, he's a guy, Richard. The nickname's from the cigarette papers."

Síle's face heated up. Haircuts could be so misleading. "Oh, I'm sorry."

"No, it's—"

"Rizla, right, cigarette papers, I thought the word was familiar," cried Síle. So much for her ability to read people.

"That's okay." Grinning.

Ah, thought Síle. *So I wasn't wrong?*

"What was your question?"

"Did I have a question?"

"Luddites," Jude remembered. "No, Rizla's all about machines; he's an auto mechanic. And I love motorbikes, so I'm not a total Luddite."

"Aren't you going to finish your *pain au raisin?*"

"Help yourself," said Jude, sliding her plate over with a huge yawn. "How do you cope with the jet lag?"

"Oh, I refuse to believe in it; it's like allergies."

"You don't believe in allergies?"

"Not unless they're the kind that make your face swell up like a balloon. You Yanks—North Americans," Síle corrected herself, "you're always claiming to be allergic to this, that, and th'other, as if a sip of milk or a bite of bread's going to murder you."

"I'm not allergic to anything," said Jude, "and I bake my own bread."

Síle rolled her eyes. "You really are a dinosaur, aren't you?"

"Whereas you're a Rechabite."

"I'm a what?"

"They were the one tribe of Israel who wouldn't settle down," Jude explained. "They were doomed to dwell in tents."

"Well, my tent is a tiny two-up-two-down in inner-city Dublin—bought cheap before our boom, mercifully. But it's true that I'm always nipping out of the country on my days off," Síle admitted. "My friend Marcus gives me cuttings in little pots but they keep dying on me."

"I live in Ireland too, with my mother," Jude volunteered. "Ireland, Ontario."

"That's hilarious!"

"Is it?"

"Like *Paris, Texas.*"

"Now that's a great movie. When he's talking to his lost wife through the one-way mirror, and he can see her but she can't see him..."

"Stop it. I've seen it five times and I always cry like a wee babby," said Síle. "So how small is your Ireland?"

"The population recently topped the six hundred mark for the first time since they shut down the train track back in the thirties."

"Oh dear."

"Actually, I like it."

"Me and my big mouth," said Síle, clapping her hand over it. "Anywhere near Toronto?"

"Two and a half hours. Pretty near, by Canadian standards," Jude added.

"I love the fact that there's nothing a tourist *has* to see in Toronto; the couple of times I've been there, all I do is go to films and eat like a beast. So what's made you get on a plane at last, Jude? Are you a student, doing Europe?" Belatedly, Síle remembered it was January.

"No, actually, I'm curator of the town's museum; it's a one-room schoolhouse. Curator translates as underpaid dogsbody," Jude added, "but still, I get to run things my way."

"What's your way?"

"Uncutesy, I guess," she said, after a second. "In North America we tend to Disneyfy the past into this sugar-coated nostalgia product, all bonnets and merry sleigh rides—"

Síle nodded. "The Irish do green marble shamrock jewelry, misty ruins, Enya whispering and moaning over the PA."

"Exactly! And let's nobody mention infanticide or lynch mobs."

The girl's vehemence delighted Síle. "So do you—" She broke off to check her watch. "Shite. Shite, I really have to run." She caught the eye of the waiter in the faux-Parisian apron with the enormous plugs in his earlobes, and gestured for the bill. "Unless you'd like another nasty coffee?"

"I'm good, thanks."

"But you still haven't told me what's brought you to England," Síle pointed out, flipping through the compartments of her bag to find some sterling. You could call it shameless nosiness, but she preferred to think she had people skills.

Jude's face had gone flat by the time she looked up. "I have to pick my mother up from her sister's in Luton. Apparently she's... not well."

"Oh dear." Síle took the bill from the waiter and handed it back with a note, waving away Jude's protests. She wished she hadn't lifted this particular stone, just before having to dash away to check-in. Her fingers were tugging a card out of her purse. *Never apologize, never explain:* She tossed it down.

"Neat design! Thanks. But actually I don't do e-mail," said Jude, picking up the card that featured a small black swallow swooping over the words

Síle O'Shaughnessy
sile@oshaugh.com

Síle frowned. "Surely your museum... you must need to answer queries, look things up online?"

"Yeah, but I don't use the account for personal stuff. I think it's the lowest form of human communication."

Síle stared at her.

"I'm a freak, I know. Here's my real address, though. In case you find out anything more about Mr. Jackson..." Jude wrote on the back of her napkin in a precise, schoolgirlish hand:

Jude Turner
9 Main Street
Ireland, ON
L5S 3T9
Canada

"Thanks, but I never send anything by snail mail," said Síle, unable to resist some tit-for-tat. "Can't bear the lag; by the time it arrives it's not really true anymore."

They started laughing at the same moment.

"Well. Enjoy your trampoline," said Jude.

"I hope your mother's okay. Go easy!" Síle considered risking a hug but waved instead, pushing her top-heavy trolley away toward the sign that said CONNECTIONS TO TERMINALS ONE, TWO, FOUR.

She put on her tiny earphones, then let herself glance back. Outside the Rive Gauche Airport Brasserie, Jude Turner was squatting down, tightening a strap on her small backpack. Not looking up, not scanning the concourse for Síle. *Oh well, that passed the time.* What was that punchline from *Waiting for Godot*? Yeah: *It would have passed in any case.*

Time moved differently in airports: It pooled, it gushed, it hung heavy on your hands and then knocked you off your feet. Síle spent her days looking after travelers who were bored, in a hurry, or both. As for the frequent flyers, she had come to the conclusion that constant transit could make a monster of anyone. Personal convenience was their goal, and their fellow passengers were only obstacles, flotsam and jetsam. Frequent fliers would push past the arthritic, step over crying children, let their seat backs down and lie with faces set like stone kings'. For their mother's birthday they brought the same duty-free perfume sampler as three years ago, and they always raided the fruit bowl for the yellowest banana on their way out.

Síle knew all this because she was a professional traveler herself; sometimes she felt like her passengers' jailer, sometimes their maid, but mostly she sympathized with their irritations and delusions. Didn't she know what it was like to walk through an airport, sealed off in a private bubble? The camera was always on her, and her private soundtrack playing. She was the heroine: the hijack victim, the brave doctor, the complicated spy. She glanced in every mirrored surface she passed.

What When Where How Why

My mind wanders like a bird which
is chased hither and thither.

—*Mahabharata* X 33

The Luton bus worked its way north, along strips of highway and winding sections of one-lane road. Everyone was driving on the left, it was a mirror-image world: Alice through the looking glass. Jude pressed her face to the chilly window. She watched the rain sleek down the green fields, polish the dark hedgerows. Strange to see a winter landscape without snow, the land gaudy with greens and ochres.

She'd put the Irishwoman's card away in her wallet. Síle's eyes were lighter than brown, she decided; nearer to pale orange, really. Was the woman this friendly with all her passengers? Maybe the Irish were like that. But there'd been moments, over breakfast... that confusion over Rizla's gender, for instance. A warm brown hand resting on Jude's for a moment. Jude couldn't have imagined it, could she?

Not that it mattered, really. An odd little encounter, sealed off from real life like a bee in a jar. The name made the sibilant chuff of a train in her head: *Síle O'Shaughnessy, Síle O'Shaughnessy, Síle O'Shaughnessy...*

Jude had the groggy sensation that time had pleated. According to *Irish Eyes* magazine, instead of fretting over what time it was by your body clock, you should adjust to the new zone fast by getting plenty of noonday sun. But what sun could push through this ceiling of English cloud? The world was going on as normal, but it seemed like none of Jude's business. What was it Gwen used to say was the basic test of mental coherence used in places like the Sunset Residence? *Oriented as to person, place, and time,* that was it. To qualify as sane, you were meant to know who you were, where you were, and what day it was. As if you were reporting on your own existence for a newspaper.

Last night's incident probably wouldn't even make the papers, Jude thought. She wondered how the *Huron Expositor* or the *Lucknow Sentinel* might have told George L. Jackson's story, a hundred years ago. "Man Expires in Flying Machine." Just the journalistic gist of the thing: the *what, when, where,* and *how,* and the *why* only if there were another half-inch to fill. The immigrants who'd come to settle southwestern Ontario had done a lot of falling through ice, onto hay forks, from topmasts, across train tracks, into fireplaces, down mine shafts or grain threshers. They swallowed buttons, got concussed in sleigh crashes, lost in blizzards, eaten by bears. Other people saw it happen: pointed, screamed, ran to help, ran away, did something. They never just sat there oblivious, reading the in-flight magazine.

At the bus station in Luton, Jude stood in a rain-streaked glass shelter and smoked three cigarettes in a row to fortify herself. When she finally managed to hail a cab, it took only a few minutes to get to her aunt's tiny row house, which had puce trim. Jude couldn't remember who it was you weren't supposed to tip in the British Isles; was it bartenders or cab drivers? At the last minute she gave the driver 20 percent, not letting herself translate it into Canadian dollars.

"No, I've got it, Louise," she heard from behind the front door. Her mother opened it.

"Hey Mom." Relief made Jude grin like a clown.

"Jude! What on earth are you doing here?" Her mother's face was startled into severity, but otherwise she looked just the same as when she'd left on Boxing Day, her brown curls a little lanker, perhaps.

Behind her, in the hallway, appeared Louise, biting her lip. "What a surprise!"

But Jude was having none of it. She stepped into the dark cluttered hallway and put her bag down. "Louise said you weren't well, that maybe you could use some company for the return trip."

"What nonsense is this?" Rachel stepped out of the hug and glared at her sister.

"I just thought it would be nicer for everyone," quavered Louise, retreating. "Now I'd better get the casserole on."

Jude went into a small lounge with lace antimacassars. She patted the couch beside her; after a few seconds, her mother sat down. "What's wrong, Mom?"

"Nothing! I threw up my eggs yesterday, that's all," Rachel added, "though between ourselves I blame Louise's cooking."

So this whole trip had been a folly, as she'd thought. Jude subsided against the cushions. "I kept calling, I left messages—"

"Did you? Louise told me nothing. She always plays the big sister. I can't believe you've been put to such trouble and expense in the middle of the holidays," Rachel fretted.

"Don't worry about that."

"I insist on paying for your ticket."

"Forget it. Actually, it's been quite an adventure." And suddenly that was true.

"You must be wrung out after that awful flight," observed her mother. "My ears are still bunged up, and my nose; I can't smell a thing."

"A man died in his sleep, in the next seat." It just slipped out. "His head slid onto me."

Her mother's stare had as much revulsion as sympathy in it.

Jude shouldn't have brought that up. "Anyway. How are you enjoying being back in England?"

Rachel shrugged her narrow shoulders. "The plumbing's atrocious as ever. There's no such thing as a pound note anymore, only a coin, can you believe it?"

Jude smiled through a wave of fatigue. She was tempted to step into the kitchen and shout at her aunt, for dragging her all this way. She supposed immigrants often found themselves in Rachel's state when they visited the homeland: their nostalgia stirred, but unsatisfied.

"But shouldn't you see a bit of the country, as you've come so far?" asked her mother. "Buckingham Palace, at least?"

"There isn't time, I'm on the same flight back tomorrow as you are. Besides, I'm needed at the museum."

"Westminster Abbey, Madame Tussaud's, though the queues are shocking…Stonehenge even. It's your heritage," said Rachel, "and you're so fond of old things."

"Next time, definitely."

"We'll have to book a taxi to the bus station."

Call a cab, Rachel would have said a week ago. It was odd to hear the old British phrases emerging. "I'll do that," Jude promised.

"Unless Bill drives us."

Jude held herself very still. She wondered if there was some allusion she'd missed. "Who's Bill?"

No answer.

Could it be a neighbour? "You don't mean Uncle Bill?" She waited. "Uncle Bill's dead, Mom."

"That's right." Rachel had the look of someone who might have left the oven on.

Jude's jaw was stiff. Had that really just happened? How could she say, *Mom, have you forgotten that Bill died of prostate cancer twelve years ago? I remember the day because when you got the phone call from your sister, I burst out crying, even though I'd only met her and Bill once; it was just the idea of someone I knew being dead. I'd been cleaning the chicken house with Dad, I was thirteen, and it was the last time I ever cried in front of you, as it turned out, and you held me in your arms so tightly my bra strap left a red mark on my back.*

Rachel was examining the slightly wrinkled hands that lay in her lap. Was she embarrassed by her mistake, Jude wondered, or mired in confusion? What other errors were infiltrating that head, still dark brown, still held at an intelligent angle? What other graves were cracking open? *Mrs. Turner. Mrs. Turner. Do you know what date it is today, Mrs. Turner? Whose house is this? Can you name the current premier of Ontario? How many children have you got, Mrs. Turner?*

"I'll take your bag up," said Rachel.

"It's all right—"

Rachel hurried off with it. Jude followed her into the hall, watched as her slippered feet disappeared up the narrow stairs. There was something askew about the woman's walk. Acid pooled in Jude's stomach. In her mind's eye, a plane plummeted through the clouds.

Genii Loci

To live in one land, is captivity.
To run all countries, a wild roguery.

—JOHN DONNE
"Elegy 3: Change"

One night at the end of January, Síle and Kathleen were sitting in a pub in Dublin's Smithfield Market. Outside the window, gigantic poles bore flaming gas torches; light gleamed across the scoured cobbles. "The architect won some prize, didn't he?" said Kathleen, sipping her wine.

"Did he? It looks like Colditz to me. I used to love walking down here on Saturdays to buy my veg, when it was a real market," said Síle.

Kathleen tucked a creamy strand behind one ear. "I don't know why you bother; they're always rotten by the time I turn up to cook them."

"They're decorative," said Síle, smiling. "And then the bloody Corpo pretty much did away with the horse fair too. I miss the surrealism of bareback lads clattering down my street. Gentrification's grand when it means people like me moving into the inner city," she added with a touch of self-mockery, "but not when it means scouring away every bit of colour or grit."

"Oh, Stoneybatter still has too much grit for me," said Kathleen with a little shudder.

Though they'd been together for—what was it?—almost five

years now, Kathleen had never expressed an interest in moving in; she still kept her high-ceilinged Georgian flat in Ballsbridge, around the corner from her tennis club. So Síle got to have a partner *and* her house to herself, which most days seemed the best of both worlds, despite the rancid spinach.

Her gizmo played "Leaving on a Jet Plane." After a brief exchange with her friend Jael, she rang off and said, "Domestic disaster, another fifteen minutes."

"There's the real difference between the New Ireland and the Old," said Kathleen: "Mobiles let your friends tell you how late they're going to be, as if that absolves them."

"Last night I got talking to a passenger who wanted to feature me in a piece on Ireland since the Celtic Tiger."

"Oh yeah? He wasn't just chatting you up?"

"She," Síle corrected her; she liked it that Kathleen still got proprietorial. "Can't you just imagine? 'Veteran crew member Síle O'Shaughnessy, chic at thirty-nine, tosses back the hip-length tresses she owes to her deceased mother's Keralan heritage,'" she ad-libbed.

Kathleen took it up. "'People are just people, under the skin,' laughs Indo-Hibernian Síle as she wheels her smart green carry-on across Dublin Airport's busy departures level.'"

"*Bustling* departures level."

"*Thronged* and bustling."

"'Her soignée blond life-mate, Kathleen Neville,'" Síle added, "is a senior administrator in one of the vibrant Celtic capital's top hospitals...'"

Kathleen grinned at that. "God, we're ungrateful mockers. In our student days, didn't we sit around griping that Ireland was trapped in the nineteenth century, and then the minute the money flowed in and it jumped to the twenty-first—"

"We've a lot to be ungrateful for, especially in Dublin," Síle protested. "You pay an arm and a leg for a fragment of sea bass, everybody's stressed and rude and booked up a month in advance..."

"At least you're not the only brown face anymore," Kathleen pointed out.

"That's true. In fact, compared to the women in chadors I hardly look foreign at all. Hey, did I tell you what happened to Brigid?"

"Which Brigid?"

"You must have met her at parties, she's ground staff. Black hair, tans easily, but County Cavan all the way back. She was on a bus the other day, got told, 'Go home, Paki bitch!'"

Kathleen looked revolted.

"She and I had a laugh about it. You have to laugh," Síle added after a second.

Kathleen covered a yawn with short cream nails and gulped the last of her wine. "I have to go to bed. If Anton and Jael do ever turn up—"

"They'll be here in a minute, sure."

"I don't wait an hour for anyone, sweetie. Give them my best."

"Okay," said Síle a little glumly. "I shouldn't be that late."

"I doubt you'll wake me." Kathleen bent to kiss her.

"We'll have a lovely breakfast."

"Sorry, I've an early budget meeting. Coffee in bed, anyway," Kathleen promised. She turned back to say, "Does the cat need another of those pills?"

"Oh yeah, bless you."

Through the pub's huge windows Síle watched her heading for the taxi rank, her blond head and sleek camel coat disappearing in the crowd; though fit, Kathleen saw no point in walking ten minutes through dark and dirty streets. Síle felt a little clenching of guilt for not going home with her. But then, Kathleen could have stayed long enough for one drink with their friends—*your friends,* she'd probably say.

Her gizmo showed a text from Orla inviting her to John and Paul's school production of *The King and I,* and yes, thank god Síle was off that day, not like the last three auntly occasions: *Keep me a seat,* she shot back. Her thumb twinged—too much texting—but she ignored it. A name she didn't recognize turned out to be a friend-of-a-friend-of-a-friend at a conference on cultural hybridities in Warsaw, wanting advice on restaurants: Síle checked her file and sent back a quick recommendation.

What a wordy species humans were, it struck her. Not content with singing and lecturing and gossiping and phoning strangers to offer them the opportunity to take advantage of a once-in-a-lifetime special offer, they also wrote. What a Babel! They scribbled anniversary cards and memos, epics and obituaries, lyrics and encyclopedia entries, books of affirmations and smut, and all for what? To reach each other, to convince, beg, placate, reassure. To stay in the loop.

That time Síle's last PDA had crashed and she'd lost her whole address book...it made her neck go rigid to remember. She'd felt like a diver whose air hose had got tangled.

She saved the text from Marcus till last, as her former colleague was her favourite man in the world (well, after her father). "Will try make it for quick one, have major news!" Síle stared at the words. Had he landed a great job? But Marcus liked his freelance technical drawing. His landlady was putting him under pressure to move out of his Dun Laoghaire flat, she knew, so maybe he'd managed to find something halfway affordable, if such a thing still existed in Dublin.

Still no sign of Jael and Anton. She called up the electronic digest of the *Irish Times,* and paused at a dispatch from the paper's woman in Baghdad. What peculiar lives foreign correspondents lived: dodging shrapnel, scribbling notes in the supermarket. They were never meant to quite settle in, Síle supposed; the moment they felt at home in the new country, they might forget how to explain things to their faraway readers.

Which somehow reminded her of Jude Turner, as a surprising number of things did. It had occurred to Síle, on and off over the month of January, to track down that little museum online and lash off a greeting, maybe in the flippant form of a cod genealogical query or something. But no, best to leave it as a self-contained brief encounter at an airport, one of the serendipitous side effects of travel.

It did bother Síle slightly that during that breakfast at Heathrow she hadn't come out with the usual phrase, "my partner Kathleen." But really, she wasn't obliged to discuss her domestic or undomestic situation with everyone she met. She'd never see the girl again, so what did it matter?

Long-limbed, Jael strode out of the crowd. "Muchos apologos," she cried, landing a kiss on Síle's cheek, "babysitter fell off his bike doing wheelies to impress Iseult. So what's the craic, what's the story?"

"Hello at last," said Síle. Jael's dark red curls were cut shorter than usual around her freckled face, and long rods of silver hung from her earlobes. When she took out her lighter, Síle clicked her fingers.

Jael slapped it down with a groan. "I keep forgetting the bloody ban. We're living in a police state."

"Have you thought of just giving it up?"

"I wouldn't dream of letting the State bully me into anything," said Jael virtuously. "No, it did cross my mind when I turned forty, but it seemed too late to bother my arse."

Anton slid into the booth with three full glasses. "Sorry, sorry, sorry. Are you on your tod, Síle?"

"Oh yeah, is Kathleen in the loo?" Jael scanned the pub belatedly.

"Actually, regrets, she wasn't feeling great," said Síle, aware of stretching the truth.

"Is it this weird lurgy that's going the rounds?" asked Anton.

She shook her head. "Mad busy at the hospital, as ever. Speaking of which, did you drive the lad to Casualty?"

"Did not," Jael snorted. "Stuck a few Band-Aids on him and told him not to ring unless he bleeds through them."

Anton straightened his tie. "I'm still not a hundred percent convinced about a male babysitter."

His wife knuckled him on the thigh. "I refuse to have this argument again. It's not teenage boys doing all the child abuse, it's priests and straight men like you."

"What, me personally?" He rolled his eyes at Síle. "As if I'd have the time or energy. Quick wank in the shower once a fortnight, if I'm up for it."

"Conor's a pet," said Jael. "I bet Yseult keeps him up half the night playing 'Demon Quest.'"

"That's your fault, by the way," Anton told Síle.

Síle nodded. "I'd never have downloaded it for her if I'd known my godchild had such an addictive personality."

"The apple doesn't fall far from the tree," said Jael, complacent.

"Marcus, my man." Anton stood up to give their tall, shaven-haired friend a hug.

"Nice jacket," Jael murmured, "though that shirt's all wrong with it."

"Nice haircut, shame about the face," the Englishman countered, squeezing onto the banquette.

Síle made room for him and kissed him on the ear. "So tell, tell. Apparently he has major news."

"You got laid," Jael decided. "You have an evil glow about you."

Marcus smiled, and scratched his head.

"That wouldn't count as *major*," Síle objected.

"Depends who it is. What about a celebrity? Maybe he's bagged some singer from a boy band."

Marcus made a face. "I've never fancied chicken. Maybe when I'm older; they say when you hit forty, you develop a taste for cradle-snatching."

"What a horrible prospect!" said Síle, who was going to pass that milestone in October. Her mind strayed back to Jude Turner. She'd looked early twenties, but how could you be the curator of anything at that age?

"Getting laid mightn't be major news," Anton put in, "but getting an actual boyfriend would."

"Give it a rest, lads," said Marcus, sheepish. "I like being single."

"Do you remember that time in the Stag's Head when some girl of all of nineteen claimed to be celibate?" Síle asked him. Turning to the others, she said, "Marcus wanted to know was she celery or halibut."

"Bet that threw her," said Jael with a cackle.

"What's—"

His wife interrupted Anton. "Oh you must have heard that one."

"Celery's when you say no to everyone," Marcus explained; "halibut is when no one'll have you."

"And you're still celery," Síle assured him.

"Crisp and crunchy."

"You never told us your news," Anton complained.

"Okay, here goes. I am the proud owner of a picturesque hovel in the North West."

A silence. "Northwest what? Northwest Dublin, meaning somewhere near Stoneybatter?" Síle asked without much hope.

"*The* North West, meaning the wilds of County Leitrim."

She dropped her face into her hands.

"Sorry, ducks," Marcus said.

"You don't sound one bit sorry," Jael pointed out.

"I can't help being excited," Marcus protested. "A great big house of my own! And it's time I got out anyway, this city's becoming a hole."

"But it isn't fair, I've lost half my friends to the sticks," Síle protested. "Trish's doing shiatsu in West Cork, Barra's tele-working in Gweedore...I know Dublin's insane unless you've the money for it, but do you all have to go so far and seem so happy about it?"

"You won't lose me, flower; I'll come up for weekends." Marcus knotted his fingers into hers. "For me it was about turning thirty-five."

"What's the big deal about thirty-five?" demanded Jael.

"You know, half the alotted *three score and ten.* The day after my party I was in my poky flat in Dun Laoghaire spritzing my little pots, and I suddenly thought, 'Sod this, I could have an orchard!'"

Well, what could Síle say to that? She shook her heavy ponytail off her shoulder and drained her drink, but it tasted like ammonia.

"Fair play to you, boyo," said Anton.

"When I got kicked out of home and went off backpacking," Jael remembered, "I used to tell people I'd shaken off Mother Ireland's bony claws for good. I thought I'd settle in Berlin or Athens, or never settle at all."

"Shows how little we know," said Marcus.

"I never chose to come back to Dublin," she went on with a frown, "I think I just dropped in one Christmas and got stuck. And now look at me! The career, the house, the husband, the child, like anchors shackling me to the spot."

"You could call it kismet," Síle suggested.

"Oh, spare me the Hindu baloney," said Jael. "It's just a long-term accident."

Anton kissed her on the jaw.

"Now that's exactly why I want to pick for myself where to live," said Marcus, "instead of letting some job or man do it."

"Have you photos?" asked Jael.

He hesitated. "They'd only mislead you."

"You mean it looks like a rubbish heap."

"Let's just say it needs some love."

As Jael interrogated him about the price and other specifics, Anton murmured in Síle's ear, "I've bollocksed up my laptop again; it won't shut down without poking the little button with a bent paper clip."

"I'll have a wee glance at it next time I'm over," she promised.

"You should charge for spoon-feeding these high-earning igno-rami," Jael cut in. "If you ever get sick of the Mile High Club, you could go into business as a techno-nanny."

"I forgot to ask about the inquiry," wailed Marcus. "So you didn't get the heave, I presume?"

"An official reprimand," said Síle with a sigh.

"Bastards."

"Management accepted not only that Mr. Jackson was dead when I was alerted to the situation, but that the doctor on board then advised me that he was hours past the point of resuscitation. However, they insisted that in line with airline policy I should still have run for the defibrillator and hauled him into the aisle, rigor mortis and all!"

"Now that would be just too *Fawlty Towers*," murmured Jael.

Síle was hot-cheeked remembering it; for all her seniority, her impeccable record, she'd been scolded like a child. Her mind slid sideways to Jude Turner's fine-boned face. (*I did offer the passenger another seat,* she'd said at the inquiry. *But as it was only half an hour till landing, she declined. The doctor did not consider that Mr. Jackson's body posed any health hazard.*) She'd mentioned the girl to Kathleen, of course; she'd said something about the Canadian in the seat next to the dead man being a bit rattled, and how Síle'd had to buy her a coffee.

"Oh, it's just typical of the industry these days," Marcus was saying, "all petty regulations and fear of legal repercussions."

"The latest is that we're meant to stop passengers from queuing for the loo, in case they're conspiring to rush the flight deck," Síle told them. "Oh, and we have to watch out for anyone reading the Koran or an almanac! Sometimes nineteen years on the job feels like nineteen years too many."

"Ah, but it must be worth staying for the, whatcha call it, the non-rev travel," said Anton.

"Yeah, you're the only person I know who can wake up on a rainy day off and wonder, *Where will I fly to?*," growled Jael.

"Though that was a bigger deal in the days before cheap flights," Marcus pointed out.

"You needn't gripe," Anton told his wife, "you were in Trieste last weekend."

"That was business. We got that EuroJoyce Festival gig, by the way, Síle; it's a two-month campaign, megabudget."

"Good on you!"

"Business, meaning champagne breakfasts," said Anton, "while Ys and Daddy were choking down stale Bran Buds at home."

Síle wriggled her way to the bar for the next round. She looked back at the animated faces of her friends. Jael was reapplying her brown lipstick in a tiny mirror and jabbing at Anton with her elbow at the same time. He was going a little silvery around the temples. Jael, she happened to know, would be entirely gray by now if it weren't for expensive monthly applications of Malaysian Cherry. In her charcoal pinstriped jacket she looked so... worldly, was that the word? Her friend had dressed so much more wildly in the days when Síle had first known her, as a perpetual student living off cheques from her parents' stud farm. Of course, Jael had been a lesbian back then, all battered leather and ties from Oxfam.

That was the early nineties, before the boom turned everything speedy and pricey, before Jael blagged her way into the business and set up Primadonna Publicity. And before Anton. Síle thought back to the phone call in the middle of the night: *I've said I'll marry him, the fat-bottomed guy in middle management. Do you think I'm out of my tree?* For as long as Síle had known them, Anton and Jael had yapped at each other like dogs. Especially when Yseult was born: Motherhood had sent Jael reeling. (*The creature pisses through everything I put on her!*) But their marriage seemed as solid as any other.

Then again, who could tell from the outside whether something was built on quicksand or rock? You could know a friend all your life and still find it a complete mystery why he or she loved this particular individual, out of all the people in the world. What did the two of them whisper to each other under the duvet? Was one of them in charge, or was there a secret power-sharing agreement? And as to whether a partnership would last, well, you might as well toss a coin. Síle had seen gorgeous, tender romances founder on the smallest rocks, and septic yokings linger on till death did them part. Couples she'd thought were perfectly content had broken up and confessed to years of complicated misery; there was an awful privacy about relationships, even in these days of tell-all phone-ins.

Her gizmo beeped. *Out of fluoride-free toothpaste. Night-night.*

Síle made a mental note to try the late-night pharmacy on the way home.

In the first couple of years, she'd often caught herself boasting about the fact that she and Kathleen didn't cohabitate: *We don't fancy domesticity.* But they'd been kidding themselves, she thought now. After five years, all couples were domestic, even if they kept two addresses. The pleasant banalities crept up on you; the comforts and irritations became equally habitual.

"Three sour apple martinis and a Murphy's," she roared in the barman's direction, waving her €50 note, but his nod was so minimal, she couldn't tell if it was meant for her.

Old Habits

Yes you did, so you did,
So did she and so did I.
And the more I think about it
Sure the nearer I'm to cry.
Oh, wasn't it the happy days
When troubles we had not,
And our mothers made
Colcannon in the little skillet pot?

—ANON
The Skillet Pot

An icy February night; Jude's first drink since the funeral.

She and Gwen were beside the fire in Ireland's bar, the Diving Duck, known to its regulars as the Dive. Gwen was staring at a poster above the rack of ill-assorted antique pistols. She shoved her sandy hair out of her face. "Jazz ballet classes. Who ever heard of a jazz ballerina?"

Jude kept on saying nothing.

Gwen pushed the basket of fries an inch in her friend's direction. "At least over here I don't run into relatives of the residents like I do in St. Mary's. I swear, I was having a quiet beer across the road from my apartment the other night and this lady came up to ask if I'd ever found her dad's cashmere cardigan, and how were his, uh, B.M.s these days?"

Jude was replaying not the cremation, not the hospital, even, but that moment in her aunt's front room in Luton: *Unless Bill drives us.* It was important to establish the beginning of the end. That way, everything before Luton counted as normal life. *I used to live with my mother,* Jude practiced; *I lived with my mother till last month when she passed on.* No, the euphemism was creepy. *When she died. Yeah, of a brain tumor. Oh, it was very quick; better that way.* Or so everyone said. For Jude, those few weeks of January—from the first hints of Rachel's disorientation in her sister's house, through the episodes of confusion back home, the morning she woke howling with pain, the CAT scan, MRI, and biopsy, the first seizure felling her in the snowdrift outside the general store, those terrible new words to learn (*high-grade, infiltrating, frontal lobe*), the radiation, vomiting, drunken slur, blindness in one eye, and so on, and so on—those weeks hadn't felt quick, but more like a sojourn in hell. She couldn't imagine how they'd felt to her mother.

When Jude hadn't been sitting in various London, Ontario, waiting rooms, she'd continued going to work, in a zombielike way. She'd presided over a board meeting in which Jim McVaddy (untiring, at eighty-two) mentioned that he might have thought twice about donating the collection that three generations of hard bargainers had built up in the McVaddy barn if he'd known that local businesses wouldn't appreciate it enough to chip in, and Glad Soontiens had countered that in her view the Ireland Museum's overhead should be covered by tax dollars handed back by those robbers in Ottawa. Jude had also overhauled the database of all known pre-1900 residents of Perth and Huron townships, and was halfway through putting up an exhibition called "Blood on the Ice: A Hundred Years of Local Hockey," when Rizla had dropped by and said, "Get the fuck out of here."

The one thing she was grateful for, in retrospect, was that the final horrors had stormed in so quickly, there'd been no need for her to pretend to get on with things anymore. For what had turned out to be the last four days of her mother's life, Jude had camped out in the hospital room. (The specialists in London had sent Rachel back to Stratford, Ontario, for what they called "palliative care," which translated as dope.) Gwen drove over from St. Mary's every day, sometimes with a box of doughnut holes. She sat there holding Rachel's hand, making conversation: "Nice day out there, Mrs. Turner. Fifteen below, but they say it'll get up to minus three or four." She gave Jude occasional bits of advice out of the side of her mouth: "She might like a bit of Bach." "Remind them to roll her over, or she'll get sores." "You know that light has a dimmer?"

"Jude? Another?"

She jerked, and covered her beer glass. She wasn't in the hospital, she was in the Dive; it was mid-February now, and her mother's ashes were a gritty mulch on the roots of the lilacs in the backyard, under a fresh fall of snow.

"Okay. Call it a night," said Gwen, heading for the washroom.

Jude took the last few fries from the basket—feeding herself had become dully automatic—and followed her old friend with her eyes. Gwen had a broad face, attractive if you liked her, plain if you didn't. She wore fleece from October to April, then switched to cotton; she claimed to be too busy practically running the Sunset Residence to bother with "all that frilly shit." In their high school it was Gwen who'd gotten called a "lez," mostly for lack of boyfriends, whereas Jude had almost never been without one. Gwen could see the joke in that; as she'd once told Jude, "My market value might be higher if I batted for the other team." But these things were in the hands of the gods, and Gwen's preference was for tall, lithe guys. (Her one grand passion had been for a giant of a hockey player who'd repeatedly trampled on her heart before turning pro.)

"How you *doing*, Jude?" Dave, the barman, set down their check weighted with two cinnamon mints. Considering Jude had gone to school with the guy, his manner was avuncular, it struck her now; maybe it came with the job.

What was the appropriate answer? *Just dandy? Frigging awful?* "Not too bad."

In her wallet she found the little card with the swallow on it, and she let herself trace the slightly raised image with her thumb. *Síle O'Shaughnessy*. Jude had thought she'd lost the card until she came across it two thirds of the way through *Dombey and Son*, the book she'd been reading to her semiconscious mother at the hospital, out of some vestigial memory that this was what you did when someone was dying. Jude never used to mislay things, but now it was happening all the time; yesterday she'd stomped around the house in search of her glasses for half an hour before discovering that they'd slipped off the hall table into her boot. She used to have a sort of quiet about her that some found enviable, others irksome; "the butch gravitas thing," a girlfriend had called it. Jude had never taken any credit for it, any more than for the smooth curve of her jaw. But now she couldn't remember how to be "solid" or "grounded" or any of those words: Loss had tipped her whole life on its side.

She rubbed the letters again. *Síle O'Shaughnessy:* She practiced saying the name in her head, though she'd never spoken it aloud. In all the dread and chaos of the last six weeks there'd been no occasion to tell anyone about the flight attendant with the Irish accent and the Indian face. But this was the peculiar thing: Jude thought about Síle O'Shaughnessy all the time. The rapid, tilting sentences; the slightly tired, ripe mouth. The memory was like a teasel stuck to Jude's heel. Every time she remembered Luton, the thought led sideways to Síle O'Shaughnessy, whose name opened like a door into another, sun-drenched world. Jude liked to imagine the woman in L.A. or Bangkok, Web-surfing on her gizmo over a cocktail, or in her lizard-green uniform bouncing high above her trampoline, her plait dancing like a cobra.

She knew this was absurd, bordering on obsessive, but she wasn't willing to give up anything that took her mind off the horror show of images of her mother, from capable retired receptionist, to frightened patient, to old lady dead in a bed. (They'd had an absurd argument about cremation a week from the end; Jude had argued for a grave and headstone—just name and dates, in the Quaker way—but Rachel had refused to waste the money. Jude had accused her mother of being a *cheapskate;* it was that word she couldn't forgive herself for now.)

"Thank *you.*" Dave again, swooping down for the saucer.

Gwen intercepted Dave and snatched the $20, tossing it back in front of Jude and replacing it with her own.

"Is this one of the stages of bereavement, getting all my drinks bought for me?" Whenever Jude tried to exercise her sense of humour these days, it came out creaky.

Gwen pulled on her beige down jacket. Jude got up, stiff-kneed; all her joints ached. Dave held the heavy door for them: "Goodnight, ladies."

"Night, Dave." Snow whirled into their faces.

"You okay going home?" Gwen asked her.

"It's where I live."

"Anytime you want to crash on my couch…"

Jude almost smiled. "Never again. I've been telling you for years, it's like being char-grilled."

"Buy me a new sofa bed for my birthday, now you're an heiress," Gwen threw over her shoulder as she headed to her car. This was a sardonic reference to the $1,391.61 that Rachel Turner had left, along with the yellow brick house, to her only child.

The wind was biting; Jude pulled her scarf up to her eyes as she turned down the deserted Main Street. It was funny that after what she'd been through, she still cared about such tiny sensations. Still preferred a warm nose to a frozen one, cold beer to lukewarm, any dinner to none. The body insisted on doing its old selfish thing, and the mind was no different. *Síle O'Shaughnessy,* she said in her head, *Síle O'Shaughnessy,* the sibilance like a tilted rain stick.

When she got to the house, Jude stared up. (Last April she'd seen Bub's porch roof crash to the ground under its burden of

snow.) The flaking sash windows were dark. Long before environ-
mentalism, Rachel had ingrained in her daughter thrifty habits
such as turning off the light as you left the room. *Next time I go out,*
thought Jude, *I'm leaving one on.*

No, she couldn't bear it; despite what she'd told Gwen, she
wasn't willing to sleep alone tonight.

A few streets away, Rizla's windows glowed with the uneven
light of the TV. There were bylaws against parking a winterized
trailer on a vacant lot and living in it year round—she'd looked
them up for him years ago—but the cops never gave Rizla any
grief; he claimed he'd smoked up with half of them in high school.

There was no answer when she tapped, but she let herself in
anyway. Siouxsie stirred and whined, but put her head back down
on her paws when she recognized Jude. Rizla was supine on the
couch, a half-smoked cigarette in his hand. Jude snatched it out of
his fingers. He woke with a long snort and sat up. "What the fuck?"

"What the fuck is this?" she asked, brandishing the cigarette.

His eyes veered to the door. "Did I ask you over?"

Jude knew he was just confused, but she treated it as sarcasm.
"No, but just as well I happened by, dumb-ass. You could have gone
up in flames."

Rizla blinked, shoving a curtain of black hair out of his face
with the heel of his hand. "I was watching *CSI* something or other."

She stepped over Siouxsie to the television, which was showing
something about penguins, and punched the power switch. "How
often do I have to tell you, put the fag out before you lie down."

"Okay."

"You say okay, but you don't do it, Riz." Her voice was unsteady. "I mean, you might as well play Russian roulette. This whole
place's going to go up like paper and there'll be nothing left of you
but cinders in the couch springs."

He got to his feet and wrapped her up in his arms. A sob jumped
out of Jude's throat. There was a density, an amazing inertia to this

man. Rizla lifted his head and she thought he was going to say something, maybe something wise that would restore her to herself, but he only yawned like a hippo. He'd had far more practice at losing people than Jude, it struck her now; his father, mother, and two of his brothers had all gone young.

She wiped her eyes on his shirt. She tried twice before her voice came out. "By the way, I never got around to saying... That time you came to the hospital? I'm sorry she didn't know you."

"Oh, just paying my respects," he said. Then, satiric, "Ma Turner never did much like the trailer-trash that led her darling daughter astray."

Provoking Jude was an old game. "That's bullshit," she couldn't help saying.

Rizla shrugged his massive shoulders, grinning through a yawn. "Gotta hit the sack."

Jude stayed, and only partly because she felt ashamed of having roared at him.

Sometimes on nights like these nothing happened, and sometimes something did; it wasn't a big deal either way. This was how it had been between them for years now, ever since they'd broken up. It wasn't an event if Jude said yes, without words, nor a problem if she said no, equally silently. Rizla was always open to the possibility—*just how guys are,* he'd once told her ruefully—but never pressed any claim.

Tonight turned out to be something rather than nothing. But it didn't comfort Jude the way she'd thought it might. Afterward she couldn't get to sleep; she threw the condom away, then turned the TV on low and watched someone wallpaper a room.

At six she walked home through icy fog for a bath before work. There was a message on the machine from her father. He called her "honey"; that must be a new Florida habit. Jude supposed one parent was better than none, but the fact was that Ben Turner was the wrong one, and about sixteen hundred kilometres too far south, besides.

She called him back, still standing in the hall beside her dripping boots, to get it over with. "I didn't wake you?"

"Lord no, I don't need more than five hours a night these days," Ben told her.

She thought of her father's sun-ripened face, in the Coldstream Meetinghouse; various Friends had stood up to give their spare, kind testimonies to Rachel Turner, but he hadn't said a word. The irony was that Ben was the birthright Quaker, and Rachel a desultory Anglican who'd become a "convinced Friend" (as they put it) after marrying him, but he'd left it behind long ago, with so much else. He'd flown in on the day of the cremation and departed the day after, although—it struck Jude now—he might never see his hometown again. Anger flew past her like a garish bird. "So you got back all right?" she said, aware it was a meaningless question.

"Yep, your uncle Frank picked me up at the airport; he says how are you looking after his beautiful motorcycle? Rochelle was so sorry she wasn't able to come for the funeral, by the way."

It bothered Jude that her father had a second wife with a name so like that of the first, but fancier. Rochelle was a few years older than Ben; she'd proposed to him on her seventy-fifth birthday, at a tea dance in Key West. Maybe the similarity of the names would make it easier for him to remember what to call Rochelle, if the day came when he started getting "confusion episodes," Jude thought vindictively.

"The little operation on her hip went just great—"

Damn, she should have remembered to ask. "That's wonderful."

"You holding up okay, honey?"

"Oh, you know." She wasn't going to comfort him, and let him tick his daughter off the list.

"Jude, if there's anything you need, anything at all…" The line crackled with static. "What's that, honey?" he asked somebody in the background.

Don't call us both honey.

"Hey, Rochelle says you should come down for a vacation, get a bit of colour. I could cover your flight—"

"I like the winter," she reminded him.

"Yeah, but under the circumstances..."

Jude had developed a new intolerance for euphemism. Why couldn't he just say *now your mother's dead?* Now Rachel, whom Ben had once loved—presumably, or enough to marry late, beget one daughter, and stay with for eighteen years before succumbing to the heavy mascara of Julia McBride from the general store—was cinders, sprinkled under the snow-bent lilacs. (There hadn't been any chance to clarify this part of her mother's wishes, after the "cheapskate" conversation. Jude seemed to remember Rachel remarking that she admired lilacs because they put forth their heavenly bloom promptly every May and then went back to stubborn green for the rest of the year. But perhaps that was one of Jude's own thoughts. Once people were gone, you found yourself carrying on imaginary conversations with them.)

"I should head off to work now, Dad."

"Sure, sure. It's marvelous how you've got that little museum up and running."

Her teeth met with a click. She knew he couldn't care less about roots, his or anyone else's. How else could he have grown up as a third-generation resident of Ireland, Ontario, spent almost sixty years there, then flitted off to Florida? Ever since Ben had shucked off his old life—and wife—his voice had had a kind of indecent merriment to it, a quality of sunshine.

Jude knew she was being absurd. Fifteen again: squatting on the creaky top stair, waiting for her parents to call her downstairs and tell her about the divorce. That was the summer everything had gone wrong. Before that, the Turners had been broke, but Jude hadn't cared; what did she need pocket money for, when all the things she liked to do were free and she knew so many of the locals, it was like living in a book?

"Keep in touch, honey, you hear?"

Keep in touch. That's what you said to old acquaintances when you bumped into them in the street.

"Will do." Jude put the phone down and listened to silence fill up the house. *My house,* she practiced saying in her head.

Foreign Correspondents

So are you in a hurry now
Or are you going away,
Or won't you stand and listen
To these words I'm going to say?

—ANON
The Black Horse

On the twenty-second of February, her mother had been dead a month. Jude marked the day by going down to the phone booth at the crossroads and calling home, to hear Rachel's careful, rather British intonation one last time. "You have reached the Turner residence…" Only when she'd trudged back through the dirty snow, tears freezing into hard tracks down her face, did she figure out that she could have heard the message from home by pressing the right sequence of buttons. She made herself record a new, briefer sentence right away: "Jude here, leave a message." She had to do it four times before she sounded halfway normal.

Jude suddenly regretted that they'd switched to voice mail a few years ago; if they'd kept their old answering machine, at least she could have held on to the tape. She had a few letters from her mother, and photographs of her, though not many—camera-shy, Rachel had the knack of evading the lens—but no video footage, no trace of her voice, even. Maybe when her mother had reached the age of eighty, it would have occurred to Jude to get around to recording her. *Textual evidence poor, artifacts sparse.* Like the traces of some obscure ancestor's life, thought Jude, for once wishing she were more modern.

She hadn't read more than a page of anything in weeks. She hadn't picked up her guitar in so long, her calluses were going soft. She hadn't made so much as a loaf of bread.

In the crammed, orderly shed that acted as the museum's archive-cum-office, Jude put herself to work removing rusty staples from a bundle of 1930s letters between Mrs. Gertrude Pleider of Ireland, Ontario—dead of complications after a fall from her motorized scooter outside the turkey factory at ninety-two, that was twenty-six more years than Rachel had got, *stop it Jude just stop it*— and her cousin Miss Jane Vorden of Wetaskiwin, Alberta. Jude was usually grateful for donations, especially of manuscripts rather than crack-backed rocking chairs or moldy snowshoes, but rusty staples got on her nerves.

She printed out this week's "From the Archives" page, slipped it into a plastic cover, and pulled her boots on to go pin it up on the notice board outside.

Some Destitute Orphan Immigrants
Arrived 6 May 1891 NOBLE, Thomas Age: 16 Sex: M indoor
      farm servant on SS Norwegian from Liverpool to Quebec
Arrived 4 June 1891 WEINER Adolph Age: 10 Sex:
      M scholar
Arrived 4 June 1891 WEINER Pauline Age: 10 Sex: F scholar
Arrived 4 June 1891 WEINER Maggie Age: 11 Sex F scholar,
      all on SS Parisian from Liverpool to Quebec

Glad Soontiens, a textile artist and Jude's best ally on the board, paused to read over Jude's shoulder. She let out a smoker's laugh. "All those little Weiners. What does 'scholar' mean?"

"Kid who'd been to school, I guess."

"Bet they got split up quick and turned into cow-herders."

"Adoption's a slim possibility," Jude told the older woman.

"By the way. Did Rachel ever finish that Stars and Stairs quilt of hers?"

"All but," said Jude, concentrating on pressing in another thumbtack. "It still needs batting, I think."

"Drop it over, I'll fix it up for this year's show."

Jude's eyes were a blur. By the time she managed to turn away from the notice board, Glad was halfway down the street.

After the CBC radio news there was an item about Pakistan, which reminded her in a roundabout way of Síle O'Shaughnessy. Jude thought of the flight attendant sitting with her sheer-stockinged legs crossed, sipping only the best Italian coffee, gazing out windows at bright squares or rainy streets, looking glamorous, anticipatory.

The beige computer was half-hidden behind a crate of microforms; Jude mostly used it to look up databases such as the "Ontario Register of Births and Deaths." It occurred to her now that none of the volunteers knew her password, which was PASSWORD.

Oh go on if you're going to, she told herself.

```
Sender: irelandmuseum@interweb.ca
To: sile@oshaugh.com
Date: 22 February 11:22
Re: Greetings
    Dear Sile (apologies for not knowing how to add
the accent over the i in your name!)
    You should take it as a compliment that this is
the first non-work e-mail I've ever sent. I just
wanted to say hi and that I owe you a breakfast. If
you happen to fly into Toronto sometime I could jump
on the highway, if you've got a break between flights
and want to "eat like a beast."
```

Jude was aiming for a breezy tone here, so she wouldn't sound like some hick from the boonies desperate for a date. The truth was she never *jumped on* the clogged highway to Toronto; she only went if she had to use research libraries or catch some major exhibition at the Royal Ontario Museum.

```
    Today I'm supposed to be indexing some letters,
and a complete run of an anti-Confederation newspaper
from the early 1860s. (Confederation was when Canada
decided to be a country, in case you're interested.)
```

Unlikely, Jude groaned to herself, and backspaced over the sentence.

```
    Looking at the "Historic Bridges of southwestern
Ontario" calendar on the office wall, I see it's been
seven and a half weeks since Heathrow (well, since I
was there; you've probably been back twenty times).
The reason I didn't get in touch till now is that my
mother turned out to have a brain tumor and has been
dying. I mean, she died on Jan. 22.
    As it's taken me about ten minutes to compose the
last two sentences I think I better call it a day
before I make it a habit of weeping all over you.
```

Weird grammar, needy tone; Jude backspaced as far as "call it a day."

```
If you've got a minute in between zigzagging all over
the known world, you could let me know if you got
this.
    Bye,
    Jude (Turner)
```

She was about to hit SEND when something occurred to her, and she edged around the paper-stacked desk to the reference bookcase.

```
P.S. I just looked you up that bit about the
Rechabites. It's Jeremiah 35:7:

    Neither shall ye build house, nor sow seed,
    nor plant vineyard, nor have any: but all
    your days ye shall dwell in tents: that ye
    may live many days in the land where ye be
    strangers.

The funny thing is, I'd remembered the Rechabites'
tent-dwelling as a bad habit, or maybe a punishment.
```

But rereading the passage, I think they're actually
being advised to stay mobile, so as not to be
vulnerable to siege warfare! Does that metaphor work
for you, Sile? Do you see yourself as an elusive
road warrior who'll never get walled up in one place
and have to barbecue rats like us settled folk?
Anyway. Bye again.

She almost thought better of it and erased the whole paragraph, but actually it read livelier than what came before it, and ending on a biblical tangent was better than with the announcement of her mother's death.

Sending Message: "Greetings." Out Basket Empty. As if the words were a flock of swallows tossed from a cage, chasing each other across the midwinter sky.

A thump on the storm door made her jump. Rizla's big brown face against the glass, eyes rolled back, tongue lolling.

"Sorry if you're desperate for some heritage, but the museum's closed on Mondays," she said, moving forward to hug him, but she mistimed it; he'd already stepped back to kick some snow off his boots.

"Can't stay, I've got the wheels off some piece-of-shit Pontiac. Doing okay?" Rizla asked.

Jude's throat locked again. "God, I'm tired of all this sympathy," she breathed out. "Did I ever tell you, Bub knocked on my door after the funeral and offered to shovel my drive for the rest of the winter?"

"Bub your mute neighbour?"

"Turns out he's got plenty to say, once he gets started. Very eloquent on death having all of us in its sights, and how my mother was the genuine article; she baked him a blueberry crisp the day he moved in. He's doing a distance learning module on electricity, and his real name's Llewellyn."

Rizla let out a hiccup of laughter. "Yep, I guess that wouldn't fly at the turkey factory." He took out a can of ginger ale and popped it with one finger. "Dropping by later for the roast beef special?" He was the sole mechanic at the Garage, the town's gas station-cum-café.

Jude shook her head. "I've got squash to reheat. Gwen's coming over this evening after I watch her snowpitch tournament, you want to join us?" She asked it without much hope.

"Would that be for leftover squash, or a real dinner?"

"If you need a burger that much—"

"Just messing with you," he told her, his grin showing his uneven teeth. He put his can down on some brown files.

Jude snatched it up. "Those are the Krebniz family letters; I only have them on loan."

"They're kinda smeary already," he said, flicking through them.

"Those are tear stains," she told him, seizing the files. "None of the three brothers ever saw each other again."

"History! What a downer," he observed, swigging his ginger ale.

"So tonight, maybe you could come by after, for a beer?"

"Nah, I think I can live without another lecture about my 'redneck attitudes.'"

"Aren't you ever going to let that drop?"

Rizla curled his lip. "Your friend may change old farts' diapers for a living, but she reckons she's pretty upscale."

"Just because Gwen didn't appreciate your Holocaust joke—"

"Hey, if anyone's entitled, First Nations are," he said with a smirk, "we got genocided too. Besides, what about that time in the diner?"

Jude sighed. "So she asked the waitress to wipe the table."

"It was the way she did it," Rizla reminisced, "kinda snitty. I figure, any gal that kicks up a stinkola about a dab of ketchup, she'll be the same way later on."

"Later on, when?"

He glared at his crotch. "You think her ladyship would ever sleep in the wet spot?"

Jude's guffaw surprised her.

At lunchtime, she walked the two blocks home through driving snow, feeling as hollow as a reed. Her right hand, holding her cigarette, was numb despite the glove. One of these days she'd have to grow up and give up smoking.

Despite the mailbox's NO JUNK PLEASE, SAVE THE TREES sign, it was stuffed with flyers as usual; she felt unaccountably annoyed. She kicked the clumped snow off her boots and unlaced them in the hall. There was one voice mail, a guy in Mitchell responding to her classified about the 1994 Honda Civic. Jude flinched at the thought of her mother's car disappearing from out front, then reminded herself that she could do with the money; without Rachel's pension, the gas bills were hitting a lot harder.

When she threw the flyers into the recycling, a wet-edged envelope slid out of the bundle. It had a blurred postmark that said *Baile Atha Cliath,* which was gibberish to Jude, but the stamp showed a carved Celtic cross and her heart started to boom. She sat on the bottom stair in the dim hall, and took her penknife off her belt to slit the envelope, her hands shaking as if she'd had too much coffee.

17 Stoneybatter Place
Stoneybatter
Dublin 2
Republic of Ireland
14 February

Well hello there Jude the Obscure. I hope you can make head or tail of my writing? because ironically enough for a techie like me (who can boast of having watched the first live birth on the Net in '98) my printer's just expired in a cloud of black smoke so I'm having to copy out this letter from my screen BY HAND. Only the fact that the shuttle picking me up for a flight to Boston is running half an hour late justifies such a waste of energy. I can't believe what a primitive business this is, making squiggles on paper with black drops from a tube...

I did wait six weeks to see would you give in and contact me first, but clearly you're the Strong Silent Stubborn Type with whom a girl should never get into a battle of wills. Or of course more prosaicly? [my spellcheck's never heard of this word] you may have lost my card, since things are always going astray in transit; over the years I've lost most of my favourite earrings down hotel drains. (In my spare time I'm happy to wear odd earrings but on the job we have to be tediously well groomed.)

Our friend Mr. George L. Jackson was Pentecostal, it turns out: seventy-five, divorced with four grown children. (The inquiry was ghastly, but I didn't actually lose my job.) Do you think about him much? I do, especially on night flights, when the lights are low and lots of passengers are asleep. He ran his own small plastics company, and he was flying to England for a trade show. No previous history of heart disease, but that's what did for him. The airline flew his eldest daughter over to collect his body and paid for the embalming. So now you know as much as I do.

My hand is tired already, I'm going to have to stop before I've actually said much. I wonder how long this will take to get to you by mule, elk, or whatever the Mounties are using these days? I'm trying to picture your little hamlet of Ireland, Ontario, and I realize the images in my head are all out of Northern Exposure, *which is actually Alaska, isn't it? Small-town life has always given me the creeps—no cinemas (I'm such a film slut I'd see two a day if I had the time) or music venues or juice bars when you need a strawberry-pear smoothie—the hideous homogeneity—how can you bear it?*

Shut up, Síle, you're being very rude...Maybe it's just me, cities turn me on. I need to feel free as a kite—I happen to be based in Dublin but it could be anywhere really (well, anywhere with a population of more than a million!), life being a moveable feast, to use the old Catholic phrase. Kathleen (my girlfriend) disagrees, she says emigrants are always a bit pathetic.

Outside the window on my street of skinny terraced houses I can see some valiant purple crocuses pushing up. (I don't know how to grow anything myself but my neighbour Deirdre and I have an MBA, she uses my windowsill as an overflow for her pots.) Clearly spring—my favourite season—is round the corner.

Hmm, handwriting's kind of like Morse code, slow and serious. It's so much more tactile than print, I'll grant you that. Here's a smear for instance of the remains of my raspberry tart:

> *Síle.*
> *P.S. Happy Valentine's Day.*

Struggling to decipher the crazy handwriting, Jude's first impression of this letter was that it was indeed written to kill half an hour. And was that "Kathleen (my girlfriend)" as in friend or as in...On the second reading, she paid more attention to the bits about waiting six weeks and a struggle of wills, and the pointed reference to Valentine's Day. It must have taken quite a while to copy by hand. She licked her finger and touched it to the brown smear at the bottom of the page, tasted it. Raspberry reawakened in her mouth, and she thought, *What a flirt!*

She reread the letter twice more; she was too excited to eat lunch. She sat down at the kitchen table with her fountain pen and a not-too-yellowed page of Ireland Museum notepaper.

22 February

Dear Síle,
Got your letter just after I e-mailed—snap! Very good to
hear from you.
I know, snail mail takes a while, but just think: If our
ancestors hadn't communicated with each other on something
as lasting as paper, over the last thousand years or so, there
wouldn't be much trace of them left.

Jude was aiming for thoughtful, but it was coming out preachy.
Time to switch topics.

Yeah, I think about George L. Jackson, mostly when I can't
get to sleep. Thanks for letting me know about him. Not that a
handful of facts tell you much about who someone really was.

Rachel Turner, *née* Dorridge, born Chichester, April 3, 1938.
Arrived Toronto September 1957. Worked Ladies Apparel Depart-
ment, Eaton's. Married—
Stop it, Jude.

I keep having to consult my dictionary. It explains
"moveable feast," but when you say you and your neighbour
have an MBA, I presume you're not talking about a shared
Master's in Business Administration?
If spring's around the corner in Big Ireland, you're clearly
not just five hours ahead of me, but a whole season. Here in
Ontario it's a shiny winter afternoon, and the sidewalks are
covered in thigh-high jagged mounds of beige snow, so I
prefer to walk on the street, which squeaks underfoot. Some
houses still have their Christmas lights hung along the eaves.
I'm particularly proud of the icicle outside my bedroom
window, which is almost as long as I am.

Oh god, this was like some schoolgirl's essay on "A Winter Day."

My mother's house is on Main Street, just two blocks from the crossroads. I keep trying to saying "my house," but it feels like one more tiny way of letting Mom disappear.

Well, what was the point of writing to this stranger at all if Jude couldn't say what was on her mind? She pressed on.

The museum is only another block away; how's that for a low-stress commute? Last summer when I busted up my knee playing street hockey with some ten-year-olds, I was able to hop to work. You know, this crossroads community (officialspeak for a one-horse town) really isn't so "hideously homogeneous." We've got flower-arrangers and fundamentalists, yeah—and last year someone did chalk RUG MUNCHER (i.e., me) on the door of the museum— but also a gay-run guesthouse, two Web-site designers, a day trader and a Buddhist. When you live in people's pockets you learn how out there some of them are. There's a guy in a rotting mansion just north of town who sets his Labrador on fallow deer and is rumoured to have an unnatural relationship with her. His wife left him a long time ago, or some say she's buried in the woods... Uh-oh, on reflection that's going to confirm all your prejudices about rural creepiness, isn't it?

It's true that if I want a strawberry-pear smoothie I've got to use my mother's Moulinex. Try again: MY Moulinex. No, cut that; it'll always feel like my mother's Moulinex. Síle, it just occurred to me that I envy you for losing your mother when you were too young to really know what was happening.

Oh lord. This was more real, but—

Sorry, that sounds cruel, and dumb. Of course it's better to

have a mother when you're growing up—but right now I
miss mine so much that all my bones hurt.

The letter was taking a rapid nosedive.

This letter is taking a rapid nosedive, but I guess there's
no use pretending I'm fully compos mentis these days. That's
another thing about handwritten letters, they're more honest.
If I'd tried to scribble over the above, you'd have seen it,
whereas e-mails let people edit their feelings.

Maybe she should e-mail a revised version of this after all. She
pulled viciously on one ear lobe. How hard could it be to answer a
letter? Not too gushy, not too cool; not too ninety-year-old, not too
seven. Somewhere in between "Dear Valued Customer" and "Dear
Woman of My Dreams."

That phrase stopped Jude short. She laid down the pen. She'd
forgotten the dream till now; she couldn't even remember if she'd
had it last night or a few nights ago. It was simple, and mortifying.
Síle O'Shaughnessy reclining on a cloud, nude and brown as a figure by Gauguin, looking straight out, unashamed.

Jude started scribbling the first lie she could think of.

There's the phone, better go answer it.
Till next time, Jude.
P.S. I like your line about flying free like a kite—except
that if you've ever flown a kite you may have noticed they
have to be anchored firmly by the string or else they flop out
of the sky?

Well, the length of that P.S. blew her story about the phone ringing, but never mind. Jude would have liked to enclose something, a
flower maybe, but there was nothing growing out there in the frozen
mud. Instead, she searched the sideboard, and ended up dropping
into the envelope a tiny inch-long feather from a Canada goose.

Virtually Nothing

Ah, but when the post knocks and
the letter comes
always the miracle seems repeated—
speech attempted.

—VIRGINIA WOOLF
Jacob's Room

Re: Technology etc
Hey Jude (as the Beatles put it), thanks for your
astonishing ginger pumpkin loaf, I take back any
aspersions I've ever cast on pumpkins. I love the old
Hudson's Bay Company tin you sent it in, I'm going
to store my bangles in it. To make this a mutually
beneficial arrangement (forgot to tell you, that's
what MBA means) I'm posting you some Irish truffles,
since North American chocolate doesn't deserve the
name.

"Rug muncher" is a new one on me, but after
several minutes of reflection I believe I've worked
it out! I still maintain that small towns are creepy,
but mercifully you don't come across like a small-
town girl; all those childhood years browsing in the
adult section of the library must explain it, I
suppose.

Got your last e-mail in my hotel in Boston--I'm
deeply flattered that I've caused this quantum shift
from post to e-mail, can I tempt you to move on to
Instant Messaging next?--or texting if you'd only get
a mobile . . .

Yes, Kathleen = girlfriend as in partner not as
in female friend, sorry. (I mean sorry for the
confusion.) Our two Englishes only pretend to be the
same language! The one that always confuses me is
"mad,"--when an American tells me he's mad I
visualize a straitjacket.

Right now I'm in the crew lounge at Dublin
Airport. No, my movements are not like "the random
firing of electrons," since you ask, they're as
highly structured as a monk's. Four days on, three
off, and we bid for our schedules in strict order of
seniority. Luckily few are as senior as me because so
many have switched to jobs on the ground, and a
third of my unlucky colleagues have been given the
heave in recent years. Our airline used to be classy,
but always on the brink of bankruptcy, so after 9/11
it had to reinvent itself as lean and mean, a.k.a.
cheap and nasty.

Still: flying's in my blood, because I was born
at 30,000 feet. My Amma--who'd been an air hostess
herself--insisted Da take her for a last-minute visit
to her parents in Cochin. (High-caste communists, a
funny combo.) She was more than eight months on, but
the rules weren't as strict in the sixties, and on the
way home to Dublin she suddenly had me in the aisle!

You ask how I "stay so charming all the time"
during flights--well, I fake it. I've never quite
expoded and screamed "Yiz are all a shower of bitches
and bastards" (as folklore has it a former colleague
once did) but I've come close. Ah no, the truth is
a flight attendant has to basically like people or
the job would start draining her like a vampire on
day one. Speaking of which, time to go through
security . . .

Re: slurs on "Frozen North"

Síle, I just checked an atlas and I'll have you
know that Ireland, Ont., is ten degrees further SOUTH
than Dublin. I admit the snowbanks are still hip-high
but the sun's dazzling.

So, a partner as well as a house; you sound
pretty settled to me, for all your talk of
freedom . . .

Re: the museum, it's a lovely 1862 schoolhouse;
when the town tried to flog it to a sinister
Heritage Village, a bunch of us formed a protest
committee. Persuaded an old farmer called Jim McVaddy
to donate his priceless Canadiana on condition the
town handed over the schoolhouse for a museum--and
then managed to beg start-up money from a private
foundation. Since I was just about the only one
under retirement age (and I'd been interning at a
Children's Pioneer Museum half an hour away while
doing my BA in the evenings), I wangled the one paid
job. In year five, *Backroads and Byways* magazine has
hailed us as "one of the more charmingly maverick
little museums in Ontario" (!).

I just had a turkey sub with Rizla. The garage/
café is run by the Leungs: see, this area is not
entirely populated by the "Waspy pioneers" of your
imagination. Gong Leung goes into Cantonese whenever
she's bitching about the customers. Their daughter
Diana looks totally Canadian and it occurs to me it's
because she wears braces. My friend Gwen always says
you can tell a Brit (meaning, from your islands) by
the bad teeth, but I've assured her that yours are
extremely white and even.

Re: Quakers
I keep picturing you in a gray Victorian bonnet,
Jude, it's unnerving. But the Quaker thing does help
explain your purist oddities. I love the way you say
"We built our Meetinghouse at Coldstream in 1859" as
if you were there--time traveler! My Amma was Hindu,
but the Church insisted she convert to marry Da
(already pretty much lapsed, ironically), and he
claims it was "simpler for her to change everything"
(country, job, primary language, religion, marital
status) all at once. Huh, rather her than me!

I chose my house in Stoneybatter because it's
handy for the airport, but I love it now. (I'm a
Southsider by birth but the rougher charms of
Dublin's Northside have grown on me, whereas
Kathleen, having grown up with five siblings in a
gray housing estate well north of the Liffey, calls
my street "grotty" and prefers me to spend my days
off in her flat in sedate Ballsbridge.) Basically
Stoneybatter's a rare example of an inner-city
village: small 1870s artisan's dwellings, plus nasty
council flats, but so overrun by artsy professionals
these days that it's nicknamed Luvviebatter. The
contrast between the indigenous population (fish
fingers and stew) and the "jumped-up trendy hoors" as
we're known in the vernacular (who buy goat's cheese
and cilantro) keeps things lively.

Re: when will you be fully "together" again, ah
come on, it's only been six weeks. My ex Ger, when
her mother died she went into a year-long slump.
Whoops, possibly not the most helpful thing to say,
but my point is, go easy on yourself, Jude, will
you?

Re: Web site
Nah, I'm not insulted that you call the museum's
site "desperately in need of a revamp," Síle. It
was set up many summers ago by the Petersons'
granddaughter, but then she went to South Korea to
teach ESL. Yeah, that would be fantastic if you could
fix it so it no longer says "School Workshops coming
soon in 2003!"

I thought of you yesterday at Paddyfest in
Listowel (about forty k to the northwest of Ireland,
Ontario), there was a great ceilidh going on. I
had to stay in my stall and hand out leaflets about
historic attractions till Cassie and Anneka took
a shift so I could go dance. They live nearby in
Stratford--C. does box office for the theatre
festival, A. wigs--and they've just managed to

complete adoption procedures for Lia, who's obsessed
with wheels. They've invited me over for Oscar night
despite the fact that I haven't seen any of the
nominees. (I hate to admit this to a "cinema slut,"
but it's a rare movie that holds my interest enough
to make me sit still for two hours.) Since Mom died
all my friends keep wanting to hook up with me, I
guess they're afraid I'll turn into Norman Bates if
left alone. (Note cunningly inserted reference to
classic film.)

Re: Canadians, mock all you like but our
inventions include basketball, insulin, the gas mask,
ketchup, and international time zones.

Re: vegging on velvet sofa
Well hello there, Jude the Obscure. I should be
meeting Trish (yes, before you ask, she's another
ex, the first in fact) at the Balkan film festival's
opening gala but it's pissing rain so instead I'm
curled up on my purple sofa with my cat Petrushka
(named for the girl in *Ballet Shoes,* which was my
favourite novel till I hit puberty and discovered
Gone with the Wind), who keeps scratching her head
on the corner of my laptop, which accounts for any
typos. I can hear footsteps going down the street and
a boy and girl having an argument in Dub accents so
strong you'd need subtitles.

Re: time zones, politics has made such a pig's
ear of the map. I just checked online and Russia's
got eleven zones, whereas China insists on keeping
all its citizens to the same time, which means the
sun comes up at 5am or 9am depending on which
province you live in. And just think, you could be
sipping tea at 4pm in Argentina, when due *north* of
you in Venezuela it's only 2pm!

Beside me is the remains of a vast carton of pad
thai--ordered in from one of the six restaurants
round the corner. For a tomboy, Jude, you're turning
out to have weirdly housewifely traits such as the
cooking everything from scratch. I bet you grow

rutabagas, don't you? (I have no real idea what a
rutabaga is, it came up in the *Guardian* crossword my
colleague Fintan was doing in the crew lounge in
L.A.) But then you also chop firewood and all that
sturdy pioneer stuff. Whereas I'm just a lazy, nail-
painting consumer, sigh. (Wretched trampoline
currently gathering dust under my four-poster.)

Re: Rizla, I think I'd like him. Since you came
out, have you and he ever wound up competing for the
limited supply of local talent?

Re: what crimes I've ever committed

Here goes. Vandalism. Defacement of currency
(at fourteen when I stamped NO NUKES on banknotes).
Driving without a license, driving without insurance,
reckless driving under the influence of alcohol and
marijuana. Grievous bodily harm: in grade eleven I
broke the nose of a bitch called Tiffany-Lou. See,
I'm not a Victorian bonneted kind of gal at all.

I have a scar around the base of my ear from
playing tabletop. That's amazing that most of you
Irish don't learn to drive till your twenties,
because all kids in Ontario do is drive around
looking for trouble to get into, like mailbox
baseball. (Can you figure that one out?) Anyway,
tabletop is when a bunch of you go on the back roads
and climb onto the car roof with your drinks (cheap
wine--Moody Blue, Black Knight, or Lonesome Charlie).
So, this particular white-knuckle ride, Rizla was
driving (fifteen years older than the rest of us but
NOT a sobering influence), hit a pothole and I nearly
tore my ear off.

Re: competing, nah, my tastes and his rarely
overlap.

Re: as to when I "came out"--hm, I'm not sure I
was ever in. I wasn't too concerned about being
"normal," maybe because Quakers aren't keen on dogma
or fitting in. I brought home some boys and some
girls, and Mom never expressed a view (though I'm
sure she had her preference). I guess my policy's

been to make no grand statements and tell no lies.
Unless you count my haircut as a statement? But I've
had that since I was four.

Re: virtual coffee
    I love it! *Gals* roaring round on *skidoos*. Jude,
your English is much stranger than mine, I'll have
you know. *Gazumping* is just a real-estate
technicality, by the way, not as exciting as it
sounds. Many thanks for the tiny zipped bag of water
labeled "Genuine Ontario Icicle Tip." I put it in my
freezer but it's come out as flat as a credit card.
(A parable about globalization?)
    I agree, it's very peculiar getting to know each
other at electronic arm's length. (We'll have to
actually meet in the flesh again one of these years.)
So today I've brought you to my favourite Dublin
Italian café to teach you what real coffee tastes
like. I've also ordered you an impeccable *torta
limone*. We're gazing out at the boardwalk erected
along the Liffey to give it the look of the Seine,
but the tourists slip-sliding along in the rain with
plastic bags over their heads do slightly spoil the
impression . . .
    Re: Coming Out (which we aged crones of thirty-
nine definitely used to pronounce in capital
letters), in my case it was a dramatic and somewhat
traumatic result of joining a feminist group at
college and falling for Trish, but had a happy ending
as Da is a die-hard liberal.
    Re: being "undomestic partners," Kathleen and I
both prefer having our own spaces, and after all,
with my schedule I'd be gone more than half the time
anyway. I cohabited with Ger for nine months while
she drove me slowly insane with her sloppiness. I was
three years, on and off, with a pilot called Vanessa,
who was memorable in several ways to do with
moodiness, alcohol, and (unproven but likely)
cheating with a girl in personnel. Vanessa would
never have moved in with me, because she was shit-

scared of the airline finding out. The irony being
that she had a Garbo-in-pants air about her and
everybody knew already.

Re: International Date Line, flying east across
it so you slip from today to yesterday is indeed
unsettling. When the captain makes the announcement,
I always get this inane impulse to glance out the
window, as if there'll be a visible seam down the
Pacific.

Re: what I do all day

Right now I'm writing 300 words on forerunners
(precognition of things not invented yet) for a
newsletter called *Pathways of the Past*. In our
archive we have an article from 1867 about a young
Mitchell man, coming home late from a dance in a
neighbour's parlour, when this roaring black machine
with white lights going "faster than a bull could
run" nearly knocked him into the ditch. Now, I know
you call me "riddled with superstition" just for not
liking to open an umbrella indoors or have thirteen
at table, but doesn't that sound like a car? Maybe
time occasionally curves back on itself, like when
you're hemming something and the thread gets knotted
into a loop.

Except you probably don't sew either, do you,
Síle?

I forgot to tell you that Mrs. Leung let me
pay for the strawberry rhubarb pie you and I were
telepathically sharing at the Garage yesterday--which
I take to mean the community now considers me
officially out of mourning. Though I'm hardly fixed
yet: Last night when I came home from a great slide
show on Ojibway arrowheads, I happened across Mom's
reading glasses in the back of a drawer and cried
for about half an hour.

Not that she was always fun to live with. We did
a lot of speculating about our neighbours, but often
she'd just watch her little TV and knit all evening,
and she'd snap at me if I forgot to keep the stove

stoked up. But nowadays I keep talking to her in my head. Which is much like a long-distance friendship, I guess . . . (Good if occasionally frustrating.)

Re: dead mothers

I know what you mean. Mine will always be thirty-five and radiant, stirring a pot of chai, blowing me a kiss. As a rather misogynist Bengali proverb puts it, "Only when a woman is dead can we sing her praise."

I can't believe you're still up to your knees in snow, in March; I almost wish I was there to wade around in it.

I remember this book about kids who make a girl out of snow; she dances round the garden in a sparkly dress of icicles. But the parents say "Bring your little barefoot friend in before she catches her death." The children try and explain, but the father says "What nonsense," chases her and drags her in, and while they're having tea she melts away on the hearthrug.

Re: snow girl

Síle, I'm due in the schoolhouse five minutes ago to help some volunteers take down the Fearful Epidemics exhibition, but I just have to tell you I know that story, it's by Hawthorne. And the worst thing is that when the kids burst out crying, the father goes into denial, and tells the maid to sweep up that pile of dirty snow the kids have tracked in . . .

Family Feeling

The sole cause of man's unhappiness
is that he does not know how to stay
quietly in his room.

—Pascal
Pensées

Sunday morning in Kathleen's flat. Síle lay six inches away, watching her tinted eyelashes against the pillow. Even in sleep, the woman's pale bob looked freshly brushed. Síle fiddled with the thin gold chain around her own waist, and waited for Kathleen to wake up.

Everybody thought it marvelous that the two of them never had fights. What nobody knew—at least, Síle had never mentioned it to anyone, and she didn't imagine Kathleen had—was that they hadn't had sex in three and a half years.

Put so baldly, this sounded like a disaster. But sex, it seemed, was one of these things that could slip away while your back was turned. For her and Kathleen it had never really been a case of fireworks in bed, and what there was had fizzled out over the first two years they were together. Síle always used to think of herself as someone with a lively libido, but perhaps these things could change, like hair going gray. (Not that hers was, not yet.)

Oddly enough, she rarely thought about it. Her life was crammed with work and play, friends and films, weekends in Brighton or Bilbao. And so much of a couple wasn't about the physical anyway. Or rather, there was an affection that was deeply physical; it just didn't lead to orgasms. Perhaps it was all the stronger because it didn't rely on the chanciness of sex, it occurred to Síle now. Kathleen tall and warm-skinned at her back, as they waved guests off at the end of a dinner party; a hard hug after a week apart; Kathleen's long hands massaging her neck, feeding her guacamole, pulling off her tightest boots.

Perhaps all that was enough. It should really be enough, if the point of the mating drive was to select a good mate. Why shouldn't it be enough?

These were tormenting questions, and Síle had no answers. (Their friends never probed; worn-down parents of small children were often assumed to have stopped having sex, but not a lively pair like Kathleen and Síle.) She really shouldn't dwell on the thing, she reminded herself; fed with attention, it swelled and loomed.

Of course Síle had minded, when she'd first realized what was happening, or rather, not happening anymore. She'd made some subtle overtures, but they'd come to nothing and she hadn't wanted to force it. You couldn't fake the spark: If you stroked a woman's back and nothing happened, what could you do but sit up and suggest a cup of tea? An article she'd come across had recommended sex toys, but the idea of suddenly brandishing handcuffs and strapons at Kathleen made Síle cringe. Lust might have given her the courage to push harder, but that was the whole problem; by the time you noticed that lust had gone AWOL, all you had left was a vague unease. Like a forgotten phone number, a lost key.

How much did Kathleen mind? Hard to tell, because it wasn't something they ever talked about. The last time Síle had tried to bring up the subject, they'd both kept their eyes on *The Simpsons* throughout, she remembered. Síle had wondered aloud whether there was anything they could do, and Kathleen had offered to ask around for a good counselor, but without much enthusiasm, and nothing had come of it. Since then, not a word, except that last year Kathleen had silently forwarded her a link to some online journal article about the high incidence of "what is popularly known as bed death" in long-term lesbian relationships "as a side-effect of the merging process." The researcher—Síle couldn't get this sentence out of her head—reported that "many subjects stated a preference for, or at least acceptance of, nongenital intimacy within the dyad." On reading this in the crew lounge, she'd felt tempted to e-mail Kathleen right back—*Sod that!*—but she'd thought better of it.

The light blue eyes were open. "Whoops, caught me," said Síle.

Kathleen produced a benign yawn. "What time is it?"

"Ten past ten."

Kathleen stretched her tennis player's arms above her head and headed for the shower, pink-skinned and limber. It wasn't about looks, Síle noted; she'd always thought Kathleen was lovely on the eye. The planets still turned, so what had become of the gravitational pull? *Stop brooding,* she told herself. *I still want to be with this woman and vice versa.* It was a fact, but it didn't make her feel any better.

"Coffee?" Kathleen called.

"It's on," Síle replied from the kitchen, flicking open her gizmo and glancing at her messages. It was so easy. They knew how to do this; they were as practiced as figure skaters, linking and lifting, keeping their joint balance.

"We must pick up some daffs on the way to Monkstown."

"Da's garden is Wordsworth territory at the moment," Síle objected.

"So? It's about manners; family feeling."

Síle rolled her eyes, but didn't say another word. Five years was also long enough to have all your arguments over and over again, till the edges were French-polished.

An e-mail from Jude.

```
Today I'm going with Gwen and her parents to a sugar
bush (here's the translation so you don't have to
Google it: grove of tapped maples) for pancakes and
sausages. The trees are all webbed together with
little hoses, you ride round in a horse-drawn wagon,
and there's pre-contact equipment like a huge boiling
tub hollowed out of a trunk. (Sorry, more history
jargon: pre-contact means before the palefaces turned
up.) You've got to go in the early weeks of March
because the first sap is the sweetest.
```

There, there was nothing in that for Kathleen to object to, if she happened to come in and look over Síle's shoulder. It was just everyday trivia. Síle read it again. *The first sap is the sweetest.*

On a tall stool in Shay O'Shaughnessy's kitchen, Síle stared at a framed photo on the wall: Sunita Pillay on her farewell visits before the wedding in 1959, black-rimmed eyes, bindi on her forehead, the traditional three-piece of pindara, rouka, and half-sari. "God, didn't our Amma look like a film star!"

"Everyone does in black and white," muttered her sister Orla, giving the roast potatoes a shake and slamming the oven door.

Was Síle being scrupulous enough? That was the question. In conversation with Kathleen over the past weeks she'd twice referred to having heard from "that Canadian girl," but in what might be termed a misleadingly casual tone. She hadn't mentioned Jude to anyone else, which was a bad sign in itself, it struck her now.

Hands on hips, still wearing the dinosaur-shaped oven gloves, Orla remarked, "Kierán was called into the principal's office for kicking."

"I didn't think that was legal anymore," said Síle, deadpan.

Kathleen smiled, as she stood arranging the carnations in a square vase.

Orla, not getting the joke, said, "It was Kierán doing the kicking." She lowered her voice so it wouldn't carry into the living room, where their father was playing sudoku. "Apparently the other boy had called him a nigger."

"At least he could have got the insult right and called him a wog or a coolie," remarked Síle. Which earned her a raised eyebrow from Kathleen. (White people were so touchy about words!) What Síle had really thought was, *At least the boy didn't call him a mongol.* Considering the Down's syndrome, Kierán was doing well at school—with intensive tutoring from his parents—but kids could be so mean.

"I swear, the Irish get more racist every year," said her sister; "those letters in the paper about the need to *save our culture from being swamped!*" Since the flow of immigrants and asylum seekers had begun in the early nineties, Orla had been running a drop-in centre with the unfortunately soupy name, Síle thought, of Ireland of the Welcomes.

"Mm, it's disgusting," Síle agreed. "I don't remember very much of that when you and I were at Sacred Heart."

"That's because you were Little Miss Loveable with the hair down to your bum and played Mary in the Nativity play," said Orla sharply.

Síle decided not to take offense. "It was more outside of school that people said stupid things like 'Where are yiz from?'"

"Besides," said Orla, "boys' schools are rougher."

"So what'll you do about Kierán?" Kathleen asked.

"I took his teacher out to lunch—that new Vietnamese in Dundrum—and gave him a course pack on cultural diversity called *Hand In Hand,* but I doubt he'll use it. Anyway."

"Anyway."

Again Síle's mind slid away sideways. Were she and Jude Turner friends, was that the idea? Síle didn't urgently need any more friends. Once, after a bottle of white wine, Kathleen had let slip her view that Síle had a few too many already. And besides, three thousand miles lay between her and Jude, for starters. (*Good if occasionally frustrating,* wasn't that how Jude had described a long-distance friendship?) Síle would never get the chance to ring up from a pub and shout over the clamour, *There's a great session on tonight, Jude, are you coming?*

She nibbled the side of one nail where the purple polish was coming off; she'd have to fix that tonight. She told herself she was making too big a deal of this. They each had their hobbies; Kathleen's tennis matches took precedence over any other weekend activities, for instance. But Síle and Jude were now e-mailing several times a day; you could call that a hobby or—the word struck her with a wave of mortification—you could call it a big fat crush.

She stole a leaf from the salad. "This needs a drop more vinegar."

"Does it?" asked Orla.

Kathleen tasted a leaf. "It does not."

Síle was all in favour of honesty, but not of causing unnecessary pain. Relationships would never last a week without a bit of tact. Besides, why risk some dramatic confession to Kathleen, when this connection with Jude, whatever it meant, would inevitably peter out? (Like with that handsome woman Síle had met at a Security Training workshop last June, for instance: a flurry of pert texts and then nothing.)

Síle hadn't had a pen pal since she was nine; the very word was juvenile. Probably only nine-year-olds were generous or hopeful enough to spend long hours writing to someone they knew they'd never meet in the flesh. Her pen pal's name had been Martine, she dug that up out of her memory now: Martine van der Haven, who lived in a suburb outside Antwerp. Síle had sent off her very favorite picture of herself—big-eyed, in Orla's discarded Victorian nightie—and written in ink on the back, PLEASE RETURN AFTER VIEWING, but the photo wasn't returned, and she never heard from Martine again. Only now, staring at her mother's photograph, did it strike Síle that instead of merely getting tired of constructing letters in English to some little Irish girl, Martine might have been disconcerted by the little Irish girl's brown face.

Kathleen was going in and out to the dining room, setting the table. "Oh, and William finished his night course," remarked Orla, picking a bit of encrusted food off a fork, "so he's now a lay minister of the Eucharist."

"Wow," said Síle, trying to adjust her face.

There was a pause, while her sister turned down the oven. "I know you don't really get it."

Kathleen gave Síle a glare: *Be nice.*

"No no, I'm happy for him." She hoped they could leave it at that.

"It's not that he thinks the Church is right about everything—"

"Well, no. You'd have to be a complete moron to think that," said Síle, unable to curb her tongue.

"Who's a moron?" asked Shay O'Shaughnessy, wandering in with an empty glass.

Síle leapt up to get his sherry bottle. "We should never talk religion on Sundays."

He sniffed the air. "Orla, that smells like very heaven. Bring back heated discussions of politics, that's what I say. D'you remember that splendid fight over Parnell in *Portrait of the Artist?*"

Since her father had left Guinness's—where he'd been something high up to do with production standards—he'd read more than ever, wading through vast biographies of Gandhi and Shaw.

"We were just saying how beautiful Sunita was," Kathleen mentioned tactfully, nodding at the photo on the wall.

"She and I met on a plane, you know."

"Did you really?" Of course Kathleen knew the story; she was just humouring him like a good daughter-in-law.

"The Flying Ranee service, on a Super Constellation, London-Cairo-Bombay, all first class!"

"Her first words to you were 'More champagne, Mr. O'Shaughnessy?,' weren't they?" said Orla.

Síle always found it exasperating the way her sister—only five when their Amma died—acted as keeper of the flame.

"Whenever Sunita had a break, that night," Shay told Kathleen, "she perched on the arm of my seat for a chat. In those days the stews called us *guests,* not *passengers;* they were hostesses in the true sense. There was no film or personal stereos of course—so the in-flight entertainment was to watch the stews walk up and down the aisles. Luckily they were all young and pretty, back then," he said, deadpan.

Síle put on a stern face and swatted at him.

"She wouldn't give me her address till just before landing..."

She caught herself wondering whether, if her mother had lived, Sunita and Shay would still be happily married. What combination of passion and stamina—not to mention luck—did it take to last a lifetime? Especially now that lifetimes were so much longer than they used to be.

She looked at Kathleen's smooth blond head, bent over the cutlery drawer, and thought of five years, and of fifty.

The front door crashed open; the boys' voices went up like dogs'. Orla opened the oven and lifted out the sizzling, black-edged salmon.

Síle picked up the pot of honeyed carrots and said, "I'll bring this in, will I? Kierán," she called out, walking into the dining room, "Dermot, Paul, John, c'mon lads, dinner!"

Human Habitation

If ye will still abide in this land,
then will I build you,
and not pull you down,
and I will plant you,
and not pluck you up.

—JEREMIAH 42:10

Síle was parked illegally, helping Marcus pack all his worldly goods into a borrowed van. She picked up a box of glass fisherman's floats and slid it under an antique sewing-machine table. "I thought you said Eoghan and Paul and Tom were coming too?"

"Mm," said Marcus, "then I realized there wouldn't be enough room in the van for all of us. But I trust your muscles. Since I left the airline, my arms have turned to goo."

Síle deposited an armchair upside down on a small sofa. "It'll be worse now you're moving hundreds of miles from civilization. Country bumpkins drive everywhere and get fat."

Marcus laughed. "I'll risk it: It's time to put my roots down. That awful Basingstoke boarding school never felt like home, and my dad had so many postings I never knew whether I'd be spending the summer in Prague or Mexico City or Jo'burg."

"Pity about you. It's not like you stopped moving the minute you grew up."

"Oh, travel's a bad habit, an itch. An unnatural lifestyle," he pronounced with priestly relish.

"Didn't you see *Winged Migration?*" She was crawling to the back of the van with a nodding asparagus fern.

"The birdie thing? I prefer my film stars human."

"They spend most of their lives on the wing, back and forth; it's like this secret pulse throbbing through the planet."

"They have brains the size of peanuts," Marcus pointed out.

"It's even written into our language. *Uplifted*—" She searched for more examples. *"Moved, transported, carried away...* Doesn't *ecstasy* mean something like 'out of place'?" she wondered.

"Dunno, but Eoghan and Tom are bringing some down tomorrow to celebrate my move."

She laughed.

There was barely room for the two of them in the front of the van, with their seat backs very upright. "Just as well we're used to confined spaces," said Marcus, pulling out into traffic. "Remember that time in the forty-seater, stuck on the tarmac at Shannon, waiting for them to change a bulb?"

Síle groaned. "Two hours of apologizing, creeping up and down that aisle like Quasimodo. I thought my neck would never straighten again."

"See? You're not going to lose me as a friend, not after times like that."

They edged through the capital's westward sprawl, and it began to drizzle. They discussed Marcus's work doing exquisite drawings of improbable inventions people wanted to patent, his dying sister in Bath—"liver disease, and the poor girl never had more than the odd sherry"—and Síle's nephews. "The irony is, Orla had two boys and was desperate for a girl, so she and William tried again and had twins, John and Paul—named for the Pope."

"That'll be Our Lord's famous sense of humour."

"Here's Kierán making his first Holy Communion, in a cummerbund," said Síle, holding up the photo. "Isn't that the cutest pair of trousers you've ever seen?"

"And I've seen some cute trousers in my time."

"Speaking of which, isn't it going to reduce your social prospects, holing up in the wilds?"

"Well, the thing is," said Marcus, rubbing his shaved head, "I've already slept with all the Dublin guys I'd ever have any interest in."

"What, all of them, you slag?"

"It's not that big a city." He turned off the wipers as the sun struggled through the clouds.

Síle stared at some unkempt horses grazing along the verge of the motorway. On the green horizon, a ruined tower kept appearing in glimpses. "You sound so world–weary."

"Do you remember your first love?" Marcus asked suddenly.

"Of course: Trish the unemployed activist."

"No, not who. Do you really remember what it was like?"

Puzzled, Síle weighed her memories. "Only some of it," she admitted. "The surprise. The glee."

Marcus nodded. "You're such a goggle-eyed baby the first time, aren't you? Having your big adventure, making landfall on a mysterious island. But then the fruit turns out to be sour or a storm blows up, and you paddle off again on your raft. Only now you're getting to be a seasoned island-hopper, and no matter how beautiful the next is, you can't forget that it's just one of many, the sea's littered with islands."

"Jaysus wept," said Síle under her breath.

"Sorry, I'll shut up and put on the radio, will I?"

A Mozart concert took them through Meath, Westmeath, Longford... The midlands of Ireland had once been a lake, and as far as Síle was concerned they should have stayed that way. After soup and scones in Carrick-on-Shannon, Marcus turned off the N4 onto a series of little winding roads, cutting north to the Iron Mountains.

"Last week, I flew to L.A. and back twice with that fluffhead Noreen Cassidy," Síle was telling him, "and by the time the shuttle dropped me home I was ready to stick a plastic fork in her Botoxed cheek."

"Is she the one with an obsession with Christmas?" asked Marcus.

"No, you're thinking of Tara Dempsey. Tara bakes her Christmas cakes in August, gets her shopping done in September," cooed Síle. "Noreen's the one—remember, we were all in a Persian restaurant in Chicago once, and I'd just had a manicure, and you insisted on explaining to the group why women of my persuasion don't tend to have long nails?"

He hooted. "When she finally got it—she was *scarlet*," he recalled in his best faux-Dublin accent. "Seriously, Síle, how do you stick it? They're not in your league."

"By what measure?" she asked.

"Brain-cell count, politics, sense of humour, ability to tell Almodóvar from Alessi..."

She shrugged. "Nuala's a decent sort, and Catherine, and Justin. And nobody gives me a hard time for being queer, not since that one pilot who moved to Qantas."

"That's the law, not a basis for gratitude," snapped Marcus. "My point is, with your talents, you should be..."

"What? If you know of the ideal job—"

He puffed out a breath. "Sparkling companion to technical artist?"

She laughed. "Buy a penthouse in Manhattan and we'll talk."

They'd been on the road more than four hours when the van rattled across two cattle grids and turned sharply right up a muddy lane. Marcus braked in the yard beside what looked like a derelict barn. "Ta-da!"

The barn had windows, Síle noticed as she walked up to it, which meant it was actually the house.

Marcus slung his arm over her shoulder. "I warned you I couldn't afford anything fit for human habitation. I'm going to turn into one of those grotesque, decaying bachelors out of a Molly Keane novel."

"It's big," she managed. "Lots of room for, for improvement."

Marcus laughed and sniffed the moist March air. "The soil's peaty but the drainage isn't bad at all, for Leitrim. See the corner where the slates have come off? That's going to be my office; it gets the morning light. All I have to do is persuade them to put in a land line, so I can get broadband Internet."

"It doesn't even have a phone?"

"C'mon, let's have a cuppa, that's the thing for shock. The kitchen's got glass in the windows," he assured her.

On her third cup of tea, Síle stared out the window at the lone sheep munching the grass. All she could hear was her heartbeat and the occasional squeak of a bird. "Well, if you don't die of pleurisy by the summer..."

Marcus threw another log into the new yellow Aga. "You're such an urbanite, you wouldn't be able to sleep without the constant shriek of car alarms. James, he's the neighbour I was telling you about, he and Sorcha run this organic farm that abuts my land—"

"Listen to you with your new country vocabulary—abutting, *mar dhea!*"

"Well, James thinks this place could be three hundred years old."

She peered up at the cobwebs. "I suppose it takes a few centuries for something to fall apart as thoroughly as this."

"Say what you like, I'm going to be blissful here," said Marcus, taking another of his homemade lemon biscuits. "Now come out and look at the best thing."

"It's raining again."

"Barely a drop." He led her across the nettle-choked yard, around several hedges, into a field that sloped away down the mountain.

Síle could see nothing but gray cloud. "The sheep?"

"No, you twit, the stones."

She stared at the nearest rock, which had a few tufts of wool caught on it. Marcus pointed to another, and then to a grass-covered lump, and another behind a blackthorn...and suddenly she could see it. "A circle!"

"I know they're not literally standing stones anymore, because half are lying down and the other half have been carted away by the locals to build pigsties. But it's still magic, isn't it?"

She slid her arm around her friend's waist. His gray Aran cardigan smelled of wood smoke. "Colonist! You Brits swan over here with your fortunes and your fancy vans, you buy up our timeless Celtic heritage—"

He let out a rip of laughter and pointed down. "On a clear day, you can see all the way to Lough Allen."

They headed back to the house with dripping fistfuls of colts-foot, barren strawberry, and herb robert (or so Marcus claimed; it was all greenery to Síle). "So I've been e-mailing this Canadian," she said out of nowhere.

"Which Canadian?"

"The one I'm about to tell you about." She produced a stiff little summary of Jude Turner.

"Is she gorgeous?"

She gave him a hard look. Then, "Yes, actually." She let herself picture the narrow shoulders, the chaste face. "But she lives five time zones away, so that's irrelevant."

"It's always relevant."

"She writes interesting e-mails," Síle snapped. They walked on, skirting a huge stretch of nettles. "Forget I said anything," she said, to keep the conversation from ending.

Marcus tucked his arm into hers. "What's going on, Síle?"

"Nothing, virtually. I don't know," she added after a minute.

"Are you and Kathleen having trouble?"

"No," she said bleakly. "Everything's fine. As always."

"Are you bored, or what?"

Síle dropped his arm. "Kathleen's not boring. I know you and Jael have never quite clicked with her, but that's partly because she doesn't want to intrude—"

"I didn't say she was boring," he cut in gently. "I asked if you were bored."

Síle didn't answer. She could have said "no," or "yes," or "no more than I've been for years." She kicked a tree branch out of her path. She spoke under her breath: "It's not about boredom. It's not about...I wasn't out looking for anything, you know."

"I know you weren't." He waited. "Is it getting serious, with this Jude character?"

"It can't be," said Síle through her teeth. "And if you look at it objectively, she and I have feck-all in common. She's so young, she's ensconced over there in Nowhere, Ontario, and her idea of a wild night out is a slide show on Ojibway arrowheads." She felt like a traitor for giving this example.

Marcus said nothing.

"And while it's great fun sending dispatches between our two planets, it'll fizzle out in the end. It's in the nature of things."

Purge

Your nearest exit may be behind you.

—passenger briefing

As Jude walked back from the museum on Sunday, the pink light drained out of the western sky. The ice shifted and slid under her boots; trees dripped loudly; squirrels hurried about their business. It was only a temporary thaw, of course, but still.

Every time she came home, these days, she had to steel herself. Not so much against the ache of grief as a sense of disorientation. When she read at the dining room table or played her guitar on the living room rug, her ears kept pricking for the front door opening, her mother's step in the hall. To be living alone in Number 9, Main Street, felt strangely surreptitious; it was as if Jude were a burglar, or no, a glue-sniffing runaway. (And the funny thing was, Jude knew she just might have gone that way, if her yen for history hadn't given her something to hold onto; after her parents split up hadn't she tried truancy, drink, and whatever toxic substances she could get hold of?) These days the house was too big for her, too dense with memory, too serious a responsibility—and yet it wasn't as if she wanted to live anywhere else.

Rizla's tangerine pickup was parked out front, and he was stretched out on the porch swing. She put her hand on his red bandana to wake him. "What are you doing, sleeping outside?"

"I like that," he said blearily. "I tell my cousins you need my

help moving your shit around, then you stand me up, leave me laying here for an hour…"

"Oh Riz, I'm so sorry! It went right out of my head."

He let out a phlegmy cough.

"Which cousins?"

"Dan and Wiggie. Where've you been, anyway? Is there some
fun going on downtown and nobody told me?" he asked, rolling his
eyes ironically toward the silent crossroads.

"I was in the museum."

Rizla shaded his eyes from the low sun. "On a Sunday? Does
somebody need some history, like, ASAP?"

"Just e-mail," she muttered, pushing the stiff front door.

"Aha, the trolley dolly!" He stepped into the hall and kicked off
his boots. "You two doing this a lot?"

Jude didn't answer at first, and then she said, "Couple times a
day."

"Get outta here," crowed Rizla.

"Well, except if we're really run off our feet," she qualified. "But
then on a quiet day we might send five or six."

He whistled. "You talk on the phone too?"

Jude shook her head. "Stop jumping to conclusions. She's got a
partner." *Kathleen (my girlfriend). Girlfriend = partner.*

"Uh-huh…"

"No, seriously. Five years," she made herself add.

"It's not a score."

Jude headed into the kitchen to put some coffee on. "I'm really
sorry I forgot about the big clear-out. Nothing's ready."

"Better this way," he told her. "Don't think about it, just keep
or chuck. Let the purge begin!" Thumping his chest like a gorilla.

Rachel had had a weakness for estate sales—well, it was a so-
ciable way to spend winter Saturdays—and strangely broad tastes.
"That ottoman can definitely go," Jude decided. "And the easel. Do
you think we can manage the La-Z-Boy between us?"

"Just open the double doors and stand aside, girlie," said Rizla, picking up the recliner in a bear hug.

"Don't slip a disc, now."

He staggered into the hall, where he knocked a small fern to the floor as he put the recliner down.

"Do you have to lean it on your bad foot?" she asked. Years ago, a car Rizla had been working on had slipped its brakes and rolled over his toes; there was talk of compensation, but he'd never seen a cent.

"Where's all this stuff going?"

"The Goodwill in Goderich, if you wouldn't mind driving it over tomorrow?"

"I could do with one of these," he panted, heaving the La-Z-Boy into the air again.

"Really? It makes me feel like I'm disabled, to crank my legs into the air. Where's it going to fit in your trailer?"

"Beside the couch," he said, a vein in his throat standing out. "Though Ma Turner's gonna spin in her grave the first time I spill pop on the velour!"

His flippancy made things easier, oddly enough. She followed him out to the pickup with boxes of china stacked up to her chin. "Hey, careful of my music system."

"This piece of crapola?" Rizla shoved it aside with his foot. "Come round some night and listen to Duke Ellington on *my* speakers."

"If you didn't spend all your cash on guy toys," Jude remarked, "you might have the down payment on a house by now."

"You are so middle-class." He grinned broadly, then doubled over with a wet cough.

As they went back inside, Jude rubbed him between the shoulder blades. "Why don't you go see Dr. Percy?"

"Last time, he read me the riot act about sugar—"

"Possibly because two of your uncles have lost toes to diabetes?"

"—then he tried to put his hand up my hole! Freaking perv."

Jude's laugh rang strangely through the building. The acoustics were different already; the house was becoming sparer, more her own.

Rizla lifted a peacock-backed wicker chair in one hand and tossed it toward her. When she lunged forward and caught it, he grinned. "Don't ever forget who taught you how to catch."

"You nearly broke this lamp."

"Sorry I missed. Put it out of its misery?"

Jude considered it, a vaguely Deco naked dancer in yellow and brown glass. With a wink, Rizla shoved over a large box full of canned vegetables past their sell-by dates. Jude's hands shook slightly as she picked up the lamp. *Sorry, Mom, but it's the ugliest thing in the world.* She let it fall into the box with a smash.

He flopped down on the old plaid couch. "So with you and this Irish chick—has the L-word been mentioned?"

Jude stared at him. "You mean lesbian?"

"I mean *luuuuuve,*" crooned Rizla in his best Elvis voice.

"No," she said, her face heating up.

"So you're what, buds?"

"I suppose." On impulse, Jude pulled out her wallet and tugged a cut-down snapshot from behind her driver's license. "Síle sent me this last week, with a packet of soda bread. You need glasses," she pointed out, as he examined the picture at arm's length.

"Yadda yadda yadda. I hate to tell you, buds don't send each other pictures. Doesn't look forty," he added when Jude didn't answer. "Or Irish."

"Her mother was from India. And she's thirty-nine: a year younger than you."

"Yeah, but gals age faster. She's pretty all right, but not my type," said Rizla. "All that gold and lipstick, kinda scary."

Jude sat down beside him and took the photo back. "The thing is, Riz, the brush-cut tomboys you like tend not to sleep with guys, which means you may never find another girlfriend."

"Fine by me. Trailer to myself, popcorn at three A.M., nobody changing the channel or bugging me to get a mortgage..."

"You're going to wind up as a headline: 'Ireland Ont. Loner Found Frozen in Trailer, Partially Eaten by Dog.'"

"Siouxsie wouldn't partially eat me," he protested. "If she went to the trouble of starting, she'd leave nothing but buttons and boots."

"She needs a new flea collar, by the way."

"Why do you keep thinking up way-out ways for me to die, anyway? I've made it through forty years in one piece—more or less," he qualified, glancing at the fingertip he'd lost to a fishing knife—"and I only had you cooking me your health-food shit for one of them." His tone had a rare touch of hardness. "And I've got family, which is more than you can say: There's thirty different doors I could knock on and they'd take me in."

Jude stared at the floor.

"I guess that was kind of a low blow," he said after a minute. "I wasn't thinking."

"Hey, you've gotten this far, why start now?"

"I take it back."

She tried to smile. "Me too. You're going to live long and prosper."

"Make it so," he answered in a *Star Trek* voice.

The guy did her favour after favour, and she acted like a cross between a petulant sibling and a scolding mother. It was so hard to climb out of ruts. Old habits, old jokes, old arguments, tease, nag, tease, nag, push, pull.

Whereas in her e-mails to Síle, Jude felt brand new. Where was Síle today—Dubrovnik, was it? Or Tenerife? Had she gone out for a raucous happy hour with the rest of the crew, or was she sleeping effortlessly between starched hotel sheets? Or home in Dublin, of course; Jude reminded herself of that possibility. In bed with *my partner Kathleen.*

The ground was almost clear of snow, but the evening was turning sharp; the small burlapped trees in front yards stood like goblins turned to stone. When the two of them had finally squeezed the La-Z-Boy into Rizla's trailer, they shared a pot of Jude's venison stew. His cousins had headed back to the rez. Jude rolled a joint, then another, then they wound up in bed.

She stared up at the ceiling, where the cracks seemed to form a map of the rivers of the Huron Tract, in the era when they were the only lines carved into the wilderness. "I think maybe that was the last time."

Rizla let out a cough of laughter. "Dang, if I'd known, I'd have pulled out all the stops." His bare chest gave off a cloud of heat. The blue snake tattoo stood out on his wrist where his hand trailed over the edge of the mattress onto the black fake fur rug. Siouxsie came over and licked it; he scratched her hard behind one crooked ear.

Jude turned on her side, and felt her exposed hip bump the floor through the thin futon. She laid one palm against Rizla's hairless chest; she heard a thumping, and couldn't tell whether it was his pulse or her own. "The thing is, I'm lying here thinking about somebody else."

"I know that."

She shouldn't ever waste her time trying to keep the truth from him, Jude decided. Or from herself.

"You realize you'll probably never see this chick again as long as you both shall live?"

"Fuck you," said Jude, turning her back. Suddenly shivery, she wrenched up the comforter. Her eyes found that dent where Rizla had punched right through the drywall, in one of his occasional rages; she couldn't remember what that fight had been about. She stared at the beer bottle on the floor beside an old moccasin his sister had made him, and the pizza crust that Siouxsie was gnaw-ing. "This place is a hovel."

"Oh, so now it's the décor that's a turn-off?" His breath was hot on the nape of her neck.

She curved her feet around his. "And if you don't cut these toe-nails sometime, they'll curl round and grow back in." She was memorizing the feel of him. Then she sat up, goose-pimpled, and reached for her red flannel shirt.

"But hey, you know," said Rizla, head back on his joined hands, "you're welcome to lie here and dream about your sweet colleen anytime; no skin off my dick."

"Síle's not mine," said Jude between her teeth. "She's taken. I wouldn't—I don't mess with couples."

"Oh yeah?"

She concentrated on doing her buttons.

"What do you call e-mailing somebody six times a day?"

Her fingers stopped moving. "I don't know," she said, her voice small. "I've got no clue what's going on." After a minute, she added, "I guess it seemed safe at first because she's so far away."

A warm, rough hand slid round her hips. "Don't worry about it. C'mere."

Jude shook her head. "We've got to break this habit, Riz. It feels...off."

"Off?"

"Peculiar. Wrong."

"Like, morally?" he asked, sardonic.

Wrong in every neuron in her brain, every cell of her body. "Just take my word for it."

"Okay."

Half-dressed, she twisted around to read his face in the orange glow of the lava lamp. "Really?"

"Hey, it's not like we're married, you know?" Rizla let out a croak of laughter.

She giggled too. Dope did that.

"If you want to be faithful to some lady you've never got to first base with—be my guest."

Jude felt anger rise like a wave, then subside. "Good night." She poked him in the armpit with one foot, then went to lace up her boots by the door.

The paths were glassy with ice; she slipped at the corner and wrenched her knee slightly, the one she'd injured last summer. She let herself in the front door.

The phone started ringing when she was halfway up the stairs. "Turner residence," she answered; she couldn't seem to shed her mother's old phrase.

"Hello at last!"

"Hi?" said Jude, then "Sorry—"

"Jude, is that you?"

She waited, afraid of interrupting again.

"It's me, it's Síle."

Jude nearly dropped the phone. This wasn't the voice she'd been remembering. Her head was still spinning; she wished she hadn't had that joint. "Síle? Are you there?"

"Absolutely," came the squawk. "Sorry it's so late. How are you?"

"Fine," said Jude formally. "How about—"

But their voices clashed again. A long pause.

"It's a bad connection," roared Jude.

"I'm on my mobile, having a nasty breakfast in Dubrovnik; I just thought I'd see if you were still up," came the tinny voice.

"I am." And Jude couldn't think of a single solitary thing to say.

"This is a bit weird."

"Sure is."

"I just suddenly thought it was time we spoke live. So you're well?" asked Síle.

"Yeah." Jude thought she could smell Rizla on herself; she wished she'd had a shower.

The pause stretched like glue.

"You've been on my mind," said Síle, as if mentioning the weather.

Jude's pulse went *bam*. "You too."

"Oh shit, I have to go, my gate's just been called," said Síle shrilly. Jude couldn't tell whether to believe her. "Another time?"

"Sure. Take care. Bye!"

"Bye." Jude put the phone down. *Well, so much for the wonders of modern communication.*

She leaned against the hall table, her hands shaking. Her father's grandfather had made it out of an old door, back in Lincolnshire. A small square of streetlight lay on the bannisters. She thought she could do with a long walk, but the streets were treacherous; she might really break her knee this time. Guilt, confusion, excitement, grief, even, were like rockets going off in her head.

She took a long breath and was suddenly stone cold sober. She went into the living room to look for her mother's box of good cream writing paper.

Dear Síle,

she wrote, and stared at the two words, and pressed the nib to the page.

I'm sorry
I'm afraid I may be
I love you.

On her way to see her naturopath about an irritating patch on the back of her left hand, Síle was stuck in a traffic jam on Astor Quay. She tried a few deep breaths. She knew if she arrived at Helen's office in a state of agitation she'd get the usual lecture about stress hormones and cellular toxins. To distract herself, she leafed through her bundle of post. Credit card offers, charity newsletters, and a couple of travel-stained kitsch postcards from friends visiting Budapest and New Zealand. There was an envelope in Jude's careful handwriting stamped *Express Delivery* that Síle had been meaning to save for the café after her naturopath, but what the hell.

Reading the first line, she felt a little dizzy. She'd have liked to pull over for a minute, but then she'd never have got back into the flow of traffic. So she kept crawling forward in first gear, but her eyes dropped every second or two to the words on the page in her lap: *I love you.*

The phrase appalled Síle. She couldn't remember the last time she'd seen it written down, except in a novel, and not the Booker-winning kind. She supposed she and Kathleen must have said it a few times, in the early days, but she couldn't remember. People were wary of the words, these days, having heard them in too many Hollywood movies. *I love you* ticked like a bomb. It pretended to be in the present tense, but it had a future hidden inside it. It was hackneyed, heavy, too much to bear.

A courier on a bicycle snaked in front of Síle, and she slammed on the brakes. She read the phrase again, and it lit her up.

She flicked through the rest of the letter. It was short, and it assumed nothing. *I suspect the right thing to do would be to keep my mouth shut and back off,* Jude had written. *But I can't sleep till I let you know what's in my heart.*

Well, what had Síle thought was happening? She was so much older; shouldn't she have been wise enough to have seen this coming, reined it in before it ran away with them? A Gilbert and Sullivan line sang in her head: *Here's a how dy do.*

She'd been busy, that was her only excuse. She'd been doing her job—*good morning, fasten your seat belts, beef or cod, thanks for choosing to fly with us*—and on her days off she'd been going to the cinema with Kathleen, and checking her stocks online, and doing an Italian intensive, and taking Yseult jeans shopping while Jael was having her roots done. And all the while, Síle's new existence had been gathering speed, rushing along like an underground stream. She'd made the mistake of thinking that dinners out and traffic jams were her real life, and this connection with Jude was just a transitory preoccupation. But now she saw that she'd been living out her real time onscreen, sentences swallowed and sung back and swallowed all over again. She was made entirely out of words.

Síle read Jude's carefully inscribed sentences again, and tasted lipstick; she was chewing her lip like a child. A tremor went right up her spine. She thought, *Yes, damn, yes,* inching along Aston Quay, her hands gripping the wheel.

Síle could have taken the lift to Kathleen's fifth-floor flat that evening, but instead she walked up the stairs, whether as some kind of penance or to buy herself a little more time, she hardly knew. She had to pause on a landing; she thought maybe she was going to be sick. Jude's letter had woken her roughly. It wasn't indecision that was wracking Síle, not at all. It was the torque of a decision that she realized she'd made some time ago. A secret she'd been carrying like a tumour through her days.

There was no answer when she rang the bell. The time-sensitive light went out with a click. Where might Kathleen be on a Tuesday evening? Not ballroom dancing, that was Thursday; she and her younger brother had been a duo for decades, and won medals for their rhumba. Was she at the deli? Having a drink with one of her old college friends? Did the dry-cleaner's stay open this late? Something Síle had always liked was that she and Kathleen didn't keep constant tabs on each other, but tonight it felt like a strange dissociation; surely she should have some idea where her girlfriend was. Kathleen might have been kept late at the hospital; the new scheduling software was acting up, Síle knew that much. She knew so many things about Kathleen—the middle toe left askew by a childhood bike accident, the terror of ghost stories, the time she'd got engaged to an orthopedic surgeon—but it struck her now, standing outside the door in the dark, that there were whole realms of the woman that were a mystery to her. Questions that, if you didn't ask in the first six months, maybe you never asked at all. Síle demanded of herself now with a clenched stomach, *Why did we spend so much time talking about news headlines and toothpaste?*

She noticed she was thinking in the past tense.

She had a key to the flat, of course; she and Kathleen had swapped keys within a month of their first dinner. But tonight she couldn't bear to let herself in, make herself at home. She sat down on the landing carpet, her back to the door, her eyes adjusting to the dark. Usually by now she'd have rattled off a text to Kathleen, *where U?,* but she couldn't bear to; this time it had to be live.

The minutes crawled by. *I'm an utter shit,* Síle thought. *I can't believe I'm going to do this. I'm throwing away nearly five years, five pretty good years.* But then it struck her like a rush of cold air that the years were gone. You didn't stay with someone because of memory and gratitude, not unless you were a wife in some nineteenth-century novel. It had to be worth it today. *How lazy I've been, drifting toward this moment! I should have got around to this before. Before Jude.*

She dropped her head onto her knees. She felt such dread of what was coming, she was tempted to get to her feet and stagger down the stairs. Had she been cheating for more than a month already, did e-mails count? Did dreams? *Jaysus, Síle,* she thought in rage, *if that's how it is, you should have done Kathleen a favour and left years ago.* What a timid traveler she'd been, clinging to her raft till the very last minute! And how obtuse! Why was it only now, with an express-delivery love letter like a bomb hidden in her handbag, that she realized all she'd been missing, all she was starving for?

In traditional matriarchal households in Kerala, she remembered her father saying, a woman could divorce her husband simply by putting his umbrella outside the door.

It seemed hours later when the lift groaned; Síle lifted her head. Kathleen walked out, laden with bags. Síle blinked in the harsh light.

"Sweetie! What are you doing sitting here in the dark?"

Síle was about to lie and say she'd forgotten her key, but she kept her mouth shut.

"Is there bad news? Is it your dad? One of the nephews?"

She shook her head.

Kathleen stared at her, and then opened the door. While she was putting her shopping away, Síle stood by the window. Dublin was a shiny jet necklace. Kathleen opened and shut cupboards, walked into the bathroom and came back. How familiar her footsteps were, the small sounds of the flat. She didn't say a word.

When Síle finally made herself turn away from the window, Kathleen had poured herself a large glass of wine and was gulping it like water. "Is there a problem?" Kathleen asked, very managerial.

She nodded.

"I suppose it's this Canadian."

That threw Síle. Kathleen hadn't seemed the least bit curious about her correspondent, and Síle hadn't brought herself to mention Jude at all in the last fortnight. But then, Kathleen was an intelligent woman, with an ear for silences. Síle hesitated, and said, "It's more than that."

"That's what they all say." As fast and poisonous as a snake's tongue.

"Who's 'they'?" asked Síle, confused.

"Fuckers who want a bit on the side."

Síle let herself down on the edge of the cream sofa. They'd picked it out together in a Habitat sale, she recalled; Síle had bargained the salesman down fifty quid because of a tiny stain on one cushion. It was still quid in those days, before the euro. Her history with Kathleen spanned the edges of two currencies, two centuries, two millennia.

"It's never as simple and grubby as 'I fancy something fresh,' is it?" spat Kathleen, setting down her glass with such a sharp clink Síle thought the stem had broken. "No, it's always something pro-founder, some unfulfilled yearning."

"I don't want a bit on the side," Síle managed to say. "But I think you and me—I don't see how—are you happy?" she asked, her voice high and uneven. "Can you really say I've been making you happy, the last few years?"

"Happy enough," said Kathleen.

"Anyway, a bit on the side of *what*?" asked Síle desperately.

She could see Kathleen's gray eyes register that strike.

She rushed on. "I'm not accusing—"

"You'd better not be. Is it my fault?" demanded Kathleen.

"It's nobody's fault, we just lost it. Maybe we should have tried harder, talked about it, at least—"

"So is that what this is all about? You want a frank discussion, Síle, fine. Why does sex have to matter that much?"

Síle stared at her.

"It's just bodies rubbing together. We're not teenagers; there's more to us than that. You and I are so bloody compatible, we get on so well," argued Kathleen, "why does that one little missing piece have to wreck everything?"

"I don't know," wailed Síle, "but it does."

"Well, you're not getting any from this girl in Canada, are you, so why are you putting me through this?"

"No," admitted Síle, "but I want her."

"What good is wanting?"

Her mouth moved like a fish on dry land. "It makes me feel alive."

"You ruthless bitch."

"I—"

"How can you sit there and say that to me?"

And then Kathleen wept so hard her mascara ran. She wouldn't let Síle touch her. She ranted and called Síle names, used words Síle had never heard her pronounce before. Then she started to hyperventilate, and crouched down on the kitchen tiles, and Síle held her by the shoulders. Kathleen's white hands gripped hers; she hid her face in Síle's tangling hair as if her torturer was her only refuge. Síle's eyes stayed desert dry.

The worst was when Kathleen started apologizing for everything unattractive about herself, every bad habit she'd slid into, every small neglect or carelessness. She even said sorry for crying. "What can I do, what can I do?" she kept sobbing. No, perhaps the very worst was when she tried to kiss Síle, unbutton her shirt; when she begged her to come to bed. Kathleen's face was naked to the bone, lit from moment to moment by terror and fury and abasement. Staring down at her, what struck Síle was, *I've never seen this face before.*

Consequences

All luggage is interchangeable.

—Aritha van Herk
Restlessness

Three weeks on, Síle couldn't shake the feeling that she'd been in a car crash; every muscle felt whiplashed.

How had she ever thought of Kathleen as cool and capable, emotionally self-reliant? The woman had cracked like an egg. She'd called in sick to the hospital, lived in her dressing gown, and stopped brushing her hair. Three evenings in a row, Síle had turned up to feed Kathleen toast and apologize over and over. They slept as tightly tangled as ropes; when Kathleen woke up crying, Síle stroked her head and shushed her back to sleep. They'd never had a more intense time together, it struck her now; it was a shadow version of falling in love.

But after a four-day rotation to Dubrovnik and Vienna, when she went over to Ballsbridge she found an envelope marked *S.* with a note in it that said *This is getting me nowhere. Please slide your key under the door.*

She felt relief, of course: Síle had to admit it. But also misery, that five years of their lives could fall away like dust.

Now the April tulips were waving like flags. "Might be best to play it a bit cool, with the Canadian," Marcus advised.

But Síle had moved beyond any kind of play-acting. Whenever she felt bad, these days, she rang Jude.

"I guess I should say I'm sorry you're going through this," said Jude, "or that I never meant to cause trouble, but that'd be a lie."

"Quaker," said Síle with a little snort. She wiped her face. "Forget what you should say, what do you want to say?"

The word went up like a rocket. "Hallelujah!"

"On Kathleen's side, or..."

"Mine," Síle admitted, tight-throated.

Shay O'Shaughnessy looked away across the clattering café. His generation of Irishmen and women married for life, she reminded herself; there'd been no such thing as divorce, in law or in their heads, and if they ended up separated they saw it as a mortifying failure.

"You've had an affair," supplied Orla.

"I have not!" But even as she was snapping at her sister, Síle knew this hair-splitting was absurd. Didn't every cell of her body spring to attention when she heard Jude's husky voice on the line? If geography had allowed, wouldn't Síle have driven to her house weeks ago, kissed that asymmetrical smile, tugged open those jeans? "There's a woman I've been writing to, in Canada," she said with difficulty. "She works in a museum. She's twenty-five," she made herself add, thinking, *cradle snatcher.*

Shay picked at his quiche.

"Are Canadians not a bit...dull?" asked Orla.

Why did everyone come out with that one? "Are the Irish not all thick and ignorant?" Síle countered.

Shay managed a chuckle.

"Fair dues," said Orla. "So. Have you actually met this girl, or is this one of those chat-room things?"

"Mm, it sounds like an assumed identity to me," her father put in with his best attempt at whimsy. "I bet she'll turn out to be a male truck driver from Swansea. *Cyber-dressing:* I read about it in the *Guardian.*"

"I met her on a flight," said Síle, meeting his eyes. *Just like you and Sunita.*

A long pause. "Well, I couldn't be sorrier about all this, especially for Kathleen, obviously," said Orla. "I must send her some flowers."

Síle stared at her plate.

"As for the new connection...all I can say is, you must have a lot of time on your hands."

Orla busied herself with her salad, and Síle watched her with hatred. *Why,* she wanted to ask, *because I'm not doing the sensible thing of staying in a sexless couple for the rest of my days? Because the things I'm feeling have no clear target, no report card, no gold ring?*

The list of friends and colleagues to tell was endless; she resorted to the vulgarity of a mass e-mail. *Síle here, I'm afraid I have to tell you all some sad news, that Kathleen and I have decided to go our separate ways...* She'd phrased it euphemistically to protect Kathleen's dignity, but only when she'd sent it winging into the ether did she realize that what it really did was cover up her own guilt. Then she wondered what kind of e-mail Kathleen was sending out.

Some replied with concern and warmth, and some didn't reply. They were resolving themselves silently into Síle's old friends and Kathleen's old friends—the couple had made no real ones together, Síle realized, which was significant in itself—and though she was hurt, she couldn't dispute the division. She didn't even have any photos of Kathleen, it occurred to her in the middle of the night; the neatly labeled albums at the Ballsbridge apartment contained five years' worth of trips and parties, but Síle couldn't imagine asking to go through them and remove a representative selection.

Kathleen had become businesslike, her old self—or some smashed, glued copy. A large box of Síle's possessions turned up in

Stoneybatter by bike messenger, with a form to be signed for closing their joint account. Her neighbour Deirdre took it in, as she always did with parcels when Síle was away.

"From your friend Kathleen," she said. Not that Deirdre was naïve, but *friend* was her generation's word for it. (The other neighbours insisted on believing that Síle was single as a result of her busy career.)

Síle had to come out with it, on the doorstep: "We're not, actually, together anymore, Deirdre."

"Ah, that's a sorry shame." A pause. "I've sometimes thought I'd give Noel the heave," she confided pleasantly, jerking her head toward her living room, where her husband read the paper all day, "only for the pension wouldn't stretch to two households."

This, oddly enough, did make Síle feel a little better.

"You're lovely, asking all the grubby details," she told Jude on the phone that night, "but I'd rather spare you."

"You can't," the girl told her. "I'm up to my neck in this."

"But—"

"I've wrecked the happiness of a woman I've never even met. I broke my own rule," said Jude sternly. "I knew you were in a couple and I didn't back off."

"Possibly because I was beaming out come-get-me signals like some dog in heat," said Síle under her breath. She couldn't tell which of them started laughing first. She groaned. "This is all so messy. If only I'd been single when I met you."

"Like you pretended to be, at Heathrow?"

"I did not! Well, I suppose it was a 'lie of omission,' as the priests call it. What did you think when I got around to clarifying who Kathleen was?"

"I felt like hammering a nail through my hand."

"Ouch! Even your metaphors are butch."

"You know, most beginnings are as messy as endings," Jude told her. "Everything overlaps; it's like a lily pond. I don't think I know two people who both had the luck to be unattached when they fell in love."

Now, sitting over the *Irish Times* and a latte in her favourite café, Síle glanced down at the Liffey and was shocked by a soaring sense of buoyancy.

"Mm," said Jael, checking up on Síle by mobile from the train to Galway, "there's a special high you only get from dumping someone you stayed with far too long."

"You didn't like Kathleen, did you?" asked Síle, letting herself face it.

"Couldn't stick her," exclaimed Jael. "It was such an effort, making conversation about tennis or bloody cha-cha."

Síle felt oddly wounded. "What was wrong with her?"

"Oh, nothing," said Jael. "Kathleen's the kind of girlfriend you'd order from a catalogue."

"You bitch!"

"You betcha."

Síle took a long swallow of coffee. "What are you doing in Galway, anyway?"

"Launching some curmudgeon's collected thoughts on impotence and death in a fourteenth-century banqueting hall. I'd name him but there might be journos on the train."

"How tactful."

"You know, Síle, you're better off single."

"Sez Mrs. Anton McCafferty," she said automatically. And then, "I don't feel exactly single."

"Careful, now. That girl in Canada was probably just a symptom of your discontent," Jael warned her. "Dykes always pair up too fast; the boys are much more sensible. Marcus can just head out to the Phoenix Park if he gets the urge, can't he, or the sauna if it's raining?"

Síle grinned at the thought of Jael's insights into what the tabloids called "the gay lifestyle" being overheard by a carriageful of travelers. "Not now he's buried in Leitrim living out The Good Life."

"Oh god, I'd blocked that, poor eejit. Sheep-shagging's his only option, then."

"Kathleen and I hadn't, in three years," Síle confided in a low voice.

The phone squawked so loudly she had to lift it away from her ear.

"Calm down," she said.

"If I ever go a month without," Jael told her, "slit my throat."

It was like being headhunted, or planning a surprise party. Síle seemed to go around all day biting her tongue. At the tiny corner shop on Stoneybatter she bought *Time, Private Eye, Wired,* and streaky bacon and a baguette, and she wanted to say to the tired eighteen-year-old behind the counter, *I've just turned my whole life upside down because of a stranger.*

She sent Jude a photo of each of the five rooms in her house; she had to borrow Deirdre's old camera, because when she sent digital ones they crashed the Ireland Museum's PC. She smiled at mothers and babies walking in the park, and gave passengers extra bags of pretzels, but was tetchy with anyone who interrupted her daydreams of Jude, and she bit her brother-in-law's head off for forgetfully calling her an "air hostess." Wasn't romance meant to make you happy? What she felt was more like palpitations, or heartburn.

Home Base

Everyone has the right to leave any
country, including his own, and to
return to his country.

—*Universal Declaration of
Human Rights,* Article 13 (2)

Above Toronto the captain announced "a little bit of nasty weather." Síle'd had three Bailey's over the course of the flight, and felt fantastic. On the descent, the wind thrust against the thin metal skin of the plane; through her window she caught glimpses of the darkening April evening, gusts of snow like the spit of a furious giant. The plane heaved, and the man beside Síle hissed with fright. This would be fun, she decided, especially as Dublin hadn't seen a flake of snow all year.

Landing, landing: an ecstatic quiver at touchdown.

Walking through a strange airport always made Síle feel like she was in the opening scene of *Jackie Brown,* which was one of her all-time favourites. (Well, how many other films starred ripely gorgeous, clever, dark-skinned flight attendants?) She walked fast, relishing the chance to stretch, aware of the movement of her hips in her purple knee-length skirt. Her red leather carry-on glided along behind her. She'd put her hair up in a French twist and applied a lipstick called Bruised Fruit. Toronto Pearson Airport was all gray carpets and oversized art; outside the walls of glass she could see nothing but spiraling white.

"Visiting friends, family?"

"Mm," Síle told the woman at Immigration with a smile, slightly breathless at the thought of trying to explain what had brought her here.

"Staying how long?"

"Just the weekend." Her passport was scanned and stamped (one mark among many on its tattered pages) and she was waved on. She sailed through customs, thinking *Don't stop me, don't let anyone delay me one minute longer or I'll burst...*

There, behind the barrier, was a small head on top of a huge padded jacket. Síle paused, blinking. Jude didn't shout a greeting; she just raised her fingers and walked toward the gap in the barrier. Her hair looked very short, infinitely soft. Síle had planned to kiss Jude boldly, with lips and tongue in the middle of the throng, but now that the moment had come she felt barely capable of shaking hands.

Jude hugged her. Síle was engulfed in down; it was like being embraced by a duvet. But on her back she could feel the hard grip of Jude's hands, and hot breath on her neck. They were blocking the stream of passengers emerging from the baggage hall. "Hey," said Síle, stepping sideways. "Hey you."

"Hey."

"Oh dear, I've got lipstick on your jaw."

"Have you?" said Jude, grinning, not wiping it off.

Síle remembered what it was all about, why she'd come all this way. Her heart drummed. "Here you are. Two feet away!"

"Less," said Jude, stepping closer for a real kiss. "Sorry about the weather," she said after a minute; "spring seems to have changed its mind. Where's your coat?"

"I'll be fine, this is lined," said Síle, zipping up her raincoat.

Jude cast a doubtful glance at Síle's heels. "It's a whiteout, out there, and the roads haven't been salted yet. We could always go to the Holiday Inn," she added after a second.

Síle frowned at the prospect of spending their first night at the

Holiday Inn. She took Jude by one skinny, warm wrist and murmured, "I trust your driving."

Jude grinned, picked up Síle's case, and staggered.

"Mind, it's heavy."

"You can say that again."

"It's got wheels, look—" but Jude was already carrying it away.
Síle followed her through the crowd, trying to remember where she'd
stowed her red kidskin gloves. As she stepped through the sliding
doors, a blast of icy wind nearly knocked her off her heels. Snow like
a cloud of needles against her face, in her ears, in her eyes. Where had
Jude got to? Síle couldn't be expected to walk through this. The evening air was like broken glass in her throat. Her hands were hurting.
The moaning wind flattened her raincoat against her; she might just
as well have been naked. *Turn it off!* she thought. *Make it stop!*

A tug on her shoulder. Jude's face inside a huge fur-edged hood.
"Where were you?"

"Where were *you*?" replied Síle childishly.

"Don't you have a hat?"

"I didn't know I'd need one, it's nearly May!" Then she tucked
her hands in her armpits, set her back to the wind, and bawled,
"Listen, let's go back inside till this dies down."

Jude shook her head. "It won't." And turned away, no discussion.

So Síle had to follow, picking her way across the road to the
parking lot through several inches of snow. Jude was still carrying
the bag instead of wheeling it; this was butch bordering on ridiculous. Her car turned out to be a white Mustang, nibbled by rust
along all its edges. While Jude was putting the suitcase in the trunk,
Síle went to the left-hand door, without thinking, and then felt a
surge of exasperation with herself for behaving like someone who'd
never crossed the Atlantic.

The heating made a desperate whirr. "Sorry about this old
wreck," Jude muttered, backing out, "but at least it's a stick shift, so
I can usually find my way out of trouble."

As they inched along the motorway in the twilight, behind hundreds of other travelers, Síle sat cupping her throbbing ears. Her ankles were wet. "I'm just not bred for this cold," she remarked with a self-mocking shudder.

Jude didn't answer. She was hunched over the wheel, peering past the headlights at the spotlit direction signs. ALL ROADS LEAD TO BRAMPTON. Was the girl really this taciturn in person, Síle tried to remember, or was it only a mood brought on by the howling blizzard? But then, what were any of us except a random sequence of moods?

"This climate's rather a thrill," she said, as merrily as she could manage. "I might have died back there outside the terminal, mightn't I, if I'd turned the wrong way in the snow and tripped over something, or just stood there waiting for you for too long? Whereas at home you could lie in a ditch for a fortnight and end up with nothing worse than a runny nose."

Jude's eyes were on the dim taillights of the jeep in front. There was no other sign that they were on a road, Síle realized. They must have turned off the motorway without her noticing. The signs were illegible with snow. "Actually," Jude began hoarsely, then cleared her throat. "Actually, this isn't too cold, because it's snowing."

Síle puzzled over that. "Am I missing something?"

"When it's really cold, snow can't fall."

She absorbed that cheering information, as darkness began to close in. The Holiday Inn was sounding more and more attractive, in retrospect. Already she'd counted four cars off the road, one of them upside down. She craned to see whether all the passengers had got out safely, but all she glimpsed was snow and blackness. The narrow file of cars crept forward. Síle suddenly wondered whether there was a road under them at all, or whether the lead car might have veered off across some desolate field, with the rest of them following like slow lemmings.

Jude turned on the radio, looking for a weather report, and for the next half hour she switched between crackling stations offering soul, classical, a panel discussion on gang culture, and Christian rock. It occurred to Síle that she hadn't seen her have a cigarette yet; maybe Jude never smoked while she was driving. "How are your legs?" Jude asked suddenly.

"Numb to the knee, actually."

Jude fiddled with the heating controls. "That better?"

"Not really."

She turned and tugged a blanket off the backseat.

Síle tried to feel grateful for that bit of gallantry, as she wrapped the scratchy, damp material around her legs. At one point she took out her gizmo and gave it a squeeze to light up the little screen. It was 8:39, somewhere in the snowbound, godless wilderness. *Distance from Home City Dublin 3285 Miles.* Nearly two in the morning back in Stoneybatter, where Síle could have been tucked up in her copper-pipe bed on her Egyptian cotton sheets.

She hadn't noticed the jeep ahead turn off the road, but it was nowhere to be seen; the Mustang was alone now. There was nothing ahead of them but the menacing whiteness under their headlights, the faint speckle of falling snow. "Not too long now," murmured Jude.

And that was it for small talk for another half hour. Síle had never met a silence she couldn't fill, but tonight she was too cold, too disappointed; she'd be damned if she was going to do all the work. *Why did I ever think I was falling for this peculiar bogtrotter who has nothing to say for herself and nothing to say to me?*

They drew to a halt two blocks short of a bare crossroads, under a feeble streetlight. "Don't say we're out of petrol?" asked Síle.

"No, we're home." Jude went out into the night, slamming the door behind her.

Síle was alone, the skin of her throat, wrists, and knees contracting in the icy air. In theory she'd known that there would be no mountains, no river, but for the first time it hit her that the hamlet of Ireland was nothing but a few silent streets. Population six hundred, but where were they all? It had taken nearly four hours to reach the arse end of nowhere.

Jude opened the door again to explain, "I can't pull into the driveway till it's shoveled."

When Síle stepped out, the snow came up to her knees. It was astonishingly wet and cold through her tights. She lurched after Jude's dark bulk. Snowflakes spiked on her eyelashes. At one point she almost lost one of her shoes in a snowdrift, but she reminded herself grimly of what it had cost and clenched it on.

Jude was waiting for her outside one of the houses, hands tucked under her arms. "Soon be warm," she said. Síle's teeth were clamped shut.

In the upstairs bathroom she cracked her head painfully on the slanted ceiling. Everything was in French as well as English, she noticed: the shampoo, the toothpaste.

Slow steps on the stairs. Jude stood in the doorway. "I guess you hate me right now."

"That's right," said Síle. She kept on chafing her bare legs with the stiff towel, aware of Jude's eyes on them.

"What you need is a hot bath."

"Oh, I always take showers," said Síle, "they're so much faster."

There it was, the crooked little smile, the one Síle'd been trying to call up in her memory, ever since New Year's Day. "What's the rush?" asked Jude. She ran the bath till it was very deep—checking the temperature, while Síle sat there on the toilet seat, suddenly drop-dead tired. Finally Jude opened a box and threw in what looked like a handful of dust.

"What's that?" asked Síle.

"Oatmeal." Jude turned off the taps, which made an old-fashioned creak.

Oatmeal? I've gone back in time, Síle thought, *I've joined the fucking Amish, like Harrison Ford in* Witness.

Alone, she immersed herself in the silky, clouded water and sank down till it covered her stomach, her nipples, her chin. The heat made her limbs throb. She felt as if she were drowning.

When she emerged in her towel, she was in a better state to notice things. Lots of bare wood; warm air puffed through intricate wrought-iron grilles in the floor. She paused at a heavy carved bookcase, her finger brushing titles: *Sisters in the Wilderness, The Donnellys Trilogy, Who Has Seen the Wind, Wisconsin Death Trip,* and a whole shelf by somebody named Pierre Berton. The first room she peeped into had an unused look, a vase of honesty beside the bed; that must have been the mother's. The next door was wide open, and her green case was standing there, incongruously executive beside a rocking chair, on the rag rug. Folded on the bed were a pair of blue striped cotton pajamas. Síle had brought her silk nightshirt with her, but on impulse she put the pajamas on and crawled under the huge, lumpy duvet. She wondered where Jude had got to. Off having a fag at last, maybe.

Two in the morning, Irish time, or was it three? Her eyelids were beginning to droop by the time Jude appeared in the doorway with a steaming mug. "Camomile tea."

"Sorry," said Síle, "but I can't stand the stuff."

The girl set the mug down on the table and sat on the very edge of the bed. "How're you doing?"

"Better."

Jude took a sip of the camomile.

The silence was getting awkward, so Síle said, "I brought you a little something," pointing to the duty-free bag on the table.

Jude pulled out the two big cartons of cigarettes.

"I've always refused to buy death-sticks for my friends, but this time I decided to make the grand gesture, to make up for biting your head off at Heathrow. When you lit up at the baggage carousel."

Jude let out a creaky laugh.

"What?" asked Síle. "Did I get the brand wrong?"

Jude leaned over and kissed her with precise and strong lips. Síle stared up at her. "You don't taste like a smoker."

"Exactly."

"You didn't!"

"Midnight yesterday, and I've been brushing my teeth a lot since then, for something to do."

"For me?" asked Síle, marveling. "You gave up smoking for me?"

Jude shrugged. "You were just...the occasion."

Síle smiled as sleekly as a cat. "That's why you've been such a glump this evening. You're in withdrawal!"

"A glump?"

"You know exactly what I mean. Riding along in stony silence like some prison escort..."

"I was concentrating on the road. It was tough driving." Jude's voice was grim, but her mouth was twisted with laughter. "And as for you, showing up in a blizzard in stilettos and a slinky raincoat—"

"Whose are the pajamas?" asked Síle, to change the subject.

"Mine," said Jude, looking at her with those transparent blue eyes.

"They're very soft. Are you coming in?" asked Síle, patting the duvet.

Jude snapped the light off before undressing. "Puritan blood, you know," she muttered.

Síle listened to the small sounds of clothes coming off, being piled on a chair. Then the bed creaked as Jude climbed in. Síle wriggled backwards till her back reached Jude's hot chest. The girl was completely naked; *not such a Puritan as all that, then*. It was odd, Síle thought; they'd never even hugged till this evening, they didn't know any of each other's curves and angles—and yet here they were; slotted together like this was the only possible way to lie on a wintry April night.

She was glad, suddenly, that it had been so long since she'd had sex with anyone but herself. Too long to be troubled by memories. *Must take off these pajamas,* she thought sleepily. *First times are crucial. Mustn't be wearing pajamas when I ravish her in some memorable way.* "Lordy," she murmured, "cold really makes you appreciate another body."

"There's a bit in the Bible about that, actually."

"Isn't there always?" she groaned.

Jude quoted it in her ear: "If two lie together, then they have heat, but how can one be warm alone?"

Síle lay still, planning a witty response to that, deciding on her moves.

But the next thing she knew, it was morning, and a gaudy yellow sun was setting their bed on fire.

Sun in their eyes, lemon yellow in the crooks of their knees and elbows. Jude shouldn't have worried. She and Síle knew what to do as if the information had been coded in their genes. There was startled breathing and shrieking. The two of them got so tangled up in Síle's hair, she had to shake it back over the headboard. This was a lucky dip, a ten-course banquet, a fruit machine where—*ching, ching!*—coins kept spilling from slots.

They lay catching their breath, their fingers slotted together. "The first sap is the sweetest," Síle quoted.

Jude's laugh turned into a hacking cough. So unfair, that it was only when you gave up smoking that your lungs broke down. She played with the delicate gold chain around Síle's waist.

"Feels strange," Síle said; "nobody's touched it in a long time. It was my mother's; it's called an Aranjanam."

Jude repeated the syllables, Síle correcting her till she'd got it right. "Didn't Kathleen touch it?" she asked. There were always ghosts around a bed; you might as well invite them in, start trying to make peace with them.

Síle looked her in the eye. "Not in a few years."

Excellent! But Jude only said that in her head, and she managed to keep her face straight. She thought of saying something like *That's terrible,* but it would be tacky to triumph over the fallen foe. "Do you ever take it off?"

Síle shook her head. "Though one of these years I may have to have it lengthened! The times I've been to Kerala, my relations tell me I look like Sunita reincarnated," she went on, "but I still feel like such an outsider there. If our Amma had lived to raise me and Orla I suppose we'd be cultural hybrids, but as it is we're just brown Irish. I've never even slept with anyone who wasn't white as paper. Have you?"

"Well, Rizla's half Mohawk—"

"Of course. I forget to count guys," said Síle with a self-mocking grin. "So, one thing troubles me: You know you say there've been no *serious* girlfriends—"

Jude shrugged. "It tends to start hot but dwindle into friendship, if anything. I don't think I'm scared of committing—"

"Clearly not! Your job, your hick village..."

"I'm pragmatic, I guess," Jude told her. "If it's not the big thing, I don't see the point in pretending it is." A pause. "And it's never been the big thing, till now."

Síle's eyes were dark orange.

"Uh-oh, is that too much, on a first date?"

For answer, Síle climbed on top of her and put her tongue behind Jude's earlobe. Things got sweaty and noisy again, and Jude forgot how much she'd been wanting a cigarette. At one point she felt sudden wet on the side of her neck, and had the crazy thought that she'd burst a blood vessel. But then Síle's face lifted, and it was blotted with tears. "What is it?" said Jude, appalled. "What's wrong?"

"Nothing," Síle sobbed. She licked her own salt water off Jude's collarbone. "Did you never have anyone weep all over you in bed?"

Jude shook her head.

"Young pup." Síle collapsed onto her back, her hair like a black vine spreading across Jude's chest. "So how do you like it, the big thing?" she asked after a minute.

"I wouldn't say I *like* it," said Jude. "It's like being Belgium."

"Belgium?" repeated Síle, shrilly.

"Wasn't Belgium always getting overrun by invading armies?"

"Ah. Ever the history buff."

"My life isn't my own anymore," said Jude, mock-belligerent.

"'Post-contact,' as you say in the trade." Síle giggled. "Don't blame me."

"I do. You and poor George L. Jackson."

Síle went up on one elbow. "I lit a candle for him the other day, in a Gothic church in Vienna."

"I'll always associate you with death now. In a good way," Jude added, when Síle made a face. "Memento mori, and all that. Did you know, they used to draw a skull at the bottom of a tankard, so when you'd drained it you'd be reminded you were going to die someday?"

"I can't see that catching on at Ikea."

"So whenever I think of how we met, I'm reminded to seize the day."

"Or the Irishwoman."

"Exactly." Jude worked her hands around Síle's waist and tightened like a snake.

"You realize this is doomed?" said Síle in an indecently hopeful voice.

"What, you mean the living five thousand kilometres apart?"

"Oh dear, that sounds even worse than three thousand miles."

"I thought Ireland was metric."

"Well, in theory, but we still talk in miles and pints," Síle explained. "But yes, the distance, and also the little matter of fourteen years..."

"*That* shouldn't matter," said Jude. "People are always telling me I've got an old head on young shoulders."

Síle grinned. "It's two generations, musically and demographically: I'm a tail-end Boomer and you're Gen Y."

"I'd like to say in my defense that I can play 'Scarborough Fair.' Couldn't we just pretend I was born in the sixties?"

"Play it on what?"

"Guitar," said Jude. "What could be more sixties than that?"

Síle let out an exasperated breath. "How could you not have mentioned that you play the guitar?"

"I'm not that good."

"You're good enough to play 'Scarborough Fair,' which makes it a big fat lie of omission." She reached for Jude's fingertips and rubbed them. "Calluses; of course, I should have guessed," she said under her breath.

"Sorry, did they—"

"I like them," Síle told her, grinning. "So what else don't I know about you?"

"A quarter-century's worth, at least."

Much later, when Síle was in the shower, Jude let her head dangle off the mattress. Her whole body felt swollen, sodden. She was woozy; she was high as a kite. She had a little headache, from nicotine withdrawal, she supposed. (Gwen had suggested patches, but Jude preferred to do this kind of thing on her own.) She rolled onto her stomach and looked under the bed. There were dust balls, and a pencil, and a pair of delicate high-heeled suede shoes with tide marks on them.

Downstairs, she dabbed the worst of the stains off with desalting fluid. She had carried the shoes halfway up the staircase when Síle appeared at the top in a towel.

"C'mere, gorgeous," said Síle, descending.

Jude shook her head, backing down. "Bad luck to cross on the stairs."

"Not another one!"

"You can call it superstition, or you can call it sense."

"And there I was thinking you just couldn't take your eyes off me."

"That too," said Jude, finding and kissing Síle's dark nipples one after the other.

Síle put on a brown suede skirt, a silk sweater, and an angora shrug—a word Jude had never learned till today, and couldn't imagine using in conversation. From the Aladdin's cave of her suitcase she took out a quantity of gold jewelry; on anyone else, it might have looked too much. Feeling Jude's eyes on her, she said, "Nomads always wear their wealth. Do you even own any jewelry? I've never met anyone who wears fewer items. Shirt, jeans, knickers..."

Jude looked down at herself. "Belt, socks...That's about all I need."

"You'd definitely lose at strip poker." Síle examined the Swiss Army knife hanging from a belt loop. "Did you know the average buyer loses theirs in three days?"

She laughed. "I got mine from my uncle Frank for my eighth birthday."

The next kiss lasted long enough that Jude thought she might fall down.

"Feed me!" Síle roared in her ear like a bear.

They had the Hungryman's Breakfast at the Garage, where Jude introduced Síle to Lynda the waitress, Johan the dentist, and Marcy the town's travel agent and desktop publisher—"had to diversify when her bakery went bust," Jude muttered in Síle's ear. Lucian and Hugo from the Old Station Guesthouse had their ferret Daphne on a harness and wanted to know how Síle was enjoying "Her Majesty's Dominion."

"Glad to see you're not the only queer in town," she murmured to Jude across the table. "All this hand-shaking and inquiries after health and happiness, it's so Old World! It must take half the day to get down the street. In Dublin we mostly just nod and mutter 'howarya.' Oh look, a pious papist," she commented as a pregnant girl pushed into the café wearing an Our Lady Peace T-shirt over a bulging sweatshirt.

"Actually that's a band," Jude told her, amused. More loudly: "Hey Tasmin. Síle, this is my friend Gwen's niece…" When the girl had gone out with her coffee and doughnuts, Jude added: "Unemployed, bulimic, and due in July. Her parents are going out of their minds."

At the next table, farmers were debating whether late feeds helped avoid night lambing: Síle was agog.

Jude paid at the counter. "All righty, see you later," said tiny, wrinkled Mrs. Leung.

"That's one idiom I find charming," Síle remarked when they were out the door. "The way it implies everybody's going to get together again before the afternoon's over. She's from China?"

"Hong Kong."

"I remember that feeling of being the only ethnics in town," said Síle with a little shudder. "You couldn't so much as pick your nose in case the neighbours jumped to the conclusion that *all you people pick your noses.*"

She walked sexily, Jude thought, even in an old pair of Rachel Turner's snow boots that had somehow escaped the purge. *Síle O'Shaughnessy's here on Main Street,* she told herself, incredulous, *right here, right now.*

The snowdrifts were translucent with sunlight at the edges, and gutters and eaves dripped musically. "This was the Petersons' surgery, before they retired," said Jude, stopping at a two-story limestone house; "when Dad's furniture business collapsed, they took Mom on as their receptionist, even though she had no experience. After school I used to read in the waiting room."

"I can just picture you, swinging your little legs," said Síle. "Dungarees?"

"Always."

She took Síle into the museum's office first. "Archivists have this principle called *respect des fonds*," she told her from the top of a set of rickety library steps, "meaning you should respect something's provenance—where it's from."

Síle's forehead crinkled. "Such as?"

"Here, for instance." Jude climbed down with a carton and unwound the string. "Miss Anabella Gurd's journal. This is one of my favourite holdings."

"Wow," murmured Síle, bending over the brittle pages.

"See this clipping about the craze for crinolines?" It had been pasted in carelessly; the paper rippled. "Provenance means you don't rip it out and stick it in a file marked Fashion. You leave it here, because it tells us that Miss Gurd of Ireland, Ontario, was worrying about her underwear on 13 December 1857."

"Context is all," suggested Síle.

"Exactly!"

Outside the schoolhouse, Jude wrestled with the padlock. "The first time I saw inside was when me and some boys broke in, in grade seven. It was totally derelict and smelled like death."

"Well it's gorgeous, now," said Síle, stepping in and craning up at the polished beams and the blown-up photos on the white-washed walls, letting her fingers trail along the back of a desk. " 'The area where you stand was a million acres of trackless wilderness probably first inhabited by the Fluted Point People (9500–8200 C.E.),' " she read aloud from a wall panel. "C.E.?"

"P.C. speak for B.C."

She examined farm tools and kitchenware, clothes hung on invisible threads from the rafters. "I was afraid there might be sinister mannequins."

"Ugh! The bane of small museums. No, I prefer real things. Like—can you guess what this is?" Jude held up an iron pincer.

"An instrument of torture?"

She grinned. "Catholic! It's a nipper, for breaking bits of sugar off a cone. But listen, I can't give you the full tour or we'll waste your last day." Ever since they'd left the house, she'd heard the hours ticking away.

She drove them out to a conservation area near Stratford. Leaving Ireland, they passed a filthy red pickup, and Síle asked, "What's that about?"

"What?"

"You nodded at them, and lifted two fingers off the wheel."

Jude hadn't even noticed. "Oh, it's the local wave."

"What if they're not local, what if you don't recognize the car?"

"Then we scowl murderously," said Jude, straight-faced.

She scanned the white-blotted fields as if with an outsider's eye: What would Síle be seeing? They passed orchards of low, twisted apple trees, tense with the anticipation of blossom, and tall houses with stately porches, sheltered by stands of cedars, that seemed to disdain any connection with the soil. A gap-toothed barn disintegrating in a riot of silvery gray; a big red one with a roof that read CROWLEY FARM CELEBRATING 150 YEARS, and another that said, unusually, VAN HOPPER AND DAUGHTER.

"It's so flat," Síle commented. "No wonder they had to use unimaginative names like 13 Mile Road or—" she craned to read the next small sign—"Line 28!"

"This road we're on, a hero of mine, Colonel Van Egmond, built it through the bush, all the way to Lake Huron," Jude told her. "He talked families into setting up inns so travelers could get their beef tallow and crust coffee, and he brought all the settlers' complaints back to his bosses."

"Bet they didn't promote him."

"Afraid not: He joined the 1837 Rebellion and died in jail." She slid her right hand into Síle's waterfall of hair and held on.

They passed a silo with a red and white candy-striped cap on it. "Check out the giant condom," murmured Síle, reading Jude's mind. She kept exclaiming over the Irish names on the map: Dungannon, Birr, Mount Carmel, Clandeboye, Listowel, Donegal, Newry, Ballymote...

"Well, that's homesick immigrants for you," said Jude. "There's also Zurich, Hanover, Heidelberg..."

But what entertained Síle the most, oddly, were the roadside signs. Apparently in her country, stores and churches didn't display folksy sayings in ill-spaced letters. "Why, is it not legal?" asked Jude.

"I just don't think it would occur to the cynical Irish. We put up billboards to sell things, but we don't offer advice on life. I mean, look at that..." She scrabbled for her gizmo as they passed one that warned A FEW LOOSE WORDS CAN LEAD TO A FEW LOOSE TEETH.

"Are you collecting them?"

Síle nodded, tapping the tiny keyboard. "I'll e-mail a list to all my friends."

"They'll think Canada's dumb," said Jude, childish.

"No no. Every country has its peculiarities."

Síle's head spun as they passed a bone-white church whose sign read GOD LOVES YOU WHETHER YOU LIKE IT OR NOT. "Scary!" The next one offered SUN WORSHIP 11AM ALL WELL COME. "They must mean Sunday Worship," she said, typing fast, "unless they all get— what was your phrase, butt-naked?"

"Buck-naked," Jude supplied, grinning.

"—and sing hallelujah to the returning sun. Solar cults would make sense, in these long winters."

"Look, outside that peach market, that's a funny one," said Jude: NOSTALGIA AIN'T WHAT IT USED TO BE.

"Peaches? Let's get some." said Síle, twisting in her seat.

"Come back in August."

"Oh of course, they'd be local."

"You're such a global citizen, you don't know where or when you are," Jude mocked her.

In the parking lot of the conservation area, Síle got out in her ladylike way, feet together. Jude noticed that the snow was tinged with blue: broken glass scattered in ermine. She went first, the sled under her arm; she stepped into the cracked foot holes of earlier walkers or waded through fresh powder, sometimes skidding. It was too bright to see clearly, but there was a drift of fog in the distance; it confused the eyes. She turned and Síle grinned back at her, shiny-faced.

"It's hard to be elegant in the snow, isn't it?" said Síle. "All you can do is stomp along like a three-year-old. And my nose keeps dripping, and I can hardly hear you through all these hoods and scarves. The air feels fantastic, though. The snowfields! When I was a kid, that's what I used to call it up in the sky, after the plane pierces the clouds and it's all dazzling white."

Jude took a narrow path through the woodland. Snow scrunched underfoot.

"There's nothing like being away from other human beings, out in the middle of nowhere, is there?" asked Síle. "I'd usually have my headphones on, when I'm walking; it's odd not to have a sound-track. It's so utterly quiet."

Jude wanted to laugh.

"Is that a robin? Oh no, of course, American robins are much bigger. I mean Canadian robins. I believe they're insanely territorial, or little Irish robins are, anyway."

Jude waited till Síle caught up with her, then clapped her glove gently over the woman's mouth.

"What?" said Síle, muffled.

"Shh for a minute."

"What were we born with tongues for, if not to talk?"

"There's kissing, for one." Jude showed her what she meant. A crow let out a hoarse croak.

After half a minute Síle stepped back, defiant. "At school I used to win public speaking contests; you'd be given a word—*fashion,* say, or *apples*—and you'd have to discuss it for five minutes without repeating yourself."

"That explains a lot," said Jude, laughing.

She'd forgotten how enlivening the cold could feel, nipping her on the inside of her wrists, the scruff of her neck. They emerged near a small pond, its white edge fringed with orange reeds. Jude stared at the drift of snow on the gray-green ice and wondered if it was a thin layer, after the recent thaw, or still solid all the way down.

A gloved hand slid into Jude's pocket. "Are you missing the fags?"

Jude let out her breath. "Since you mention it—I'd empty my bank account for one."

"Oh, my love." The endearment startled Jude, but it sounded oddly natural. "How much is that?"

"Actually, only about $75," Jude admitted.

Síle laughed. "And our phone bills can't be helping."

"Best money I've ever spent. Besides, giving up the smokes is going to save me big bucks."

"Was it really all about my visit?" Síle asked coyly. "All you had to do was smoke on the porch for two days."

Jude shrugged. "I'd always meant to give them up before I was twenty-five, so I'm late already. And Mom would approve; she always called it 'your filthy habit.'" Taken off guard, she was blinded by tears.

"Careful, your eyes might freeze over," whispered Síle, pulling off one glove to wipe Jude's face with the heel of her hand. "I'm sure she'd be chuffed. *Is* chuffed," she corrected herself, "looking down on you, hoping you'll live to be a hundred."

Jude buried her face in the dark cloud of hair sliding out of Síle's hood. "Time to toboggan," she announced.

When they got home, Jude opened the garage to show Síle her bike.

"Ooh," said Síle, crouching to peer at the sleek coils of the pipes, "I bet this cost five times what your car did."

"Just about. She's a 1979 Triumph: the year I was born." Jude stroked the icy paintwork. "My uncle Frank customized her, rode her every day from May to October, till his arthritis got so bad he moved down to Florida, near Dad, and left this baby with me. You're just a few weeks too early for a ride," she added regretfully.

"Next time," said Síle, and Jude's pulse thumped with delight.

Jude heated up some parsnip gratin, making the kitchen fragrant with onions and sage. "Oh, did you want to listen to the news?"

Síle shook her head lazily. "Not this weekend. You notice I haven't even checked my messages?"

"I hadn't. But now that you mention it, I'm impressed."

"Well, if you can go cold turkey, so can I..."

"I still can't quite believe any of this is real."

"I can," said Síle, her hands decisive on Jude's hips, pulling her close. "You're no figment: I've never met anyone so here and now."

In bed, it got dark without them noticing. They were shattered and sore and the sheet was pleated with wrinkles. Jude found a little notch in the knuckle of Síle's index finger. "Aha!" she said, "now I'd know you anywhere."

Jude felt ridiculously nervous as they crunched up Main Street hand in hand, toward the crossroads.

"Shades of Narnia," laughed Síle under her breath: "one streetlight and a lot of snow."

There were about a dozen drinkers in the Dive. "Jeez," boomed Rizla, "the honeymooners managed to stagger out of bed."

Jude said in his ear, "Remember I promised you could meet her if you promised not to be a jerk?"

He shook her off, enclosed Síle's hand in his beefy one, helped her off with her jacket, and insisted she take his stool. "Go right ahead, my fat ass's had enough sitting around."

Síle crossed her legs seductively, despite the borrowed snow boots, and smiled up at him. In her bright skirt and beaded Rajasthani jacket, she stood out against the comfortable casuals the locals were wearing, quite apart from being the only South Asian face in the village.

"Dave," said Rizla, "may I present Síle O'Shaughnessy from Dublin, Ireland?"

The bartender wore a wary smile. "Whatever you say, Riz. Now, what can I get you, ma'am? Sleeman's, Upper Canada..."

"Actually, Dave," said Síle, her accent strengthening as she leaned over the bar, "I'm not too fond of the old beer. What I'd love is a chocolate martini, if it wouldn't be too much trouble."

"A chocolate martini?"

Rizla wiggled his eyebrows at Jude.

"Made with crème de cacao, you know?" said Síle.

"I'll have a look in the back," Dave said abstractedly.

In his absence, Jude told Síle that she might have to settle for a straight martini.

Síle widened her eyes. "Place your trust in the global economy. My local supermarket stocks Ontario maple syrup."

And indeed, five minutes later, Dave came in brandishing a dusty bottle of crème de cacao. Rizla and Síle looked up from their discussion of their favourite *Simpsons* episodes to applaud. Jude thought, *This woman is a magic wand.*

Dave rested on his elbows and examined the visitor more closely. "That sure is a nice accent you've got. I thought Rizla here must be pulling my leg, because you don't look Irish."

Jude stiffened.

Síle beamed back at him. "And the funny thing is, Dave, I've been told I don't look like a lesbian, either."

Dave blinked once, twice. "Well, pleasure to meet you," he said blankly, taking a swipe at the counter with his cloth before heading into the back.

Rizla pounded the bar in silent mirth. "Two-nil to the Fighting Irish! You shut that dickhead up."

"Poor Dave," Síle murmured, "and after he made me a perfect chocolate martini…"

"I bet you don't take any shit from your passengers."

"I take infinite amounts of shit from them," Síle corrected him, "which is why, when I'm off-duty, I speak my mind."

Jude felt all the strings in her body loosen.

"Yeah, this whole area was Mohawk hunting grounds," Rizla was telling Síle when Jude tuned in again, "till we sold it to the Crown in the early eighteenth century."

"You mean early 1800s," Jude reminded him.

He ignored that. "I'm not actually Status, though."

"Sorry, you've lost me," said Síle.

"Mom wasn't a Status Indian once she married a Dutchman. She had to leave the rez," he explained, "so they raised eleven of us in a farmhouse a ways west of Brantford."

"Eleven!"

He shrugged. "Well, you know, it's that or disappear."

"But you haven't had any yourself?" Síle asked.

"Nah," he said, "just lots of nieces and nephews. See, it's like sports: I'd rather watch hockey players smash each other's heads in on TV than actually play a game myself. Aren't the Irish big breeders too?"

"Less so, nowadays, since we don't kowtow to the Church so much," she told him; "I think the average family's down to three point nine. And my parents only had two."

"Got bored of the old bump 'n grind?" suggested Rizla. "Took a vow of abstinence?"

"My mother died when I was three." After a second, Síle grinned. "Now don't you feel like a crass bastard?"

"Not for the first time nor the last," he said, and insisted on buying the next round.

Dave was still subdued, eyes averted. "He'll be lying awake half the night, wondering what to make of you," Jude whispered in Síle's ear. "I bet he'll share it with his Bible Encounter Group."

"Whoops, have I muddied your reputation?"

"Too late for that," she said, laughing.

Síle looked around the bar speculatively. "So what's the local demographics—mostly farmers? That pair behind us have been discussing their alfalfa yield for half an hour," she whispered.

"Yeah, mostly dairy and cash crop," said Rizla. "Those guys playing euchre work for Dudovick's Turkeys."

"Luke Randall—" Jude nodded at a man reading the *Globe and Mail*—"is a manager of a bank in Stratford. Behind us is Greg Devall, the TV executive whose bloody SUV killed my red setter Trip," she added under her breath.

Síle narrowed her eyes, like a mobster memorizing his face.

"But you know, unless you're old stock, here at least a hundred years, you don't count as local," said Jude. "Dad was third-generation on his father's side, but his mother was a Home Child; she was sent out here from England at the age of nine."

"What'd she done?" asked Síle.

"It wasn't meant as a prison sentence! Though in some cases it turned out that way," Jude explained; "in theory it was a fresh start as farm labourers for orphans from the home country."

"You've got great triceps for a girly gal, Síle," Rizla remarked, gripping her bare arm. Jude thought Síle might object, but instead she tensed it for him. "You work out?"

"No, she stacks trays at ten thousand metres," Jude reminded him.

"Right. *I'm Síle, Fly Me!*" he said in a lewd falsetto. "Hey, so when I was flying round the world, I noticed you trolley dollies disappear for hours. Whatcha doing, chewing the fat back there?"

"Yeah, we pass round the duty-free vodka," Síle told him, "that's how we manage the permanent glazed smile. Actually, the real money's in the sex; it's €50 for every hand job, and €100 for a fuck in the toilet."

Rizla blinked at her, and then released such an enormous laugh that the euchre players looked up. Licking his finger, he chalked one on the air for Síle.

They had a game of pool. "I taught Jude here all she knows," Rizla explained.

"So how come I beat you nine times out of ten?" asked Jude, racking them up.

Síle kept messing up her shots. "Everything's the wrong size here, I'm getting vertigo," she complained, laughing. "The table's too low, the balls are too big, and spotted instead of red or yellow…"

"If you stayed a week you'd get the hang of it," Rizla told her. "I could give you a crash course in being a Canuck."

"I already fell off a sled twice today."

"That's a start, but you gotta skate and Ski-doo, you gotta shoot things—"

"Don't listen to him," said Jude.

"—and you gotta tell Newfie jokes. You hear about the Newfie who's so lazy he married a pregnant woman?"

"I know that one," Síle protested, "but it's about a Kerryman."

"Yeah," Jude put in, "and the Spanish probably say it about the Portuguese."

"This other Newfie, he goes to the hospital in St. John's, says, 'I want to be castrated.'" Rizla's eyebrows leapt up. "'You sure about that?' says the doctor. 'Yeah yeah boy,' says the Newfie, 'I'm telling you I want to be castrated.' So after the op, he wakes up in a room with another patient. He says 'Hey, you boy, what operation you got done?' The other guy says he's been circumcised. 'Dammit to hell,' says the Newfie, '*dat's* de word I was looking for!'"

Jude groaned, but Síle and Rizla were raucous with mirth.

She breathed in and thought, *forty-six smokeless hours down, only a lifetime to go.* Her lover was Síle O'Shaughnessy. Her head was a shaken kaleidoscope. Anything was possible.

But coming back from the washroom (where, as happened every couple of months, some stranger had given Jude's hair a startled look as if to say, "This is the Ladies!"), she got the impression that the atmosphere had cooled.

"Another quick one?" said Rizla.

"I don't think so," said Síle, covering a yawn.

On the street outside, he gave them both crushing hugs, and strolled off in the direction of his trailer. The night was clear and starry. "You have a good time?" asked Jude.

No answer. Síle was looking down at Rachel Turner's boots as they squeaked on the flattened snow. "Rizla thinks you must be really into me, to give up smoking."

"You know I am," said Jude warily.

"He said, and I quote, 'She's a closet romantic, is my wife.'"

Bastard, thought Jude. Had he been planning this masterstroke the whole evening? All that broke the silence was the creak of their footsteps.

"Is that just his little nickname for you? *Wife?*"

"Well," said Jude, her chest tight, "I mean, it's technically true—"

"*Technically?*" Síle pulled up short, and almost slipped on the ice.

Jude put a hand out to steady her, but Síle shook it off. "We split nearly seven years ago."

"But you're telling me you two were actually married?"

"For less than a year." Her voice was uneven.

"Why didn't I hear about this before?"

Jude shrugged. "There's a lot of details you and I haven't got around to swapping yet."

"Details?"

"Getting married at eighteen was a dumb mistake; I hadn't even reached the legal drinking age. I prefer to forget it."

"Still, you could have told me. My jaw fell into my lap, back there; I felt like a complete feckin' eejit."

"I'm sorry."

Síle started walking again, slapping her gloves together to warm her hands, and Jude thought maybe the conversation was over, which was fine by her.

"Sure I know loads of Irishwomen who got married before they knew better," said Síle, her tone softening into exasperation. "So you got divorced, what, when you were nineteen?"

"Well, that's when I moved out." Jude made herself add, "We haven't actually got around to finalizing the paperwork yet, because Rizla's broke, and I wasn't going to pay for it all myself."

Síle turned, her tawny eyes hawklike in the streetlight. *Cheapskate,* Jude thought; *I should have borrowed from the bank.* "You didn't ask much about him," she said, going on the offensive; "you don't seem to count guys."

A tense pause. "Well, it's true that's my blind spot."

"C'mon home before we freeze," she said, tucking her arm into Síle's and heading down Main Street.

After a minute, Síle said "Okay, sorry to harp on, but just to clarify—you're still legally married, but you haven't been involved in over six years."

Jude tried to swallow. *Involved,* what did that mean? One cigarette, that's all she needed. "Right, we haven't been a couple."

But of course Síle heard the equivocation, and her eyes turned on Jude like a searchlight. "The last time you slept with him," she said, spelling it out as if to a child, "it was more than six years ago?"

Messy, messy. "Well, no," said Jude, letting out a long plume of steam.

Síle had dropped her arm. "When was it?"

"Beginning of March."

"Which March?"

"This one just gone."

"Last month?" Síle stood and stared up at the cavernous sky, breathing in and out like a horse. "Then what the fuck am I doing here?"

She was one of those women who looked superb when angry, Jude thought; her hair stood out like a crackling halo. Jude was waiting for the right words to turn up in her mouth, but—

"What exactly was the point of this mad trip to the frozen arsehole of the world?" asked Síle, breaking away to the other side of the street. "I thought you were a dyke. So you're still bi, is that what you're telling me?"

"Those are your words," said Jude thickly.

"Well go ahead, pick one you like." Síle waited. "You certainly let me believe you were single."

"Because I am. Was, till now, I mean," she corrected herself miserably. "You don't get it."

"Get what? The erotic appeal of a not-quite-ex-husband with oil under his nails? Who *are* you people?"

Jude caught her by the sleeve. "Shut up for a second."

"Oh, now you want to do the talking," Síle almost screamed. "Go ahead, delight me with some more little *details.* Next you'll be telling me there's a kid! I can't believe I left Kathleen for you."

Now, that was low. "It was your decision."

"Decision?" Síle repeated, sardonic. "It was a leap in the fucking dark!"

Jude took a breath. "Why are you doing this, Síle?"

"What? What am I doing?"

"Making some big old volcano out of a molehill," said Jude. "There's no kid. There's no sinister conspiracy. So I wound up in bed with my ex once in a while; haven't you ever done that?"

"I've never been that desperate," said Síle with scorn.

"We weren't desperate," insisted Jude. "It only happened a couple of times a year. It was about... company. Comfort." She had a hunch all these words were getting her nowhere. Her newfound happiness was teetering like an icicle in a thaw. She took a step nearer to Síle. "So the last time it happened to happen was at the beginning of March, and I told Riz that was it, over and done with, because it felt wrong, because all I could think about was you."

Síle blew into her gloved hands. "You're the one who doesn't get it," she said, gravely. "This isn't about sex. I don't care who you slept with last month, though from this weekend on I care a lot. What I can't stand is being fooled."

"I—"

"This was a big fat lie of omission! You should have told me what I was walking into and you know it. I'm a stranger in this peculiar little world of yours." A ragged breath. "I've gutted my whole life like a fish because you said you loved me."

"I do," Jude groaned.

"I don't just want to fuck you, I want to know you."

"I was always going to tell you the whole story of me and Riz," Jude said weakly. "There's things that are hard to explain in writing or over the phone. Sometimes it's better to wait for the right moment."

"What, like this one?" asked Síle, waving at the deserted street, the black speckled sky.

Peak Time

If I was a blackbird,
I'd whistle and sing,
And I'd follow the ship
that my true love sails in,

—ANON
If I Was a Blackbird

Síle, Marcus, and Jael were eating overpriced sushi in a Temple Bar restaurant made entirely of hard, noisy surfaces. "It's like lunching in a xylophone," Marcus complained at the top of his voice.

"This is what burying yourself in the sticks does," Jael told him, "you've lost all your urban armour already and it's only been two months."

"I'm growing lettuce, parsnips, leeks, and kale, and building a solarium," he remarked.

"Yeah, and I'm growing sick of smug, back-to-nature gits. And what's that on your head?"

"Tweed has made a comeback," Síle put in, nibbling a bit of pickled ginger.

"Not in the form of an aul-fella's cap."

"The shaved head seemed a bit much, in Leitrim," said Marcus sheepishly, adjusting his cap. "I suspect the neighbours think I'm having chemo."

"And as for you—" Jael threatened Síle with a chopstick. "I thought this Canadian thing was meant to be casual?"

Síle was caught off guard. "No, *you* said it sounded fun so long as it stayed casual." She was failing to hide her smile.

"I hope you realize she could keep succumbing to the hairy charms of the Neanderthal around the corner?"

"Mm," Marcus chipped in, "hubby in the caravan does sound like a bit of an obstacle."

"He is neither hairy nor an obstacle," said Síle, her voice rising. She almost wished she hadn't told them the full story. "It only happened in a very occasional, low-key way; it wasn't like they were in love."

"No, just married," said Jael with a snigger.

"Divorced, bar the paperwork," she snapped.

"Okay, but even if she's mad about you, long-distance relationships are sinkholes for time and energy," Jael warned her.

"Sure, anything more than lying on the sofa takes energy," she protested. "Anton's busy, but he finds time for tae kwon do, doesn't he?"

"Don't talk to me about tae bloody kwon do! It's just an excuse to get away from me and Ys on Saturday afternoons. No, but remember when I was wooing that ex-nun in Portugal?" asked Jael. "What a load of faffing about, waiting for the post to arrive!"

"That was pre–e-mail, Granny," Marcus put in. "Between the Internet and cheap fares, it's never been a better time to fall for someone far away."

Síle grinned at him. "Anyway, it's happened, so it's not as if I have a choice."

"Of course you do. Dykes and their tortured romanticism!" Jael bolted her saki. "If you must keep it up, keep it light. What about phone sex? I tried it a few times with that policewoman in Australia."

"Why only a few?" asked Marcus.

"Did it make you feel lonely?" asked Síle. "I've often thought it might be sad—you know, the unbridgeable gap between word and flesh."

"No, it was just too expensive," said Jael. "It took her so long to come, it cost about thirty quid a go."

They howled. "I suppose you could have got the Aussie to warm herself up beforehand," said Síle, "then ring you for the big climax."

"Oh, and once with Anton," Jael added, "when he was overnighting in Belfast and he'd had too much coffee to fall asleep."

"Was he easier?" Marcus asked.

"Two minutes, max! I kept *Six Feet Under* on mute; I barely missed any of it."

"I can never tell whether you make things up to sound outrageous," said Síle, "or live outrageously so you'll have things to tell your friends."

"Live outrageously? I wish! To think that I used to be truly wild," Jael lamented through a mouthful of rice. "Promiscuous, peripatetic, breaking hearts hither and yon. And now I'm a suburban mammy with an easy-maintenance haircut."

"You've still got a pierced tongue," Marcus comforted her.

"No, it's grown over," she said thickly, sticking it out.

Síle let out a cry of disappointment.

"You know what the worst of it is? We send Yseult down to Kildare on the train, and Mummy and Dad take her to Sunday school."

"No!"

"She better not grow up to be some scary homophobe," said Marcus.

"Trust me for that much," Jael told him. "To be honest, it gets her out of our hair for a few hours so we can have a shag."

"I used to prefer chat rooms to phones," said Marcus, "because there's pictures."

"Used to?" Jael repeated.

"Does this mean your libido's been sublimated into gardening?" Síle wanted to know.

"Actually..." He took a bashful sip of saki.

Jael leapt in. "Don't say you've found some action in the badlands of the Northwest?"

"No, the badlands of Temple Bar," he said, jerking his head. "He lives above Vintage Vinyl. I've spent the whole weekend there."

"So that's why you've been ignoring my texts," said Síle accusingly.

"You whore!" Jael congratulated him, loud enough to startle the occupants of the next table.

"Name and serial number!" Síle felt an absurd pang: She should have been the first to know, but she'd been so preoccupied with Jude recently...

"Pedro Valdez. He knows you, Síle."

"Pedro from Barcelona? Jaysus, small world! He did the photos for that Pride Exhibition I ran back in, what, '93?"

"So you could have introduced us all those years ago?"

"How was I to know you two would like each other, out of all the nellies of my acquaintance?"

"Of course we do," said Marcus. "He's gorgeous, he's hilarious, he's a brilliant designer—"

"I'd have thought Pedro might be a bit quiet for you," she said.

"Not at all! He's self-contained, that's all."

Jael shrugged. "There's no predicting these things."

"I'm so glad," Síle told Marcus, her arm around his shoulder.

"Bet you wish you'd stayed in Dublin now," remarked Jael.

He stuck out his tongue at her.

"The last bit of matchmaking I did was such a disaster," said Síle, "I've sworn off it."

"Which was that?"

"My sister, Orla. I set her up with William—he was my trainer on a management skills course—but over the years he's gone creepily ultra-Catholic. But listen," she said to Marcus, "how come you and Pedro never ran into each other before?"

"We think we must have, once, at some fetish night on the Quays round about '98—"

"He's using 'we' already, do you notice?" said Jael grimly.

"—but he was wearing a rubber mask, so I don't remember his face."

The women snorted with laughter.

"So, Jude Lavinia!" Síle was lying by the fire in her purple velvet dressing gown, spreading her hair over an embroidered silk cushion to dry.

"Shut up," said Jude. "I wish you hadn't wormed my second name out of me."

"You veell tell me ayvrysing," drawled Síle in a Transylvanian accent.

"It must be pretty late, your end."

"I'm just waiting up for *The Sopranos.*"

"A choir?"

"Jude! Sometimes your ignorance of TV makes you sound like a Martian."

"Ah."

"So has spring come to Ontario yet?" Síle asked.

"Oh, it's practically summer. The lilac in the backyard started blooming on Mother's Day, which I took as one of Mom's rare jokes."

"Sweetheart," said Síle, sorrowful. A silence. "Our Mother's Day is in March, not May; it must be a matter of when the flowers come out." She pictured Jude wiping her eyes with her cuff. Which shirt? The black cotton one? "I wish you were here; you could cry into my very absorbent hair."

A wobbly laugh. "I remember it well."

"By the way, Jael and Marcus think it's a bit suspect, your falling for an older woman just after losing your mother."

There was a distinct pause before Jude said, "Wow. That hadn't occurred to me."

"You're joking."

"The two things aren't connected."

"Everything's connected, sweetie," said Síle.

"Well, call me naïve—"

Síle wished she hadn't started this. "I didn't mean—"

"But I think your friends are too quick to jump to conclusions."

"Well, that goes without saying," she hurried to agree. "We Dubs, we talk faster than we think."

"Rizla's your age; maybe I just don't find young people that interesting. And if you'd ever met Mom—well, let's just say you and she have absolutely nothing in common," said Jude briskly.

Síle wriggled to get more comfortable on the sheepskin rug. "I wish we were having this conversation in bed."

"Mm," said Jude, a long drawn-out sound. "The thing about you older women is, you really know what you're doing."

"Why, thank you! But I'm not vastly experienced. Jael's got this concept called sexual density," said Síle, "it's the number of people you've had a *genital encounter* with, divided by the years you've been sexually active. She says anyone whose density's under one has ripped up the invitation to life's party."

"What's Jael's density, then?"

"It was up around five when I first knew her, but since she married Anton it's been slipping badly."

"What about yours?"

"Let's see—counting you," Síle decided, "that would be six over, what is it, twenty years . . . that's only about nought point three women per year."

"One leg," suggested Jude, "or an arm and a few ribs."

Síle laughed.

"I can't believe there've been only five lucky winners before me."

"What, leathery whore of the stratosphere that I am?"

"It's just that...you've traveled so much, you know? You've swum in enough oceans to be able to draw comparisons. You like so many different kinds of food, music, movies..."

"Why hasn't my love life been equally eclectic? I don't know," Síle told her. "Maybe I've been too busy traveling and eating and going to the cinema."

"Just dialing your number makes me wet."

Síle sat up, and her hair fell in damp veils around her. Neither of them said anything for a minute. Odd, she thought, how much people would pay in peak-time charges to listen to each other's silence.

"Síle? Are you there?"

"Yeah. Just speechless."

"Now that's a first."

With the shuttle beeping outside at dawn, and the blackbirds screeching, Síle pulled on a new pair of black tights while signing off on an e-mail to Jude.

```
The thought of you's a constant shock to me, like
the smell of a cut lemon. All yours, S.
```

"Nuala and Tara, you've got Spanish, yeah? Any Japanese, anyone?"

"A tad," said Justin.

She examined his lapel. "Great, but where's your pin?"

"I don't know how it happened, Síle—"

"Not left on the hotel table again? Next time this'll have to go in your file," she warned him.

"Yes, Mammy," under his breath.

She grinned back at him. "Now I'll be in the main cabin tonight, with you, you, you, you, you, and you," she said, pointing. The other five would be in premier, which was lighter work than economy but more servile, she always thought. "Captain says there's a bit of chop expected over Greenland and his is grapefruit juice. Clamato for the first officer."

"What's the passenger load?" asked Coral, adjusting her jade neck-scarf. She looked hungover; more than once, this year, Síle had caught her taking a restorative suck on the on-board oxygen supply.

"Ninety-six percent," Síle told her. Grimaces all around: In her early days it had been more like 50 or 60 percent, with whole stretches of empty seats.

"I heard that Russian airlines let passengers stand up, to pack more of them in," volunteered Lorraine.

"Old aviation myth," said Justin a little snottily.

Scanning the manifest, Síle noted a minor TV celeb, a passenger who'd been turned back for lack of medical clearance for a broken leg, and three who hadn't shown (which meant, in her experience, they were still in the bar). As she went forward to help fold up the baby buggies, a waft of cold air stiffened her smile. Síle thought about her friend Dolores, who'd fallen asleep with her face against a train window and had a paralyzed cheek for months.

"Is this your first time flying, aren't you a great lad? Sir, I don't think that's going to fit . . . Well, sure, try it the other way round, but if not I'll be happy to check it for you. Yeah, this is 12E, there's no 12F. I know, it's not logical, there's no I or J either."

She noticed one red-faced woman who looked well over thirty-two weeks along, now that her coat was off, but if she'd made it past the gate agent Síle wasn't going to give her any grief. Up the length of the plane, pressing bins shut, silently counting heads. A man plucked at Síle's sleeve wanting to know if they served Drambuie, so now she'd have to start her count all over again.

"We thank you very much for choosing to travel with us," Síle concluded over the PA, "and we wish you a very pleasant flight. *A chairde, tá fáilte romhaibh inniu,*" she began from the start in practiced Irish.

A Cork woman defended her daughter's electronic bear. "You're not seriously telling me that a Talking Teddy's going to banjax the navigation system? What kind of tin can are we flying in?"

"Please turn it off now," said Síle. Iron voice in a velvet smile. "Sir, would you like an aspirin for takeoff? The pressure can build up inside a cast."

The moment of liftoff brought her the usual surge of pleasure, as she sat strapped into the jump seat. She wondered whether Jude would ever learn to like it: Were passions contagious? Síle couldn't remember when, at three or four, she'd first become aware of the magic trick of hopping between countries, continents even. But what she'd loved from the start was the way that houses became boxes, cars insects, humans specks of dust, in a miniature play world. And the abstract patterns: plough tracks looped across rectangular fields, rivers like gigantic lazy worms, mountains mere folds and wrinkles in a quilt. That sense of strangeness, of possibility. You felt you were gliding slowly when in fact you were going faster than anything. And as the plane angled up through cloud, the dull fog gave way, and you found yourself hovering above the infinite, dazzling reaches of the snowfields.

Of course, the irony was that once Síle had started working as a flight attendant, she'd been too busy stacking, storing, serving, and chatting to look out the window.

A call from the flight deck; the first officer told her the smoke sensor in the premier toilets was lit up. She sent Jenny to knock on the door and threaten a fine. Síle bounced a carrot-stained baby up and down the plane for five minutes, and managed to make him stop crying by singing "Row, Row, Row Your Boat" in his ear. They passed an old woman hawking phlegm into a sick bag, and she thought of George L. Jackson, and stopped to offer a glass of water. These people were under Síle's protection: thousands and thousands of them over two decades. She did a quick sum, and discovered that over a million passengers had passed through her hands.

"More sugar? No decaf, I'm sorry. They should, I know, I've suggested it before." Nuala spattered coffee on a passenger's cuff and had to rush down the plane for a dry-cleaning claim form. "Don't fret about it," Síle said in her ear, squeezing by a few minutes later, "in my first year I spilled hot tea on a two-year-old and thought my career was over!"

"Oh thank you, sir, it is a striking uniform, isn't it; it's by Louise Kennedy."

Flashback to the ghastly eighties one: the long boxy green jacket with big pocket flaps, the blue sleeveless woolen number. Early nineties wasn't any better, with all those military buttons, shamrock buckles, and coy blouse collars. For someone who thought of herself as stylish, Síle had spent an alarming percentage of her life in ugly uniforms, it occurred to her now. She summoned up an image of her mother in the crisp lines of the Air India uniform, jaunty cap, pearls, gloves... Her mind strayed to *Twilight Girls,* that 1959 pulp classic about an affair between two sultry stewardesses.

The first spare moment Síle got, she checked her messages. An e-mail from a cousin in Delhi announcing yet another new baby, and one from Jude.

> I should be calling the Society of Canadian
> Archivists to thank them for the loan of their
> humidity measuring machine but instead I've been
> looking up your clan (online, you'll be glad to
> hear). Did you know you're a direct descendant of
> Heremon, fourth-century King of Ireland? There
> was also a Sir William Brooke O'Shaughnessy who
> introduced the telegraph to India, and cannabis to
> Western medicine...
>
> Sometimes I say it out loud just to make it real:
> Síle Sunita Siobhán O'Shaughnessy. When I walked past
> the General Store an hour ago I saw you buying
> stamps, but I guess it was a hallucination.

Síle shot off a reply.

```
(((((((((jude)))))))))))
```
        (If you were a visitor to chat rooms you'd know
this means a big hug.)
        A small boy in a psychedelic tracksuit is playing
with his yo-yo and staring at me as if he knows I'm
writing to a woman half my age (okay, 64% of my age)
who somehow loves me back despite the fact that my
sentences (if you can call them that) run on and on
and on. At LAX the other day I saw an ad for "Apple
a Day" Vitamins that advises "When you don't have
the time or opportunity to eat an apple, take the
equivalent nutrients in one easy-to-swallow tablet."
I can literally *hear* you cracking up at that--
telling me that if you ever don't have the time or
opportunity to eat an apple you want to be put out
of your misery with a shotgun.
        Love Síle (that's an order)

Paperwork and gossip in the galley: When would management cough up the long-promised pay raise, and what good had last year's work-to-rule strike done at all? Lorraine, verging on the plump, had received an oh-so-subtle letter from personnel inviting her to join the airline's free Weight Watchers program. There were rumours about a bag of coke stashed in a cistern in the block-booked set of top-floor rooms the airline's crews used in New York. Apparently it was true about the Denver security screener who put himself through the X-ray machine to see what his brain looked like.

"Padraic, I'll hold it for you, the latch is bollocksed; Nuala's lost a nail to it already. Yeah, I've inputted it in the log twice. The bathroom's the other way, madam," Síle told a passenger, reverting to her professional voice. "Oh, you're doing your stretches, excellent. Mind your head on the locker."

And she was off on her rounds again like some peculiar nurse. "If it's in Spanish you're probably on Channel 3, try Channel 1. 400 Benson and Hedges, here you go, that's forty U.S. dollars." Peddling

tobacco was the bit of her job Síle liked least. "Hang on, let's see…
miniature plane, ages three and older, no, not for a newborn. Six
Waterford Crystal Tot Glasses, a Connemara Candle, and a pair of
J Lo Shades, certainly."

In five hours they'd be on the tarmac. Arab airlines followed all
pronouncements about time with "God willing," which seemed
sensible. Unless that was another old aviation myth.

More paperwork, hot towels. "Euros or dollars? Sorry, new
rules, only soft drinks are on the house in economy. On the plane,
yeah, ha-ha. Yes, madam, dinner's on its way."

Considering how many passengers left their food uneaten, they
were always in a hurry to get it. Since the airline had downgraded
its meals, Síle brought her own: There was a Camembert and apple
panino waiting for her in the rear galley. "Mind, the foil's hot. Did
you ask for a non-dairy low-sodium vegetarian meal? Ah, I'm sorry,
you have to order in advance. We've just run out of the chicken, I'm
afraid; can I interest you in the beef? It's in…some kind of gravy."

Síle's mother had served five-course dinners from a three-by-
four-foot galley, Shay never tired of reminding his daughter. *Yeah,
I know, Da,* Síle would throw back with a roll of the eyes, *waltzing
and discussing Gandhi all the while.* Everything had been more chic
in those days; Síle imagined that lost world in slo-mo black-and-
white, violins surging on the soundtrack. Sunita Pillay offers that
first clean smile to a young Dubliner flying to Bombay on his brew-
ery's business. *My name's Shay O'Shaughnessy, and what might yours
be?* Worlds touch, tremble, spin into a different orbit. The aisle of
the narrow plane fades into the aisle of a church and "Here Comes
the Bride."

Síle caught herself yawning, even though this was only leg two
of her Friday-to-Tuesday rotation. The trick to long flights was to
keep moving. What was it airlines used to say, in the bad old days
when flight attendants were forced to retire upon marriage or the
first crow's foot, the era of secret weddings and hidden pregnancies?

The job calls for young legs, that was it. Ever since Marcus had taken a buyout package, he'd been nagging her about the health hazards: Cabin crew had three times the injuries of miners, apparently, and more radiation exposure than nuclear plant workers. At least schedules were better than in her mother's day, she reassured herself: Sunita had flown up to 120 hours a month, whereas Síle did an average of only seventy-three. Sometimes when she felt the energy draining out of her, in the middle of a flight, she closed her eyes, then opened them wide and became her mother, ever soignée, ever gracious, gliding down the aisle on ever-young legs.

It was at night that time went haywire, Síle thought in her hotel room, waking with a jerk from a miserable dream of playing tennis with Kathleen, the balls coming down on them both like hail. You could drop your head on the pillow and then, what felt like a moment later, struggle up to slap off the alarm: Where had those eight hours disappeared to? Or else you could lie in the dark in restless anxiety, dipping in and out of consciousness, with every hour feeling like forty days in the desert.

She conjured up Jude, or rather her absence, a hot ghost for Síle to wrap her body around. She reached for her gizmo and lit up the screen.

```
I used to be a great sleeper, but since meeting you
I seem to have lost the knack. Sometimes I recite
old pop lyrics; sometimes I work my way very slowly
over your body, checking I remember every crease,
every freckle. Does it count as consensual if my
spirit ravishes you in your sleep? What if we're both
asleep?
    Last night you showed up in a sinister bonnet
and a dress with a bustle--clearly this dream was
inspired by your hilarious description of the school
workshops. I'm insulted that I haven't infiltrated
your dreams yet, Jude, but I'll just have to believe
you that new people take about ten years to get
```

```
processed by your subconscious. It's just that I
resent being a "new person." I find myself wishing
that (here comes a perverse one) I could have been
present--as a fourteen-year-old towel-holder or
water-boiler--at your birth. I miss all of you I
know, Jude, and all of you I've never known too.
```

Dreams pulled so unpredictably on the fabric of time. Sometimes the night was one leisurely picture show, a cinema where you could wander from screen to screen. Identities blurred and swapped: It was your father, but he was a woman, or at least you thought so...There were dreams that seemed to go on forever; Síle had once dreamed a whole life sentence in prison for murder, and woke up with her face clenched from years of weeping but found her cheeks quite dry. At other times you could conjure up a whole world in seconds, creating an elaborate backstory to explain the ringing of the phone that had woken you.

Why did people assume that daytime was the real life, it occurred to Síle now? It would be hard to explain to a Martian that diurnal events counted and nocturnal ones—no matter how dramatic or memorable—didn't. In the night people journeyed far from the ones they slept beside, they lived out infinitudes of time, and in the morning they all behaved, like adulterers, as if nothing had happened.

At home on her purple sofa, lips to the receiver, she told Jude, "We never calculated your sexual density."

"Uh-oh," said Jude at the other end of the line.

Síle grinned. "Don't panic, I'm really not a jealous fiend. Full disclosure and burning love, that's all I demand."

"Okay. Chronological order?"

"Aren't you an archivist?"

"It's possible to classify in other ways; thematically, for instance—"

"Get on with the genital encounters," Síle told her.

"In high school: Sven, Pete, Dave—then Mike, oh and the other Dave..."

The rush of names startled Síle. "You had sex with all those monosyllabic boys?"

"Well, not always, uh, intercourse, but we necked. Made out in the backs of cars."

"*Necked* and *made out,* meaning, genitally?"

"Sure, we had to keep warm in the long winters. Mike was the abortion."

"That's a cruel way to describe any young man."

"You know what I mean," laughed Jude, "it was his condom that burst. And, give the guy credit, he drove me to the clinic in Toronto."

"The Dave I met, the bartender at the Dive, he wouldn't be one of the Daves you mentioned?"

She could hear Jude squirm. "He's the second, but really that was only one night at a drive-in."

"What was showing?"

"One of the *Aliens* movies."

"The first, I hope—or no, we must be talking nineties here, yeah?"

"Dunno. I think it was set on a prison planet."

Síle rolled her eyes. "The third, *not* Sigourney's finest hour. So what are we at, five? This sounds like an all-male lineup," she commented.

"Yeah, they always get that wrong in the movies, they make the girly-girl the one with all the guys in her past," remarked Jude. "Whereas in my experience it's the tomboys who hang round pool halls and cars with the guys, and fool around with them, too. But no, there were some girls too: Hannah, Sue...some girl from Quaker Camp who used to cut her arms; this is awful but I'm blanking on her name."

"Did it feel any different with the girls?" Síle wanted to know.

No answer for a second. Then, "Sex is always different, depending on who you're with."

"Your generation's really ditched the old labels, haven't you?"

A pause. "Classic case of the limitations of phones," Jude told her. "I can't tell if you just sounded impressed or sad."

"A bit of both," said Síle, laughing a little.

"In my case—in a bunch of cases—the labels don't fit," Jude said gently. "I could sleep with just about anybody. In fact," getting there first, "I have! But I've never lost my heart till now."

"Shut your eyes, this is where I kiss you." After a minute, Síle said, "Go on with your list; you haven't even left school yet."

"'Reader, I married him,'" said Jude in a determinedly sprightly tone. "Rizla proposed the night I turned eighteen."

"What possessed you—"

"You know Gwen asks me that at least once a year?" Jude sighed. "I was furious with my parents for splitting up, but that's no excuse. Riz seemed kind of glamorous, as well as being my best bud. I guess I thought life with him would be a trip."

"Was your wedding the last time you wore a dress?"

"Actually we both wore jeans. Then when we got back from our trip to Detroit and moved into his trailer—"

"He took you to Detroit for your honeymoon?" said Síle. "The city where they can film post-apocalyptic disaster movies without building a set?"

Jude laughed. "We heard a couple of good bands. Rizla got into a stupid fight and broke his thumb. Anyway, that year we were mostly unemployed and often wasted, my mother thought I'd thrown my life away, and I was beginning to see her point. And then I realized I fancied the check-out girl at the Valumart in Mitchell much more than my husband. So I told Rizla it'd all been a big mistake."

"How did he take it?"

"Pretty well. Then I went off to plant trees in northern Ontario. It's what kids do, here, to make some cash," Jude explained.

Síle frowned. "Hang on, what about the check-out girl?"

"Oh yeah, she was Lina," said Jude.

"I'm running out of fingers," Síle commented, starting on her right thumb again.

"I had a thing with another tree-planter called Steve—though we sometimes fell asleep halfway through, we were so wiped out! Then I worked in a bar in Goderich, and I slept with..." She ransacked her memory. "Another Dave. Sorry! In Stratford there was Gwen, then Kay; Kay and I had a nice few months..."

"Not Gwen as in your straight friend?" interrupted Síle.

"See what I mean about labels?" asked Jude wickedly. "Nah, you're right, Gwen only likes guys, in fact only tall jocks. She and I were tanked at the time, we never meant it to happen. Not that much happened, actually, just enough to make us mortified in the morning."

Síle shook her head in wonder.

"Then there was Lynda."

"Not the waitress at the Garage?"

"Mm. And I think she may have had a little encounter with Rizla too, just after he got hired as the mechanic there."

"Small-town life," murmured Síle with a shudder.

"She's getting married to Bud in June."

"Your neighbour with the big mustache?"

"No, that's Bub the turkey plucker; Bud's a contractor. There'll be a marquee in the field behind the elementary school."

"Are you invited?"

"Of course. I'm playing 'Amazing Grace' on guitar after the vows. Our little...moment was years and years ago; Lynda's probably forgotten it ever happened."

"I doubt that," said Síle seductively.

"Next is Clarisse at the Children's Pioneer Museum. Oh, and I forgot Mrs. Lubben."

"*Mrs.* Lubben?" She folded down another finger.

"I never knew her first name; I was about fifteen. She was the mother of a girlfriend of mine."

"Girlfriend as in lover?"

"As in friend, sorry. We need a translation machine!"

"So," said Síle, "I make that eighteen, including me. What a varied crowd!"

"Well, you know, growing up in the country, you tend to hook up with whoever's up for it. Hey," Jude asked, "are we including *everything* genital? Even if it's, like, one-sided?"

"Absolutely."

"And...incomplete?"

A rueful laugh from Síle. "If it didn't count as sex till somebody came, I'd have to exclude my whole first relationship!"

"Okay then, I'll add some semi-stoned fooling around with a turkey-jointer called Marsha."

"Can no one resist your seductions?"

"Blame those long cold winters," said Jude, sheepish.

"You're sure that's it now?" Síle asked. "Nineteen, going once, going twice...Nineteen it is. Starting at age..."

"Fourteen. That's what, eleven years ago. So my density's nineteen over eleven. Does your little gizmo do math?"

"Yeah, but so does my brain," said Síle. "One point seven partners per year."

"Wow. I guess Jael would approve. More than you do, I suspect," said Jude lightly.

"No no," said Síle.

"I wouldn't worry," Jude told her, very low. "I've never felt this way since the day I was born."

———

A mild May night, Jude's birthday. She'd celebrated at lunchtime with a fifty-minute call to Síle, to hell with the cost. Now she was taking her Triumph out for the first long ride of the season. High beams on, she wound her way along country roads, the air faintly floral already. Riding her bike at night felt oddly safe to her, as if the dark were one vast cushion. She went all the way to Lake Huron, and climbed down to a little beach she knew. Somebody had a campfire going, behind the rocks. She sat on the damp sand and let it trickle through her fingers. Twenty-six. She felt a sudden longing for a cigarette, but now she knew it would pass.

On her way home, she braked at Rizla's trailer and knocked on the window. He put his head out. "Thanks for the key ring, you freak," she said, pulling out of her pocket a little wooden naked woman attached to a heavy bunch of keys.

Rizla continued blowing his nose. "Just a little something I whittled in front of the box."

"'TV My Inspiration, Says World-Renowned Folk Artist Richard Vandeloo.'"

"Happy birthday, anyhow. Coming in?"

Jude shook her head. "I'm going to drop in to the office, check my e-mail."

"After midnight?" He did an impression of a panting dog.

"Yeah, yeah, I've got it bad." Jude got back on her bike. "When I'm being rational I know there must be lots of other brilliant, beautiful women out there—"

"You figure?" asked Rizla, scratching his neck. "Maybe you could give me their numbers."

"—but for some reason the only one I'm interested in is Síle."

"Beautiful's not much use, if you can't see her," he pointed out.

"I can, in my head."

He guffawed, leaning on the corroded windowsill. "It's all a bit suspicious."

"What is?"

"You just-so-happening to lose your heart to someone so out of reach. I mean, you gals are meant to be into commitment; I was reading about it at the dentist's."

Jude stared up at him, briefly distracted. "You finally let Johan see to that molar?"

"Well, he looked at it."

"It needs a root canal?"

He waved that off. "Sometime when I've got the dough."

"Ah, Riz—" Jude reminded herself that this was none of her business. "Anyway—you were saying you read about me and Síle in a magazine?" she asked confusedly.

"No, all of you muff divers."

"Oh speak up, I don't think Mrs. Bayder-Croft heard you."

Mrs. Bayder-Croft, in the house next door, was too vain to wear a hearing aid.

"It's a true fact," Rizla insisted. "So what's the matter with Jude, we ask ourselves? Finally lands a serious girlfriend, but she lives halfway round the planet—"

"A quarter of the way," Jude corrected him.

"It ain't healthy, is all."

Jude laughed, and revved up the Triumph.

The next evening she had a drink with Gwen at the Shakespeare's Head in Stratford. They had no particular love for its Ye Olde décor, but at least it wasn't full of squealing nineteen-year-olds.

Gwen was deep into an account of her recent snowboarding trip to Blue Mountain. Jude thought she was listening, she really did. But Gwen stopped and said, "You're miles away."

"Sorry."

Gwen lifted a nacho heavy with melted cheese. "Five thousand k, in fact?"

"Not that many, actually; less than a thousand, tonight. She's on the Boston rotation for the next month."

"Did she send you a birthday present?"

Jude grinned. "The most fantastic saddle bags, for the bike." With a scrawled note, *So you can take me for a long ride.*

"Geez Louise." Gwen had some odd expressions she picked up from her elderly residents.

"Isn't it weird, how love kind of warps time?" said Jude suddenly. Gwen narrowed her eyes, and Jude felt a wave of embarrassment, but pressed on. "When you're falling for someone, everything slows down strangely. A bit like that time we took mushrooms in the woods in grade eleven."

"Mm," said Gwen reminiscently.

"Daily life becomes this sort of epic: The First Time I Saw Her Face, Our First Walk by the Lake, The First Phone Call, The Night I Stayed Up Making Anagrams of Her Name..."

Gwen stared. "Anagrams?"

"When I can't sleep...," admitted Jude.

"What can you make out of Síle?"

"I use her surname as well, O'Shaughnessy. The best so far is *She Is Enough Lassy;* I figure *lassy* with a y could be an alternate spelling."

Gwen hooted with laughter.

"No, but my point about time is, then the minute you start feeling happy, the days start to zip by."

"I don't usually get as far as the happy stage," Gwen reminded her.

They gossiped about various schoolfriends of theirs who were currently pregnant or bankrupt. "Oh, hey," said Jude, "what were you up to at the Darlene Motel on Tuesday?"

Gwen looked blank.

The Darlene was one of a rash of motels on the outskirts of Stratford. "Tuesday, just after five? I saw your black Chevy."

She shook her head. "Lots of them around."

"Okay," said Jude, confused.

Gwen took another nacho. "My folks were asking after you on the weekend. They said, 'How's she getting on with that holiday romance?'"

Jude couldn't help bristling at the phrase. "You could tell them it's a long-distance relationship."

"Aren't they all," said Gwen enigmatically, into her beer.

The conversation was in a lull. "How's work these days," asked Jude, "have you managed to fire that care assistant yet, the one who left bruises on the old ladies?"

Gwen set down her glass. "I can't lie to you. I mean, I guess I have been, but now you've brought it up—"

The care assistant? Bewildered thoughts began slowly lining themselves up in Jude's brain. "Is this about the motel? I didn't mean to bring anything up."

"It's okay."

"Gwen, I wasn't—I just thought maybe you had a relative staying at the Darlene."

"He's somebody's relative," said Gwen wryly, "but not mine."

"You don't have to do this."

"Oh heck, I might as well."

Let her speak, Jude told herself.

"He usually comes to my place," Gwen began in a low voice, "but I've had the plasterers in, on and off all week, so we went to the Darlene. It's only maybe the second or third time we've had to do that; I can't believe you spotted my car."

"It's your plates," Jude apologized, "the second half's always stuck in my mind: XOX, like hugs and kisses."

Gwen grimaced. "His wife's not well. That's how I justify it, though some would say that makes it worse."

"What's wrong with her? Is she dying?"

"I wish," said Gwen under her breath, then shook her head as if to disperse the evil words. "Depression, mostly; agoraphobia, on and off. Some OCD stuff like hand washing and calling him every half hour."

"Oh, Gwen." Jude could see what a haven her most sane friend would be to a man in that position. "Is he—" She didn't know what she was allowed ask. "Did you meet this guy in St. Mary's?"

A peculiar grin. "A ways before that. I've known him about as long as you have." Leaning to Jude's ear, she breathed the name: "Luke Randall."

Jude covered her mouth. The bank manager lived just outside Ireland on a curve in the road. He was a short, stocky guy, not Gwen's type at all. He came into the general store quite often, but nobody ever saw his wife.

"I knew you'd look at me like that."

"Sorry, I—"

"You must think I'm a worm."

"I'm just taken aback, that's all." Jude struggled for words. "How long—"

"Three years, give or take. Maybe I should have told you before, but keeping secrets is a hassle so I thought I'd spare you."

Jude was silenced. She thought of three years of compromise, three years of waiting.

"And before you ask, he'll never leave his wife."

Síle had dragged Marcus and Jael out to what sounded like a really interesting Danish one-man show, and now she was paying for round after round of martinis in an attempt to make it up to them.

"The way he kept going behind the screen, and taking painfully long to come back out in the mask of his mother," Marcus recalled.

Jael shook her head. "That wasn't the worst."

"Could it have been a reference to *Hamlet*?" suggested Síle.

"The worst bit," announced Jael, "was when he played that

footage of the Twin Towers, and he stood naked in front of the screen and made flapping birdies with his hands."

Síle groaned. "I'd almost managed to forget that bit."

Marcus pointed at her. "You dragged me up from Leitrim on the first warm Saturday of the year for this multimedia caca."

"I've said I'm sorry! But at least you can spend the rest of the weekend with Pedro."

"Well, there's that," he said with a dirty grin. "So when do we get to meet this Jude character?"

"When she can find the price of the flight," said Síle, trying not to sound sullen.

"Bad sign," said Jael, shaking her head.

"Her job doesn't pay well."

"Maybe, to coin a phrase, she's just not that into you."

"Shut up, you cow," said Marcus.

"So what does Pedro think of your rotting manor?" Jael asked him.

"He drives down nearly every week; he says it's the only place where he can really switch off."

Jael rolled her eyes. "With the hormones bubbling away in the pair of you, Pedro would think a urinal was the Taj Mahal."

"Actually it's not so squalid now the roof's on; you and Anton and Yseult should venture down for tea," Síle told her.

"But I do miss him a lot of the time," Marcus was saying quietly.

"Blame Síle," said Jael, "she started all this."

"All what?"

"Falling for inappropriately faraway people."

"Leitrim to Dublin's only about four hours, hardly a long-distance relationship," Síle scoffed. "Canadians drive that far for a picnic." She knew she was exaggerating, but she couldn't help resenting the men's luck in being just a drive apart.

Marcus stole the olive out of her glass. "Oh, that was far enough when you were whining about all your friends moving down the country."

"Anyone beyond arm's reach in the wee dark hours is too far away," said Jael, draining her martini.

Síle was oddly moved by the image of Jael curling herself around Anton's sleep-fragrant body in the middle of the night.

"No insult to the Catalan or the Canadian," said Jael, "but they can't be worth the grinding effort of it all."

Síle and Marcus shared a conspiratorial smile. "Blame the zeitgeist," he said. "The new technologies let us get ourselves into tangles: They make these arrangements just about possible without making them liveable. Everyone's at it: I know several L.A.–New York marriages, with kids, even."

"Mm," said Síle, "I'm finding it's like some obscure health problem—irritable bowel syndrome, or head lice—as soon as I confess I'm having an LDR, people say 'Me too!'"

"Then cure yourself, woman," said Jael in exasperation. "Sure, spend the occasional weekend in the Toronto Hilton rutting like rabbits till this girl's out of your system. But don't get overinvested, when you've only just escaped from Kathleen!"

"I know it's a tad inconvenient that I fell for Pedro just as I'd moved out of the city," said Marcus, "but I can't wish it undone."

"Which," Síle asked, "the falling or the move?"

"Either! I'm mad about my house and land, and he wouldn't ask me to give them up."

Jael caught Síle's eye and jerked her eyebrows infinitesimally. Síle knew what this meant: *Maybe Pedro's got somebody else in the city.*

"I admit the timing's unfortunate," Marcus went on, "but hey, that's fate for you."

"Oh well, if it's *fate*," said Jael, pretending to be impressed.

"The funny thing is, it might have stayed casual longer for me and Jude if she lived here." Síle was thinking aloud. "We could have gone to gigs, dinner parties—"

"Multimedia caca," offered Jael.

"—watched the news together." The idea of sharing these simple, proximate pleasures with Jude gave her a pang. But then, she didn't want some simulacrum of her life with Kathleen, did she? "Whereas on e-mail, or on the phone—"

"You're forced to say what you mean," said Marcus, nodding. "Toss it out into the void."

"Jaysus, if we've reached *the void*, it's time for the bill," said Jael, looking around for the waiter.

"Síle, could a suburban wife of our acquaintance be having a little visit from the green-eyed monster?"

"Oh please," Jael scoffed. "Been there, shagged that, up down and sideways, sniveled down the phone and flew Air Cesspit...Remember that disastrous entanglement of mine with the Genevan dermatologist?"

"The one who turned out to have a wife and four children," Síle recalled.

"Five. Distance is romantic, I grant you, but so is leaping off the Golden Gate Bridge. At least Marcus is only a drive away from his boyfriend, but Síle, seriously!—I can't bear to see you signing up for the time zone tango."

"Where d'you get that phrase? It makes it sound quite sexy," said Marcus.

Jael was grim. "Oh, all very sexy till someone loses an eye."

Síle shut her front door, stepped around her suitcase, and went straight for the phone. Waiting to talk to Jude was like the prickling sensation before thunder. She didn't even take her trench coat off; she dropped onto the sofa and punched Memory 01. *Please be in.* Six in Dublin, that was one in the afternoon in Ontario. *Don't make me leave another message.*

"Jude?"

"Hey. Hey there!"

"At last. There's a bit of an echo…"

"Is there? It's fine on my end," said Jude. "D'you want to try—"

"No, it's okay," Síle interrupted. Their voices were slightly out of synch; it was distracting. About a century and a half since the invention of the telephone; surely the bugs could have been ironed out by now? "You know, we could talk live over the Internet if you got a grant to upgrade your system—"

"What the museum needs is more basic funding, like to pay our heating bills," said Jude. "Besides, I'd never get any work done with you whispering in my ear; the thought of you is distracting enough."

Síle smiled, watching dust motes spiral in the window light. "Were you at your Quaker Meeting this morning?"

"Yeah, I just walked in the door actually."

"Why do you stick with it? If that's not a rude question," Síle asked belatedly.

"I guess it's partly the history: We've been stubborn cranks for nearly four centuries now. And the politics," Jude added. "We're about three-sixty degrees to the left of your Pope."

"He's no Pope of mine, I'm ninety-nine percent lapsed," Síle reminded her. "So is nobody allowed to say a word?"

"Oh sure, you stand up if you get a *leading,* but often in a small Meeting nobody does, and those can be the best times."

"I do like you being odd," murmured Síle.

"*I'm* odd? You're the Hiberno-Indian jet-setter with hair like Rapunzel."

"What I mean is, all my Irish girlfriends had shared reference points. Like Maria Goretti jokes."

"Who's Maria Goretti?"

"There you go! Every Irishwoman would know that she was *the* girl saint. Resisted her rapist to the end, and died of multiple stab wounds, but not before forgiving him."

"That's gross," Jude objected.

"I'm delighted you think so. You're a fresh eye on my entire life."

"Hey, did you get the baby pictures yet?"

"Yeah," said Síle, laughing, "that one of you at six months, having a bath in the sink! They're up on my fridge, attached by little Magritte magnets."

"Which Magritte?"

"The bowler-hat men."

"You know, last night I was just trying to imagine the first long-distance phone calls," said Jude. "Imagine if one night you were talking to your cousin in Melbourne, and she said, 'The sun's just come out,' and you had to look out the window at total darkness—"

"You'd realize that where you lived was just one tiny spot on the globe."

"Exactly! And that all knowledge is relative."

"So when are you paying a visit to my tiny spot on the globe?" asked Síle, in what she hoped was a seductive rather than a nagging voice.

A little release of breath. "I can't tell you how much I'd like that."

"Ah go on, just stick the fare on your credit card!"

"I don't have one."

"You don't have a credit card?" Síle asked, taken aback.

"I've never wanted to get into debt."

"None of us *want* it, exactly, it just happens. My god, you're the only person I know outside the credit economy. Is this some freaky Quaker thing?"

"No, just a freaky Jude thing."

"This is a nonsense! It's medieval. I financed my BMW with the equity from my house," Síle told her.

"It's just not my way."

Strange how you could feel such a surge of rage, with an undertow of love. Síle kept her tone light. "Listen, Sinatra, if you're this absolute at twenty-six, I dread to think what you'll be like at fifty. Tell you what, let me find you a ticket."

"I thought the airline only let you transfer free travel to immediate family?"

Síle cursed her employers, and herself for having let this fact slip. "Yeah, but I can swing an enormous discount."

"That's really kind, but—"

"*Kind?* I'm not your maiden aunt," she barked. Then, softening her voice again, "Money's so randomly distributed. Why punish me for the fact that curators of tiny museums happen to be underpaid? C'mon, let me buy a few nights in bed with you."

"No." For such a stubborn Puritan, Jude had a very dirty laugh. "I'll ask the bank for an overdraft."

Síle bayed like a triumphant wolf.

That Which Moves, That Which Changes

> Like a bird who wanders from her
> nest, so is a man who wanders from
> his place.
>
> —Proverbs 27:8

Jude felt only the occasional jolt of panic this time. She'd taken a daytime flight, on Síle's advice, so as not to miss a night's sleep. After Greenland she saw icebergs: newly smashed, as if a god had dropped a plate on a floor.

In what the pilot called a "holding queue" over Dublin, Jude peered down at a brighter grass-green than she'd imagined a country could be: little irregular patches of light and dark fields, and then the gray and black and brown scatter of the city. No skyscrapers, she noticed appreciatively. And then they were down, the plane as smooth as a rollerblader along the tarmac, while the engines screamed.

Síle was waiting for her at the exit, her hair loose down her back. "I can't believe you're here," she cried. "'Jude Goes to Big Ireland!'"

The early evening sky was a tight-fitting gray cap. As Síle wheeled out of the airport in her little green car, Jude smoothed a hand over the silvery leather upholstery. Most of the vehicles on the road seemed brand new and minute: Instead of station wagons and pickups she noticed Mini Coopers and those little Smart cars that looked like they'd been rear-ended. Síle edged through the stop-

and-start traffic, past large sculptures in red metal or stone. At one point she took a back road to avoid construction, and Jude spotted an incongruous clump of trailers on the verge. "Why would anyone spend their vacation on the side of the road?"

"What? Oh, they're Travelers, they move from place to place. Irish gypsies."

"Excellent," said Jude.

"Yeah, except they get treated like shite."

Jude was relieved to find that Síle was an excellent driver. "It's like a movie set," she murmured, as they turned down a cobbled street with a row of old corrugated iron roofs.

Síle pressed a button, and all the locks slid down with a thump. "For some forties prison drama, maybe! This is one of the worst slums left; they'd set fire to your car while it was still moving."

"I'm on such a high, everything looks good to me," said Jude, as they slid by a huge new office building, all gray granite and greenish glass. "There sure is a bunch of litter, though," she added, noticing the plastic bags that tangled around every tree, the chip bags hooding the pointed railings.

"Oh I know, we're a filthy nation."

Many pedestrians—and drivers, too—were talking into cell phones. And how similar people looked—except for the occasional black face, and a lone woman in a veil, waiting for a green light. Very pale faces, mostly; flat profiles, light brown or sometimes red hair.

It was starting to drizzle as Síle turned onto a narrow street of tiny red brick row houses, their doors painted scarlet, cream, or navy. She edged into what Jude considered an impossible space, bumper to bumper. Putting a key into a canary yellow door, she gave it a shove with her hip to get it open. Jude—skirting some dog shit—followed her in.

It was like a doll's house. Bright velvet modern furniture filled a room you could cross in three steps; fairy lights edged the window.

Behind the front door, a big framed silkscreen print lay on its side. "Amelia Earhart?" Jude wondered.

"Good guess! I picked it up in Berlin last year, I can't imagine where I thought I'd put it..."

It was true, there was no wall with a space big enough. Jude saw an old cast-iron fireplace with relief carvings of exotic birds, and bent to trace them with her fingertips. A steep staircase in the corner, barely wider than a ladder. A tiny open-plan kitchen with wrinkly apples in a fruit bowl made of a swirling orbit of metal. "Is this a sculpture?" she asked, touching a tall spider shape in stainless steel.

Síle threw her an odd look. "Doesn't everyone have an Alessi lemon-squeezer by now?"

"Not on my planet." All at once Jude was reeling with fatigue.

"Petrushka?" Síle called. "Petrushka?" She thudded up the stairs, past a glittery gauzy hanging. "My cousins sent this from Mombai, it's technically a bridal veil; I did warn them it would end up nailed to the wall. Petrushka?" Her voice floated down the stairs. "Deirdre from next door feeds her when I'm away, but she tends to sulk and hide in my wardrobe. The cat, I mean, not Deirdre."

Jude read a small yellow note on the counter that said *Leave cash out for Neela Saturday!!! and ask rugs.* She concluded that Síle must have a weekly cleaner, and, which amused her more, that she sometimes relied on old-fashioned paper to remind her of things. Jude went back to the purple sofa, stroked the fine pile of the cloth. She flicked through a magazine called *Simplicity,* which seemed to offer very elaborate instructions for buying, sorting, and storing your possessions.

A long ring at the door made her leap. She could hear voices outside in the street, only two feet away. She figured out the latch and tugged the front door open. At first she thought there was no one there, then three small kids edged into view. They were wearing remarkably shiny track pants and two of them had Roller Blades. One of the boys said something in an impenetrable accent.

"Excuse me?" said Jude.

"Got yer cat!" squealed the girl.

"Oh, that's great. I'm not the, uh, homeowner, actually," Jude explained.

"Are you American?" asked the bigger boy, squinting.

"Canadian," said Jude distractedly, feeling jet lag settle around her like a cloud. "Canada's a big country just to the north of—"

But she was interrupted by the hard-faced girl, who'd rolled forward, to the sill of the door. "Will you tell the missis we've got her fuckin' cat."

Jude stared at her, then looked up and down the street for an adult.

Síle was in the doorway, shunting Jude to one side. "Bring her back this minute."

Another front door scraped open, inches away, and a woman with gray hair in curlers leaned out. "Are you home?"

"These little knackers are at it again, Deirdre."

"It's a kidnap," crowed the smaller boy as if he'd suddenly remembered the word.

"Yeah," said his brother, "and we want a ransom, we want €20."

"A good strapping's what you want," cried the neighbour.

"We'll stick a firework up its hole," said the small girl.

Síle seized her by the front of her sweater. "I'll stick a firework up your own hole quick as look at you."

Jude edged back, appalled.

The girl wrenched herself out of Síle's grasp and spat at her, dry-mouthed. She and the boy zoomed off on their Roller Blades, the smaller child thumping along behind them.

"Bring Petrushka back this minute," Síle roared, "or I'll have the Guards out. I know your names!"

"Do you?" asked Jude in a low voice.

"It's a figure of speech."

"You don't really think they'll hurt her?"

"Ah, they wouldn't have the nerve," said Deirdre.

"Extortionist bullshitters," said Síle through her teeth.

To fill the silence, Jude introduced herself to the neighbour. She got a vertiginous flash of what she might look like to this middle-aged Irishwoman: a grubby bull-dyke backpacker who'd ousted *that lovely Kathleen.*

"Give it five minutes," Deirdre advised Síle, "then ring the Guards."

Inside, Síle hunched over on the sofa. Jude bent to kiss her on the forehead. While she was making tea with the unfamiliar electric kettle, she heard a knock at the door. Síle had some words on the doorstep, and finally came in, cradling a small dove-gray cat on her chest.

"Well done!"

"I bargained the bloody gurriers down to a tenner," said Síle, stroking Petrushka's narrow head, "but it should have been less. I'm losing my touch."

"That'll be the sapping effects of love," said Jude, risking flippancy.

"Too true," said Síle, setting the cat down on the narrow counter and leaning over it to give Jude a long kiss.

Over tea, Síle relaxed visibly, and Jude set herself to finding out where Petrushka liked to be scratched. "Deirdre seems like a great neighbour."

"Oh, she's a star. She puts milk in my fridge, lets the plumber in...And all I do for her in return is give her the odd lift into town. But that's Stoneybatter for you: The old-timers even pay each other daily visits."

"My kind of village," Jude joked.

"Apart from the kidnapping of small animals."

"Ah, we had some dogs poisoned last year; we all know it was Madge Tyrrell, but it can't be proved."

"Listen," Síle told her, "we're having dinner at Jael and Anton's, they insisted. Do you mind? You do."

"Well, I'd always rather take you straight to bed," Jude answered, "but I'm up for anything, as long as I can look at you."

Jael and Anton lived on the south side of the River Liffey—the expensive side—in a suburban neighbourhood where all the houses hid behind high hedges. The house had moss-deep rugs and intimidating, abstract oils on the walls.

The skinny girl, Yseult, talked nearly as fast as her mother. "Do you know what age I am? Guess," she instructed Jude.

"Uh, I don't know."

"Of course you don't know, eejit; that's why I said guess."

Jude decided she loathed Irish children. "Nine?"

A roll of the eyes. "I'm seven. Do you know how to spell my name? Bet you don't."

This time Jude was prepared for failure. "Let's see. I—s—"

"Wrong!" said the girl. "It's a Y. Y-s-e-u-l-t."

Jael clapped one glossy-nailed hand over her daughter's mouth. "Stop harassing our guest. She's just come all the way from Canada."

"You told Daddy Canadians are boring."

Jael's cheeks twitched. "I did not, I said that was a common misconception."

Jude met her hostess's eyes and nearly laughed.

"I'm desperate for a fag," Jael announced. "Jude?" She cocked her head.

"Sorry, I'm an ex-smoker."

"So I hear, but half the ex-smokers I know like to bum the odd one off me."

Jude shook her head, and the redhead grinned back at her flirtatiously.

When his wife was outside, Anton said, "She did give up while she was pregnant. It nearly killed us both. She kept growling 'Never again!'"

They didn't sit down to eat till ten: Moroccan stew with apricots in it. Jude was expecting the child to go to bed, but Yseult just got more exhibitionistic. Jude waited some time for a gap in the conversation, which was mostly about the awful two-tier health system (a friend of a friend of Anton's had spent three days in agony on a gurney), Iran's nuclear capabilities, whether the new tram line would make any difference to the Dublin traffic, genetically modified featherless chickens, and rip-off prices each of them had been charged for a cup of tea or a ham sandwich. They'd got onto whether music really made children better at algebra when Jude managed to come out with "This is amazing." They all looked at her. "The food, I mean. And the wine," she said in Anton's direction.

"What were you expecting, bacon and cabbage? Or just a trough of spuds?" said Jael with a bray of laughter.

"You'll have to excuse her, she's not used to culinary compliments," said Anton, rising to collect the plates.

"Yeah, I've come to cooking late in life," Jael admitted. "Last November, Fat Bastard here was away on some junket in Prague, leaving Yseult and me to subsist off frozen tikka masala, and I suddenly thought, I'm an intelligent woman, I run my own PR company, why don't I try cracking a cookbook for once in my damn life?"

Jude was about to say something about the first time she'd ever barbecued an arctic char, but she'd missed her moment; the conversation had swirled on, to cover digital TV, bilingualism (here Jude tried to say something about Canada's French immersion schools but fumbled her chance again), a particularly brutal recent murdersuicide, and whether very hairy men should wax their backs. She sank into a weary fugue and let it all flow over her head.

At one point their hosts were all out in the kitchen, and Jude turned to smile at Síle. But her lover's mouth was tight. "What is it?"

"You haven't opened your mouth in forty-five minutes," whispered Síle.

"I haven't had a chance to get a word in edgeways! You talk right over each other, all the time."

"The Irish are highly evolved," Síle snapped. "We can listen and talk at the same time."

"Well I can't."

Síle chewed her lip. "I just want them to like you."

"I'm not a performing seal," muttered Jude, and then the mango brulée came in, heralded by Yseult, blowing through a paper trumpet.

Jael went out for another cigarette after dessert, and Jude was sorely tempted to go with her. But on the couch, Síle reached for her hand, and their interlocked fingers made up the quarrel. The child reluctantly went to bed at 11:30. Half an hour later, Anton came down and murmured, "She's out for the count."

Jael, sprawled on the other couch, like Sarah Bernhardt, perked up at once. "Who's for a little coke?"

"Yum," said Síle.

"I'm fine with coffee," murmured Jude, thinking, *Who'd want to drink pop after a meal like that?* She only got it when Anton brought in an old striped can that claimed to be mouse poison.

"It's hell to get hold of these days," Jael was complaining. "Worse than reliable babysitting, and nearly as pricey."

Anton waited till Jael and Síle had inhaled their lines off the mirror. "Sure you won't join us?" he said graciously, holding the mirror out to Jude.

She was suddenly sick of being predictable, being silent, saying no to things. She was a woman with a foreign lover and an overdraft she couldn't clear; she was a long way from home. Casually she took the rolled-up note. Síle was watching her a little warily. Jude snuffed it up, then sat back, feeling nothing except a bit numb in her nose. But a few minutes later she found herself participating confidently in an argument about voting systems, despite the fact that all she knew about proportional representation was based on a half-forgotten skim through of a New Democrats leaflet. She didn't feel drugged, she felt at her own healthy best, the dinner party guest she'd always been meant to be. "For some unknown reason this reminds me of one time I was hiking in the back country—Algonquin Park—and I turned a corner and nearly walked smack into this huge black bear. They say the thing to do is to stick your arms above your head so you'll seem taller, and sing as loud as you can…" She was playing the self-deprecating merry Canuck for all she was worth, and Jael was laughing so hard she claimed she was going to be sick, and Anton at some point, for a reason Jude could never remember afterward, demonstrated a Highland sword dance on the Persian rug, using poker and tongs.

When Síle was in the washroom, Jael announced she needed another smoke. Jude went with her, for a breath of cool air. Irish houses didn't have porches, she was discovering, so they made their way onto the damp lawn—Jael slightly unsteady from the wine. "Does it still smell good?" she inquired, waving her cigarette in front of Jude's nose.

Jude let herself breathe in. It did. "Temptress."

"It's the taste I like," said Jael, kissing her.

At first Jude was too startled to react, and then a giggle escaped from her mouth. Her hostess had stepped over to some scented bush and was tapping ash onto the grass, as if nothing had happened. Jude considered letting the moment go by, but some obscure fighting instinct roused her. "What was that?"

"Just taking your measure," said Jael in a reasonable tone. She had a few more puffs, then ground her butt into the lawn, before picking it up to bring into the house.

At one in the morning, Síle got Jude into the little green car and they all waved good-bye. "Well, that went rather splendidly in the end," said Síle, backing out of the drive.

"Mm." Jude's impulse was to mention the bizarre little incident right away, but she was thinking better of it. She'd heard enough stories about Jael to know that before marriage she'd had the sexual ethics of a bonobo chimpanzee, but her sense was that the woman hadn't been seriously hitting on her; she'd been making mischief, at worst. This was probably not a moment for full disclosure.

"Thank god for the coke," she said instead. "From now on I'll be tempted to bring a little cache to every party." She reached over the gearstick and slid her fingers down Síle's raw silk wrap-around skirt. She stared out the window as the neon signs of Dublin melted by: B&B, ANGELO'S CHIPS, DANGER CONSTRUCTION, SACRED HEART CONVENT, CAR PARK FULL. "So Yseult's your godchild?"

"For my sins. All I have to do is spend an afternoon with her and I'm glad to be childless again. Anton would love a second, but Jael says fuck off." She turned with a wide smile. "Listen, as it's only eight in the evening for you—"

"It is?"

"When I was on the Dublin-Heathrow rotation last year, I went back and forth three times a day. I never knew what country I was in. Anyway, what I was going to say was," stroking Jude's nape, "there happens to be a monthly club night on called Colleen."

"As in, girl? Sure, why not? I've only got three days; I should pack in as much as I can."

Jude had expected some shiny chrome-and-glass venue, but it was a ballroom upstairs in an old hotel. The girl selling tickets at the door looked about fourteen, and pretty with-it. "Thank god for the new generation," roared Síle in her ear. "When I was your age I'd have known every single raddled face here."

"By the way," Jude asked over her first pint of Guinness—it really did taste much better in Ireland—"did Jael ever try to get you into bed?"

"Just once," said Síle, with a grin that was half-wince. "She felt me up in the back of a taxi, but I swatted her away. Jael's really mellowed, but sometimes I don't know how—being her—she can stand her life."

By grabbing the odd stranger on the lawn, maybe, thought Jude.

Then a pack of Síle's acquaintance were on them, and it was all shrieked hellos and pecks on cheeks. It comforted Jude, the familiarity of this small world: roughly the same proportions of leather jackets and denims, lipstick and cleavage, smiles and chips-on-shoulders as she might find at a women's night in some mid-size Canadian city. A lot of the music was familiar, but not too much so; mercifully, she hadn't yet heard "I Am What I Am," or "Sisters Are Doing It For Themselves." For the first time today, Jude felt more or less at home.

The only problem was, she couldn't understand a word these women were saying. Síle was engaged in rapid, bellowed conversation with two of them; they were probably interrogating her about why she'd left the flawless Kathleen.

Síle squeezed over to her, now, kissed her on the jaw. "I know most of the girls in here," she remarked. "I've probably slept with half of them. I've lived with half of the half I've slept with. I've loved half of the half I've lived with. What does it all come to?"

Jude stared.

Síle fell about laughing. "Don't you recognize the quote? It's from one of the Beebo Brinker novels. Nineteen fifties lesbo trash."

"Oh," she mouthed in some relief.

"My other favourite Beebo line is 'Nine months of desire exploded like a firecracker between her legs.' "

Jude grinned. "I know that feeling. Sure beats *The Well of Loneliness:* 'That night they were not divided.' "

Swapping quotes was not the ideal activity in this noise. Jude took hold of Síle's hips and steered her onto the light-rimmed dance floor. Síle seemed to hang back, which Jude only understood halfway into the first track when she was forced to conclude that her lover's odd, off-the-beat, bouncing movements were not some highly sophisticated dance style that hadn't yet made it to rural Canada.

"Can I please sit down now?" Síle shouted in her ear.

"Good idea."

"I know, I know, it's mortifying!" Settled back at the table with her martini, she wailed, "I look like someone who can dance, don't I?"

"You look like dance made flesh, darlin'."

"I like clubs, I love music. But some bad fairy godmother decided not to give me a sense of rhythm."

Jude started laughing again.

"Whereas you, you beast, are a very funky mover. Get back out there; look, there's Lisa and Sorcha waving."

"You sure?"

"Go on, I want to watch."

Hours later Jude was splashing her face in the washroom when a tall blond woman at the sink beside her said under her breath, "You must be the Canadian."

Jude blinked. "Guilty," she said with a foolish grin. "You must be a friend of Síle's."

The woman shook her head, and applied her brownish lipstick in two moves. Jude's stomach tightened. The blonde snapped her little bag shut and smoothed her satin skirt. "I suppose you think it's all a great laugh," she said, turning to face Jude.

"What—"

"A zesty, international fling, who cares what havoc it creates?" The woman's voice was still level. "I wonder, have you any scruples at all?"

Jude took a laborious breath. "Listen, Kathleen—"

"Shut your mouth." The woman's nose was only inches away from Jude's. "You don't know me, you don't call me *Kathleen*. You're a greedy little home-wrecker and you turn my stomach."

The door swung open and two girls came in giggling. When

they'd gone into two stalls and locked the doors, Jude tried again, in a low voice. "I know you loved Síle—"

"You know nothing about me." The elegant features contorted. "She and I had a life, for your information, we had something you're too young and ignorant to understand, and it was lasting, it was working, till you happened along and shat all over it."

Jude didn't know what to do. The whole washroom seemed awash with pain, and Kathleen was already out the door.

When Jude found her way back to the table, it was empty. She looked around in irrational panic. Síle wouldn't have left without her, would she? Gone off with Kathleen? *That's ridiculous.*

She had to ask two different friends of Síle's before she finally tracked her down in the lineup for the coat check. Síle's voice was ragged, but her cheeks were dry. "I was just getting our jackets."

Jude put both arms around her. "What did she say to you?"

"I shouldn't have brought you here: bloody small world," said Síle instead of answering. "She was always so scathing about gay clubs, I never thought—"

"I've had a great time," Jude insisted, which had at least some truth in it.

In Síle's extraordinary four-poster made of copper piping, they had sex half the night, and then Jude slept as if she'd been felled with a club.

In the morning, she took a shower in the narrow tiled stall, which was fine until she was rinsing her hair and the water turned cold all at once. "I should have warned you," said Síle, laughing as she rubbed Jude all over with a big orange towel. "We're a cradle of civilization, but our plumbing's rubbish."

"That's okay," said Jude, "it woke me up."

Síle's house always rang with music; there were speakers in every room. It was good music, everything from salsa to Bach, but it never stopped. Jude was tempted to ask for a little quiet time, but *when in Rome...*

After what Síle called "a dirty great fry-up," they went walking downtown, along the docks; Jude smelled Guinness brewing, at one point, and then a waft of the sea coming upriver. Plants spilled down stone walls; she recognized clematis, and Síle managed to identify a red one as fuschia. She pointed out to Jude a bewildering assortment of cathedrals, crypts, and Georgian buildings. The streets were thick with bodies; people pushed past muttering "Sorry" (if anything). There was an old man with a twitch shouting obscenities, and a woman preaching out loud on an upturned crate.

They were crossing a busy road to Trinity College when Síle paused on a traffic island. "This is it. The holy spot."

"Which holy spot?"

"I was thirteen. This girl at school, Niamh Ryan—"

"As in the gal with the golden hair who lured Oisín over the sea?"

Síle laughed. "I suppose. But this Niamh had flaming copper hair. We weren't best friends or anything, but I always knew where she was in the classroom, without looking; I could hear what she was saying from twenty feet away."

"Ah." Jude remembered crushes like that.

"This one time, Christmas shopping, we bumped into each other. Niamh's bus stop was on Fleet Street and mine was on Nassau Street," said Síle, pointing in opposite directions, "so I said I'd walk her halfway, but we couldn't agree exactly where halfway was, so we ended up on this traffic island. It was freezing—well, by Irish standards!—and there was even a sprinkle of wet snow; we kept shrieking 'Snow!' and trying to pick it up. We stood here all afternoon talking, till it was dark. I was numb to the knees, because I was in tights and court shoes, but I wouldn't have moved off this spot if a bomb had gone off."

Jude nodded. "The first time you have a conversation like that—you feel like you've been slapped awake."

"Exactly!"

They wound up having a drink in a quiet, shabby pub, "the last one that hasn't been overrun by twenty-year-old millionaires," according to Síle.

"I do kind of get it about cities, you know," Jude told her. "The vrumm, vrumm, all that rough energy spilling over…"

"You're adapting surprisingly well for a country girl," Síle teased her.

"There's this bit in the Koran—"

"Oh, getting very nondenominational all of a sudden."

Jude quoted, "'Live every moment in this world as if you were a traveler in a strange land.' Which I guess means, noticing everything."

"Or it could mean, always constipated," Síle suggested, sipping her martini. "I spend my working life with 'travelers in a strange land,' and they're a tense bunch."

Jude kissed her cherry-red lips.

They had cod and chips while waiting for the musicians to start playing. There were fiddles and a banjo and a hand drum pronounced *bow-rone*. Síle texted her friend Marcus twice—it was an irritating habit, but one Jude knew better than to object to—and at eleven he turned up, tall and baby-faced, in a smart pale brown suit.

"I *thought* you might be at Pedro's for the weekend," said Síle, hugging him.

"No no," he said, deadpan, "I was down in Leitrim, weeding my cabbages, but as soon as I got your text I saddled the heifer and galloped across the country."

Jude grinned at him and held out her hand.

"Sure I wouldn't have missed my chance to meet the famous Canadian," he said, leaning to give her a kiss on the cheek. "As a keen observer of the O'Shaughnessy, I can tell you I've never seen her quite so smitten. She could barely find your homeland on a globe, before, but now she plagues us with trivia she finds online, like all the Canadians that nobody knows are Canadian."

Síle took a breath. "Joni Mitchell, Mary Pickford, William Shatner—"

"Stop it now, girl," he said, "or you'll have to be slapped."

Settling in Ireland, Marcus told Jude, was the natural course of action for maverick Englishmen. He'd been a flight attendant for a British airline, then for another based in Chicago, before taking a year off to work for a whole-food co-op in Sydney. "Then a Dubliner dragged me over here for Pride '93—to celebrate the decriminalization of gay sex—and I discovered that I had an inner Irishman."

"More than one, if I recall," said Síle lewdly.

"So you just...stayed?" Jude asked, fascinated by the idea of a weekend that lasted a lifetime.

He nodded. "Now I'm a Paddy, to all intents and purposes; my mother complains I can't say my *T*s anymore! I love being settled, voting in elections, knowing who to cheer for in the Olympics..."

Síle snorted. "Much good it'll do you. Ireland may be littered with Nobel Prizes, but we're hardly world rulers in sport."

"Last orders," called the barman, "last orders."

"Is it closing already?" asked Jude, startled. She was digging notes out of her wallet, but Marcus slapped her hand away. "Síle hasn't given me a chance to spend any of my euro yet," she protested. "I feel like a gigolo."

"Pity about you," said Síle. "Save them for next time."

"Síle," said Marcus, holding out a note, "I can't seem to get off my fat arse..."

As soon as she was gone he turned to Jude. "So what are your plans?"

"For the rest of the weekend?"

"No, long-term."

That threw her. "I don't think we've got any. Yet."

"Fuck, listen to me," said Marcus, throwing back the dregs of his pint, "Mr. Barrett of Wimpole Street! It's just that I couldn't bear her to get her heart broken." His gray eyes were very searching.

"Me neither."

"And with these long-distance things, there's potential for disaster."

"More than there always is?" Jude looked at him levelly.

"Fair enough. Sorry for the interrogation." He gave her an uneasy grin. "I get edgy, meeting Síle's girlfriends."

"How many—"

"Only two...no, three," Marcus decided. "Ger was a good laugh, and the pilot was fun but just too neurotic—the thing was, none of them seemed quite worthy. And Kathleen was too...unruffled," he added before Jude could bring herself to say the name.

Jude snorted slightly. "She accosted me last night, at a club."

"No!"

"Ruffled wasn't the word. I thought she was going to whap me."

Marcus stared. "Well, I suppose pain brings out hidden traits. Like invisible ink and a hot iron."

Jude tried to smile at the image.

"Síle and I always joke that back in the bad old days, we'd have had one of those theatrical marriages of convenience—silver cufflinks, Noël Coward dialogue, cocktails at five..."

She grinned properly, then. "Listen, Marcus, I don't know if I'm worthy, but I promise I'll treat her right."

"Okay, that's a deal. My boyfriend wears cufflinks with his silk shirts," Marcus said abstractedly, "that's why they're on my mind. Mostly reds and greens—the shirts—but I think he'd look better in cream. Speaking of the devil—" He half stood and waved across the crowd.

Pedro was a small, beautiful, olive-skinned man who kissed Jude on both cheeks.

"So you guys are living pretty far apart too," she said to kick off the conversation.

"Isn't everyone," said Pedro, sliding in beside Marcus.

"Madness," said Marcus in what she deduced must be a Noël Coward voice, *"sheer madness!"*

"You liking Dublin?" asked the Spaniard.

"Very much," Jude assured him.

"She hates cities," commented Síle, arriving back with the drinks.

"I guess I'll have to make an exception," said Jude, looking up at her.

"And you've been together how long?" asked Pedro.

"Counting from when?" Marcus objected. "If it's consummation, that was only in April."

"New Year's Day," said Jude, decisive.

"Oh yeah?" asked Síle, grinning.

"For me, anyway. That's when the big ol' rock dropped into the pond."

"Six months, then," said Pedro judiciously. "So you should come here," he told Jude.

Wasn't she here? "Uh..." Was this a language problem?

"To live."

She laughed. Then she felt bad, because it wasn't as if she'd been scoffing at the notion, she was just startled.

Síle was nodding back at Pedro. "A splendid notion." Her tone was slightly sarcastic, but then it often was. Jude couldn't read her face.

"Well, that's them sorted, anyone for a packet of crisps?" asked Marcus, which raised a general laugh.

Later, Jude and Síle stood in a queue for cabs with rain drizzling into their collars. "Oh, and when you were getting drinks," Jude remembered, "Marcus grilled me about my long-term intentions."

Síle groaned. "I'm so sorry. Total strangers harassing you to emigrate on the spot." A strand of her hair was slicked against her cheek. "I'd never—I mean, in an ideal world," she corrected herself, "of course I'd love to find you in my four-poster every time I came home! But I know you have your own life."

Was that a way of saying, *Don't intrude on mine*? Jude kept her tone light. "Well, not entirely my own, since Belgium got overrun."

Síle kissed her, rain-chilled mouth to mouth. Somewhere in the line behind them, drunken lads started making mwah-mwah sounds. Jude flinched. Síle kept on kissing her. Now one of the guys was pretending to puke. Síle tucked her arm tightly through Jude's and stared ahead at the taxis.

On Sunday, Jude woke up with no idea where she was. Then she recognized the tiny square room she'd gone to bed in, the glittering hangings nailed to the wall.

"We don't have to shift for another hour, Da's not expecting us till noon," murmured Síle through her hair, and Jude's stomach formed a knot.

Driving to Shay O'Shaughnessy's house, Síle flipped between CDs. "Bhangra, Sharon Shannon, Dolly, or Franz Ferdinand?"

"Eh, whatever."

Síle narrowed her eyes. "Since when have you taken to saying, like, *whatever*, dude?"

Jude sighed. "Full disclosure: I haven't heard of any of them."

"Ha! You may have turned heads on the dance floor the other night, but I shall have to take your musical education in hand," said Síle, and put on some country and western singer who turned out to be Dolly Parton.

"Am I the youngest woman you've ever brought home?" Jude asked. She meant it as a quip, but it came out anxious.

"Oh no, when I turned up with Carmel, we were both about nineteen."

"The biggest age gap, I suppose I mean. And the poorest?"

"We don't charge admission to Sunday dinner," Síle murmured.

"The most foreign, then?"

"Not at all. Ger was only from Liverpool, but Da could barely understand her."

"The most likely to be called Sir in a women's washroom?"

"The most beautiful," said Síle, holding her gaze.

All Jude had going for her was the look in her lover's eyes. *I should have saved the coke for meeting the family,* she thought. Jude was the invader, the evil fairy, the thirteenth at the table. All the havoc was her doing.

Shay O'Shaughnessy's house was alarmingly grand, a three-story gray terrace looking straight out at the sea. Only the father and sister were there; the brother-in-law had taken all four boys to somewhere called Croke Park to watch a game. *Damn:* Jude had been hoping the kids would provide some kind of protective cover.

Shay was as pink-pale and white-haired as Orla was dark—she had Síle's skin and hair, Jude thought, but harder features. Father and daughters had exactly the same mannerism of pursing their lips. Lunch was roast lamb, and in her eagerness to show appreciation Jude ate far too much of it.

"Scrambled animal vaults nicely, in twelve..." murmured Síle in the living room, examining an almost-finished crossword.

"Oh leave it, it's been tormenting me all weekend. It'll come to me in my sleep," said her father, lighting another cigarette. "Jude, I understand you've only recently thrown off the shackles?"

Did he mean marriage? Jude blinked, startled. Was he calling her a *greedy little home-wrecker?*

"Yeah, and you're not helping," said Síle, swatting at the smoke.

"He insisted, as the kids aren't here," Orla apologized. "Though technically this house comes under the workplace ban, Da," she added slyly, "now you've got a cleaner."

Did no one in this family mop their own floors, Jude wondered? Perhaps the O'Shaughnessys could be described as—what was that great phrase she'd heard at Jael's the other night?—*smoked salmon socialists,* that was it.

Shay took a long suck and held the cigarette behind his chair, like a teenager. "I apologize for tempting you, Jude. I'm full of admiration."

"That's okay," she assured him. "I really only get the craving late at night." Curled up on the porch swing, insomniac, holding to the thought of her faraway lover. What did Orla and Shay think she and Síle were up to? Did they imagine that it was nothing but sex, or did they prefer not to imagine it at all?

"You tried to give it up once, Da, didn't you?" asked Orla.

"Mm. Nineteen sixty-nine, when I turned forty: the worst eleven days of my life. Barring your mother's death, of course," he added quietly. "But you know, the demon weed doesn't harm everyone."

"That is such bollocks," said Síle.

"At my last checkup," he confided in Jude, "Dr. Brady said he didn't know how it was possible, but I have the lungs of a teenage mountaineer."

The father was a charmer—and he showed no signs of bearing a grudge against Jude, she had to admit through her fog of paranoia. The sister was harder work, but Jude warmed her up by asking about her Ireland of the Welcomes drop-in centre.

Orla went off on a rant about the denial of citizenship to children of non-nationals born on Irish soil. "The day we voted to deny citizenship to children born on Irish soil to non-nationals—I was mortified! It's not like people arrive on a whim! This family I know left Bosnia the day the war broke out, without so much as nappies, and one of our volunteers arrived from Rwanda missing a hand."

"The irony is that we're all boat people," said Jude. Orla stared. "If you go back a generation or two, I mean."

"True enough."

"In Canada, you can't help being aware you're on stolen ground."

"Whereas here, an Irishman like me—a pale one, at least,"

Shay added jokily—"tends to imagine his ancestors sprang up out of the bog."

Jude shrugged. "Everybody's from somewhere else, originally. Even my friend Rizla—he's from the biggest native community in Canada, the Six Nations of the Grand River Territory, but I tease him about the fact that they're actually blow-ins from New York State."

"Really," Shay marveled.

Síle was smiling, and Jude wondered whether she was being a bore. She turned back to Shay and asked about the age of the house.

"1850 or thereabouts. But Monkstown dates back to the thirteenth century, when the Cistercians built the Castle."

"It must have been a thrill to grow up here."

Orla made a face. "I used to long for a *new* house like my best friend's, with cupboards that shut properly and a swing set in the garden."

"My daughters have a tin ear for history," Shay lamented to Jude. "And Sunita—my wife—she didn't much care for it either. They have a different conception of time in India, of course. Did you know, the Sanskrit word for the world literally means 'that which moves, that which changes'? Hindus believe things happen over and over again. For Brahma a single day is—hold on, I used to know this—"

"Four million human years," Síle supplied.

"Good girl," he said, gratified. "And each Brahma day starts with creation and ends with dissolution, and has fourteen subdivisions, each ended by a deluge."

Jude was experiencing something like vertigo.

"And lunch is ended by strawberries," said Orla, heading for the kitchen.

They were small, and sweeter than Jude had ever tasted. By now the June sun had come out weak and clear, so Shay proposed that Síle drive them down the coast to a spot called Greystones.

"I get it, gray stones. I like it when names make sense," Jude told Síle on the pebbled beach.

"Ah, but these are all English names, foisted on our landscape," she said with a touch of mockery, as she crunched along.

"How can you move in those heels?"

"Don't you like them?" asked Síle, doing a Marilyn Monroe as the breeze whipped up her skirt.

"More than you know," said Jude, grinning.

"I've worn heels so long, flatties would make me feel I was falling backwards!"

Orla and Shay were having a serious skimming match, and Síle and Jude joined them. Jude tried not to show off, but she was the best by far. Had Kathleen come here with the family, every Sunday, before she'd been banished with no warning? Had she skimmed well, or found it a childish game?

"You throw like a girl," Orla told her sister.

"I'm just out of practice." Síle spun a pebble at Orla, hitting her on the leg.

"Now, children. Behave, or you won't get an ice cream," said Shay.

"Ah, now I feel thirty-nine again," said Síle heavily, "because there's no way I could make room for an ice cream."

Nobody had slipped up yet by mentioning Kathleen's name, Jude realized. That meant they were all being very careful. Facing the cobalt waves, she breathed in deeply. "You're a lucky guy to live by the sea," she told Shay.

He sniffed. "Clears the old head out."

"It must be weird to swim in salt water, though."

"If you've any little cuts they sting like the devil," he told her, "but when you come out you're tingling all over."

"The Indian Ocean is the best," Síle put in; "it's so saline, it's easier to float."

"I can't imagine it ever getting hot enough to swim here," said Jude with a little shiver.

Síle laughed. "I'll have you know, this is high summer! But it can be a bit of an endurance test on a windy day. Da used to put up a prize of tenpence for the first one in up to her neck."

"Who won?"

"Usually me," put in Orla.

"Yeah, she's more of a stoic. But Da's an old softy," said Síle, tucking her hand into her father's arm, "so whoever came second got fivepence."

Síle could feel the minutes dripping away like a leaky tap. Back in Stoneybatter, she took Jude around the corner to buy fish and chips, "the best of Irish cuisine."

On the way back they passed some kids sitting on a wall. "Are yiz lezzies?" sneered a girl.

"We are," Síle called back with a steely smile, "and thanks for asking."

"Kiss her, then, would you," contributed a boy.

"Kiss her yourself!"

They turned the corner. "That's twice in one weekend," said Jude under her breath. "You don't seem to let it bug you."

"Sticks and stones," said Síle with a shrug.

That night, their last night, the rain came down in sheets. Síle fingered the wooden slats of the blind to one side; the street was as black as an oil slick, and a passing car made a long hissing splash. Jude lay on her side, looking like a statue of a sleeping faun. But her eyes were open, and caught the streetlight.

Síle was tired but didn't mean to waste a moment of it on sleep. She let herself demand and insist. She banged her ankle on a bedpost. She forgot she lived in a row of terraced houses, and cried out like a banshee in the night.

She fell asleep without meaning to, between one hard hold and the next, and woke to the alarm at seven on Monday morning, feeling like a child who didn't want to go to school.

Through the living room blinds came the lights of the waiting taxi. "I wish I could drive you," she told Jude. "If only I didn't have to do recruitment at this bloody Graduate Fair—"

"Maybe it's better this way."

"Yeah. The good-byes are killers, aren't they?" She pressed her face to Jude's small breasts, and roared, "I demand asylum from a harsh world! I claim this as my true homeland!"

Jude managed to laugh.

As Síle stood on her doorstep in her cream satin kimono, watching the taxi turn the corner, Deirdre popped her head out.

"How are you, Síle love? Y'all right?"

"I'm grand."

The older woman took a step nearer. Her face was tight. "If you ever need anything, just knock on the wall."

"Sure, thanks," said Síle, wondering whether Deirdre had been shocked by the youth of her visitor.

"No, but...if there's ever any problem, don't hesitate, just bang on the wall. Any hour of the day or night at all!"

"Will do." And Síle gave her frowning neighbour a little wave and stepped inside, wondering what to have for breakfast.

Only when she was halfway through her third slice of stone-ground toast and gooseberry jam did she figure it out. Perched on her kitchen stool, she felt mortification and delight shaken together like a cocktail. She remembered the sounds Jude had squeezed out of her, cries that must have sounded as much like suffering as plea-sure. *Great*, she thought, *now it'll be all round Stoneybatter that the air hostess is getting battered by her little bit of rough.* She started laughing, sitting alone in her kitchen, and couldn't stop.

"I'd give you two another couple of months, at the most," was one of the things Kathleen had said to her in the club the other night. "My curse on the pair of you," was another.

Songs of Absence

Put your sweet lips
A little closer to the phone.
We'll pretend that
We're together, all alone.

—JIM REEVES
"Put Your Sweet Lips a Little
Closer to the Phone"

When Jude opened her backpack on the plane home, she found a white rose from Síle's tiny yard inside the cover of *The Way the Crow Flies*. It was huge, creamy, with yellow at the heart. Half a dozen times during the flight she lifted it out to bury her nose in its cool satin. It smelled like lime juice, like light. By the time she landed in Toronto the rose was only a clump of bruised, dog-eared petals.

On the phone, her father teased Jude a little sadly about the fact that she'd only visited him once in the five years he'd been in Florida, the time she'd driven down for his wedding. "You know, there's courses you can take to tackle the fear of flying."

All of a sudden Jude regretted her reserve; if Ben Turner knew nothing about his daughter's life, whose fault was that but her own? "Actually," she said, "I'm getting over that. I just got back from Ireland."

"What do you mean? You live in Ireland."

"No, Ireland the country. I've been—I'm seeing this woman, her name is Síle."

Ben whistled. "It must be a big deal, to make you go all that way."

"Actually, yeah." She steeled herself: He might be annoyed that she hadn't mentioned this before, or hurt that she'd fly to Dublin but not to Tampa.

"That's wonderful, honey."

Was that relief in his tone? Gratitude that his peculiar daughter, her marriage over before her nineteenth birthday, had found someone to be serious about at last? Jude told herself to stop being so perverse.

Re: Toute Seule
    You're only gone three days, Jude, and I'm missing you sorely. Ring me tomorrow morning, as soon as you're up?
    Jael just texted to say "girl seems right stuff even if temporarily nonsmoking and born in Eighties" (grr, I've told her twice it was '79!).

Re: Chez Moi
    Síle, I swear when I close my eyes I can still feel your hands.
    In half an hour I'm due in my professional capacity at the Clinton Fair, which features team penning, area youth showing calves, mutton busting, round bale rolling, porcelain pony races and a hoedown/jamboree. Am I ringing your bells yet?
    I was just filing the following clipping from the *Irish Clarion* (9 February 1861) and thought I'd include it as a heavy hint . . .

        Urgent!
        Thousands of nice girls are wanted in Canada. Tens of thousands of men are sighing for what they cannot get--Wives!
        Shame!

```
Don't hesitate--COME AT ONCE.
    If you cannot come, send your sisters. So
great is the demand that anything in skirts
stands a chance. These men are all shy but
willing. All prizes! No blanks. Hustle up now
girls and don't miss this chance because some
of you will never get another.
```

"I don't know, it's understood between us," Síle told Jael in the long, rain-spattered queue to get into a gig at Mother Redcap's. The friends were stuck behind a hen party from Liverpool in frilly skirts that said *Kiss Me Arse,* one of whom had just thrown up on the path.

"It's absurd," scoffed Jael. "What's it been, a grand total of two weekends together in the flesh? So why on earth would you grudge each other a bit of fun?"

Síle shivered in her little red lambskin jacket.

"And don't give me that I-only-have-eyes-for-her line." Jael hunched over a cigarette to light it in the wet breeze.

"Sorry, but it's true."

"You've always fancied so few people," said Jael disapprovingly.

"But it's not just that. Even if I did take a shine to somebody else—" She broke off, trying to find the right words. "The point is, if Jude and I aren't committed—"

"It's not a coincidence that that word means 'locked up in an asylum.'"

"You're the one who's bloody married," protested Síle.

"Exactly. Face pressed against the asylum window, waving at you, shouting *Hold onto your liberty!*"

"I thought you liked Jude."

"I'd have her on toast with jam and butter."

"I didn't mean—"

"I like her as a person *and* as a ride. I think both of you should enjoy your freedom."

"That's a meaningless word," Síle argued. "Put it this way, if Jude was just one of a number of possible lovers, then given the distance between us, given all the inconvenience, what would be the point?"

Jael released a plume of smoke from her nostrils like a dragon. "Sounds like all the hassle of being in a couple, and none of the pleasure."

"Well, it's true that LDRs depend on masturbation," said Síle under her breath.

Jael cackled, as the queue surged forward briefly. The rain began to thicken; the two of them squeezed farther into the lee of the building. For a minute, Síle couldn't even remember the name of the fiddler she was queueing up to see. These days, she was constantly distracted from her own life. "Can I ask you something?"

"No, I'm afraid not," said Jael, "a friendship of only fifteen years doesn't entitle you to ask questions."

Síle grinned. "I was just wondering why you went off women."

A brief pause. "Did I?"

"Didn't you?"

Jael stamped her cigarette out with one pointed boot. "I think I just met Anton. Ironic, isn't it, that I became a has-bian in the early nineties, just when the lot of Irish queers was about to improve?" She lit another. "Maybe I'll take it up again later, when he's dead of furry arteries. I'll cut a Vita Sackville-West swathe through the old-folks' home."

"So you didn't actually stop fancying them?" asked Síle.

"I didn't stop fancying anything," said Jael. "The night before our wedding, I told Anton that I'd tried monogamy and it didn't suit my complexion. I suspect he thought I was being funny. But the laugh's on me, as it turns out, because I've been far too busy and knackered. *Nonmonogamy*, we used to call it," she reminisced, "as if it was some philosophical principle, instead of simple sluttishness!

Anyway, getting back to the fair sex, I'm sure they're grateful to have been spared my attentions."

Síle nodded. "You were a nasty lesbian," she risked saying. "You make a much better wife and mother."

Jael's mouth twitched. "Well, women bring out the worst in me, they're so fucking sensitive: rabbits in the headlights. Whereas Anton's such a rubber ball, whenever I try to crush him he just bounces up again."

Síle was trying to sleep in, after a four-day rotation, but the postman woke her with a padded envelope containing a cassette labeled, in Jude's careful script, *Songs of Absence*. She was overwhelmed with fond exasperation. "A tape! You're about three generations of technology behind," she told Jude on the phone.

"Do you like the mix, though?"

"Very much, despite the abysmal sound quality. It's like something out of a time capsule. I had to borrow Deirdre-next-door's boom box to play it on."

"What's your favorite?"

"It's a close tie between 'All by Myself' and 'Walking after Midnight.'"

"Mine is Ella doing 'Every Time We Say Good-bye,'" said Jude.

Something occurred to Síle. "Do you think all the best songs are songs of absence?"

Jude laughed. "There's certainly something to be said for it. No yawning together in front of the TV or squabbles over who forgot to buy milk."

They rang each other at any time of day or night they thought the other might be reachable and awake. They spoke from airports, in bed, or in the bath. (Síle had started taking occasional baths now, to remind her of Jude, and because there seemed more time to kill.) "This must be costing you a fortune, I'll ring you back," Síle would say, and Jude would answer, "It doesn't matter. What are you wearing?" Jude couldn't figure out which phone company offered the best rates. She didn't need a "Family 'n Friends!" discount package, she told Síle; she needed a special deal for "Obsessive Romance."

"Jude, I have to confess I've been staring at the phone and willing it to ring like some girl in a fifties film. Oh well, I suppose you're out, enjoying the hamlet's glittering nightlife? If you're in by midnight your time, you could try me but I may have gone to Italian by then. Big kiss…"

"Síle, really sorry, if I'd known you were going to call I'd have come home earlier, I was just having dinner with the Petersons next door…"

"Damn! I thought I'd catch you over breakfast today, but you've clearly headed off to the museum at the crack of dawn. You work far more hours than the board pays you for; I'm going to report you…"

"Oh sweetheart, I was just clippering my hair. The phone rang again a minute later, so I raced downstairs, but it wasn't you, it was somebody trying to sign me up for a diploma in accounting, so I've scattered hair all over the floor for nothing. Guess I better go get the broom, then there's some election signs I've got to hammer into the front lawn. This phone tag is getting slightly annoying."

"*Slightly?* I'm back, I was only in the supermarket replacing my rotting greens. Anytime before midnight's fine for ringing me back… no, later's okay, actually, I can always get back to sleep…"

Sometimes they booked their calls in advance, which took some of the spontaneity out of it. Once Síle tried Jude repeatedly all Saturday and Sunday, working herself into a state of panic, before finally remembering that this was the weekend Jude was at a conference in Toronto called Southwestern Ontario's Past: The Way Forward.

They could never say good night or good morning without laughing at the incongruity of it, the dissonance. The timing was awful: Their biorhythms never matched. Sometimes Síle was going to bed, wanting to flirt sleepily, and Jude was frying garlic or dashing out to a meeting or off to play pool with Rizla. Sometimes over her porridge Jude tried Síle and caught her in crisp, busy mode at an airport. Once, insomniac at four in the morning, she called and got Síle making tea for an eighty-five-year-old neighbour who'd dropped in to use her scanner.

Out of sight, not out of mind, Síle told herself at solitary moments. This was like prayer, she supposed: talking in your head, keeping faith with the invisible.

Here and Now

All of your life
that has gone before,
All to come after it,
—so you ignore,
So you make perfect
the present

—Robert Browning
"Now!"

Toronto Pearson Airport in early July. Síle started to laugh as she ran through the sliding doors.

"Mm," said Jude at last, emerging from the curtain of hair. "Where's your baggage?"

Síle threw her arms up. "You're not going to believe this. Last night I got in late from dinner with Orla at this new Lebanese place, and I swear I set my alarm in plenty of time, but it must have been P.M. rather than A.M., because it didn't go off! Such a beginner's mistake! In my dream I was at your funeral," she said, clutching at the sleeve of Jude's white T-shirt, "and I couldn't stop crying, and your friends—your mother was there too—they kept looking at me and whispering, 'Who's this gal? We've never seen her before in our lives.' And then the priest started banging on the coffin with the spade—"

"I was getting a Catholic burial?"

"Shut up, it's my dream," said Síle, kissing her neck. God, it was good to be here, no distance at all apart! "And of course the *bang-bang* was actually the taxi driver whamming away on my knocker. Thank god he did—he'd been there about ten minutes. I had to run downstairs in a towel—"

Jude grinned at the image.

"And I barely had time to throw this on," she said, looking down at her amber linen shift. "They were paging me at the departure gate. I was scarlet! Thank god it wasn't my own airline."

"You look very presentable," Jude murmured.

"Well, I got some duty-free makeup," Síle told her. "I've nothing else with me but credit cards. I was in such a fluster, I even left my gizmo on the kitchen counter. You're going to have to take me shopping in—" she tried to recall what the in-flight magazine had recommended for Toronto—"Yorkville, is that what it's called?"

"The problem with that is," said Jude, leading her toward the door, "we're meeting Gwen at the Summer Squash Fair at four."

"Is she competing?"

"Yeah, in the imaginative appetizer category, and she always runs the chutneys and preserves."

Síle did a double-take.

"Oh, you thought I meant squash, the sport?" Jude laughed.

"Can't we call her and change the time?" Then Síle sighed. "Right, she probably doesn't carry a mobile..."

"I believe it's the only Summer Squash Fair in the world."

"Well then! Lead on," said Síle, slipping on her new shades as they stepped out into the white sun.

Jude looked at her sideways. "Are you mad?"

"No no, I'll manage without any possessions somehow."

The Mustang had no air conditioning, and with the windows down, on the highway, the roaring air made it impossible to talk. Síle kept her hand on Jude's denim thigh and relished the sensation of doing absolutely nothing. When they got off onto smaller roads, driving past fields of stubble and gold, with the warm manure-scented wind flaring her hair, she felt ridiculously happy. She noticed fruit stalls, art studios, guesthouses, tearooms, Angel Treasures, Porch Geese, and other Traditional and Totally Unique Collectibles. "Has there been some kind of boom around here, since April?" she asked.

Jude shook her head. "Lots of businesses only open in the summer, to catch the tourist trade," she shouted back.

Síle slid her hand up under the soft T-shirt. She observed that having one nipple squeezed didn't affect Jude's driving, but it did alter her breathing. "Look," she said, pointing at a church sign, GOD RECEIVES KNEE MAIL! Damn, without her gizmo how could she be expected to remember anything?

Creamy sheep, brown cows, and a black horse and foal lying down in their field as if stoned. On the side of a barn in tall fresh letters: MARRIAGE = 1 MAN + 1 WOMAN. A garden furniture store with a sign that said GROW WHERE YOUR PLANTED. Jude said something that was lost in the warm wind.

"What?"

"I like that one, apart from the spelling."

"You would," Síle roared back.

The Summer Squash Fair, on a farm just outside Ireland, was packed solid. Under striped canopies, people were queuing up for zucchini ice cream with deep-fried squash blossoms, and there was a squash carving final coming up at five (the categories included Funny, Horror, and Celebrities). In the big tent, a troupe of eight aging couples were square dancing with ease: the men in cowboy shirts with shoelace ties, the women flicking up their ruched, starched petticoats. "My god," said Síle, "where have these hordes come from?"

Gwen was writing $3.99 on the lids of a batch of jams. "Which ones are the whores?" she asked mildly, looking down the field.

"*Hordes,* crowds, lots of people," said Síle, appalled. Jude howled with laughter.

"Oh, from all over, really," Gwen told her. "This event's pretty famous; I just met a family up from Ohio. That's my niece Tasmin over there, she's two centimetres dilated—"

"At last!" said Jude.

"—and she's going to keep walking round till her labour really kicks in. Jocelyne here"—Gwen nodded at an angular blonde collapsed in a deck chair behind the stall—"she's been in *Troilus and Cressida* and *Private Lives* over at the Stratford Festival all summer."

"Which sounds almost as exhausting as labour," murmured Síle. "You really treasure your English heritage here, don't you?"

"Not mine," Gwen corrected her. "I'm German; it was English pilots who firebombed my folks out of Dresden."

"Ah, history," murmured Jude into the brief silence; "never a dull moment."

"D'you find the drive from Toronto long?" Gwen asked Síle.

"You mean, because the entire island of Ireland could be hidden in any park in Ontario?" asked Síle wryly. "No, it was fine, Gwen; my job is all about spending time in tin cans." She noticed, with mild irritation, her professional habit of repeating people's names.

"That Mustang should be torched. I'd do it for you, Jude, as an act of friendship."

Jude nodded. "The only problem is, the insurance money wouldn't even buy me a new motorbike helmet."

The Giant Vegetable Marrow was big enough for Jude and Síle to sit on and have their photo taken. Síle blew $2 on guessing its weight. (Canadian currency still seemed like Monopoly money to her; everything was so astonishingly cheap when she translated it into euro.) She had a slice of crisp barbecued zucchini slathered in pesto, and a plateful of tiny yellow ones sautéed and sliced to fan out, with their flowers still on and filled with some savoury mousse.

The maple-glazed squash pie was her favourite. By throwing hoops at a wall of hooks, Jude won a basket of decorative gourds, and presented them to Síle, who was transfixed by the yellow knobbly crookneck with the goblin painted on it. "Hey, I could borrow your Swiss Army knife and whittle these into replicas of my missing baggage," she told Jude. "Soap dish, comb, ear plugs..."

"Jewelry box, castanets," Gwen contributed.

"Wonderbra," said Síle, putting two round gourds over her chest. "It'd be the development of civilization all over again."

Jude took her off for a Rustic Ride in a Pioneer Hay Wagon. "I thought you hated the peddling of nostalgia?" asked Síle.

"Only when it pretends to be history. If it's just a wagon ride, I'm all over it."

While the kids jumped up and down and threw hay at each other, Síle and Jude lay back in the scented, scratchy stuff. "You're such a skinnymalinks," Síle murmured, finding a soft spot under Jude's shoulder for her head, "I have to place myself carefully."

"So, are you a squash fan yet?"

"Fervent! Especially those striped Cocozelle; we never get them back home."

Jude gave her a slow kiss. "You know those movies about big-city Yanks visiting the innocent Old Country? Well, you seem to be doing it in reverse."

"I wouldn't call rural Ontario *innocent*, exactly," said Síle. "Just backward."

For that, Jude rubbed a lot of hay into her hair. When Síle had stopped fighting she lay quietly for a while, the sun scorching her legs as the wagon bumped them along the field.

Gwen came over for dinner, contributing a zucchini date walnut loaf. Síle was finding her a little bit of work, as quiet types always were, but they were usually worth the effort. "Why do you have to wear a pager on your day off?"

"Mostly in case a resident goes AWOL," Gwen told her.

"How can they wander out, don't you lock the doors?"

"Oh, you know. Human rights," said Gwen drily. "Freedom of movement and all that."

"Even if the Alzheimer's ones end up under a tour bus of theatre-lovers," Jude pointed out.

Síle got Gwen reminiscing about her previous job in rural health outreach. "Only fifteen minutes from here, we're not talking the Yukon," said Gwen. "You've got your elderly and your Amish and your farm families, and none of them go to the doctor."

"Why not?" asked Síle. Gwen was kind of handsome in a pioneer way, she decided.

"That'd show weakness, wouldn't it? Be making a fuss in front of the neighbours. So they wait till the cancer's tertiary—that's the women; the men don't come at all unless they've had a leg sliced off in a thresher."

"Jaysus. I thought Irishmen were bad."

"Bad at what?" came a booming voice behind Síle, making her jump.

"You could call, you know, before strolling into my kitchen," Jude told Rizla.

"It's an ancient custom of my people to drop in, all spontaneous-like," he said, taking a chair and the last two slices of cake. Gwen curled her lip. "Besides, my phone's been cut off again."

Síle registered that she was the reason for his coming over, which was oddly flattering. She was ready for him this time. "To answer your question, Rizla, Irishmen are bad about neglecting their health. Cigarettes, dirty cuts on their hands," she said, her eyes dropping to his scarred fingers, "and too much cake."

His laugh was like the bursting of a balloon. "She's a quick one," he told Jude.

"Don't I know it."

"Anyway, these Amish ladies think it's immodest to eat too much, so their babies are born tiny," Gwen continued. "I roared at this one gal; I said, 'Aren't you supposed to *be fruitful and multiply?*' As for breast self-exams—we had to call it a Women's Flu Information Night and hand out diagrams on the sly."

"More power to you." Síle laughed, draining her martini. "Country living, ugh!"

"Whatcha doing here again, then?" asked Rizla.

Síle grinned at him, tightening her grip on Jude's thigh under the table. "Lapping up the local delicacies," she said with precise innuendo.

He whooped, and she thought, *in spite of everything, he likes me.*

Rizla started telling them about this great recording contract his sister had just got.

"What's her music like?" Síle asked.

He shrugged. "New Age Aboriginal, I think she calls it. She performs as Falling Feather because she says Ann Vandeloo sounds like a brand of apple pie. So there'll be a big party at her place all next week; you two should ride down on the bike," he said, pointedly leaving out Gwen. "Unless it's raining again."

Apparently the summer was proving weirdly cool and wet, though it seemed scalding to Síle. Rizla started warning her about tornadoes. "On the highway, never try to outrun one or your ass is dead meat. Jump out of your car and dig your way into any kind of hollow."

"Don't let him scare you off," Gwen told her. "Immigrants from all over the world are banging on the door to come settle in southwestern Ontario. Not that it's too hard to get a visa if you've got the skills," she added hastily.

"I'm sure," murmured Síle, amused at the lack of subtlety. Jude caught her eye and gave her an embarrassed little grin.

"Why would I be trying to scare her off?" sneered Rizla. "We could do with a looker like Síle, there's so many dog-uglies around here."

Gwen met his stare.

"I reckon Síle should move right in, right away," he said, his finger indicating the bedroom upstairs, "jizz the old house up a bit."

"Work at Dudovick's?" suggested Síle.

"Why not, I bet you'd make a mean turkey plucker."

"Or maybe I could cash in my mutual funds, buy that garage-café place where you work, and be your boss."

That threw him, but only for a split second, she could tell; soon he was down on his knees demonstrating how readily he'd lick her boots. Gwen was looking revolted.

Later they played Pictionary. Gwen's drawings were hilariously bad, while Rizla's big hands proved expert with a pencil; when Síle got muddled about the differences between a whale and a seal, Rizla made her a handy diagram of each as well as a dolphin, a shark, and an otter for good measure.

"How come you're such an expert?" asked Gwen, dubious.

"I did work my way round the world when I was twenty-five," he reminded her.

"What, swimming with sharks?" Síle asked.

"Washing dishes and hitching rides with truckers," Jude told her. "He only knows wildlife from late-night TV."

"Mohawk wisdom has many mysterious sources."

"Oh," Síle remembered, "and Jude says you can do the sound of those birds on the dollar coins."

"Loons, sure." He cupped his hands and made a sad, wavering call. "But Jude shoulda shown you herself; I taught her how when she was a kid."

"That's not all you taught her," said Gwen under her breath.

He gave her a cold look. "Something to say, spit it out."

Jude made a feeble attempt at a loon call. "See, I've lost the knack."

"If you ask me," Gwen told Rizla, "you were lucky her mom didn't call the cops on you."

His eyes bulged.

"Hey, hey—" Jude began.

"I mean what kind of so-called adult hangs round a teenage girl, plying her with rotgut, playing stupid driving games that nearly rip her head off?"

Síle smiled into her hand.

"It was a cut ear, that's all," said Jude. "And we all *begged* him to buy us liquor."

Rizla exploded, his finger pointing at Gwen. "You make me sound like some kind of slimeball serial killer."

"I'm just saying, any daughter of mine—"

"She wasn't a freaking vestal virgin, you know. I didn't get anything some pimpled tenth-grader hadn't got already."

Jude winced visibly.

Rizla roared on. "Listen, Goody Two-Shoes, just because you spent your whole adolescence doing extra softball practice because nobody ever had a hard-on for you—"

Síle was pleased to see that this observation didn't crush Gwen. "And then you *married* her," Gwen accused him, "in some lame attempt to keep her from escaping your sweaty clutches by going off to college—"

"I didn't plan to go anyway," Jude put in, but nobody was listening.

"—and it's just typical of you that you *still* haven't come up with a penny toward the cost of the divorce. And don't try your old trick of blaming racism or Tory fiscal policy for the fact that you live in a rotting trailer, you bum."

Rizla produced a teddy-bear smile. "Thing is, though, I'll always be her number one bud. You're just the backup."

Gwen spoke through her teeth, leaning across the table. "You are a fungus on her life."

"Might I have a moment?" Síle spoke with serene authority, as if to a plane full of fretful passengers. "Now it's Jude's misfortune that her two old friends can't stand each other, but given the limited options in an underpopulated area, she's unlikely to replace either of you—unless you go on behaving like three-year-olds at dinner parties. So might I suggest we call it a draw, and call it a night?"

Later, Síle had to remove her makeup with moisturizer and toilet paper. It was quite fun, all this improvising, though she couldn't imagine getting through the whole week without shopping.

Jude fished out a new toothbrush from the back of the cupboard.

Síle looked at it quizzically. "I hope I remember how to do this without the help of electricity."

"You know, come the apocalypse, you're going to be helpless."

"Come the apocalypse, I have a lot more expertise on handling panicking crowds and first-degree burns than you do."

Once Síle was settled in bed beside her, Jude said, "Okay now? Any more core needs I can supply?"

"Very possibly," said Síle, wrapping one leg around Jude's hip.

"What time is it for you?"

Síle made a quick calculation: *three in the morning.* "Here and now."

Jude had to work the next day, so that she could take a three-day weekend after that. Síle smelled her linen dress and made a face.

"I guess this afternoon we could check out the stores in Stratford—"

"No, this is a learning exercise. I've gone twenty-four hours without baggage already; let's see how long I can last. People pay hundreds of euro for courses on simple living, you know."

Jude snorted.

Síle managed to find some low-slung black jeans that were loose on Jude but bum-hugging on her; with the cuffs folded up several times they made a reasonable approximation of capri pants. She added a belt with a snake's head, and an old red bandana to keep her hair out of her eyes. "Wow," said Jude, stroking her white vest as it clung to the curve of Síle's shoulder, "everything looks different on you."

They had breakfast on the tree-shaded back deck, where various bird feeders hung. Jude pointed out a mourning dove, a red-wing blackbird, a yellow chaffinch, and a grackle with a jade head. The air was heavy, sticky already, as Síle walked Jude to the museum and kissed her good-bye. There was a sulphurous tang in the air that Jude said was skunk.

Síle spent the first part of the morning looking around the old house. It had clean lines, and Jude kept it uncluttered and serene. There were red and blue quilts hung on most of the walls; she thought Rachel Turner had probably made them. Síle felt like a detective, leafing through old filing cabinets and photo albums. Inside a wardrobe she found *J.L.T. 1989* cut in a ten-year-old's careful print. Nineteen eighty-nine: That was the year Síle and Ger (who found they got on much better as exes) had gone snorkeling on the Great Barrier Reef. Sometimes the gap between her past and Jude's gaped so steeply, it made her dizzy.

She wandered the length of Main Street. At the Garage she had a homemade lemonade; the only other customers were a fat teenage boy and girl silently holding hands, and two women lamenting the closure of two more rural mail routes and discussing the peculiarities of their cows, tractors (also referred to as *she*), and husbands. Síle listened to the rolling vowels; she thought she was beginning to distinguish the local accent, though Jude had only a trace of it, probably because of her English mother. The menu included a Little Eric (*1 fish w. cheese*) and a Foot Long. Looking out through the little lace curtain, Síle thought she spotted Rizla's legs sticking out from under a Jeep. For all his famous travels, he didn't seem to have any further ambitions to leave town. He seemed oddly content, considering how little his life amounted to: fixing cars, free lunch on the premises. *Shut up, Síle,* she scolded herself, *how do you know what his life amounts to?* He had a best friend to whom he just so happened to be legally married. She knew her jealousy was absurd, but that didn't make it go away.

At the Olde Tyme Gift Shoppe, Síle did her bit for the local economy by buying herself a Shaker-style jewelry box and some tea towels made of old flour sacks. On the street she noticed a lot of baseball caps, denim, shorts. Also bad hair, racks of white teeth, heavy mustaches that made the men look like gay clones. The cars were mostly Buicks, Chryslers, Dodges, and GMC trucks—some old, some new and expensive-looking. She passed a shiny yellow SUV and wondered whether it was the one that had killed Jude's red setter. She counted three motorized scooters; back in Dublin, old ladies simply had canes, but then at home the paths were never knee deep in snow. Two girls in long dresses shot by her on Roller Blades; she thought they were probably Mennonites. The small cemetery had some familiar names—Malones, Meaghers, O'Learys, and Feeneys—but also a Looby, some Soontienses, Krauskopts, Schoonderwoerds, and (this one made her grin) Heuver-Poppes.

In Replay Used Books and Video Rentals a man with a tragic face charged her a dollar for a book of love-letter poems called *Flesh and Paper.* At the door, she turned back to say, "Excuse me, this was a furniture shop once, wasn't it?"

He nodded. "Ben had a yellow velvet chaise sitting in that window for five years, I swear. The stuff was too fussy; he hadn't the business sense of a frog, though you don't need to tell Jude I said so."

Síle's face heated up; of course the man knew who she was, she kept forgetting that she wore an invisible sign: THAT TURNER GIRL'S LATEST.

There was a mysterious booming coming from inside the turkey factory. Síle paused to read the Soviet-style slogan: REACHING SAFELY BEYOND OUR GOALS, IN THE PAST SIX YEARS WE HAVE LOST NO TIME TO ACCIDENTS.

Lots of houses had those wooden chairs outside, with flat arms to hold drinks. There were Daffy Duck weathervanes, gnomes, elaborate slides and swing sets, a huge trampoline just like her nephews had in Dublin. Basketball hoops, tinkling chimes, plastic wagons and bikes left out with no concern for thieves, maple-leaf flags, and banners featuring teddy bears. Some Catholic had propped an Infant of Prague in a dormer window. She passed a porch strung with white washing, and recognized a dial-up modem's distinctive whine coming from the room behind.

"Well hey Jim, how're you keeping?" she overheard on the street.

"Pretty good, Loretta, and yourself?"

"Good, good. All righty, see you later."

Dublin had never been like this, Síle thought, though it had possessed a certain easygoing sleepiness back in the eighties, before the tidal wave of money had crashed in.

The retired G.P.s next door to Jude were selling white peaches off their porch; Síle bought a basket and introduced herself. "What a pretty accent!" they told her, as several others had that morning; she feared she was playing it up. The male Doctor Peterson assured her that when he was growing up it was all bush around here; he used to take his shotgun and bring a couple of bunny rabbits home for supper. "In those days you could shoot a cannon down Main Street, but now, the traffic!"

Síle agreed, straight-faced. It wasn't that she looked down on the residents of Ireland, Ontario; she just couldn't take the place quite seriously.

They wanted to know how poor Jude was doing since losing her mother. "These serotonin reuptake inhibitors do wonders for bereavement," the female Doctor Peterson assured her. Síle was startled by this shift into the contemporary.

On the porch of the old red general store, kids were sucking those frozen tubes Síle remembered from her own childhood, except these seemed three times longer. Inside, there was a post office counter and dry-cleaning drop-off. The counter had herb pots, a rack of beef jerky, and a dish of pennies labeled LEAVE ONE, TAKE ONE, WHEN YOU NEED ONE. The notice board offered a GARTH BROOKS TRIBUTE, a DRUMBO/INNERKIP FISHING DERBY WITH PRIZE FOR LONGEST TROUT, and DEWORMED SIBERIAN HUSKY PUPPIES, $250 AS IS. Paul specialized in live trapping and would solve all your problems with skunks, possums, raccoons, pigeons, bats, and mink. There was an opening for a PERSON (she liked the attempt at gender neutrality) in a mineral plant in the Goderich area, DRIVE FORKLIFT, OWN BAGGING EQUIP.

At half past twelve she made up some peculiar sandwiches from whatever she could find in Jude's fridge (Brie and mango chutney, prosciutto and cucumber) and brought them down the street to the museum. Jude was excerpting some letters for a forthcoming feature on economic depressions called "Hungry Times." "Did you know," she said, "that the recipient owns the piece of paper itself—like, the body—but the sender owns the words, like the soul of the letter? So it's a present you've half given and half kept."

"How romantic!" Síle perched on the desk and leaned over to try to make out the spidery brown handwriting. "A permanent thread between the two of them."

"But a huge hassle if you're trying to track down two sets of descendants to get permission. I'm now wondering whether I should just summarize Mrs. Alfred Vogel's thoughts about her dead children rather than quoting her not-particularly-eloquent words...So how're you liking things?" Jude asked, taking another sandwich.

Síle wasn't fooled by the casual tone. "Charming," she assured her. Honesty made her add, "If a tad Stepford." Jude grinned. "Oh goody, a pop culture reference I don't have to explain."

"I read *The Stepford Wives* when I was twelve, and I swore I'd never get married."

"So what happened?"

"I guess I forgot."

"Hamlet in the secondhand bookshop was rude about your father's business sense," Síle remarked, "though I doubt the guy's making enough to pay for light bulbs, himself."

Jude laughed. "That's Joe Costelloe. Alma's the cook at the Old Stationhouse Guesthouse. She and Joe split up years ago; now they live on different floors of their house but have to share the kitchen and bathroom. Each of them's waiting for the other to crack and leave town."

"Jaysus," Síle groaned, "are they under a spell?"

Jude shrugged. "Bad enough to lose your marriage without having to lose your home too."

Privately, Síle thought it would be the best thing for both the Costelloes. "Oh, and I've been glued to the *Mitchell Advocate* and *Huron Expositor.* All those blurred photos of grinning prize winners or sales staff called Wayne or Agnes or—inevitably—Dave! Warnings about *animal rightists* sneaking into poultry farms. And I love the way they juxtapose international news with local—like, "Asia Faces Currency Crises" alongside lost terriers and in memoriams—and the way the stock listings include grain and hogs!"

"You've probably never read an Irish local paper, have you?"

"Hmm," said Síle, "but it couldn't possibly be quite as wholesome. There's a charity bicycle race on in Seaforth next week in which the slowest rider wins!"

"You've really been doing your research," said Jude, with a slight edge to her tone.

Síle decided she'd been laying on the satire a bit thick.

"In the general store, who served you, was it a young guy? That's Neil McBride, the Evangelical who won't hold the door for me and my haircut. I can tell he pictures me sizzling in hellfire. Was his mother around?"

"An oldish woman? Blue rinse?" Síle recalled.

"Julia McBride."

"No way! The one your father—she's still here?"

"Where else would she be? Dad moved to Buffalo, and there were terrible fights between her and Hank—she was seen with a shiner, once—but she never left him."

"So your poor mother had to buy her morning paper from the Whore of Babylon?"

"She had it delivered," said Jude, "but yeah, she and Julia even served on the Quilt Show Committee together for a couple of years. They were civil."

"Do you think your mom's jealousy just faded away?"

"Not a bit," said Jude, shaking her head. "But in a place this small, running into each other twice a day, they had to come to some kind of terms."

"Why do you stay, really?" Síle asked, despite her best intentions.

Jude shrugged. "This is where I was born and raised."

"But that's utterly arbitrary—"

"Sure, but so's the fact that I speak English, have blue eyes, and fancy you."

Síle smiled, trying to keep the tone light. "It's just that...we don't have to stay where we're put anymore. We've been cut loose, set adrift; we can live where we want."

"I don't want to be adrift," said Jude. "What's that line of poetry? Something about seeing the world in a grain of sand."

"Yeah? When I look at a grain of sand, I see a grain of sand," Síle told her. Then she burst out, "A population of six hundred people, that's barely enough for a party!"

Jude's eyes were hard.

It's been six months since the woman died, Síle thought, *it's time.* "I think you stayed here to look after your mother, didn't you?" she asked as gently as she could. "Especially after your father dumped her."

"Mom was a very capable person."

"I'm sure. But then to move back in with her, after you split up with Rizla—" She was tempted to add that she thought Jude had stayed in town to keep an eye on him, too.

"Out there is the garden where I grew my first tomatoes," said Jude, jerking her head. "My first kiss was with Teresa Guderson in a storm overflow pipe off Main Street. I came off my motorbike at the corner of Huron and MacKenzie, and if I look closely I can still see a little bloodstain on the wall."

"We've all got a past," said Síle. "But to cling to the spot where it happened is a bit pathetic." As soon as the words were out, she wished them unsaid.

A cold stare; a shrug. "Amnesia's a form of brain damage, you know. Is that what you'd recommend? Fresh start, clean slate?"

Silence.

"I didn't mean that. Sorry. I just...Stasis gives me the creeps," Síle admitted. "I can't stand to feel walled in. I need a little breeze of possibility." After a minute, she added, "I'm talking about us now."

"I realize that." Jude came up close to her and blew on her ear.

Síle smiled, trying to shed her bad mood.

"There is no stasis. At Heathrow, on New Year's Day—when you marched off with your baggage cart," said Jude, sliding her hand into the small of Síle's back, "I knew I wanted to see you again, but it seemed impossible. And now look at us!"

"Yeah, squabbling away like long-timers," remarked Síle, which won a laugh from Jude. "Well, I suppose every couple has one argument they replay over and over. One, if they're lucky: Vanessa and I had about fifteen!"

"Listen," said Jude, looking reluctantly at her desk, "I really have to finish this big application, so I can get it into the mail by five."

"Oh yeah, can I read it?" Síle didn't want to leave while their quarrel was still lingering in the air.

"Would you, seriously?"

"Sometimes an outsider's eye—"

"That would be fantastic," said Jude.

They worked on the application together for almost two hours; it was far less tedious than Síle had expected. "You meet every criterion on this foundation's list," she told Jude; "I don't see how they can turn you down."

"If we get even half of what we ask for, it'll cover overhead for the next three years," Jude told her, grinning.

But the humidity was really getting to Síle now. She went back to the house and lay on the sofa with *The English Patient*.

Jude woke her with a kiss and a glass of cold fresh mint tea. "Three people stopped me on the way down the street to say they'd met my friend from Dublin. You're a big hit."

"Is it still baking hot out there?"

"I know how to cool us down," said Jude, beckoning Síle outside, where the Triumph stood at a rakish angle outside the garage. "A ride to the lake."

"The saddlebags look fantastic," said Síle, playing for time. This had seemed a very sexy idea, but... "The last time I was on one of these was student days," she mentioned, "and when the guy went up a hill I started sliding off."

"You can't," said Jude, patting the black leather seat back; "this is known as the sissy bar." She handed Síle a helmet.

She tugged it down over her face; it was heavy, claustrophobic, like something an astronaut would wear. "Ugh," she said, spitting out her own hair.

Jude flipped up the visor and leaned in to kiss her. "Here's my old jacket. Oh, and roll those pants down or you'll burn your leg on the tailpipes. And don't forget, lean into the corners."

Síle let out a faint moan.

But as soon as they were moving—her arms tight round Jude, leather on leather—the breeze cooled her beautifully. This had to be like what driving a car felt like, circa 1910. Such a sense of cutting through the air, and the air play-fighting back; Síle could feel the hungry tug of it on her helmet. Behind her back, her hair whipped and cracked like a flag; she'd never get the knots out. "This is wild," she yelled through her visor, but she could tell Jude couldn't hear her over the roaring of the engine and the wind.

And then they turned a corner and Síle thought, *We're going to crash, the whole side of my body will be scraped off.* She forced herself to lean in on the next corner, curling fetally toward the tarmac. *Centrifugal force,* she reminded herself. *Oh Lord, I believe, help thou my unbelief.* The whole world was vibrating; where the back of Síle's borrowed jeans met the sissy bar, her skin was itching madly, but there was nothing to be done so she just clamped her teeth together and held on, held on. Mostly all she saw was the back of Jude's helmet (*ITQ Nad,* it said enigmatically), and yellow and bronze and green fields flashing by in the corner of her eye, but if she tilted her head to the side she could catch a glimpse of the little road snaking ahead of them.

Jude lifted her gloved hand in a minimal wave to the first biker they passed, then the second, then the third—at which point Síle figured out that she couldn't know them all, it must be some biker solidarity equivalent of the local wave. When they were between a truck and a minivan full of children, Síle wanted to ask Jude to slow down, but couldn't think how; she thought if she tugged at her sleeve, Jude would assume it was an emergency and pull off onto the soft shoulder.

The sea, she thought, finally, catching a sparkle of blue, and then corrected it to: *the lake.* When the bike puttered to a stop, Síle got off dizzy and sore. "Forty-five minutes, and not a word out of my mouth," she remarked.

"At last I've found a way to shut you up!"

Síle swam in her silk knickers (well, it was a Monday, so there weren't many people about); in the high waves they played tourist and shark. Though it was Síle who should have been jet-lagged, back on shore it was Jude who fell asleep, head pillowed on her jacket. Síle wandered down to the waterline to look for colourful stones, like a child. She looked back over her shoulder at Jude, curled up in the shady lee of a dune; she could see her better from here, glimpse her entire. You could say that much for distance, it sharpened the image. She was with Jude so rarely that when she was, every cell of her body rang with grateful knowledge of it. And a tinge of resentment, too, she registered. Like that of someone starving who was offered only a morsel to eat.

After a while Jude woke up and tried to teach Síle to whistle through grass. Jude's sounds were like plaintive curlews, Síle's like retching gulls. The two of them lay on their backs and stared up at the sky, clouds scudding by.

"I remember being seven, walking behind my parents, down this sunny hill in West Cork," Síle remarked. "I started running, and suddenly I couldn't stop; I was heading straight for the edge and I hadn't the breath to shout."

"What happened?"

"Amma turned her head and saw me hurtling down; she grabbed Dad's hand and they got in front of me, they caught me in their net. I was five feet from the cliff, I swear. That's what I think of when I hear the word love: that feeling of being caught, all the breath knocked out of your body."

"Wow," murmured Jude after a minute, "what a memory!"

"The only problem," said Síle, "is that she died when I was three."

Jude frowned. "So maybe it's a memory of being three, not seven?"

"But we only went to West Cork the summer I was seven. It happened all right, Dad says I did nearly run off the cliff, only it was him and some German tourist he was chatting to who saved me. I must have written my mother into the film, afterwards, and now I can't remember it any other way."

They lay silently for a while. "What was it your father said the Sanskrit word for 'world' meant?" Jude asked.

"That which moves," Síle supplied. "That which changes."

"That which never stands still for a damn second."

Síle watched the surf rush in. She'd never known that lakes could have waves. "Did you know that every maritime culture comes up with its own selkie story?"

"What's selkie?"

Síle tried to remember what the word meant. "Half seal, I think, and half woman."

"Like a mermaid?"

"Mm. The man lures her out of the sea and hides her sealskin or comb or whatever—she's sort of tamed, has kids with him—"

"Oh, I know that one. Some day she finds her things and gets overwhelmed by the longing to go back," said Jude, nodding. "Like your Oisín in the Land of Youth. So the poor jerk comes home to find wife and kids have disappeared into the sea."

"My sympathies were always with the selkie," said Síle with a grin. "If you've gotta go..."

They ate local perch outside Casey's Clam Shack. On the ride home, pinky-orange forks fractured the sky; flashes lit up the whole flat landscape. Síle tried to remember if any of Rizla's warnings had pertained to lightning storms. Did lightning like to strike motorbikes, because they were made of metal, or avoid them, because of the rubber tires? She felt disjointed, and thrilled, and safe.

The rain held off till they were back in the house. "It always seems to rain when we're in bed," Síle remarked, throwing aside the pillow. "Of course, there haven't been that many nights yet."

"This is the sixth," said Jude.

She sounded amazed, Síle thought. That there'd been so few, or that they'd been granted so many? On this trip there'd be five more, she calculated; that made eleven. She caught herself wondering how many nights they'd get to sleep together, in total. She thought she might cry, but she went to sleep instead.

Geography Lessons

Ye Gods!
annihilate but space and time,
And make two lovers happy.

—"Martinus Scriblerus"
[Alexander Pope]
Peri Bathous: or,
The Art of Sinking in Poetry

Re: death in the skies
    Jude, you say "high-risk job" as if I'm an
astronaut! You realize your dread of my being in a
crash is just a metaphor for my discarding you the
first time Sigourney Weaver's name turns up on my
manifest? Seriously, sweetheart, it's not cabin crew
but pedestrians and cyclists who have the highest
rate of accidents.
    But it does get on my tits when people (I
suppose I mean Americans) go on about their fear
of flying "these days." Did they kid themselves that
the world was a cozy place before 9/11? Even leaving
terrorists aside, big machines can always get into
big trouble. A duck can dent a plane's windshield,
and aviation's greatest loss of life happened on
the ground (Tenerife, 1977) when two jets ran into
each other.
    Oh dear, I've wandered from the point, which was
to reassure you about my personal safety...

Re: missing you

By now I've acquired quite a good collection
(fonds, as we say in the trade): framed photos, a
file of letters and e-mails, a lipstick called
Bruised Fruit you left here in July...But somehow
documentation and artifacts aren't doing it for me,
Síle.

Here's your quote for the day. This one's from a
woman called Catherine Talbot to one called Elizabeth
Carter, back in the days (1744) when women who fell
for each other had to stay at home with Mamma and
write a lot of letters...Anyway, here goes:

We must be content with loving and esteeming
people constantly and affectionately amid a
variety of thwarting, awkward circumstances,
that forbid all possibility of spending our
lives together.

I was babysitting Lia last night so Cassie and
Anneka could go to bed--anyway, she said a whole
sentence that I'd swear was Japanese. Cassie told me
something interesting, that language is a side effect
of love. Apparently hunger or tiredness wouldn't be
enough to motivate Lia to learn to speak, because she
could just gesture or cry. It turns out that language
is pure fun, a game played with those you love.

Of course, from my current point of view language
is looking like a side effect of loss. I guess
absence makes the heart grow louder. Writing to you
reminds me that you're far away, but it also throws
a kind of bridge across the abyss. It's a sad fact,
couples who spend blissful lives together don't leave
much trace in the archives. Whereas a love letter
will outlive us both, if printed on acid-free paper
and kept in a dry place.

Síle was down in Leitrim, recuperating after seeing nine films in
three days at the Dublin queer film fest. Lying in Marcus's meadow,

she smelled honeysuckle and cowpat on the August breeze. She could still taste the home-grown raspberries and white currants he'd served up for dessert. "So here's the latest," she told him: "The airline is in dire straits and wants to ax *another* thirteen hundred of us. They've proposed a voluntary severance scheme—"

"Sounds like slitting your own throat," observed Marcus.

"Doesn't it!"

"I have news too," he said, going up on one elbow. "Brace yourself."

"What? You're pregnant?" she asked.

"Ha ha. Pedro's moving in."

"In where? In here, into your ruin?"

"The indoor toilet now has cold *and* hot water, and the bats have been banished. It's an eighteenth-century farmhouse with a view of Lough Allen and rock stars would kill to own it."

"But…" *But you've only been together since April,* Síle wanted to say. As if that were the measure of anything. As if it weren't possible to be entirely serious about someone before you even got to kiss her.

"The thing is," said Marcus, "the drive is hell, and weekends aren't enough for us anymore."

"Well I never," Síle said, playing for time. She thought of what it would be like to see Jude every weekend, as easy as hopping into her car.

"And besides, the rent's shooting up in his flat in Temple Bar. This psychic he met said his life's at a fork in the road."

Síle couldn't help rolling her eyes. "Since when have you believed any of that guff?"

"Whatever works on Pedro," said Marcus with a grin. "So he's persuaded his boss to let him work from home. We're going to finish the solarium, maybe add an extension if we can get permission."

"And make mad, passionate love among the nettles."

"Hourly." After a few seconds, his smile faded. "You don't get it, do you?"

"I do! Sort of."

"I thought, because of your Jude woman…"

Oh, Síle understood that love could come up behind you and grab you by the throat, all right. She understood about no amount of time together being enough, when the heart was a hole that couldn't be filled. "I do," she repeated weakly. It was true, so why this vague dread, this cynicism? "It just seems sudden."

He shrugged. "When you're ready, you're ready."

Her friend never used to make such meaningless remarks, Síle thought. "What if all the wild romance gets stifled by domesticity?" She was afraid that might have come out sounding malicious, but Marcus only laughed. There was grass embedded in his shirt; she'd never seen him look so handsome. "Oh sweetie," she said, "I do wish you luck."

"They were only living a four-hour drive apart anyway," Síle told Jude on the phone; "geography's never been a major problem for them the way it is for us."

"Is it?" A pause. "I mean, sometimes I think it's part of what attracts us," said Jude.

The notion took Síle aback. "Well, we're not the girls next door, that's for sure," she conceded. "Do you mean we wouldn't actually like living together?"

"No no. But it would be a whole new dynamic," said Jude. "Right now, my pulse starts hammering the second I hear your voice."

Síle smiled at the wall. After a second, she went on: "So Marcus and Pedro are having their wedding in the cow pasture on the thirtieth—"

"Oh? I didn't think it was legal in Ireland yet."

"It isn't; this is a *ritual of handfasting,* or so says the invitation."

"I didn't know Marcus was a pagan," said Jude.

"It's Pedro's shtick," Síle told her. "Apparently he goes off on camping trips with the Radical Faeries, and Marcus is so besotted he'll plight his troth in any language. Anyway, you have to come."

"But I've only met them once—"

"Not for them, you thick, for me! Weddings bring me out in a rash. So I hope it's okay but I've booked you a flight to Dublin the day before."

A silence. "Darlin', you can't do this."

"I already have," said Síle, hoping she sounded masterful rather than childish. "Don't worry, it was an amazing Web bargain," she lied. "Besides, how often do you get to take part in a pagan ritual in a Neolithic stone circle?"

"Oh, right, play the Ancient History card!" Jude's sternness sounded like it was easing off. "And what about the fact that I used up all my vacation days lolling in the porch swing with you last month?"

"Aha, well your ticket was so dirt cheap—only ninety-nine euro," Síle improvised— "that you can take a week of unpaid leave and I'll top up your salary."

"Don't push your luck," Jude told her, but she sounded like she was smiling.

Unfortunately, Síle had managed to forget that airlines always e-mailed the passenger a full receipt. Which in this case included the line "Total charged to credit card Ms. Síle S. O'Shaughnessy, €803.92."

When she answered the phone, she made the mistake of using the phrase "little white lie."

Jude said she didn't care for lies of any colour.

Síle told her she was a poker-arsed prig. "It cost me no more than a couple of pairs of good shoes, and god knows I don't need any more shoes."

"I just prefer to pay my way," said Jude.

Síle could feel her temper bubble up. She was tired; she needed a cup of strong chai and some satellite television. "Yeah, well I just prefer to see you once in a while."

"You should have asked me, instead of tricking me into it. You're older, and a lot wealthier," Jude went on before Síle could answer, "and sometimes I feel like I've been sucked into your orbit, and I'm swirling round like a rag doll."

"That's ridiculous," snapped Síle. "You're so rooted to the spot, it would take a tornado to dislodge you."

"I'm just saying—"

"It's stubbornness and pride, that's all. Now would you please accept the bloody ticket before you make me cry?"

Síle's little BMW was ailing at the garage, so she accepted a lift to Leitrim with Jael's family. She and Jude sat in the back beside Yseult, who was watching *The Incredibles*.

She found it endearing how enthralled Jude was by everything old. When they passed the sign for the Hill of Tara (STONE AGE TOMB, IRON AGE FORT, SEAT OF THE HIGH KINGS OF IRELAND) Jude asked if they could stop, but Jael snapped, "We're not even past Navan yet, we've got half a lifetime to go."

"In her village, the oldest surviving building's what, 1830s?" Síle put in.

"Eighteen forty-seven," said Jude, "ever since the McPhee homestead burned down."

Anton snorted. "I grew up in a 1780s house, and there was nothing glamorous about it. Spidery high ceilings and a dank basement kitchen."

"There were five great paved roads in early Ireland," Síle told Jude, "and one of them went from here—the Hill of Tara—all the way south to the monastic site of Glendalough in Wicklow, and the bit that passes through Dublin is called *stone road*—Stoneybatter!"

"Did you dig that up just to impress me?" asked Jude.

"She did of course," said Jael over her shoulder.

"Googled it when I was bored in the crew lounge in Boston last week," Síle admitted.

Somehow they got onto the subject of border crossings. Jael's worst had been in Seattle. "This balding prick takes a glance at my well-stamped passport and grunts, 'How come you can afford to travel so much?' So I look him in the eye and say, 'Because I have a better job than you.'"

Síle squealed.

"What a prime bitch!" murmured Anton to Jude appreciatively. "Isn't she just the most almighty bitch you ever met?"

"Uh—" Jude began.

"It's all right to say yes," put in Síle. "He likes her that way."

"What do you mean, likes?" demanded Jael, changing lanes too fast. "Adores!"

Yseult pushed back her headphones. "I'm going to be a prime bitch when I grow up."

"Of course you are, pet," Jael told the child, meeting her eyes in the rearview mirror. "The primest."

"But Ys, remember our little chat about only using words like that at home?" Anton asked his daughter.

"Duh," groaned Yseult, and pulled her headphones back on.

"So what did the immigration guy say to that?" Síle asked Jael.

"Not a word."

"But he must have punished her by scrawling something mysterious on our customs form," said Anton. "We got pulled over and they went through our dirty underpants."

"Which must have been worse for them than for us," said Jael magnanimously.

Jude spoke up in her husky voice. "My friend Gwen grew up in Windsor where you drive over the bridge just to go to the Detroit malls, but her mom escaped from the Nazis as a child, so whenever she had to cross the border she had a panic attack."

"No!" said Anton.

"So of course the Americans would get suspicious, yank her out of line to interrogate her in a back room…"

"Borders are a bugger," said Síle. "I think they should all be done away with."

"It'll never happen," said Jude. "The human mind needs boundaries. Without them it would fall in on itself, like a crushed honeycomb."

There was a brief silence.

"Jaysus, that's a bit fucking deep for nine in the morning on the N3," murmured Jael.

They all roared with laughter, including Jude. "Sorry, blame the jet lag."

"No no. You have to remember, at twenty-five you have about twice as many brain cells left as the rest of us," Anton told her.

Yseult yanked her headphones down again. "Haven't I the most, though, Dad? Haven't I about ten millions of times as many brain cells as you and Mum?"

"Oh, go on, rub it in."

"No, Jude's right about boundaries, though," Jael muttered as she sped up to get around an ailing truck. "Take the whole straight-slash-queer thing."

"Yeah," said Jude, "society tries to bully everyone into one camp or another."

"Who slashed who?" Yseult wanted to know.

"It's just a punctuation mark," her father told her. "Are you watching that film or not?"

"And god help you if you fancy a trip across that border," Jael complained, grinning at Jude, "with a few duty-free goods in your bag!"

After Cavan the roads were bad, but the views got better. They reached Marcus's by noon. The yard was full of cars already, so Jael parked behind the old pigpen with a rattle of gravel. "It's even worse than the photos."

"I think it's gorgeous, in a mouldering-pile sort of way," Síle told her.

Yseult writhed and plucked at her seat belt. "Off, off!" Jude pressed the button for her, but the girl said "No, I'll do it," shoving the Canadian's hand out of the way, and clicked the seat belt back into place so she could open it again.

Brat, Síle mouthed with a silent grin.

"I see no balloons," remarked Anton.

Jael had a quick cigarette while applying more brownish lipstick in the mirror. "Maybe there's been a lovers' tiff and it's all off."

"Balloons wouldn't be very pagan, would they?" Síle pointed out.

Jude came back and opened Síle's door for her. "There's a big bonfire in the field behind the house, and people in rainbow robes."

"Spare us," hissed Jael, taking two long drags on her cigarette before grinding it into the gravel. "The champagne better be excellent."

There was only mead, passed around in big horns. Síle managed to splash some on the collar of her orange silk tunic, and had to nip into the house to rinse it out before it attracted wasps. "I thought you were luring me away for nefarious purposes," murmured Jude, "not to help with your laundry."

"Oh, I wish," said Síle, relaxing into her arms. "I just don't buy this."

Jude frowned in puzzlement.

"The notion that Marcus and Pedro will stay together a day longer because they've exchanged garlands and vows. It's bollocks, the whole till-death-do-us-part thing."

Jude shrugged. "The Petersons next door to me have been happily married for nearly sixty years."

"Of course it sometimes happens to happen," conceded Síle, "though who can tell from the outside who's *really* happy? But what I mean is, it's not the wedding that glues you together."

"That's true. It sure didn't work for me and Rizla," Jude admitted.

Síle grinned at her. "I'd rather a lover than a wife."

"Why, because the word has a better ring to it?"

"Because then it's a choice, not a promise. *One day at a time,* as the alcos say," she added drily.

The afternoon had that end-of-summer tint, and the ceremony was oddly moving, despite the fact that men in robes always made Síle think of *Monty Python's Life of Brian.* Pedro and Marcus looked stunning in matching white linen as they jumped the broom together. Síle got to throw a basket of mint leaves and rose petals over their heads.

"What are Quaker weddings like?" she whispered to Jude.

"Guess."

"Silent?" Somehow they started giggling and couldn't stop; Síle blamed the mead, which had quite a kick to it.

By the time the banquet was served—by girls in garlands, on unsteady trestles set up in the meadow—the guests were raucous. A small black sheep wandered past, bleating. Síle and Jude got talking to the neighbours who ran an organic farm; Síle couldn't for the life of her remember their names. They had a daughter who was studying economics in Galway.

"Is she one of these lovely damsels in daisy chains?"

"Oh no, they're from an agency," Mr. Organic assured her. "We're the only locals here. No, Marcus gets on grand in this community, but nothing's spelled out, you know?"

"You mean—"

Mrs. Organic's laugh had a drunken edge to it. "Everyone knows he and Pedro are bent as forks, and that's no bother, but they'd rather not receive a wedding invitation!"

Jude was nodding. "Some bits of rural Canada can be like that."

The husband talked about two men he knew who'd been holding hands on a beach in Sligo when some teenagers threw stones at them. "Like something out of Leviticus!"

Síle gave a theatrical shudder. "It all goes to show that queers should head for the biggest city they know and stay there."

"Oh come on, that's such a cliché. Bad things happen in cities too." Jude spoke sharply. "To me it's more important to be able to see the sun rise without a hundred skyscrapers in the way than to be able to buy a skim-double-latte from some tattooed transman."

"Different strokes," said Síle with a little laugh that sounded affected even to her.

"What's a transman?" Mrs. Organic wanted to know.

Marcus had been hovering on the edge of the group, and now he stepped in. "Dublin should suit you, then, Jude. Nary a skyscraper and very few tattooed transmen, either."

"Ah, but could she afford the skim-double-lattes, at Dublin prices?" asked Mr. Organic.

"Who can!" said Síle pleasantly, her eyes searching for her lover's. Why had she been so stupid as to bring up their perpetual argument?

Mrs. Organic was congratulating the bridegroom.

"Apart from a slight mead headache, I'm having a ball," Marcus assured her.

Later on there was dancing under the full moon: to Latin rhythms, rather than pan pipes, which was a relief to most of the guests. Jude insisted Síle dance one slow number with her, holding her very tight and moving Síle's hips on the beat. Jael drove her lot off to stay in the most luxurious B&B in County Leitrim, but Síle and Jude ended up on a single mattress in Pedro's office, a barely renovated hen house. Saying good night, he kept kissing Jude on both cheeks and exclaiming over the present she'd brought them, a photo of two bachelor farmers in Waterloo County, Ontario, in a frame she'd made herself out of a cedar shake. "Circa 1873, maybe as late as '76," she said scrupulously. "I liked the way they're leaning on the same pitchfork."

"Which shoved my overpriced glass fruit bowl rather into the shade," complained Síle as they were going to sleep.

Jude set her teeth against Síle's nape and breathed hotly.

"Are we all right, then? I really must stop being rude about rural life."

"You never will," said Jude, kissing each vertebra in her neck. "I guess it's good that we can quarrel; it shows we're not on best behaviour anymore."

"Oh, great. Next we'll be cutting our toenails in bed and farting in the bath."

They shook with laughter.

The next morning, Síle asked Jael if they could take the N4 because Jude wanted to see the bit of Roscommon that Síle's branch of the O'Shaughnessys were from. Jael and family stayed in the car, which pleased Síle. She and Jude walked up to the small lake and stared at its glassy darkness. Clouds scuttled off, and the sky was suddenly the blue of a baby's vein. The clover smelled sweet where their feet had bruised it. "My great-granda used to earn his living rowing Yanks round this lake," Síle told her, "till one night he took a big boatful out and they all drowned."

"No!"

"Apparently he was stocious—drunk," she glossed. "That's the house where Da grew up, the one behind that big granite erratic," she said, pointing down toward the village.

"So he's a hick like me, then."

Síle laughed. "We came down to see Granny and Granda every month or so. We were here the weekend our Amma died."

Jude slid her hand into Síle's. "I was telling Gwen about it, she wanted to know: Was it hypo or hyper?"

"Hypo," Síle told her. "They never found out why she slipped into a coma, but low blood sugar can come on really fast—confusion, tremors, convulsions...I found one site that said sometimes if you've had diabetes for years you stop noticing the danger signs. That's the real tragedy of it—if she'd drunk a glass of orange juice it would have saved her. Or an injection of glucose might have, if we'd even got home a bit earlier that Sunday and rung an ambulance in time."

"Oh, lord. I hope your dad doesn't blame himself?" Jude added after a minute.

Síle shrugged. "No idea. He's happy to talk about her, but not about the death. I think it took ten days till he switched off her life-support. Anyway!" She pointed down the hill again. "The rock's known as Diarmaid and Gráinne's Bed, but I should warn you, so is every flat-topped stone or dolmen from here to Kerry."

"Who are Diarmaid—"

"Oh, this is a good story for a wedding weekend! Remember Fionn Mac Cumhaill?"

"Oisín's dad?" said Jude.

"Very good. Well, Gráinne the High King's daughter was supposed to marry old Fionn, but during the bridal feast at the Hill of Tara she ran away with one of his young followers, Diarmaid. So he rounded up the Fianna, and they hunted the pair all over Ireland. Diarmaid and Gráinne could never sleep two nights in the same place."

Jude smiled. "Rechabites! So did it end in disaster?"

"Ah, they had a good run of it—sixteen years," Síle told her, "then Diarmaid got gored by a wild boar and she had to marry Fionn after all."

They turned down the hill toward the car.

"Come for a fortnight, next time, and we can do a proper Magical History Tour."

"I'd love that."

Síle's pulse was thumping in her throat. "Better yet, come for good."

Jude didn't answer. She turned her light eyes on Síle's.

Síle forced a smile. "I know you imagine it'd choke you to move townships, let alone continents."

"It's not that," said Jude carefully. "But I don't think I'd know myself in Dublin."

"Stoneybatter's a sort of village—"

"Inside a city. And I'd be an unemployed, disoriented foreigner, waiting four days at a stretch for you to come home."

No you wouldn't, Síle protested in her head, but what was the point?

"I'm flattered. And touched."

This didn't mollify Síle. *Damn, damn,* why couldn't she have kept her mouth shut till she had a strong case prepared? Now there was a big, raw crack in the ground that they'd have to edge around for the rest of the visit.

Yseult was lying down on the backseat. "I'm bored, is there anything to eat?" she asked, rising with a yawn as they climbed in.

"Did you know snails sleep for up to three years?" Jude asked her.

A cold look. "You can't fool me, I'm eight now."

Heavy Weather

> The heart may think it knows better: the
> senses know that absence blots people
> out. We have really no absent friends.

> —Elizabeth Bowen

Re: Diarmaid and Gráinne

   Only early October, and all the leaves have
fallen off the cherry tree in front of my house.

   In my nephews' *Treasury of Irish Legends* I was
checking out the tale of the lovers on the run,
Jude, and I'd forgotten this great piece of advice
someone gives them:

> Never enter a cave that has only one opening;
> and never land on an island that has only one
> harbour; and where you cook your food there
> eat it not; and where you eat, sleep not
> there; and where you sleep tonight, sleep not
> there tomorrow night.

Ring me today?

Re: cave

   My cave has got several openings, lovely Síle,
and you can take your pick.

   I think I'm in withdrawal. I can't sleep, not
hungry, sit in the museum breathing in dust and
talking to you in my head. It seems to get harder
after each visit, curiously enough. This is
definitely worse than giving up the smokes...

Re: dating

   I know, I know, after we say good-bye it's like
some awful lurching gear change, and then as the
weeks go by the car gradually grinds to a halt. The
ground staff coordinator mentioned she'd heard I was
"dating some woman in Canada." It struck me not only
as one of the many Americanisms sneaking into
Hiberno-English (Da would say "doing a line with," I
grew up with "going out with"), but what a strange
concept, "dating," like something they do to
Phoenician ruins . . .

Re: re: dating

   Maybe it's the right word for it, though, Síle,
because don't we live by dates these days? I know
without having to check my "Black Ontario History"
calendar that it's been thirty-four days since you
waved at the cab taking me away down Stoneybatter.
What I don't know is how long it'll be till your
next flying visit to my side of the world.

   Hm, that's a glum opener, let's try again . . .

   I guess your sister may be right that we're
making--what's that great phrase she used?--"heavy
weather" of the distance between us. We're certainly
luckier than many couples. Gwen works with a care
assistant from Uzbekistan who only gets to see her
husband about every two years. I keep reminding
myself that in the days before cheap(ish) air travel,
you and I would have been sunk. This thing between
us depends entirely on those big noisy tin tubes in
the sky I so dislike. In the old days, letters were
the only lifeline, and they were always going astray.
My archive is full of migrant workers who rarely saw
their families, wives emigrating to join husbands but
dying on the ship, men who went off to the Gold Rush
and lost touch . . .

This was certainly the oddest year of Jude's life. It was hard to pace
herself, that was all. She didn't know when she'd be able to climb

into Síle's nut-brown arms again, dropping the rock of absence. Between trainings and meetings, chiropractic appointments and kids' birthday parties, the two of them couldn't seem to find three days when their schedules allowed for a visit. Their next reunion shifted like an oasis on the horizon, and Jude couldn't plot her course. She trudged through her days, haunted by the feeling that real life was happening five thousand kilometres away.

Doing the time zone tango, that's what Síle called it, *and you know how awful a dancer I am!* Jude pictured the two of them thumping across a vast ballroom, joined at the shoulders and hands, heads cricked to the side. It was a peculiar dance, the tango; a desperate yoking.

"That must be such fun," people said when Jude told them she was seeing a woman on the other side of the Atlantic, and she never knew what to say: Sort of? Sometimes? Less fun, now the gaiety of the first few months was sobering, but more necessary. What stratagems and devices, what compromises and deals would it take for her and Síle to last? The thought of another year of e-mailing, phoning, and waiting—let alone twenty—made Jude queasy.

Every time she went over it again in her head, she felt bad about the curt way she'd rejected Síle's suggestion on that hillside in Roscommon. Yet what else could she have said, without misleading the woman? Something Jude had always known about herself was that she wasn't the emigrating kind, not like her schoolfriends who'd ended up in Ohio, Amsterdam, or the United Arab Emirates. And for all the good times she'd had in Dublin on both her visits, the noisy capital of a foreign country wasn't somewhere Jude could ever feel at home. Trips were different, she argued in her head; the whole point of a vacation was that it was an exception to the rules. Jude could snort cocaine or Síle could snooze in a porch swing: They were just playing at sharing each other's lifestyles.

Jude had fantasized about Síle moving to Canada, of course she had, though to ask it aloud would only be to embarrass herself. At least Dublin had a certain slapdash glamour; what could Ireland, Ontario, hold for Síle Sunita O'Shaughnessy? Jude let herself imagine Síle in the house on Main Street only briefly. Like the way some women dreamed about being pregnant, she supposed. It was just the contrary heart wondering if it could have it both ways, live more lives than one.

"I guess you and I are just rooted kind of people," she said to Gwen as they pushed their way along the forest path through the lush overgrowth of early fall.

Gwen snorted.

"Wouldn't you say?"

"Sometimes it feels more like trapped," said her friend, slapping a leaf off her sweaty cheek. "If I met some god from Paraguay, I might just go there."

"You would not."

"I might."

"The thing about your situation..." Jude didn't know quite what she meant to say.

"It's a trap in itself," Gwen said drolly. "I might as well be on the other side of the planet from Luke, some days. I sit around biting my cuticles, wishing I could call him without his wife picking up."

"Oh, Gwen."

A shrug. "He's a nice guy."

"Nice enough?"

"You take what you can get."

Did this mean Luke Randall, out of all the men available for affairs in this corner of southwestern Ontario, or Gwen's meagre share of him? Jude didn't ask; it was too sad either way.

"My point is, you and Síle should quit bitching and moaning. There's nothing keeping you apart except for an ocean," said Gwen. "You can dial her number and talk to her anytime you like, say whatever comes into your head. You can see each other every month or so without anyone standing in your way."

"I guess so," said Jude grimly. It was like wanting ice cream instead of meat loaf, and being told that children in refugee camps would be grateful for the meat loaf. Yes, of course she had nothing to complain about, compared to so many people, but when had that ever stopped anyone from complaining? Happiness was a balloon that always hovered just out of arm's reach.

Work helped, some. For the next month, Jude would be organizing the third annual 1867 Day, which took place on the second of November, All Souls. She had to wangle loans of period clothing from the costume workshop at the Stratford Festival, argue with the insurance company about covering the children's haystack climb, and track down a replacement for the blacksmith who'd succumbed to carpal tunnel.

"I'll really try to make it down this year," said Estelle, her old boss from the Pioneer Museum, on the phone. "You've done wonderful things with that little schoolhouse."

"I have, haven't I?" said Jude, laughing at her own cockiness. "And now we've got a good shot at substantial funding from the same foundation."

"But you know, if you ever wanted to stretch your wings, there are some interesting opportunities in Toronto—"

"I thought it was all cuts, cuts, cuts?"

"True, but there are two retirements coming up in a special regional collection that just so happens to be run by a good friend of mine…"

"Thanks for thinking of me, Estelle, but I've got big plans for my little museum," Jude told her.

That afternoon she borrowed Rizla's pickup to bring a slightly rusty Dominion Cheese Company churn down to a museum in London, Ontario; it was just too big for her to display. In return, the curator gave her a copy of a clipping from the *London Free Press* of January 9, 1883, headed "Ireland Ont. Farmer Stabbed in Market Day Brawl, Liquor to Blame."

Jude found herself reluctant to start the drive back. In the city's handsome covered market she found a café called The Little Red Roaster, and sipped Fair Trade Organic Sumatran from a tall blue mug. She thought even Síle would call this a good cup of coffee. She was quite enjoying the energy of the surging, chattering shoppers. She shut her eyes and pictured the building in 1883, full of liquored-up, brawling farmers.

At the next table, below a spindly coffee tree in a pot, a young woman with jaw-length brown hair was deep in conversation with a boy of six or seven. Her son, he had to be, he had the same dark-eyed charm; she must have had him very young, thought Jude, watching out of the corner of her eye, pretending to read a pamphlet about Falun Gong. They were talking like friends; there was none of that "now let's wipe our mouth" stuff. Suddenly the woman burst out laughing at something the boy said, and the flash of teeth transformed her face. He dropped his muffin on her folder, glugged his milk, then jumped onto her lap, and she wrapped her arms around him. Jude angled toward them unobtrusively, catching a few lines of a conversation that was either about a bush or George W. Bush, she wasn't sure. She glanced at the pages sliding out of the folder; an essay headed (ah, her radar was working)

Yana Petronis
"Bad Little Sisters: A Case Study of Cross-Border Censorship"
Women's Studies 253 (Lesbian Issues)

Time to head home. Jude tried to catch the young woman's eye for a quick smile but didn't manage it.

As the sprawl of new subdivisions gave way to open fields, she found herself imagining another life. A no-distance-at-all relationship. You met your girlfriend at the market, saw her again at dinner, slept a hairsbreadth apart all night. A life measured in minutes and hours, instead of weeks and months; plans wouldn't need to stretch any farther than tomorrow's bike ride or Saturday's music festival. Not necessarily perfect, but made up of one fresh day at a time.

But why had this never happened to Jude, in the years between leaving Rizla and meeting Síle? Why, despite all her *genital encounters,* hadn't she fallen hard for someone local? Look at it pragmatically: There was probably someone in every town whom Jude could love, who could love Jude. What perversity had made her fixate on a foreigner instead? Why was she sweating out her heart for a faraway woman when no doubt there were people just as intriguing, all around her? It was like some sinister fairy tale in which the prince fell into a decline: *I long for the fruit of the tree at the end of the world. Nothing but that fruit will satisfy my thirst: only its juice can save me.*

THINK GLOBAL, BUY LOCAL said an ad in the window of the general store as Jude drove into Ireland, and she gritted her teeth.

```
Re: Keeping Busy
     Today I was in London--yup, another place named
by lonely emigrants. They have this weird 1826
miniature castle that was the courthouse and jail, it
turns out it's a copy of Malahide Castle near Dublin.
(Take me next time?) Before anyone had actually
settled in London, there was a public execution that
folks came from all over Upper Canada to see. The
rope broke, so they had to string the guy up again,
and the worst thing is that he was Francophone, but
his confession's in perfect English, which suggests
he was framed...
     In the market I saw a woman in a café and thought,
why can't I love someone like her instead of you?
```

On second thought—Jude highlighted that sentence and hit *Delete.* There were things you could chance face to face, but e-mail was a blunt medium.

One day without a call from Síle was okay-ish; two days were lonely; three days of silence led to paranoid thoughts. (*She's pissed at me, I've slipped her mind, she's got better things to do.*) Jude was fighting to keep her overdraft the right side of $5,000, and the sight of an envelope with Bell Canada on it made her stomach knot. Síle kept telling her to set up a line of credit backed by the house, but Jude could just picture her mother's pursed lips. "It's not borrowing," Síle insisted, "it's just liquidating a little bit of an asset." For lovers who'd slept together for a grand total of fifteen nights, it occurred to Jude, they spent a ridiculous amount of time discussing money.

"Sounds like marriage," Rizla sniggered, over a hot dog at the Garage.

Jude didn't rise to the bait. "I was thinking of selling the Triumph. The insurance just went up again, they're killing me. I might be better off downsizing to an eight-fifty cc, seven-fifty, even."

Rizla was goggle-eyed. "Man, she's got you by the balls."

"It's not Síle's idea," she snapped.

"The bike's a freaking family heirloom. What would your uncle say if you flogged it to some Toronto lawyer to pay your phone bill? Here's the line in the sand," he went on, his finger scoring in the air. "You're a biker with a vintage Triumph, you don't cash that in. Geez, sell the house first."

Jude was aware of a certain relief. "Dumb idea, I guess. I just... I really need to see Síle. She's been sounding exhausted; she's on this heavy rotation to New York and L.A. I wish I could be there when she gets home, making her some risotto."

"Why can't she make herself some risotto?"

Jude shook her head. "It's too slow; she always turns up the heat and burns it."

He chewed one broad, leathery thumb. "If gals can't cook, you might as well have stuck with guys."

She fixed him with a look.

"Hush up, now, Richard," he scolded himself, "your little friend's got *luuuuve* problems."

"Love isn't a problem, geography is."

"But geography wouldn't be a problem if you weren't in love, right? I mean, I live thousands of clicks from Céline Dion but that's fine by me."

"Okay, so it's the intersection of love and geography." It sounded to Jude like a surreal street address. "The what and who and why are easy, it's just the when and where."

"And the how much," he laughed, reaching for their bill.

Jude picked up a napkin to dab ketchup off his chin. "It isn't that Síle would want me to give up the bike," she insisted. "She'd rather pay for everything herself."

Rizla threw up his hands. "Shit, forget the cooking, then: If I had a sugar mommy, I'd lay back and take it."

Jude rolled her eyes.

"She's something else, that gal," said Rizla with a grin. "When she was over in July, the way she shut Gwen up!"

Well, if that was how he chose to remember the incident—

"But you'd better face it," he said mildly, "it's only ever going to be a vacation thing."

Jude stared at him.

"You've hooked the big fish, and she's a beaut all right, but you're never going to land her."

"You don't know that." Why were her own thoughts so unbearable when he spoke them? "Why would you say that?"

His mouth twisted with something like compassion. "Who's going to be the mountain and who's going to be Muhammad? It's not going to happen."

"It could, theoretically!"

"Well, so could me becoming the next Dalai Lama," said Rizla. "Tell you what, let's put some money on it. Let's say, if you and the lovely lady are shacked up together anywhere in the known universe in, what, two years, I'll pay you...the cost of our divorce," he finished with a grin.

"You think you're funny, but you're just mean." Jude's voice was ragged.

"Hey, no skin off my fat ass, either way—"

She shoved back her chair and walked out, and only halfway down the street did she remember she hadn't paid for her hot dog.

Síle stood demonstrating the nearest exits with smooth fluting hand movements. She'd done this mime so often, she could have completed it with her eyes shut, only that might have alarmed the passengers. Then she strapped herself into the jump seat at the back, between two colleagues who were discussing the risks of rain for a January wedding. As the plane thrust away from the earth, Síle waited for the familiar rush in the stomach, the pure, sweet liftoff as gravity was shed.

But it didn't come. They were in the air and Síle didn't feel any bliss. Only a heavy craving not to move anymore, not to go anywhere anymore. She felt as if she'd suddenly forgotten how to have an orgasm.

That day passed in a blur of conversation, hatch-latching, rubbish-collecting, discreet yawning. Some days, this job was like working in a very cramped burger joint during an earthquake. The plastic food-handling gloves were making Síle's palms itch, but she refused to call it an allergy. *Jude, Jude, why aren't you here, in Seat 39D, grinning up at me?*

Sometimes, these days, when Síle felt the plane touch down she had no idea what country she was in. She woke up in hotels and stared at the ceiling in bewilderment. The aeronautical term was "losing situational awareness." In the privacy of her head she was thinking *Jude, Jude, how long,* like some cadence from the Psalms, though she knew the comparison was absurd. *How many visits can we manage without losing momentum, grinding to a stop? How far can this go?* Sacrilegious thought: She tried to remember whether she'd been more content in the old days, before she'd ever laid eyes on Jude Turner.

Cabin crews had all voted, last week, and the union had got its mandate to strike if the airline imposed the mass redundancies. But Síle could think of a few colleagues who were ready to go on any terms: Nuala, for one, and possibly Jenny. They'd all had it up to here with the tussles and changes—new short-haul routes every month, schedule snafus, ludicrous performance targets—and the only thing that seemed to stay frozen was their pay. And if the airline did manage to carve away another thousand-odd jobs on top of the two thousand already purged, Síle thought with a surge of anxiety, the survivors would have to work harder than ever.

"So it's all going great with Pedro, you lucky buggers?" she asked Marcus, speaking into her gizmo in the back of a taxi.

"Yeah, though we mostly talk about vegetables, these days," he said benignly. "No, your situation's much more romantic: the great lovers doomed to live separate, Heloise and Abelard and all that."

"Oh, well there's a comfort," she said, sardonic.

"Wasn't it Socrates who said we only really love what we lack?"

"You're disgustingly well-read, my boy."

"Actually I think I heard it on BBC2. But it is an interesting question: How far apart should lovers live?"

"The space of a kiss," she suggested.

"Well, sometimes, yeah, you need the amazing proximity of skin," Marcus agreed. "But at other times it's probably better to be farther apart than you can bear, so you can really see each other, realize what you want, what you're missing. Maybe it should be like muscles contracting and relaxing: near, far, together, apart."

"Yeah, that's what I thought at first, but I'm burning out. Just together would do me grand," said Síle, mulish, and then Marcus had to ring off because his mushroom consommé was boiling over.

Off-duty, Síle retreated from October rain into Polish film series or Crawford double bills. She loved that about films: They sucked you into their world so it didn't matter where your body was. You could walk into the most garish, blaring multiplex, or the grottiest old country cinema, and the film would still be the same. (Well, apart from that one time in Carlow town when it had slipped off the reel and got snagged.) When she tried to recall her life with Kathleen nowaday, that was what she saw: The two of them sitting side by side in a cinema, hands touching maybe, eyes on the screen. It was very strange, how little she missed Kathleen. It was like coming across old clothes neatly folded in a drawer, clothes that you couldn't remember yourself ever having worn.

Walking down Grafton Street, Síle was handed a flyer headed "Ireland of the Welcomes."

> Are you an immigrant or asylum-seeker? At our Drop-In Centre we can help you make the often difficult ajustment to life in Ireland today. Legal/medical/benefits advice, counseling, creche for under-fives, free refreshments (tea, coffee, soup).

Darkly amused that she'd been targeted, she made a note to tell Orla that whoever wrote her leaflets couldn't spell *adjustment.*

For the first time in her life, Síle would get into bed in the dark, bone tired, and find herself unable to sleep. She switched her gizmo's sound programme from white noise to forest calls, ocean surf to whale music, but nothing worked; the waterfalls track only made her need to get up and pee.

Síle had to have her Jude reservoir filled up, that was all that was the matter; she was feeling hollow and shaky. No matter how often they went over their schedules, they couldn't seem to find an opening for a visit. Like dancers who couldn't get in synch, lurching and stepping on each other's toes. *Fuel exhaustion,* that was the term; she remembered reading about a plane that, because of delay and communication problems at JFK, had simply run out of petrol and dropped out of the sky.

She put her tiny framed photo of Jude beside her bed, in every hotel, and nearly lost it once when it slipped behind a table. Absence in love turned you into an idolator. Síle's gold hung heavy on her throat, her ears.

"Excuse me. Excuse me, Miss? I rang my bell hours ago. My light won't come on..."

"I've got to sit with my fiancée. There's been a mistake, we were meant to be together, but this woman won't move..."

"Miss, Miss? My daughter says the film is in English in one of her ears and French in the other—"

"But how do you know she hasn't been sleeping with the Mohawk brave," asked Jael, "or somebody new, for that matter?"

Síle's purple sofa was so small, their curled-up stockinged feet touched. "She just isn't. Look, Jude and I talk about everything. That's all we have, is talk."

"The most eloquent love letters I ever got were from that ex-nun in Lisbon," Jael remembered, eyes on Síle's ceiling, which was strung with fairy lights. "They were so passionately written, so alive, they nearly burned my fingers. I even kept them, for a couple of years," she added, in her more usual tone.

"Sister Snake?" asked Síle, bristling at the comparison. "She borrowed money off you, infected you, then dumped you by postcard."

"Oh, Anton says I had it coming, karmically. The letters were deceptive, yeah," said Jael with a curious gentleness. "I think now that she meant every word of them, at the moment of writing. But yes, there was a lot she left out, including the younger girlfriend and the chlamydia. It's in the nature of letters to be selective. And e-mails," Jael added, before Síle could get a word in, "and texts, and phone calls, and whatever devices we use to keep in touch when we're not living the same life."

"Doesn't Jude seem honest to you?" demanded Síle.

"This isn't personal. Stop defending your true love and switch your brain back on for a minute."

"This is such bollocks," said Síle, the back of her head starting to ache. "Deception and distance are unrelated variables. Can't people who share a house tell lies too? In fact, maybe living together is so claustrophobic, it makes people hide things just to win themselves some breathing space." Síle wasn't sure she believed this, but she was provoked. "Marriage, even more so!"

Jael shrugged. "I don't know the stats. My only point is that correspondence has room for lies *built in*. It's inherently misleading. When you're writing to Jude, or on the phone, I bet you talk as if your whole life is given over to love."

Síle struggled for an answer.

"But then you say bye-bye, and you get on with things till the next time, don't you? Work and friends and shopping and coffee and smelling the roses. This is your busy-busy world and she's not in it." Jael's tone was almost vengeful. "You live on your own, and for all the romantic angst—this is your life, Síle, and you like it."

Síle looked away, as if examining the tiny bronze that stood in a niche in the wall.

"You're not—" Jael took her by the jaw. Síle slapped her away. "Have I made you cry?"

"Why, was that your goal for the evening?" she asked, standing up and wiping her cheekbones.

"Ah ducks. I'm a terrible killjoy," said Jael.

That was probably the nearest Síle would get to an apology. "I need to go to bed."

"Don't we all. I've to be up at the crack tomorrow to drive the fucking child to rehearsals; she's Dorothy in this forty-minute version of *The Wizard of Oz*." Jael couldn't hide the pride in her tone. Standing up with a slight wobble, she pulled on her trench coat. "Lunch next week?"

"Probably not. Busy-busy," said Síle meanly, holding the front door open. When she'd shut it behind Jael, she knelt to unplug the fairy lights.

Flying Visit

Time, you old gypsy man,
will you not stay?

—Ralph Hodgson
"Time, You Old Gypsy Man"

Every time Síle had bid for the Dublin-Heathrow-Detroit run that would have put her within a long bus ride of Jude, she'd lost to someone even more senior who had a sick sister in Michigan. But at last someone else agreed to swap with her for just one run, and from Detroit she hopped on a prop plane to Toronto for the afternoon.

The city hugged the lake like a glittering dress. Jude took a half-day off and rattled up the highway in her Mustang. They met at—Síle's choice—a vintage clothes shop in the heart of Kensington Market. "Wow, what a daring haircut!" she said, when she'd stopped kissing Jude long enough to take a proper look.

Jude rubbed the uneven pattern and laughed. "Last night my old clippers finally quit, halfway across my head."

"I like it," said Síle, pulling her close.

Toronto was full of Indian and Sri Lankan and Bangladeshi faces; it was the first time in years that she'd felt so visually unremarkable, and the effect was oddly relaxing. After half an hour wandering around tattoo parlours and Chinese greengrocers, Síle said, "Let's go to bed."

"I wish," said Jude.

"I've booked us a room for the afternoon."

"You haven't!" Jude's clear eyes looked very young.

At the Honeysuckle Arms, in the gay ghetto, Síle hung up the *Privacy, Please!* sign, and the world narrowed to a white square. The two of them were starving, sticky, worn out in the strong autumn sunshine that poured in through the *broderie anglaise* draperies of their antique tester bed.

"I have to go."

Jude kissed the naked inside of Síle's left elbow. "You only just came."

"Let go, badness. Really!"

"Honestly!" mimicked Jude softly. "Don't worry, in a little while we'll hail a cab; it'll get you to the airport in fifteen minutes, twenty max."

"What if there's traffic? Sweetheart, seriously, if I don't catch that short-hop flight I won't be at my plane in Detroit an hour before takeoff."

"It can't take a full hour to trundle the meal carts on."

"I do more than trundle carts..." But Síle was lost already, straying into bliss, her knees dropping her onto the quilt.

Afterward, when she was lying with her face pressed against Jude's delicate collarbone, she held her breath and stayed very still, as if playing hide-and-seek with time.

Jude said she would grab a sandwich, then find a barber to neaten up her head, after she put Síle—still buttoning up various parts of her emerald uniform—into a cab. She was a tiny waving figure in the back window. Síle immediately turned on her music and hit the Shuffle function, but between trying not to worry about being late and feeling her toes curl with remembered pleasure, she didn't hear much.

There was indeed traffic, lots of it; a three-car pileup had brought things to a standstill. It took an hour and ten minutes to get to Pearson Airport. Hurrying past a mirrored wall Síle caught sight of herself, cheeks glowing. The small plane that was to have taken her to Detroit was gone.

When she got through to the flight supervisor on her gizmo, he turned out to be a Corkman she'd never met. He barked at Síle on the line as if she were an escaped convict. "You've ruined the day for nearly three hundred passengers, and that's just this leg, not to mention the knock-on effects."

She bit her lip, tasted lipstick. *Síle, get a grip!*

"You're on Flight 592 tomorrow morning, that's if you manage to crawl out of bed."

In almost two decades in the job, this was the first time Síle had missed a flight. What had got into her? *Jude.* She wondered what the report sent to personnel in Dublin would say: *irresponsible, unprofessional, unacceptable?* This time it was all true.

She shut her eyes briefly as she walked. She was other things, too. She was beloved. She was succulent.

And if she moved fast enough, it occured to Síle now, she might even catch Jude at the barber's, and they could have a whole night together. Maybe their room at the Honeysuckle would still be free, the sheets not even changed...

If Jude weren't such a Luddite, of course, she'd be reachable by mobile, a sudden thought that filled Síle with rage. Still, surely she could track Jude down; no queer ghetto was that big. "Church and Wellesley," she said to the driver. The taxi shot along the road that looped between the city and the dark blue lake. Síle put her head back and thought of everything she hadn't had a chance to do to Jude yet. If she was going to be irresponsible, by god she'd enjoy herself.

There were two barbers and a hair salon on the block where Jude had waved good-bye. Síle popped her head into the first and said, "Excuse me, I'm looking for someone who might have been in for a cut in the last hour—a young woman, white, slim, short hair?"

The Italian gave a mirthless laugh, and Síle realized that she'd probably described half his clientele. She thought of trying to describe the ways in which Jude's slim-boned face was different from all the others, but she realized that lovers saw peculiarly.

Well, surely Jude would have lingered for a coffee before her long drive home? She talked loudly in her head: *Hang on, gorgeous. On my way.* The afternoon was warm, for all the pumpkin and cornstalk décor in shop windows, and the boys (and occasional girl) sitting in shorts on café steps with enormous iced lattes all seemed to glow with health. She passed a place that offered bubble tea: Would Jude be likely to go in there? Nah, too contemporary.

She should have planted a bug on her lover, slipped a microchip into the almost-grown-over hole in Jude's earlobe, so she'd be able to track her everywhere. What right had the girl to be out of Síle's reach? This was ridiculous; they couldn't miss each other entirely, not after she'd blotted her record by missing a flight for the sake of one last delicious fuck. She suddenly thought of Jude's car, parked behind the Honeysuckle Arms. But when she got there, breathless, the parking lot was full, and none of the cars was a rusty white Mustang.

Then Síle saw her. Walking along in blue denim, head down. "Jude," Síle shrieked. "There you are!" And thundered across the street. But the head lifted and the jaw was too heavy; the haircut belonged to a moody boy whose lip and eyebrow were connected by a light chain. "Sorry," Síle said, laughing, almost sobbing, "I'm really sorry."

She sat with a sour apple martini, watching the crowds go by. The crisp October evening had turned dusty. Later on she had gnocchi with sage, but didn't taste a thing. It occurred to her to go back to the Honeysuckle and ask the nice owners for the same room, but then she told herself that it would do her no good to spend the whole night sniveling into the pillow. Besides, by now it would probably have been rented out to a pair of Minnesotan dermatologists celebrating their thirtieth anniversary.

Instead, Síle taxied back out to the airport, past the darkening disc of the lake. She browsed through the book racks for something to read, but all she could see were titles with time in them: *The Time Trap, Recipes in No Time Flat, Finding Time for the Timeless*. In the Hilton she watched three episodes of *South Park* back to back, then turned the TV off and slid down on the pillows. She tried to think of this night as an offering on the altar of love, but she wasn't convincing herself. She wondered whether she'd tell Jude, when she called her from Dublin. (She wouldn't let herself call tonight, in case Jude insisted on climbing back into her car, so tired she'd probably rear-end a truck.) There was no valid reason to mention it at all; it would only cause Jude frustration to know that they'd missed out on a whole night together (and who knew when the next would be?). But Síle would no doubt spill out the whole story, tomorrow, as soon as Jude picked up the phone.

In the bag that held her velvet-lined eye mask, she found a small package wrapped in newsprint. She ripped it open and found a strange, humanoid figure made of flat stones glued together. The note said

Made you this Inukshuk one night when I couldn't sleep. It's an Inuit thing, a beacon for travelers, meaning "meat buried here" or "try coming this way" or "evil spirits begone" or maybe just "hang on."

All yours, keep believing, Jude

Spring Forward, Fall Back

And once I went
over the ocean,
Being bound for
the proud land of Spain,
Some singing and dancing
for pleasure,
But I had a heart
full of pain.

—ANON
*The Maid with the
Bonny Brown Hair*

Síle's fortieth birthday began well, at home in bed, when she opened the parcel with the Canadian postmark and found a tiny Japanese notebook in which Jude had written, one item to a page, four hundred things she loved about Síle.

Your flair for argument.
Your orange eyes.
The way you let Petrushka shred your couch.
Your zest.
Your wrinkled instep...

But then she had to hustle to the airport for her flight to New York, which turned out to be a stinker. High winds on approach made them abort their landing; the plane was diverted to Philadelphia, and sat on the ground for three hours. Food ran out, passengers fumed about missed connections, and one got stuck in the bathroom and went into hysterics. Síle managed to remove the lock with a screwdriver, which would have made a nice story: *How I spent my fortieth earning Mrs. Walson from Alabama's eternal gratitude.* Except that Mrs. Walson exploded from the tiny bathroom and knocked her down; Síle found herself lying across a passenger's feet, with a twisted knee and orange juice in her hair.

"I've wangled an extra day's layover in New York to rest my knee," she told Jude on the phone.

"I thought you said it was all better."

"Oh it is, but not officially. Meet me there on Tuesday?" she begged.

That little intake of breath that meant her lover was marshaling her stubbornness.

"Come on, for once, just let me pay for everything. I could have post-traumatic stress disorder!"

"You're such a bullshitter," said Jude, laughing. And then, "I'll get the Greyhound, it's cheaper."

Manhattan was a dazzle, a confusion; Síle watched it through the eyes of someone who'd never seen it before. She rode the elevator to the forty-ninth floor of their hotel, and when she let herself in she found Jude curled up asleep in the wide bed, her hair still wet from the shower. Síle stood and watched her. A fairy tale: Snow White in her glass box. She bent over to wake her with a kiss on the eyelid.

They'd meant to hit the town, as they had less than forty-eight hours, but they ended up not leaving the room that night. It had a view of the Chrysler Building, lit up in icy Deco curves. At two in the morning Síle insisted on calling Room Service for her delayed birthday dinner. They had oysters, grilled pear salad, and BLTs served with parsnip chips, a pretentious detail that made Jude laugh like a two-year-old.

Everything was a little too fast and frantic. Síle's body felt like sandpaper, then like mercury. Jude didn't take her hands off her, not for a minute. When Síle went to brush her teeth, Jude followed and held onto her hips.

"Doesn't summertime end tonight?" asked Síle. "Or is it different over here? No, I think I'm right."

"So have we lost an hour?" Downcast.

"Gained," Síle assured her, putting back the hands of her watch. "Look, it's not even three A.M., all over again."

"Spring forward, fall back," murmured Jude, leading her to the bed. "I can never remember which way it goes unless I say that. It's a depressing phrase."

"You think?"

"Like that math problem about the snail that climbs ten centimetres up the well every day but slips down five every night."

They had brunch in a revolving restaurant above Times Square, which moved so slowly you didn't notice until you glanced up and found the view had changed. "I'd have an old house in Florence," Síle decided, "with a week or two of skiing in the Rockies, then Sussex in March to see the bluebells, oh and Sydney for Mardi Gras, and lilac time in New England, then a month in West Cork, then, hmm, Bangalore's pretty nice any time of year because it's so high up. You must see Bangalore, Jude, it's what the future looks like. Maybe late summer in San Fran—I always feel exhilarated there even if it's foggy, it's so improbable the way it's built on all those hills. Autumn in New York—or maybe Toronto, why not, there's the big film fest, and drives to see the leaves," Síle offered, aware that she was juggling the conversation single-handed—"then back to the Med. What do you think?"

"I don't like this game. The whole point seems to be to make you restless," said Jude.

"I was born restless," said Síle with her best approximation of a devilish grin.

"The answer's never going to be Ireland, Ontario, is it?"

"Maybe for the Summer Squash Fair," she said weakly.

"Besides, living's not tourism," Jude pointed out. "We stay in one spot on the planet because of real things like jobs and families, not because of the scent of the bluebells."

Christ, sometimes the girl sounded sixty-five. "Bluebells are real."

"You know what I mean."

"It's only a game," said Síle, taking a bit of bacon from Jude's plate, more to be cute than because she wanted it; it was cool and clammy. "Where I'd really like to live, actually, is a little-known hideaway known as J. Turner."

A pause. "Oh yeah? Whereabouts, specifically?"

"The Inter-Mammarian Plain," Síle suggested. "Or, no, a little valley between Leftleg and Rightthigh."

Jude smiled, after a brief delay, and they went back to their hotel.

Later that afternoon they took the ferry to Ellis Island. "It's great to be arriving by sea, just like the immigrants did," said Jude, leaning over the rail.

"Who would you be?—if I'm allowed any more Let's Pretend?" Síle asked cautiously. "What about a humble but hard-working button girl?"

Jude shook her head. "I'm a tomboy who's passing as a sailor because men get twice the pay."

"Cheat!"

"It happened a lot," Jude assured her. "It was doable if you kept your cap tilted down."

"Okay," said Síle, delighted by the image. "And I'm an exotic ayah traveling with a boorish English family, and my dark eyes cannot leave your narrow mysterious form. I discern your secret and we make a pact to run away to the Wild West together the minute we're through customs."

Jude craned up at the green giantess rearing up out of the gray water. "She doesn't look quite as...welcoming as I expected."

Síle lifted the camera attachment on her gizmo, and its lens went erect like a nipple. "Mm, I know that's meant to be a torch she's holding up, but it looks more like she's saying *Stop!*"

The Museum of Immigration was vast. On a CD-ROM, Jude found a Shawn O'Shawnassy from 1893 who could easily have been a great-uncle of Síle's.

"His surname isn't spelled the same way," Síle objected.

"They'd have written it down wrong," Jude told her. "Like Bukovski becoming Booker, or Cohen, Cole."

The Interrogation Hall was empty except for a vast Stars and Stripes. A little exhibition hall displayed the tests used to weed out applicants of subnormal intelligence. Síle laughed at this, but when she was doing the Spatial Relations puzzle and Jude said "Ten seconds left," she panicked and couldn't finish it in time. "Well, that'd be me and Great-Uncle Shawn back on the boat."

"How can a world traveler be bad at spatial relations?"

"Ironic, isn't it?"

They read stories of applicants who spent years on Ellis Island, waiting; women who were effectively held prisoner until their menfolk turned up. On their way out they passed a huge pile of old-fashioned trunks and barrows. "Must be Hollywood props left over from some set," said Síle.

Jude looked up from the plaque. "Actually, they're real. Unclaimed baggage."

"No!" Síle stared at the handsome old trunks, bound or nailed shut, and the skinny barrows. She reached for her gizmo. "Pose beside them, sweetie. Look sad."

Jude turned away.

"Go on, go on!"

She shook her head. "I don't feel like playacting."

Síle bit her lip. Every way she turned, she seemed to step on glass.

On the boat they had a dull conversation about solar energy. It was understandable, Síle reassured herself. Days together were so strange, so short. They couldn't be having a fabulous time every minute.

When Síle woke the next morning, the first thing she knew was that it was very early; there was only a faint light at the edge of the curtains. The second thing was that the sound that had woken her was Jude crying.

She enfolded the shaking woman in her arms. "Don't."

"I want a cigarette.'

"Don't cry, love. Don't cry. We still have half a day."

"And after that, when do I get to see you again?"

Síle couldn't answer. She thought of saying "Soon," but it sounded feeble. Darkness nibbled at the edge of the word.

Jude sat up, hunched around her knees.

"Do you really want a cigarette?" Síle asked.

Her lover shook her head and stared out the window, where a hungry-faced gull shot by.

Síle considered various arguments she could make. Her knee was aching again. She thought of suggesting they ring room service for breakfast.

What came out of Jude's mouth was, "I can't do this."

Síle waited: silent, for once.

"All this. Any of it. The waiting," Jude growled. "I know I should be grateful that we've been able to meet six times in seven months, I know we've got it so much better than most. But I'm tense all the time, it's like this gigantic rubber band about to snap in my face…"

"I know. I know," Síle crooned, "it's brutal, it's the pits—"

"But you've got the knack," Jude interrupted. "It's as if you can breathe at these altitudes."

"No I can't."

"Well, you seem to."

"How does it help," said Síle frantically, "to moan and groan? Are you trying to pick a fight on our last day?"

"No," said Jude, so low Síle could barely hear her. "I'm trying to say this is over."

For several seconds, the only sound was the delicate whir of the heating. Síle spoke in a clipped voice. "I don't know what you mean. It's clearly not over, is it? I mean, here we are, the feelings haven't evaporated overnight." She waited. "You mean you'd like it to be over, is that it? You don't want me to visit, you don't want to come to Dublin, to e-mail me or ring me or think about me?"

"Sometimes," said Jude into her kneecaps, "I almost think it was better in the old days—simpler, anyway—when you just waved good-bye to the ship or train, pulled your shawl over your head, and got on with surviving." The pause stretched out like spun glass. "Let's face it, Síle. When you're gone you're gone, and we don't even breathe the same air."

Síle stared at her. But couldn't deny it.

They were oddly courteous with each other after that. They packed their bags like zombies. Jude offered to come to the airport, but Síle said it made more sense for the taxi to drop Jude off at the bus station. Their hands were only inches apart on the backseat. "I'm sorry," Jude said, once. Síle spent so long trying to think of the perfect reply—the magic phrase that would move her lover, persuade her, catch her in a web all over again—that the moment had passed. They kissed good-bye like strangers.

Living History

I'll go no more a roving
with you, fair maid,
A roving, a roving,
since roving's been my ruin
I'll go no more a roving with you

—ANON
The Maid of Amsterdam

On All Souls, November second, it was 1867 Day, when the inhabitants of Ireland, Ontario, were possessed by the spirits of their ancestors. Or that was the idea. Jude stared blank-eyed at the passing parade. In her head, voice mail replayed over and over.

Me again. I can wait, while you're thinking about this, Jude;
I just need to know roughly how long I'm going to need to
wait. Ring me back, leave a message; that's all I'm asking.

1867 Day was Jude's idea, though it was inspired by other living history projects she'd visited, like Plymouth Plantation. She'd picked the year because of Confederation, when Canada West had become Ontario, a province of the new nation. She supplied each participant with a fact sheet about the resident of Ireland, Ontario, he or she would be playing, as they were on November 2, 1867: *Patience Toofer, forty-one, spinster, raising two sons of dead sister, runs a laundry, pocks from scarlet fever*...From the sofa-bound vicar's

mother to the bloody-nosed brawlers drying out in the cell, everything going on today was researched, everything was real.

But over the four years Jude had been running it, the locals had
come to claim 1867 Day in an increasingly flippant spirit, and now
it struck her that the whole thing had degenerated into a feel-good
family day out. Marcy the travel agent went by waving in leg-of-
mutton sleeves that were at least twenty years too modern; when
Jude had pointed this out this morning, Marcy'd said, "Let's not
sweat the small stuff," in a most un-Victorian way. Hugo and Lucian from the Old Stationhouse Guesthouse were dressed right but
swung their pitchforks over their shoulders like dapper golfers. A
boy ran by with headphones on over his flat cap, and two tiny nuns
followed on pink scooters with tinsel streamers flying from the
handles.

Why had Jude ever thought that playing dress-up would give
people any real insight into the strange, intractable past? These
comfortable citizens of the twenty-first century hadn't the least idea
what it was like to hack a space out of an endless forest; to grapple
with a bureaucracy for roads, schools, or churches; to somehow
settle what had been a mosquito swamp. Nor did Jude, for that
matter, she reminded herself grimly; she'd just read lots of books.

*Did you get the letter I couriered? Will you at least read it? It
took me half the night to write. I'm in a bad way here. Come
on, Jude, pick up the phone; you owe me that much.*

Gwen stood beside her. "Have you seen Tasmin, over by the
mulled cider stall? Really getting into the spirit."

The girl was breast-feeding her baby through an unlaced
bodice. "Looks more like a seventeenth-century harlot than a
nineteenth-century farmer," muttered Jude.

"You're just jealous of those tits," Gwen joked. "It's all going
good, eh? Very festive."

"It's not meant to be festive. It's meant to mean something."

Gwen's eyebrows rose.

"Sorry. Ignore me."

The messages replayed themselves in Jude's head till she felt like a lunatic. The worst were the abased ones.

I know I was careless, I didn't look after you well enough, I mustn't have loved you well enough; I swear I'll do it better if you'll give me another chance. Please? Jude, please?

"You know, this could last for years," Gwen remarked.

Jude watched the bedraggled procession of decorated carts down Main Street. "No, they're nearly at the turkey factory already."

"Not the parade. You, in this state of suspended animation. If you ask me, which you haven't," added Gwen after a second, "I still think you should have hung on in there."

Jude's mouth was frozen shut.

"It's like childbirth, or what I've heard of it: You can always bear more than you think. When I first took up with Luke," Gwen confided in an undertone, "the first six weeks, I didn't imagine I could do it for long. The squalor of being so secret, and brooding about his wife—I really thought I was going to have to call the whole thing off. But it passed."

Jude turned and looked at her. "Great, now you've been unhappy for three years."

Gwen's eyes were hard. Jude had never seen her cry, and perhaps she never would. "I'm not setting myself up as an inspiration here. My only point is, you can get used to anything."

"Then someday I'll get used to being on my own again."

A sigh of exasperation. "Are you still refusing to talk to the poor woman, even?"

Jude knew she'd never done anything crueler than this. Síle lived and breathed talk: Silence choked her. To leave her in limbo, to refuse to even acknowledge any of her messages, was an act of brutality. But Jude could find no other way.

Fucking hell, Jude, how can you cut me off and pronounce the case closed?

Joe Costelloe went by in a pair of anachronistically clean overalls (*Eddie Bauer,* said the big label). After a minute, Jude said, "I want a clean break, not like Joe and Alma."

"That's nothing like," said Gwen scornfully. "They're divorced, but they still share a toilet!"

Jude, I'm telling you for the last time: Pick up the damn phone!

She was being beckoned over to the information booth to deal with some crisis, and Gwen said she'd go try a candy apple. Jude held onto her friend's sleeve briefly. "Bear with me."

"As if I have a choice," said Gwen.

There were two new messages when Jude got home, many hours later. The first was in the rapid, malevolent voice of a crank caller.

I don't understand, and I don't forgive you either. People think you're so strong: What a joke! You hadn't the stamina to hold onto me for even a year. You hadn't the balls.

The second was nothing but low sobs.

As soon as she'd got off the Greyhound from New York, Jude had done all the right things, just as if she'd been packing away an exhibition: She'd taken down the framed photos (Síle on the Triumph, Síle asleep on the couch, Síle and Jude sitting on a giant vegetable marrow), taped up the box of letters and e-mails, put away the atlas so she wouldn't be tempted to turn to the British Isles page. Every time something reminded her of Síle—an espresso pot, a crookback gourd—she put it in the basement. This time last year the house had contained Jude and her mother and all the clutter of their joint lives; now it was beginning to have an uninhabited air.

Always Jude felt the tug, the hook in her ribs. *The fish can't be landed.* The thousands of kilometres between her and Síle should have provided insulation, padding, soundproofing, but somehow they didn't. If only the woman had never come to Ireland; if only the town hadn't become imprinted with memories of her. The stool she'd sat on in the Dive (third from the wall) still bore her silky stockinged ghost.

It's over, it's over, Jude kept telling herself, like a mantra. But the phrase didn't seem to mean anything. Like those teenagers who boasted, "I broke it off with him on Saturday night but Monday lunchtime we got back together": These weren't actual events, only declarations. Why were people such fools as to think they could stage-manage love's confusing entrances and arbitrary exits? All Jude could see to do was suffer through, keep her mouth shut, get to the end of one day, then the next, then the next. In the hope that one day she would get her life back.

She had turgid nightmares of trudging across fields of snow that turned to black ice and cracked beneath her feet; of tangled ropes, barking huskies, grappling hooks. But one night, when she finally dropped off at three in the morning, she had a lovely dream. They were sitting on a windowsill together, a hundred stories up. Síle kissed her lightly on the cheek—heat blooming on the spot—then took her hand, and they dropped together into the air. Fearless, soundless. Jude woke cringing, as if someone had snapped on the light and ripped off the quilt.

Rizla had this notion about a trip to Detroit, that it might cheer Jude up. Eventually she agreed to a single overnight, just to shut him up. He did the driving, because as he pointed out, Jude was in such a fog these days, she'd go off the road. It was weirdly mild weather for November; Jude wished she hadn't worn such a thick jacket.

On the outskirts of Detroit, they got lost in the tangled high-ways. She kept the pickup's windows shut and stared out, remembering their honeymoon. What a child she'd been; it shouldn't have been legal. Downtown, certain burned-out blocks looked like Godzilla had just stomped through, though the riots had happened more than thirty years back. Steam puffed up from vents in the street, clouding Jude's vision. She thought of all those white people who'd fled to the burbs and never come back. She pictured Síle, her dark face gliding through a crowd of pallid ones.

They passed empty-eyed buildings with trees growing through them. "Betcha there's pheasants and shit in there," Rizla murmured. "Wish I'd brought my rifle."

"That would really have endeared us to the border guards."

"Ah, they like guns down here. Land of the free!"

By luck or some homing instinct from his drinking days, he found them a blues bar with a good house band. He bought Jude one of their CDs, but she felt only irritation that he was wasting money. They ate their way through a vast order of chicken fajitas. After a couple of hours they were hoarse from trying to talk over the music, so Jude suggested they move across the road to a bar with a rainbow flag she'd glimpsed on the way in. It turned out to be called Lip Sink; they sat through the semifinals of the Best Chest in Detroit competition. Jude was managing a pretty good imitation of a girl having a good time. She tried to enter Rizla's name for the prize, but he twisted the slip of paper out of her hand.

"Ow," she said, rubbing her wrist.

"That'll teach you."

He reminisced about their wild days, rides on dirt roads, slamming on the brakes to do doughnuts; he folded back her ear to find the old scar from that game of tabletop.

"Cut it out." She pulled away.

When the table beside them filled up with female twenty-somethings, Rizla grinned. "That's better. Remember that fetish night you took me to in Montreal that time, and those gals with the live snakes?"

"You're a very strange guy."

"Ten o'clock," he muttered, and she checked the clock on the wall, which said five past midnight. "Ten o'clock," he repeated, "nice little blonde!"

Jude glanced over, then shook her head.

"Thought you liked 'em girly?"

"There's girly and then there's scary, Riz. She's got sequins on her nails."

"What about her?" He jerked his thumb the other way.

"In the red dress? You're picking all the straightest-looking ones."

He shrugged. "Just trying to see through your eyes, babe. Personally I'd go for the little cutie in the shirt and tie."

"Pervert!"

Several beers on, she was finding it harder to keep up the act. When Rizla quoted "Time wounds all heels, as Marx says," she snapped "*Groucho* Marx, moron."

"You know what your problem is, Grouchy?" he asked, sipping his beer.

"If there's one kind of person I hate," said Jude, "it's the kind who says, 'You know what your problem is?'" In the background, she realized, they were playing a CD of Irish songs.

She went away from me, and she moved through the fair,
And fondly I watched her move here and move there...

"You gotta let this one go," Rizla told her.

"*This one,* meaning Síle?" The name was like a sharp pebble in her throat.

He shrugged. "Roll credits. The distance wore you out: end of story. Sad but true."

For a light drinker, Jude thought, he could sound like the most sententious of drunks. Sinéad O'Connor moaned on:

And I smiled as she passed me with her goods and her gear
And that was the last that I saw of my dear.

"Show's gotta go on," said Rizla. "If it was meant to be, it would have been. Some meet, right, and some part, and the world keeps on turning."

Jude turned to look at him. It was like a light snapping on; she only marveled that she'd been so naïve. "Oh spare me the hippie bullshit. You couldn't be happier."

He sat back, with a *who, me?* look.

"You did everything you could to sabotage me and Síle. The jokes, the needling, the bets that we'd never live together...It was jealousy, pure and simple!"

"I don't think so," he said with a chuckle. "Wives are work. I gotta tell you, I wouldn't have you back as a gift."

"No, you don't want me back as a wife," she said; "that was what confused me. You want me single. Isn't that right? Unattached and available for long evenings watching TV, smoking dope, or *whatever.* Your best bud, right here to hand, no strings!"

"Aw, fuck this shit," said Rizla, rearing to his feet. "I didn't drive three hours to get my head bit off."

Jude followed him to the door, at a cold distance. Rain was lashing down. Diana Krall was singing a mournful "Danny Boy." Jude turned up her collar and stepped out into the sheets of biting rain.

"Truck's this way," Rizla barked, pulling her under the canopy of his big leather jacket. They went up and down the parking lot twice, like a four-legged puppet staggering through puddles.

"Are you sure it wasn't the other way?" she asked.

"We turned left to the bar."

"No, you dick, that was the first bar, the other side of the street."

A jeep screeched in reverse out of the parking lot, passing within half a metre of Jude's hip. "Jesus, H," Rizla roared. He left her holding the jacket over her head like an umbrella and lunged after the car.

"Riz," she shouted, "forget it."

He planted his fist on the hood with a terrible bang.

Oh no.

Through the sheets of rain she could see a head stick out of the window. "What the fuck you doing, asshole?" said the driver.

"No, *you* asshole," said Rizla, "you practically crushed my friend, why don't you look where you're going?"

Jude felt a surge of hatred. Why did he have to do this, right here, right now?

"No, why don't you fuck off back to the hole you crawled out of?" The guy climbed out of the jeep and slammed the door.

White, thirty-looking, that was all Jude could tell through the blinding rain as she peered out from under Rizla's jacket. She wanted badly to be at home.

"Yeah, why don't you go fuck yourself, faggot?" Two more men stepped down. The shorter guy told the driver, "They came out of that gay bar down the street, I saw them, they were all over each other."

The driver spat. "This your little boyfriend, faggot?"

Before Jude knew it he'd got her by the shoulder, his fingers gripping painfully. She was about to speak; she was picking the right calming words to let them know that she was a woman, that nobody wanted any trouble, that her friend was really sorry for touching their car. But all that came out was a high-pitched gasp.

Rizla head-butted the guy, who let go of her and staggered backward, holding his face and making a guttural sound. There was something wonderful about the moment, Jude registered, even as terror was sending up its mushroom cloud in her head. Rizla and the shorter guy grunted, landing hard blows. She thought of running for help but the third guy was coming at her, he had her in a chin lock, his arm was like a steel forklift on her windpipe. There was something Jude had learned in that self-defense workshop all those years ago, something about stabbing an attacker's foot with your stiletto heel? She was in running shoes, there was no time, she was on the wet ground, how did that happen? Thrown down like a sack of garbage into a puddle, and gravel hard as diamonds under her cheek. She managed to curl up before something stove in her ribs, and the worst pain in the world came down on her hand.

Afterward Jude could never quite remember how Rizla had got her to his pickup. She was on the floor with her head on the seat and there was a lot of vomit. "Stay face down, or you'll choke," he ordered, swerving round a corner. Pain came and went in waves over her head.

The next thing she fully understood was Rizla arguing with somebody. "Listen, all we bought was a CD, I don't remember to what freaking value! Maybe ten bucks. Look, my friend's bleeding, can we speed this up? Her passport's probably in her jeans—She's my wife. Ex-wife. What do you mean, did I hit her? I told you these assholes jumped us, I think my nose is broken. No I don't want to go to the police station, I just want to get back into Canada. No we don't need an ambulance, man, just let us through!"

When she woke up, Rizla was sitting on the side of her bed and a thin gray light filled the room. "Morning, you. We're in the hospital, just across the border in Windsor," he added after a minute.

"Yeah." Jude's voice came out raw, as if she'd been screaming, though she didn't recall screaming. She seemed to be wearing a big white glove on her left hand, with her fingers coming out the end like pink worms.

"I was afraid if I took you to emergency in the States they'd charge ten thousand bucks to let you in the door."

She nodded, then wished she hadn't; her head felt as if it might come off.

"I ate your breakfast, to pass the time," he said, nodding at a tray. "You've got bruised ribs, and something called a Colles fracture where that bastard stamped on your wrist."

Ah, so that explained the cast.

"No concussion though, that's something," he said, cheery. "You didn't happen to catch their license plate?"

She shook her head, carefully.

"I can't tell all these new jeeps apart," he complained. "Could have been a Ford, but I'm guessing. You think it's worth going back to Detroit to make a statement?"

"No," she growled. She took a big breath, and it hurt.

"You pissed at me?" Rizla waited. "What do you want me to say? I get riled up, I go in guns blazing; it's a guy thing."

Jude spoke thickly. "Other guys have the same amount of testosterone but they don't act like dumb fucks all the time."

"It's not all the time," he said, childish.

"Too often. That Australian you punched, the night of our wedding. Or that time you wrapped your sister's car round a stop sign. What about when you put your fist through the wall of your trailer?"

Rizla rubbed his eyes. "Gimme a break, I'd just heard my wife was a dyke."

Adrenaline was bringing Jude to life; she managed to half sit up, despite the stabs in her ribs. "Ah, so it *was* meant for me, not the wall."

"I would never hit a woman."

It was his tone that got to her. "Well excuse me, O perfect Christian gentleman! But you'd pick a fight in a parking lot and get her beaten up by other guys."

He let out a long groan. "I'm sorry, okay? I never meant for anything to happen."

He's been nothing but trouble since the day you met, her mother commented in her head; Jude could hear every crisp syllable. But it seemed to her that for all his flaws, this man was all she had left. The two of them were damaged goods; they would never get free of each other.

"I've got a broken nose, if that helps. The doctor had to wham it back in line."

The corner of her mouth turned up on its own. "Nothing else?"

"Bruises, probably a black eye tomorrow."

She let out a scornful puff of breath. Her life was a tangled thread looping around on itself; she might wind up back in that trailer yet. Jude choked at the thought. *I'm only twenty-six,* she thought, *how come I feel so used up?*

"The last shiner I got was for being an Indian; I guess getting gay-bashed has novelty value," Rizla offered, and she half smiled. "Next time we go out, I'm making you wear a skirt and heels. I can't believe we got taken for a couple of fags!"

"I need to stop talking now," said Jude faintly, and wormed her way down in the bed. Silence: She shut her eyes, fell back into it.

When she opened them again, Rizla was standing against the window, like a paper cutout of a man. "Kinda sleety now."

She struggled to reach the paper cup of water with her right hand. He came over, pressed a button that tilted her pillow upward, and lifted the cup to her lips. "How you doing?" he asked as he set it down, and dabbed the spilled drops from her blue gown with his knuckles.

"Not good," she whispered.

"Your ribs? Or your hand?"

Tears crept out from under her eyelashes. "My life."

"Ah," said Rizla.

Jude knew she'd been punished. She'd thrown away her lover and the stupid thing was, she couldn't quite remember why. She was baffled and battered, ground into pieces. She couldn't quite imagine picking herself up and going on from here.

"Your life is fine," he told her, "it's structurally sound. It just needs, what's the Shawn Colvin album?"

She cleared her throat. "My life needs a Shawn Colvin album?"

"The one you kept playing on our trip to Montreal. *A Few Small Repairs,* that's it."

Jude almost managed a laugh.

A startled Caribbean face came around the curtain. "Check your vitals?"

Rizla went outside so the woman could take Jude's temperature and blood pressure. "You in much pain?" she asked.

Jude tried to shrug.

"One to ten?"

"Five?"

"Nearly everybody says five," the nurse observed. "I get you a pill."

"How long—"

"Doctor will be in later; maybe your friend take you home tomorrow."

Home: Jude thought of the house on Main Street, as hollow as an eggshell. Her friends, her neighbours, the museum: She tried to summon up some interest. How a life could deflate as fast as a balloon!

The light leached out of the window. November dusk thickened in the room. Jude listened to the silence, as if she were at Meeting. *Here I am. Help me. Here I am.*

Behind the curtain the door swung open, letting in a stripe of yellow light. "Jude?" A whisper. A pause. "Are you asleep?"

Jude thought she was probably hallucinating from the drugs.

A head came through the gap in the curtain. All Jude could see was the silhouette. She fumbled for the switch and the light snapped on.

"Hello, stranger," said Síle, leaning over the bed and smiling like it was Christmas.

Jude blinked, blinded. Finally she managed to speak. "How—"

"Rizla got a message to me via the Dublin office this morning. Didn't he say? I picked it up from New York, grabbed a flight to Toronto, and hired a car to get to Windsor."

Her mind was in a blur at the thought of all those cities.

"I would have called to say I was on my way," said Síle, "but I was afraid you might say no."

Jude shook her head vehemently enough to hurt it.

Síle put out her hand, stroked Jude's hair very lightly, as if touching some wild creature. "Rizla's gone home. He apologized for the merchandise getting dented on his shift."

Jude thought she was going to cry again.

"I'll be driving you back tomorrow, if you're in a fit state. I've never seen you look so awful," she remarked.

"I've never seen you look so beautiful."

Síle bent and kissed her, her mouth like a ripe plum. "If you'd died, and I wasn't here, I swear I'd have murdered you."

The stern tone made Jude smile. "I've got no idea what I thought I was doing, trying to end it."

A serious nod.

"I've caused you so much hurt—"

"Make me happy from now on, and I'll write it off," said Síle with a stylish little shrug.

"I guess it was…a failure of nerve."

"I tried rock-climbing once," Síle remarked. "It was all great gas till I couldn't find a foothold and my whole body froze up. They called out instructions, they bawled at me, but I was ice. In the end they had to winch me down the cliff like a sheep."

Jude was surprised to find herself still capable of laughter.

Going the Distance

Either the well was very deep, or she
fell very slowly, for she had plenty of
time as she went down to look about
her, and to wonder what was going
to happen next.

—Lewis Carroll
Alice's Adventures in Wonderland

Three days later, Síle put her bags in the trunk of the rental car. She went back up onto the porch where Jude stood, shivering a little in her hoodie. "Go on inside, you're not well."

"I'm fine." Jude grinned at her and scratched the place where her cast rubbed against her hand. property of sile sunita siobhan o'shaughnessy, it said in dark capitals across the plaster.

Síle bent to pick up a scarlet maple leaf, and everything seemed to shift, like a minor earthquake. She straightened, dizzy, still staring at the leaf's sharp points.

"What is it?"

She put the leaf in her handbag, inside her copy of *The Time Traveler's Wife*. "It won't be long, this time," she told Jude.

The blue eyes lit up. "You don't mean you're coming for Christmas?"

Síle shook her head. "For the rest of my life."

Jude watched her, arms wrapped round her own ribs. "Don't

mess me around, darlin', not when you're about to head off to the airport."

"No, I've just decided: I'm making the move."

"Which move?" she asked suspiciously.

"Eejit! If we want to be together, we have to make it happen. And the fact is that I'm a more moveable feast than you are. So Ireland, Ontario, it is." Síle pronounced the name as breezily as she could.

"No way! We can keep going as we are," Jude protested; "we'll cope."

"What was that Bible line you quoted me, our first night?" Síle stared up at the bedroom window. "Two lying together..."

"If two lie together, then they have heat, but how can one be warm alone?"

"Precisely." After the kiss, she checked her watch and headed toward the car.

"I don't believe you're going to do this," Jude called.

"Watch me," said Síle over her shoulder, her smile curving like the wing of a bird.

Síle's high lasted two days. It took her through the flight home from Toronto, into a damp morning where she stared out the taxi window at Dublin's gray streets and thought, *Okay, if this is what it takes. I've spent four decades here; it's time for a move.* Her exultation lasted right through her next rotation to New York and back. She was wrapped up in the romance of that moment on Jude's porch, when her life shook and she knew exactly what to do; the memory crackled like leaves underfoot. There was to be no more making do, no more muddling along; all the cautious phrases had given way to one certain *yes.* Síle knew there'd be difficulties; her arms were open to embrace them.

The third day she woke early, though she wasn't working. She felt weirdly tired, as if she were coming down with something. In her head she drew up the list of pros and cons. On one side was *old friends, Da, Orla, nephews, job, cinema, urban buzz, cafés*... That list went on for some time. On the other side was just one word: *Jude*. Why was she making a list, she scolded herself, when she'd already made up her mind?

Síle turned practical. She found the Canadian Government's immigration Web site, and was immediately disheartened. The laws were progressive, all right, but they didn't seem to apply. Jude could sponsor Síle's immigration as her "common-law partner"—but no, dammit, they hadn't "cohabited in a conjugal relationship for a period of at least one year." (They'd never cohabited for more than a week at a stretch, in fact.) Síle noted that "conjugal partners" were subtly different from "common-laws"; they didn't need to have actually lived together, if there was some impediment—but blast it, they still had to have spent at least one year "in a committed and mutually interdependent (marriage-like) relationship" where they had "combined their affairs to the extent possible." Hmm. "Affairs" sounded juicy but seemed to mean joint bank accounts, wills, credit cards, property, life insurance... What had Jude and Síle *combined* over the past eleven months except words and bodies?

The sponsorship form was surreal. *Did anyone (individual or organization) introduce you?*

George L. Jackson, deceased.

On first meeting did you and your sponsor exchange any gifts?

A cup of vile coffee, a pastry.

And then, over a five-line blank box:

Describe how your relationship developed after first contact. Provide photos and documentary evidence of activities in which you both participated. For expediency and security reasons, do not include documents with electronic components such as musical greeting cards.

Oh dear, here was another problem, Síle saw, on skipping down to the list of "Excluded Relationships": You couldn't sponsor a partner if you were "the spouse of another person" at the time. Meaning, in this case, one Richard Vandeloo, blast him. Jude and Síle's situation was sounding more disreputable every minute.

"How're your dented ribs?" she asked on the phone.

"Much better," said Jude.

"And your wrist?"

"Mending nicely, the doctor tells me; I just have to resist the temptation to pick up a snow shovel."

"Snow, already," marveled Síle.

"This is what you're letting yourself in for, if you're really moving here," Jude warned.

She grinned. "Hey, just checking something: You don't want to marry me, do you?"

A beat. "I thought in Leitrim you said weddings—"

"I wasn't proposing!"

"Oh."

"I hope that's not disappointment I hear?" asked Síle, regretting having brought it up so flippantly. Wishing they could be having this conversation on a pillow somewhere, anywhere at all, even the nastiest Super 8 motel.

"No, just momentary confusion," Jude told her. "Once was enough for me, honest."

Her lover's firmness on this point reassured Síle. "It's just that I've just been looking into ways of getting me into Canada, and you divorcing and re-hitching is the most obvious, though even going that route would take quite a while. But there's loads of options," she said more confidently than she felt.

"So who've you told about this mad notion of yours?"

"Nobody, yet," said Síle. Sometimes she could actually hear Jude's thoughts, like faint radio. "I just need to arm myself with a plausible plan first," Síle assured her.

"Listen," Jude said, "if you get qualms—find you can't go through with this—"

"Shut up with that nonsense."

"I wouldn't hold it against you. So if you change your mind—"

"I'm putting down the phone," Síle sang.

She could apply for a visa as a skilled worker, she discovered from further research, but what kind? A news report on the troubled air industry in Canada confirmed that there were no flight attendant jobs a-going, and even if there were, the airlines wouldn't hire an Irishwoman over one of their own. To Síle's surprise, this fact didn't depress her, far from it: It was a new life she wanted, not a copy of the old one. For years now, hadn't she been feeling weary of pushing past belligerent tourists and serving up foul-smelling omelettes? A fresh career at forty would be just the thing.

The list of desired occupations issued by Immigration Canada made her laugh out loud. What could a positive artist be, or a hair examiner, a switcher, an all-round furrier, or a camp cook?

Síle ordered herself copies of *Pursue Your Passion: Making Career Choices From the Heart, Dream Up Your Dream Job,* and *What Are YOU Doing For the Rest of Your Life?* Then she thought that perhaps instead of spending $62.59 on dodgy self-help books she should start saving for the many costs of emigration, so she canceled the order. She ended up buying just one book, called *Downshift: Learning to Live the Life You Love On Less.* It turned up two days later (Síle always ordered books express delivery), and it enraged her so much with its preachy, make-do-and-mend suggestions—shred old phone directories for a no-cost garden mulch, stay out of shops, bake your own birthday gifts—that she was tempted to mulch it.

She chose Marcus as the first friend to tell, so she waited till he was up for the weekend, and—thrift be damned—took him to the Shelburne Hotel for tea on silver service in the plump armchairs.

His clotted-cream scone froze in midair. "I knew this was coming."

"Really? That's more than I did."

"Why can't Jude move here?" Marcus demanded.

"Because she's not the kind of shrub that bears transplanting," said Síle.

"Shit, shit, shit."

"Come on, now," she said, "if anybody understands I thought it would be you, Mr. Love-Will-Find-a-Way!"

"I do understand," said Marcus, putting his scone down, "but I don't feel like being an advocate for romance today. More like a five-year-old whose best friend's about to move to the moon."

Síle tried to laugh; she sipped her tea. "It's not like you and I were living near each other anymore, anyway." That sounded like a reproach, so she hurried on. "I'll ring you from Canada just like I ring you from Dublin, and persecute you and Pedro with long visits."

Silence, as Marcus weighed the credibility of that.

"I'm sorry," said Síle in a flatter tone. "It seems it's one of those moments when friends come second."

He nodded. "I do wish you and Jude luck; you're lovely together."

She leaned over to kiss his stubbled cheek. She took a cream-cake, but it stuck to her tongue like glue; she swilled it down with lukewarm tea.

"Leaving aside my own personal loss," he said, "how are you going to cope with the move?"

She shrugged. "People do these things all the time. Pedro managed beautifully, didn't he?"

"The difference is, you've no interest in the joys of the countryside. If it were a city you were going to, at least..."

"I'll be within arm's reach of Toronto," she said unconvincingly, thinking of those two and a half hours on the road. Three and a half, in a blizzard.

"And besides, you're Irish through and through."

"Whatever that means!"

"It's your setting, your frame. You're a Dub," Marcus told her, warming to his theme. "This dirty old town is your, what's the German word, your *heimat*." She didn't answer. "What the hell are you going to do with yourself at some little Canadian crossroads?"

"Be with Jude," she said furiously. "I want to live with her full-time, sink into it, feather our nest. Be stationary, for once."

"And there's another thing, when you leave the airline—"

"—which you've been at me to do for years now, by the way!"

"But not without a new job. How will you pay the rent?"

"Jude inherited the house from her mother."

"You know what I mean," said Marcus. "What are you going to *be*?"

"Well, that's something I need your help with, since switching horses is something you've done already." Síle's tone strained to maintain the fiction that this was a chat instead of a spat.

He sighed. Then, after a second, he said, "Something online."

"Like what?"

"I don't know, but the point is, the Internet's your playground, so you might as well make a job out of it. A job that isn't tied to any one location," he added darkly, "just in case this turns out to have been a disastrous mistake."

Later, thinking about it, Síle was rather taken with this idea. She tried to picture herself as an online something-or-other; a travel advisor, maybe? But the problem was, these days everybody seemed eager to offer information and expertise for free, just for the pleasure of seeing their own words onscreen. Maybe Síle could milk her cousins for contacts and run a business selling cheap mirrored hangings from Rajasthan to customers in Red Deer, Alberta, or

Nacogdoches, Texas. Hmm, that sounded both exploitative and unlikely. But the Internet was clogged with people who apparently made a good living from selling weirdly specialist items: doll's furniture, soy candles, baseball cards...

One evening, when she and Jude had both had bad days—Síle's involving a cracked front window (she blamed those little yobs who'd kidnapped Petrushka back in June), Jude's hinging on an eight-year-old who'd gone into hysterics when Jude had smacked her desk with a willow switch during a workshop—they decided to get drunk together. Jude hadn't had a drink since Detroit, but her various bones were feeling so much better that she was ready to open a bottle of Glenfiddich. At Síle's end she'd prepared a cocktail shaker of martinis. She went through the list of careers she'd considered so far.

"Supermodel," suggested Jude.

"Flatterer! Something more consultational, I think, if it's to be the beauty world. Makeup Tips for Mixed-Race Lovelies?"

Jude howled. "Snow shoveler? Rizla says I should be paying him a hundred bucks a week."

"Cat masseuse," she countered, scratching the back of Petrushka's head.

"Premier of Ontario?"

"Ha! I'd give your Medicare a kick up the arse."

"So how long's it going to take to get this visa?" Jude wondered.

Síle groaned. "I was hoping you wouldn't ask. Have some more whiskey."

"That bad, eh?"

"You have to put together this elaborate application with photos and birth certs and CVs and your addresses for the last ten years, you get police clearances and notarized copies of records of employment and and and, you courier it all in to the nearest Canadian High Commission—oh, and I forgot the medical. The form's alarming, listen to this," said Síle, fingering through her pile of printouts.

> *Have you received treatment, attention or advice from any physician or practitioner for disease of the heart, tumour or polyp, disorder of the intestines, dizziness, abdominal bruits, nephritis, pus or blood in urine, paralysis, deformity of bone, lung masses, thalassaemia, disorder of testes, impairment of throat, murmurs, thrills, or convulsions?*

"Wait up," said Jude, "I believe I may have seen you experience murmurs, thrills, and convulsions."

"Every time you've taken my clothes off," Síle admitted, grinning. She read on. "'Have you ever been advised to reduce your alcohol consumption?'" That one made them both laugh. "Only every bloody Christmas, by my sister. Then there's all these mysterious parts of me the doctor has to give a clean bill of health to, like my *fundi*; I dread to think where that is…"

"This reminds me of the Irish ships arriving at Quebec in the 1840s," said Jude—"the terror of the dirty, disease-spreading immigrants." After a second, she said, "But you haven't told me how long it all takes."

Síle knew she'd been stalling. "It's really hard to track down figures on processing times. One site says currently it's anything between six and forty-two months. Average more like twelve to eighteen."

That silenced them both.

"Oh, my love," said Síle. The mouthpiece was damp with her breath.

"If I know you're on your way, if I know it's really going to happen, that makes all the difference," Jude told her. "These days I walk around grinning like a clown."

Halfway through a sleepless night at an airport hotel in JFK,

Síle sat up in bed and turned on her gizmo. She went back to the immigration Web site, then checked her airline for the latest details on the voluntary severance offer. Next she had a look at real-estate listings for Stoneybatter. Then she found something called *ancestors.com* and tapped in "O'Shaughnessy."

"I've been looking at this all wrong," she told Jude, yawning at 6 A.M., when she called her from the hotel over an elaborate breakfast tray.

"Oh yeah?" The small sound of coffee being sipped from that ghastly handmade mug.

"Did you heat the milk?"

"It's fine," said Jude.

"You have to heat the milk," Síle told her.

"Oh, the joys of domesticity. In forty-two months or less you'll be able to nag me in person."

Síle laughed. "I can't wait that long. See, where I've gone astray is, I've been asking myself how to get a Canadian visa."

"To be a landed immigrant, right."

"Actually, it's called permanent resident nowadays. But what I should be asking is, *What do I need in order to move in with Jude?*"

"Why is that a better question?"

"Because the answer is, *nothing but my passport!*"

"You've lost me," said Jude.

"If I come in as a *visitor,* initially," Síle gabbled, "I'll be allowed to stay six months, and I could probably renew that while I'm applying for a visa to stay. I'll be fine for money; I'll have my golden handshake and the proceeds of my house. Meanwhile I'll still be domiciled at Da's house in Dublin for tax purposes while I'm starting up my Web business as a genealogical conduit—"

"As a what?"

"You'll like this bit. You know how you get pestered with queries about great-grandmothers who might have lived in Huron

County? Well, it turns out heritage-hunting's the biggest hobby on-line—if you don't count porn or gambling," Síle conceded—"and people will pay surprising amounts for help tracking theirs down."

"Not to undermine you, sweet thing, but what you know about history—"

"Could fit on my gusset, I know. I've only just learned to spell genealogy and what a GedCom file is. But my job will be to link up clients in Iowa or Melbourne with researchers in Lyons or Water-ford or Minsk or wherever," Síle explained. "It's just people skills and a fast grasp of information."

"Without the vomit in the aisles."

"Precisely! I'm going to call it Origins."

"Yeah, actually," said Jude, sounding much more awake, "I can see you making a go of this."

"Can you really? I might have to hire you as an archival consult-ant. Maybe we can talk about it when I arrive. That's on—" Síle set the receiver down on the bedside table, and did a loud drumroll, then snatched it up—"December fifteenth."

"No way!"

"I've bought my ticket. That's just thirty-two days, thirteen hours, and twenty minutes from now."

She'd been avoiding Jael, till now; she had a childish fear of being talked out of her plans. But that afternoon, when she spotted her friend in a sandwich bar in intense conversation with a blond woman, she decided to get it over with.

Jael blinked, and pushed a red curl away from her face. "Síle, howarya." After a second, she added, "Remember Caitríona, from the office?"

Síle smiled. "You organize Primadonna's music events, don't you, Caitríona?"

"Actually I've been promoted," said the woman with a slightly sheepish nod at Jael, "I'm head of marketing now."

"Marvelous!" It was funny to see Jael as an authority figure.

"Take my chair," Caitríona told Síle, picking up her sandwich and coffee.

"Oh, no—"

"Really, I need to head back and chase up a package."

Síle sat down and helped herself to a mushroom from Jael's plate. "So, brace yourself."

Jael heard her out in untypical silence.

Síle wound down. "Go on, what do you think?"

"What do you think I think?" Jael countered, rolling her eyes. "You got the girl back, without any concessions; she was lying there in the hospital bed, slightly dented but fully contrite. You won by a fluke," she reminded Síle. "So what possessed you to throw in your cards?"

"It's not a game." Síle thought of trying to explain about that moment on Jude's porch when her future had slammed into her like a car. "I don't just want her back, I want her happy."

"Couldn't you have prised her out of her incestuous little hamlet, even?" asked Jael. "Vancouver, Montreal . . . You'll wilt without a bit of metropolitan buzz."

"I'm not going to haggle. What I need right now is to stop clock-watching and live with the woman I love."

"Every fucking folly gets committed in the name of love," sighed Jael. "Women are still such suckers for self-sacrifice. Listen, Síle, love's what makes you miss a bus or stay up all night, fine. But it's not enough of a reason to abandon your friends and spend your prime years chewing your nails in Zilchville, Ottawa."

"The province is Ontario. Ottawa's the capital."

"Come off it. Wake up. You don't have to see this story through like it's *Patience and Fucking Sarah*."

Síle's voice came out so wrathful it startled her. "In forty years, Jude is the best thing that's happened to me and if I have to go to the Rings of Saturn to be with her, that's what I'll do. And if you can't give me your blessing, like I did when you suddenly announced you were marrying Anton, then get the hell out of my life."

There was a long moment. Then—"Okay, bless you, my child," Jael said in her best Father Ted imitation. She dipped her fingers in her water glass and flicked drops at Síle's head, mumbling, "Ominy pominy dominy..."

Síle managed only a small smile. Jael picked up the rest of her sandwich. Síle thought perhaps the conversation was over, but then she saw a dark mark spread on the black tablecloth. Another tear dripped from Jael's jaw. Síle stared at her. "Ignore me," said her friend through a mouthful of ham.

"What—"

"Blame parenthood."

Now Síle was really confused.

"I was never like this before Yseult," complained Jael, pressing her eyes with the back of the hand that held her sandwich. "Having a baby, it cracks you like an egg. Leaves you so bloody permeable. I cry when the child gets a mouth ulcer, though I don't let her see me. I cry when I'm listening to the news in the car, sometimes."

"Oh pet—"

"Don't you *pet* me. Yseult's growing up so fast, she'll probably swan off to Thailand any day now. Nobody stays in one place anymore. Call yourself my best friend, fecking off to Canada."

Síle reached to grab her arm. "I'm really sorry."

"What good does that do me?" Jael's wet eyes met Síle's, for a long second, then she produced a horrible grin. "Besides, you are not sorry, you're a woman on a mission. You're wetting your knickers with excitement."

"I love you to bits, you know. Do you believe in long-distance friendships?"

Jael put her head back and groaned like a walrus.

———

Telling people was like breaking the news of a terminal disease, Síle found. Only in this case, of course, it was her own fault.

Shay stared at his daughter at the other end of the sofa. "Moving to Canada? Fully? So...you two must be in for the long haul."

"That's right, Da," said Síle, hiding her irritation. Why did no one believe any two people felt strongly about each other until they set up home together? And why did these metaphors—*going the distance* was another—have to make love sound like trucking?

"Till death do you part?"

"That's the idea," said Síle, dry-mouthed.

"Well!"

She'd been afraid he might scold her for impulsiveness, but he claimed to be very taken by her business plan for Origins. She was glad he was taking it so well, but also absurdly hurt. How could her father be so urbane about this when her friends had given her such grief?

"Certainly you couldn't have picked a nicer girl than Jude," he murmured.

"I didn't pick her," Síle said. "I never imagined someone coming along and knocking my life into a spin."

"Ah well," said Shay. The pause stretched. "Of course I'll miss you terribly, but that's by-the-by."

Her wail burst out. "It's not by-the-by, Da!"

They were holding hands. "I only mean it's neither here nor there," he told her. "No parent would want to clip your feathers... It's our job to raise you right, then stand back and see you launched on the wing." Her father put his hand to his watery eyes, and she noticed, for the first time, the dark insignia of liver spots. "No, it's an excellent idea to change country. Gets you out of your rut."

Shay had lived all his adult life in Monkstown. "Did you ever think of living anywhere else, Da?" she asked, expecting him to shake his head.

"Tanzania," he answered promptly. "The time I was there, on

Guinness's business—I've never felt so relaxed. You didn't have to dither among fifteen kinds of toothpaste or pore over a bus schedule, you just asked, 'Is there toothpaste?' or 'Is there a bus?,' and if there wasn't, too bad."

On impulse, Síle asked, "How long did it take for Amma to adjust?"

He looked blank.

"To the new weather and religion and everything, here in Ireland. It must have been a strange time to arrive, when the Irish were fleeing the country as fast as they could."

"In 1961 Kerala was on the brink of civil war," Shay reminded her, rubbing the bridge of his nose where his glasses had left a mark, "so there was really no question—"

"No, I see it made sense for you two to settle here rather than India," she interrupted, "I'm just wondering how fast Amma got through the blahs and actually felt at home."

"Hard to say."

Was it making him sad to harp on his marriage, she wondered belatedly? Widowed at thirty-seven.

"But this move of yours will be a great adventure," said Shay. "There's an Indian proverb, something about a bridge..."

"We can probably find it online," she told him quickly. She hated to see her father fret over memory lapses. He was seventy-five; what was male life expectancy nowadays? How many years would he be around, after her departure?

He snapped his fingers. "'Life is a bridge,'" he quoted. "That's it."

"That's it?"

"Hang on. 'Life is a bridge: cross over it, but build no house on it.'"

That left Síle uncomforted.

She kept a list of tasks on her gizmo and updated it hourly. She worked out the final details of her redundancy package with the airline. (It turned out that in the teeth of their union's protests, sixteen hundred of her fellow flight attendants were fleeing too.) She tidied her house—taking down at least nine-tenths of what was hung on the walls, on the estate agent's insistence—and it sold in three days, after a bitter bidding war between a child protection officer, a cellist, and a director of an Irish-language reality TV show. Neighbours stopped her in the street to tell her how much she'd be missed, and to ask who was moving in, *and are you really sure you're sure now?*

The whole thing had the unreal feeling of a dream. Some days this emigration project made Síle feel like a smuggler, or a giver of gifts; Joan of Arc with a gleaming, noble face. But other days she felt dull and floppy as she faced the stack of paperwork to do with her job, the house sale, Petrushka's rabies certificate, the thousand unromantic details. Occasionally she caught herself thinking *Jude, you're going to owe me big-time.*

She went through her possessions, dividing them into three piles: Canada, Da's Attic, and Give Away. The Canada pile got winnowed down to winter clothes, shoes, a few small pictures, and the gadgets she always traveled with. Two suitcases, plus Petrushka in her travel box as hand luggage: It wasn't much more than she usually packed for going on a week's holiday.

"Are you going to let me mess up your austere house by hanging up my gaudies?" she asked Jude on the phone.

"Anywhere you like."

"Oh, you say that now, but you haven't seen the barbed wire crucifix I picked up in Louisiana."

On reflection, she put the crucifix into the Give Away pile.

"People keep telling me that emigration's a great opportunity to reinvent yourself," she said to Orla, over artichoke soup at a café counter.

"Really."

"A chance to shed accretions," Síle went on, feeling like a poorly scripted TV ad. *Come on, Orla, work with me.* "Did you find that, in Glasgow?"

Orla sipped her soup. "I don't think I'd gathered many accretions by twenty-two. But yeah, I suppose I made new friends there."

Politicos, Síle remembered; Orla had even sold *Socialist Worker* at demos for a while, and brought a boyfriend home who'd done three months for throwing eggs at an M.P. So when had respectability hardened around her sister like amber around a fly?

"When we were at college," Orla observed, "didn't it seem like everyone we knew was moving to New York or Brussels? But then the minute the Boom happened, most of them came rushing home. You've picked an odd moment to leave, I must say; you're pushing against the tide."

"Oh, well that settles it," said Síle, caustic; "I'd hate to be statistically anomalous."

Orla set down her spoon with a clink. "Why don't you just buy a Porsche?"

Síle stared at her. "Why don't I *what*?"

"You've got every other symptom of a classic midlife crisis. Turn forty, start chasing change. Dump the devoted partner," said Orla, counting on her fingers, "take up with some exotic young thing, jack in an excellent career, and flee the country!"

There was a strained silence. "Bitter old cow," said Síle under her breath. They were seven and nine again, and somehow they were laughing.

Some days, as Síle puzzled over Canadian government Web sites and browsed through the *Globe and Mail* online, she felt adrift in confusion. What was this Canada she was going to humbly petition to be let into? She'd only seen a couple of square miles of one of its provinces, a couple of times. The country was 142 times the size of Ireland, but with only eight times the population, a full quarter of them immigrants. Bilingual, in theory. Liberal and diverse; cautious and provincial. Sport-fixated, snowy, scorching; a sedate Stepford with a Wagnerian climate. Red leaves, good manners, civil rights, God Save the Queen, doughnuts. Socialist, Americanized, dull or a thrill, Síle had no real idea yet, and besides, all that mattered, in the end, was whether she and Jude would master the trick of being happy together.

As she sorted and packed, she was listening to a lot of trad these days, sorrowful ballads of exile that she'd once derided as Celtic schmaltz.

Till sad misfortune came over me,
And caused me to stray from the land,
Far away from me friends and relations,
I followed the black velvet band...

But the people in the songs had been forced to go, by the Queen's soldiers or the Famine or plain old poverty. Síle was choosing to go; shouldn't that make it easier?

She drank strong homemade chai as she looked through her mother's Netturpetti, her rosewood and brass treasure chest that still smelled of sandalwood after all these decades. Shay hadn't asked for any dowry, Síle remembered, but the Pillays had insisted on giving one, in case the Irish might look down on their daughter. What were the six hundred souls of Ireland, Ontario, going to make of Sunita's daughter? How far would a bit of blarney get her?

It occurred to Síle now that it must have been her father who'd divvied up Sunita's possessions between their daughters after her death; had he done it at random, or guessed what each girl would like best? Orla had inherited the pearl, enamel, and stone bracelets, the sandalwood figurines, the traditional metal lamp and bronze hand mirror. Also all Sunita's red, gold, and white woven mundo: Orla had sometimes draped herself in them for a fancy-dress occasion and looked like a maharajah's wife. Síle had been given the Netturpetti and lots of gold jewelry including the delicate Aranjanam she kept strung around her waist, plus a model snake boat and caparisoned elephant (her favourite of all, when she was a child). And the thing that meant the most to her now: the tiny gold leaf that had been strung on the holy nuptial thread, at the Hindu ceremony in Cochin forty-three years ago, before her parents' Catholic wedding, and which still dangled from its thread today, very bright against Síle's hand.

Kneeling beside her lemon yellow filing cabinet to sort papers for storage in her father's attic, she let herself glance through some bundles of old letters from pre–e-mail days. She noticed wryly that she'd used rubber bands to hold each correspondence together, so the effusions of one lover wouldn't get mixed up with the yearnings of another. The paper was yellowing already, like ashy remnants of the hot flesh. How awkwardly she turned the pages, like a nervous researcher who knew the head librarian was watching over her glasses! She didn't recognize some of the handwriting; this felt like spying on strangers. She was trespassing on her own sealed-off past.

She'd kept printouts of some of her replies. *You're the most beautiful woman in the world,* someone signing herself Síle had written in a distant time and place to Carmel, a not particularly good-looking art student who'd been settled for many years now in Dorsetshire with a veterinarian named Pete; they sent the occasional funny Solstice card. Síle had sworn *I'll never get tired of writing to you* to a Heathrow-based gate agent called Lorn, and that flurry of correspondence had died out three letters later, before they'd ever got near to reaching consummation. (The last letter never gave any indication of being the last one, she found; you just turned over the page and there was the void.) She was particularly embarrassed by overlaps in time, such as the valentine posted to Síle by one woman on the very date Síle had started writing to another.

The letters made her both sad and elated: to think that she'd been repeatedly in love, and loved, her heart renewing itself as ruthlessly as a snake sloughed off its skin. She skimmed over the hectic paragraphs, now; she didn't want to slow down enough to be caught up in any old spell. The letters were like a riddle because they captured moments but never explained what happened between one letter and the next to make love or rage flare up or fade to nothing. *I miss you all day and all night,* she read in a typed note to Kathleen in month three, and she felt moved, and slightly sick.

Other phrases jumped out at Síle, and the terrible thing was, she had no recollection of what they meant.

> *Roll on the 23rd!*
> *Will you ever forget the moment that door opened?*
> *I'll be saving you a y.k.w.*
> *Went to the beach with D, very noli me tangere.*
> *Always your Speranza.*

It was like a wartime code. It was beginning to repel her, the fevered opacity of it.

The worst was when she found, at the bottom of the cabinet under several bundles of letters, a neatly folded pair of white underpants, bearing the faintest marks of having been worn. She had no idea whose they were, though there were only five viable candidates. What did the Síle who'd preserved that little relic have in common with the Síle who loved Jude today? Was she one Síle or a million, an image built up from tissue-thin layers of time?

She suddenly thought of the other filing cabinet, the one on her hard drive, stuffed with every e-mail Jude had ever sent her and every one Síle had ever sent back. She considered some terrible future self who might scroll through them (if their technologies were compatible) and sit in judgment, as if on the dead.

December, and Dublin was the colour of charcoal, the leaves churned to mud in the gutters. She'd usually have bought her Christmas tree in Smithfield, but this year she'd be celebrating at 9 Main Street.

(She'd tried, once or twice on the phone to Jude, to say *Ireland* meaning Ontario, but it gave her a vertiginous feeling, and anyway Jude tended to assume that Síle meant the country, not the village.) Síle forced herself to imagine her daily existence after the fifteenth of December. She supposed she'd work on her business model, and e-mail her friends a lot; maybe even learn to cook. There'd be time for everything—so much time, she'd be tripping over it. *Stop brooding, Síle.* She and Jude talked about it a lot, in a speculative way. It would be a new life for them both, Síle knew, but still she felt alone: Only one of them had to make this journey.

By January, or February at the latest, the purple crocuses would be pushing up under her father's apple tree, and on Deirdre's windowsill. But by then Síle would be locked into the Ontario winter, which wouldn't relent till the heat of April or May. Spring was her favourite season, and she was moving to a part of the world where it lasted about two days.

"We should wake you," commented her father. "I mean, give you a wake."

"I'm not dying," said Síle, too sharply, though she knew that someone with a terminal diagnosis might look at everything the way she did these days, with a hungry, lingering gaze.

"Surely you've heard of an American wake?" asked her father. "In the old days in Roscommon, they'd have it the night before the youngsters were going off on the ship. They'd get the emigrants so fluthered they'd hardly feel the parting."

"Did they call it a wake because they didn't expect to ever see them again?"

"That's right."

"But I'll be back all the time," said Síle, tasting the lie on her tongue.

The Give Away pile was beginning to look like a rubbish bin. How had Síle acquired so much stuff over the years? Tubefuls of posters

she didn't even remember buying; moulting feather boas; six pairs
of scissors! She drove the shabby stuff down to the Vincent de Paul
shop. "For the rest, I'm considering throwing a potlatch," she told
Jael as they dashed through Stephen's Green, laden with Christmas
shopping, toward Yseult's drama studio.

"Oh no," groaned Jael. "Somehow that always means five
troughs of potato salad and no dessert."

"That's a pot*luck*," Síle corrected her. "A potlatch is a Pacific
Coast feast where somebody gives away all their possessions."

"Oh well in that case, bags your Alan Ardiff gold pendant."

"My which?"

"You know the one, with all the tinkly dangly bits."

"That's copper, not gold."

"I still maintain you're going to regret this grand gesture," muttered Jael, picking up speed and switching her bags to her other
hand. "You must admit, changing job and country and all, for a
lover...let's just say it's not a soundly diversified portfolio."

"Could you sound more middle-aged?" Síle taunted her.
"Come on, moving in with someone is always a risk, even if you
stay in the same city. You're putting your heart in their hands. But
who are you to tell me it can't work out? I remember you panicking at your hen night, taking me off to the loos and bleating *Síle,
how can I possibly be content with one person for the rest of my life?*"

Jael grinned oddly. "Anton was the only Irishman I'd met who
was taller than me."

"You play the old cynic," Síle panted, "but actually you're an inspiration to me."

Jael stopped, straightened, put her hand in the small of her
back.

"What is it?" Síle walked back to her. "Have you a stitch?"

Jael shook her head. Her shopping bags were on the ground;
her hand was over her mouth.

"Come on, we'll be late for Yseult's star turn as Dorothy!"

"You're such a fucking innocent."

Síle's forehead contracted.

Jael spoke despairingly. "That's what I like about you, Síle, you have this sort of transparency, this *shine,* and it reflects off the rest of us..."

"What are you on about?"

"When you saw me and Caitríona in the café," said Jael, "what did you think we were talking about? Budgets?" she suggested after a second. "Press releases?"

Síle viewed the scene again in her memory, the heads bent together, red and fair. She felt so mortified, she had to turn her face away. "You mean—"

"One person isn't enough." Jael spoke the words as if giving dictation. "Not for a lifetime."

"Oh, Christ."

"Or maybe it's just me." A violent shrug.

"Are you—are you and this Caitríona—does she want you to leave Anton?" Síle asked awkwardly.

Jael half laughed. "She's married too, she's got twins going into secondary school. Nobody's leaving anybody."

Síle should have been glad about this, but her chest hurt.

"It seems I need a little bit extra. Something of my own," said Jael hoarsely. "Without it, I swear I couldn't hold it all together: the house, the husband, the job, the child. Maybe I need a secret."

Síle nodded.

"So, sorry to wreck your illusions, but I couldn't bear you holding me up as some kind of bloody role model." Jael glanced at her watch and snatched up her shopping bags. "Come on, we'd better leg it, they'll be halfway down the Yellow Brick Road."

And the two of them broke into a run.

"Mm, it's true, I'm moving to Canada," she told colleagues and acquaintances, "I'm emigrating." Why was it, Síle wondered, that *emigration* sounded noble and tragic, *immigration* grubby and grasping?

Immigrants had everything to prove, with documents or witnesses or even with their bodies: Shay told her an awful story about Indian women, coming to join their fiancés in Britain in the seventies, having to submit to virginity tests at Heathrow. Crossing borders, for so many people in the world, was a perilous business: guns behind, hunger ahead, possessions and relatives scattered. Only the other day she'd been reading about a Palestinian woman in labour, delayed by Israeli guards, who'd given birth in the bushes, and the baby had died. There seemed no limit to what people would endure in order to enter the country of their (perhaps arbitrary) choice: extortion, bureaucratic humiliations, being spat at in the street. One of Orla's Nigerian clients at Ireland of the Welcomes had just had a backstreet abortion because she was terrified to go to England for a legal one while her application for asylum in Ireland was pending. Síle tried not to think of the worst stories, like that tomato truck full of suffocated stowaways.

On the phone, she and Jude had got in the habit of shutting their eyes, pretending they were in bed together, and telling stories. Tonight, Jude had an Inuit one about a girl named Sedna who lived with her father way up north. "She was so handsome that young hunters from far and wide came to ask her to marry them, but she thought she was too good for them. Then one spring when the ice was breaking up, a fulmar flew into the bay and started singing to Sedna."

"What's a fulmar?" asked Síle.

"A seabird. It sang—" Jude put on an eerie voice—" 'Come with me, beautiful Sedna, to the land of birds, where there's no hunger or want. My tent is made of soft skins, and you'll be dressed in feathers; your lamp will always be filled with oil, your pot with meat!' "

"Uh-oh," said Síle. "Shades of Tir-na-nOg. Does she stay three weeks but it turns out to be three hundred years?"

"These aren't the Celts," Jude warned her. "So Sedna climbed on the fulmar's back and it carried her over the sea. When they finally got there she realized she'd been tricked: Her tent was made of tattered fish skin, and all she got to eat was old fish scraps. So she sang, 'Oh father, come in your little boat and take me home.' After a year her father turned up."

"At last. Hurray!"

"He killed her fulmar lover, and he and Sedna set off in his little boat. But the other birds discovered their dead friend and they started weeping and wailing, and they do to this very day."

"Ah," said Síle, "that's a sad one."

"Wait," said Jude. "They chased after the boat, and stirred up a terrible storm with their wings. So Sedna's father threw her overboard."

"He *what?*"

"But she clung on to the edge, so he took out his knife and cut off her fingers, and she went down. Once the fulmars thought she was drowned, they flew home and the storm died down. Her father pulled Sedna back into the boat—"

"Minus fingers!"

"—but she hated him now," said Jude. "As soon as they landed at their own bay, he lay down to sleep. Sedna called to her dogs, and told them to gnaw off his hands and feet. The father woke up with no hands or feet and started cursing; he cursed himself and his daughter and the dogs and the fulmars, too. And the earth split open and swallowed them all up."

"Jaysus," said Síle, into the silence. "Celtic myths are cuddly by comparison. All the Wee Folk do is swap their skinny children for ours, or sour the milk." Then she added, "It's about emigration, isn't it?"

Jude laughed.

"The moral is, never fall for a foreigner and let them carry you off to their godforsaken country."

"You think everything's about emigration."

"Everything is! Last week on telly I saw a random selection of old movies—*Casablanca, Journey to the Center of the Earth, Wings of Desire, Castaway*—and every bloody one of them was about swapping one world for another."

Crossing from Trinity College to Dame Street in a hurry, arms full of rolls of wrapping paper, Síle paused on the traffic island and remembered a similar cold day, twenty-seven years earlier, when she and Niamh Ryan had stood and talked on that spot. Her eyes shut and she was back then, watching white specks land and melt in the orange waves of the girl's hair. Feet gone numb, like Lucy after she walked through the wardrobe into Narnian snow. She and Niamh hadn't been particularly close friends after that day, and Síle had no idea what had become of her since school. Síle had been to the reunions ten years after, then twenty, but Niamh Ryan had never been there. Just as well, really; her hair wouldn't have been the colour Síle remembered. Probably rusty brown now, speckled with gray.

These days she felt as if she were living in a film. Every song she heard on the radio, every random choice her headphones threw at her, formed part of the soundtrack of *Síle's Last Weeks in Dublin*. As the shuttle took her home from the airport, she examined every grubby shopfront or littered gutter as if it were precious. She was often on the verge of tears, for no reason; she caught herself laughing wildly at some crass joke about three blondes a taxi driver told her. *We've all got a past*, she'd told Jude scornfully in July, *but to cling to the spot where it happened is a bit pathetic*. Well, now Síle was clinging like a baby. She walked along old Northside streets, in one memory and out of another, and every corner was a touchstone. Would Dublin miss her at all, she caught herself wondering? To think she'd once claimed to be a citizen of the world, with no particular allegiance to this place! *My arbitrary domicile, my grain of sand.*

"I never bought that citizen-of-the-world stuff," Jude told her on the phone. "Of course you love Dublin. That's why I can barely believe you'll go through with this."

"It does help that you get it," Síle told her.

"Of course I do. *Respect des fonds,* remember? Context is all, and you're ripping yourself out of yours. I'll just have to spend the rest of my life trying to make it up to you."

Warmth like a flush all over Síle's body.

Provenance

Emigration may, indeed, generally be
regarded as an act of severe duty,
performed at the expense of personal
enjoyment, and accompanied by the
sacrifice of those local attachments
which stamp the scenes amid which
our childhood grew, in imperishable
characters upon the heart.

—Susanna Moodie
Roughing It in the Bush

December seventh was Síle's last flight, Heathrow to Dublin. The sunrise was particularly lovely. Yellow light slanted in the portholes as in a religious painting, touching heads, shoulders, cheeks. Síle watched the sleepers, the report-readers, the gazers, the chatters. So many strangers she'd shepherded through the skies. They weren't all rude and irascible, she thought now; she'd been forgetting how many of them sat peacefully reading or chatting to their children.

That sense of slow dropping to earth; the ungraceful scrape and rumble as the wheels caught the tarmac, and the engines screamed. Then a lull, a gliding along the runway. A scattering of applause went up. Safe landing.

The Canadian wake took place that night in an upstairs room in her local in Stoneybatter. Familiar faces turned up from school and college, from the airline (the small handful she would miss, and a few others she wouldn't), from Pride committees, her Italian course, a night class in early French cinema. Deirdre had brought her husband and half a dozen other neighbours. Síle was touched by this turnout, in a city where everyone was always claiming to be madly booked up for months to come. Orla was there, having left the boys with William; beside her, Shay nursed his pint. No sign of Marcus and Pedro yet.

Her old friend Declan was just home after six years in Stockholm, as it happened, and about to take a short-term contract in Glasgow. "We're ships in the fecking night," he declared to Síle with a sloppy kiss. She remembered now that when she'd come out, he'd kept gallantly offering his services if she ever wanted to "give us lads a try."

"What did you miss, when you left?" Síle asked in his ear.

Declan shook his head. "The sad thing isn't the going."

"Isn't it?"

"The sad thing, Síle, is when you come back for a visit and you find yourself bitching about everything. Maybe not the first visit or the second," he said, "but sooner or later you find Dublin isn't home anymore. But nor is the other place. And then you're sunk."

Jael came to rescue her with another martini. "Ah, stop it," said Síle. "I won't remember a thing about tonight at this rate."

"Jael's forgotten everything about our wedding but the hangover," Anton joked, at Jael's side. "Listen, I wish you luck," he told Síle in a more serious voice. "My year in Japan, I felt like a complete feckin' outsider all the time."

"You're such a mammy's boy," Jael told him. "Running back to suck the withered dugs of the Shan Van Vaun!"

She had her arm slung around his shoulder. Husband and wife looked so good together, you'd never know a thing, thought Síle. Did Anton know anything, guess anything about his wife's affair? Maybe he had secrets of his own, unlit chambers in his heart.

Ching-ching: Síle's inner circle were clinking their mobiles and pens on their glasses to hush the crowd.

"And now," said Shay, rising to his feet, "if I might say just a *cúpla focail* about my beloved daughter—*in whom I am well pleased,* to quote the Man Upstairs—"

A hail of laughter. Orla was recording the whole thing with Síle's digital videocam. Síle couldn't imagine when she'd ever sit down and play it back.

"She's going off, as I'm sure you all know, to throw in her lot with Jude, a remarkable young woman whom we wish was here for this knees-up, and we only hope they'll both zip back over the Atlantic to see us on a regular basis."

Síle grinned at him across the room, willing herself not to cry.

"Now you may think I'm going to blab on and embarrass you all night, Síle, but indeed and I'm not. In honour of your mother, who I'm sure is with us in spirit," he said as matter-of-factly as if Sunita were at home with a bad cold, "I'm going to wind up by quoting a marriage hymn from the *Rig-Veda,* the address to the bride, and in this case I'm addressing it to both lassies. 'Be ye not parted, dwell ye here; reach the full time of human life,'" he intoned. "And now I'll dry up." With that Shay sat down, to cheers and applause. He leapt up again, to say "—so that the lady herself can favour us with a little speech."

"I will not," Síle protested, but eventually the pressure sent her to her feet. Her mind was blank. And then she began, in familiar professional tones, her hands tilting forward and back. "Ladies and gentleman, if I could have your attention for just a few moments while I explain some crucial safety features of this aircraft..."

Raucous laughter.

"Seriously, now, folks. Jude sent me a quote the other day that I think is applicable," Síle said, hoping she'd get it right. "It's by some Frenchwoman called Madame de Boufflers; I never heard of her before. Apparently she said *oui,* she'd be perfectly willing to go to England as ambassadress—*if* she was allowed to take with her twenty or so of her intimate friends, and also sixty or seventy other people who were necessary to her happiness."

More guffaws, though actually Síle found the line more sad than funny.

"So if that's all right with you all, I'm planning to stuff you all into my carry-on at the end of the night, because to be honest, if I could bring my nearests and dearests with me, I could live without the rain, the Guinness, or the Tayto crisps." Wild applause. She caught sight of Marcus's shaved scalp at the back of the room, and gave him a wave. "And now, as none of you love me enough to want to hear me sing, I'm going to call on my friend Marcus to come forward—"

But he shook his head very sharply, and she knew she'd blundered, somehow.

"Go on, boyo!" somebody roared.

"Give us a sad one."

Síle's gaze landed on a musical cousin, who was willing to be persuaded to try out the pub's piano, and her neighbour from two doors down got up and launched into a quavery rendition of "The Parting Glass."

She worked her way through the crowd to Marcus's side.

"Sorry I'm late," he said in a voice so flat it alarmed her.

"No bother," she told him. "Where's Pedro?"

"London."

She did a double-take. "For how long?"

An abrupt shrug.

Síle pulled him out into the corridor for privacy.

"He's with James," Marcus told her.

"Who's—"

"Our neighbour, remember?"

"Mr. Organic?" Síle was still bewildered. "You mean—"

"Pedro's never been faithful to one man in his life," said Marcus, gravel-voiced, "but I suppose I deluded myself that I'd converted him."

"Sweetie!" Why hadn't Síle known any of this? Why hadn't she asked? She'd been entirely preoccupied with her own big move. "Is he coming back?"

"Oh, probably." Marcus said it without enthusiasm. "I don't know. We'll see what there is to salvage."

Síle felt an awful dragging sensation. "Was it—was moving down the country too much for Pedro?"

A snort. "I had the impression he adored it. But then, I had the impression he adored *me*."

"I'm sure he did, both. Does," said Síle with some desperation. "I suppose people and places are similar that way, that you can't tell how long you'll end up staying." *Shut your trap, woman, you're not helping.*

But Marcus was nodding. "Yeah, but if love's a country, there's no such thing as a permanent visa. Deportation without notice," he added bitterly. "Free fucking trade."

Síle held him very tightly. Then the door swung open, and "There's herself!" She was pulled back into the party, for big hugs, requests for one last coffee or drink before the fifteenth, the endless, maudlin good-byes.

Only when she was going down the stairs with the last few stragglers did she realize who it was that she'd been scanning the crowd for all evening: Kathleen. Not that Síle had contacted her, but she supposed she'd had an absurd hope that some friend might have passed word on, and that Kathleen would have dropped in for a minute, just to say good luck, to offer some kind of pax, or release—as if life were ever that neat.

Shay and Orla came back to her house to wait for the taxi to bring them to the Southside, since the company said it could be up to three quarters of an hour. Síle made them tea and toast. "It's a fascinating story," Shay was saying, "someone from the Iraqi Children campaign sent me a clipping. This fellow bought a tape on how to do bird imitations, and decided to focus on owls. He tried out his calls in the back garden: *hoo, hoo, tuwit, tuwoo*. And one night he heard an owl hooting back! The two of them sounded identical—at least to his ears—and he was thrilled to find himself talking to a bird, like a boy out of Grimm's fairy tales. Though of course he had no idea whether the two of them were swapping territorial claims, or mating calls, even."

Her father's excitement made Síle smile.

"He kept this up for months, till one night—"

"It turns out to be his neighbour, practicing owl calls," she finished for him.

"What a twit!" said Orla.

Shay frowned. "You should have stopped me."

"I liked how you were telling it. It did the rounds online, years ago."

"But this article was from a recent newspaper," he objected.

Síle shook her head. "It's an urban myth, Dad."

"Ah."

Then she regretted having made him feel foolish. "Which isn't to say it never happened."

"Are you nervous?" Orla asked when Shay had gone upstairs to use what he called the facilities.

"I am of course."

"I worry about you."

"Me? I'll be grand."

Orla was sitting on the very edge of the couch, eyes on the rug. "I know you think you're just like Da," she said hoarsely, "but she's the other half of you, remember."

"Who, Amma?" asked Síle in puzzlement.

"It was the move that did for her, even if it took eight years." Orla didn't look up. "You've always preferred the official version, okay, that's what I tell people myself, because it's none of their business. But I've always wondered, Síle, do you actually believe it?"

Fatigue had Síle in its grip; she wished the taxi would come. "What are you on about? What official version?"

"Oh come on," said Orla. She glanced up the narrow stairs, but there was no sound from the bathroom. Her fingers formed quotation marks. *"Our beautiful young mother died of diabetes."*

"But she did."

Her sister spoke in a furious undertone. "Tell me this, then: How come she managed just fine for two years after being diagnosed as Type 2, then when Da took us away for a long weekend she just so happened to lapse into a terminal coma?"

Síle's throat hurt. "The signs of low blood sugar aren't always obvious; I read this article..."

"Oh, Síle, cop on." Orla counted on her fingers. "Tremors, sweating, headache, dizziness..."

"Confusion! Confusion is one of the main symptoms—"

"What, with no warning, all at once she was so utterly confused that it never occurred to her to drink some juice? She kept sweets in her purse, in the car, in the kitchen drawer! I remember nicking one and Dad told me off, they were our Amma's special medicine for emergencies."

"These things happen," said Síle, almost stuttering.

"Yeah, mostly to stoned rock stars," said Orla. "Or to depressed immigrants who pack their family off down the country and take a triple dose of insulin."

Síle was shocked into silence. Then she put her face very close to her sister's. "You're paranoid. You're making this up. You were only five!"

"Old enough to notice that Amma was one of the walking dead. She'd got really fat, lethargic; did you never wonder why there are no pictures of her from the final year? I'd come home from school that winter and she'd still be in bed." Orla spoke in a rapid whisper. "Back in my teens I figured out, there's only two logical options: Either she took too much insulin or she starved herself all that weekend. Maybe she thought if she just curled up in bed and ate nothing, it wouldn't count as suicide."

The word hit Síle like the boom of a boat.

The sound of a flush, the tap running. The sisters stared at each other, unblinking.

Shay came down the stairs carefully. "The place looks much better purged of all your clutter, I must say."

"Doesn't it," she managed to say.

A beep from the street, and she pulled the blind aside: Their taxi was here. Orla hugged her too hard and muttered something about meeting for a last lunch early in the week. Síle pulled away from her without a word.

As soon as she was alone, she rang Jude, and spilled the story out in a shaking voice. "I was so oblivious!"

"You were three years old!"

"I mean, since, looking back. I suppose I loved the smiley pictures of Amma in my head, and love makes you stupid."

"Darlin'—"

"It's not that I want to believe it, but it all makes a sick kind of sense," said Síle, beginning to sob. "She must have felt bits of her starting to crumble off as soon as she landed. She settled in Da's family house, with all her neighbours goggling over the hedges; she turned Catholic, stopped speaking Malayalam, got a little less Indian every year. She must have felt she was *withering*—"

"Wait up a second. Even if it's true—"

"It has to be true, damn it," she shouted. "Orla says Amma was so depressed she stayed in bed all day. It's just too much of a coincidence that she'd fall into a coma the one weekend we were away!"

Jude's tone was reasonable. "What I want to know is, why would your sister drop this bombshell tonight, of all nights in your life?"

"She was warning me."

"What, that if you emigrate you're doomed to despair like your mom, even though your circumstances are totally and utterly different?"

Síle felt rage like spit between her teeth.

"It just sounds to me like Orla's trying to punish you for leaving."

"You don't understand."

"I—"

"Look, you've won, all right? I'm giving up my whole family for you; don't slag them off as well."

A silence, as loud as a slap.

"Sorry," said Síle, only half-sincerely.

"I didn't mean to butt in. I'm really sorry about your mom, if it's true."

"Forget it. Thirty-seven years on, what's the difference?"

"You sound tired," said Jude after a minute. "Get some sleep, my love."

"Mm."

Síle turned out the lights, but halfway up the stairs she had to sit down. Her head was a wasp's nest. She wanted to wail aloud for Sunita Pillay, glamorous Air India stew, who'd swapped everything she'd known for a rain-green Dublin suburb: followed her man, gone into exile, surrendered her country and family and friends in the best tradition of womanhood. Who'd done it all for love, and discovered that love wasn't enough to live on after all.

Síle thought of the *cave with only one opening,* the *island with only one harbour,* and panic rose like a wave over her head. The snow girl was melting on the hearthrug. Síle seemed to feel the knife along her fingers, and hear the shriek of the birds as they dived.

Place Markers

Our nature lies in movement.

—PASCAL
Pensées

The last yellow leaves were clinging to the branches that slapped Jude's bedroom window: Persephone had gone back under the ground. Jude always longed for the first snow of winter, and here it was.

In the back of a kitchen drawer she came across a set of tiny heavy silver frames. She went next door to ask Dr. Peterson if she had any idea what they were.

"They're place markers, you silly, for name cards. Hold on to them for when you host a big dinner. Maybe you should have one to welcome Síle: a landing party!"

"Maybe in the New Year," said Jude, grinning.

The village had the air of a dressed but empty stage set. Jude kept looking around and thinking, *Síle will do this, like that, hate that.* Sometimes she could see it, it was just about plausible, and neighbours like Bub seemed to take it as a matter of course that Jude's beautiful friend was moving into 9 Main Street. At other moments she thought paranoid things like *One winter and she'll be off.*

Out shoveling, trying to go easy on her weak wrist, she peered into the bright haze at Rizla coming down the street.

"Hey, you. How's Jet-setter Barbie?"

She hadn't minded the teasing, since Detroit. She knew that the battle was over the minute he'd picked up the phone to summon Síle. "Busy packing."

"You must have worked some voodoo shit on that chick," he marveled. "Emigrating's more than I could do."

"You went all around the world," Jude pointed out.

"Yeah, but I came home. The eagle has landed!"

"So you'd never live anywhere else?"

He shook his head. "Just because I don't hunt or farm doesn't mean this isn't my territory. A Jew's a Jew, even in the Bahamas, but a Mohawk abroad would just be a stray."

"Actually, that's a genealogical term," Jude told him, and when he looked blank she said, "A stray's someone who shows up in the historical record far from where he started. We fill in forms on a database—*young male*," she improvised, "*Michael Buchanan, sty on left eyelid, died in threshing accident, Seaforth, 1893*—and suddenly someone in Ayrshire's tracked down her Great-Great-Uncle Mick."

"Huh. Neat, I guess. By the way," said Rizla, "that settlement came through."

"What settlement?"

He wiggled his right shoe.

"After all these years! When did you hear?"

"A while back. Should be enough to get us unhitched."

"Excellent," said Jude, startled. *A while back? When did he make up his mind to do this?*

"Your gal'll be happy."

"Mm. Now I just need to come up with my half," she said, visualising her bank manager's face.

He waved his hand. "Nah, the thing's done; I talked to the lawyer last week. Told him I wanted a divorce on the grounds of you being a big ol' bulldagger," he said with relish, "but apparently all we need to do is declare we've been living apart all these years."

She was touched. "You could have bought something you really wanted, like a giant flat-screen TV."

"Believe me, I wanted this." He sang falsetto, miming a shampoo: *"I'm going to wash that girl right out of my hair..."*

Not that it would, Jude thought. She and Rizla would always be in each other's hair, one way or another. She picked up her shovel again, worked it across the path with a grinding scrape.

"It's next week Síle's landing, eh?"

"Tuesday," she told him, her grin as quick as a fish.

Jude was utterly distracted. She immersed herself in cataloging, but was troubled by tunnel vision: Every document seemed to be about travel or love. Scandalous mixed marriages between Catholics and Protestants; the expulsion of Acadians from eighteenth-century Nova Scotia; bombastic advertisements to persuade prospective settlers that Upper Canada was a new Eden. In an 1822 collection of games for young ladies, Jude happened across a description of what was clearly a yo-yo, but it was called an Emigrant. The painstaking instructions for use concluded, "It would in fact return of itself into your hand, only that a part of its impulse is destroyed by the friction and the resistance of the air." Jude rested her head on her folded arms and thought about that.

On the notice board outside the museum, she pinned up the latest plastic-coated display:

Some Criminal Assize Indictment Records
for Huron County.
Hockey, Hubert; Uttering Forged Note, 1863
Jardine, John; Attempt to Carnally Know a Girl under 14, 1894
Johnston, Marshall; Nuisance, 1861
McKeegan, Malcolm; Bestiality, 1862
Naebel, Doris; Unlawful Disposition of Dead Body, 1923

Pratt, John; Obstructing Free Use of Railway, 1893
Sturdy, John; Unlawful Voting, 1882

Sturdy, that name rang a faint bell. Wasn't one of the Malones married to a Sturdy, a few generations back? Oh well, it was only voting fraud the guy was accused of, not bestiality.

Canada geese went by in arrowhead formation, honking glumly. Mindless birds, didn't they know it was nearly Christmas? They should have been in South Carolina by now. What were they still doing here, flapping back and forth all day; what were they waiting for?

In the mailbox Jude found a letter from the foundation to which she and Síle had made that application, back in July. She ripped it open right there, on the snow-choked steps. Phrases struck her like darts.

In the current climate, the scarcity of resources is such...
Whether there is indeed a pressing need for another small
museum devoted to the history of Perth and Huron Counties,
given that...

She stared around her at the glittering white that covered everything like a parody of a Christmas card. Her wrist was hurting. She knew she should make some calls, set up a meeting of the board. She could anticipate exactly how Jim McVaddy would denounce her for her failure, how Glad Soontiens would appeal to everybody to just calm down.

The awful thing was, Jude didn't care. Or rather, of course she was devastated about the foundation's refusal of funding, but the thing was, this was the fourteenth of December, and tomorrow was Landing Day. So there really was only room in her head for one thought, which was Síle. Síle coming through the sliding doors at Toronto Pearson Airport, with her cat and her bags; Síle here to stay, somehow; Síle unlimited, miracle made flesh.

No need to tell anyone about this letter yet, Jude thought. *I'll call the board in the New Year; we'll come up with something. New approaches to fundraising, appeals to the community...* But already her mind was sliding sideways to Síle in tall fur-lined boots, slinking down Main Street.

Tuesday afternoon, Jude was at Arrivals, hands tightened on the barrier. Her heart ticked like a clock in a room where someone was trying to sleep. She and Síle had left each other phone messages over the past few days, but never managed to speak. Jude had been waiting forty minutes; put another way, she'd been waiting all year. She stood still, as passive as a ghost.

Other passengers from Heathrow emerged and were greeted lovingly. At first, Jude enjoyed watching them. Then she began to resent every face that wasn't Síle's. Gradually the crowd dispersed, and the flow of emerging passengers dried to a trickle. "Excuse me," she asked a man with a briefcase, "have you come from Heathrow?"

A shake of the head. "Bonn."

Jude told herself not to panic. *She must be coming, she had her ticket bought a month ago.* But that proved nothing, now Jude came to think about it. It wasn't even a piece of paper: Síle always got e-tickets. Just a few letters and numbers somewhere on the Internet, a fragile sequence of code.

She stood where she was for another fifteen minutes, till the passengers from Bonn had all emerged. She clung to rational possibilities. Síle was being grilled by Immigration, having rashly answered "How long do you intend to stay in Canada?" with "Forever!" No, customs officers were going through her bags with probes and sniffer dogs; Jael must have planted some coke on her. Actually, Síle was still at the baggage claim, waiting for a missing suitcase that contained all her favourite clothes. Unless she was ill, locked into a washroom cubicle. Or had come through already and somehow sailed right past Jude.

Jude told herself not to be ridiculous. She waited, stiff-kneed, for another ten minutes. Then she went off in search of a pay phone so she could check her voice mail, in case Síle had left a message.

Driving out of the airport in the looming twilight, Jude felt cold chew at the back of her neck, slide its claw inside her cuffs, deaden her fingers inside their gloves. She talked to herself soothingly as if to someone standing on the railing of a bridge. The fact that Síle was not on this particular flight, because something must have come up at the last minute, didn't mean that she wouldn't be on another flight to Toronto, another day. *Cold feet, it could be that. No biggie. She'll call tonight.* But Jude's heart was a pebble.

Outside Stratford she felt the sickening glassiness of black ice under her wheels, and before she could slow down the skid had begun. How slowly, how gracefully the Mustang lost its grip on the road! She hunched over the wheel, shut her eyes in the darkness. The car came to a standstill, and she opened them; she was facing back the way she'd come. When she wound down the window and looked out, her back wheel was at the edge of the snow-filled ditch. The road was still empty. Jude knew she might have been killed, but she was unmoved. She turned the car around and headed on home.

When she got in, there was no message. Jude didn't tap in that familiar number. What could she say? *I was at the airport, you weren't* seemed redundant. *Where were you?* was pathetic. Instead, she made herself a pot of espresso and sat on the floor by the wood stove, trying to warm up. The coffee beans had been too long in the freezer, she could taste the burn; she knew the difference now.

Bone tired, she lay down on the sofa and waited. She was hollowed out; she was nothing but longing. There was a line from Jeremiah that kept nagging in her head: "There is no hope: no; for I have loved strangers and after them will I go." But Jude couldn't go anywhere, could only stay where she was, lying like a fossil in the house where she'd been born.

———

For three days Jude hadn't gone out.

Gwen left a message welcoming the new Canadian, and inviting the two of them to come watch her hockey game, as the Stratford Devilettes had reached the quarter-final. Rizla left a ruder one, encouraging Síle and Jude to *stop boinking one of these days* and join him at the Dive. There were other messages, to do with various Christmas bazaars and fairs that Jude was supposed to attend; she erased them all.

She didn't see the need to tell anyone what had happened. What was there to announce? A nonevent; a failure; a blank. It wasn't divorce till you'd been married. It wasn't moving out if you'd never moved in. Only some kind of breaking off, like the abrupt silencing of a tune. Only her life cracking in on itself like a rotten tooth.

The predictable feelings filled her—grief, and rage, and fear—but flickered away. Jude found she couldn't even really blame Síle for not turning up on the plane; the whole project had been a fantasy. Síle wasn't calling, but wasn't that exactly what Jude had done to her, back in October? It was all a matter of timing, she supposed. They'd missed their moment; the baton had dropped between their fingers and hit the ground.

To pass the hours, she looked out the window a lot. Ireland had a strange, fictive look to her: an old cracked photo, a creepy ghost town. *What am I doing here, still here at twenty-six?* Jude felt a sudden nausea. Those pragmatic settlers would have despised her for clinging to home. They carried their nostalgia like their framed photos and heirlooms, but they never let it get in their way.

A place was nothing on its own; it hit her now; it was only people who carved it into meaning. She'd misunderstood the old myths. It was when Sedna tried to come home that she'd lost her fingers; it was when he touched his native soil again that Oisín felt his flesh withering away. You couldn't stay in the womb; you had to go voyaging.

Not that Jude had the energy, right now, to get to the general store for milk.

She had no desire to go to work, either. What difference would it make if the Ireland Museum opened today, or tomorrow, or ever again? It wouldn't break anyone's heart. Perhaps with a great effort by all the board members and volunteers, it could crawl on for another year or two. But the fact was, there were bigger museums that covered the same themes, only better. If it hadn't been for Jim Mc-Vaddy's stubbornness about the terms of donation, the museum would never have come into existence; his collection might well be better off in Goderich or Stratford.

Jude had a bath, to kill half an hour, then lay down on the sofa again and shut her eyes. Síle walked through the crazy architecture of her dreams, her hands indicating doorways or corridors or chutes, her plum-coloured lips moving silently.

When the phone sent up its shrill clamour, Jude woke with a start in darkness. She had no idea what evening it was. Saturday? The ringing had stopped, but she felt her way to the hall table and listened to the message.

What she heard first was silence, but she could tell who wasn't speaking; she recognized the sound of this woman's breath in any mood. "Jude? It's me. I—Listen, I'll try you again in a minute, will you please, please pick up the phone?"

Jude put the receiver back in its black cradle and stood very still, holding her breath. She was dizzy, and her mouth tasted foul. When the phone rang again she snatched it up so hard she thumped her cheekbone.

"You must think I'm a monster," said Síle, so near, so clear.

It seemed a year since Jude had heard this voice. She was speechless.

"I hadn't been sleeping," said Síle. "I kept telling myself it would be all right once I was with you. I was all ready to go, on Tuesday morning, I'd booked a taxi. And then I just…couldn't."

"I know," Jude whispered.

A release of breath. "Sweetheart," said Síle, and the word was like crushed strawberries. "I've missed you. I'm sorry I didn't turn up, I'm so sorry."

A giddiness filled Jude from her toes to her scalp. "That's okay," she said, still hoarse. And then, to stop the call from ending, she rushed on: "You know, I never meant to rush you into this whole emigration thing. We can let it go."

"Let it go?"

"For now, anyway. I'm thinking of moving."

"Moving?" squawked Síle. "Moving where?"

"The museum—there's a distinct possibility it's not going to last much longer," said Jude. "A while ago my former boss said there's jobs coming up in Toronto, she'd give me a great reference." She was improvising, but it was all true. "So what do you think—is there any chance that would make the leap possible for you, if we split the difference? Between Dublin and here," she explained when Síle didn't answer. "Could you imagine living in Toronto?"

"Yes, but—are you serious?"

"Why not? I guess I could get used to a city if you can get used to a new country." Jude leaned her face against the cold wood of the bannister. "Síle, are you still there?"

"Yeah, I'm right here."

"But I'm getting ahead of myself; let's drop it for now. It's enough just to hear your voice. The thing you have to understand is," Jude went on, the words tripping over themselves, "I feel the same about you no matter where in the world you happen to be."

"Really?"

"From the day I met you"—her voice was uneven—"from the very first day, you've been, you're the only, I mean—"

Quiet laughter.

Jude never knew what small sound made her turn and glance out the glass panel in the front door but there coming up the drive, out of the dark, was Síle, gizmo pressed to her ear. Her suitcase cutting a trail, her cat in a small cage, snowflakes snagged in her hair.

Acknowledgments

Portions of "Home Base" appeared as a short story in *No Margins,* edited by Nairne Holtz and Catherine Lake (Toronto: Insomniac Press, 2006).

For conversations that have left their traces on this novel, I want to thank friends in London, Ontario (Judy Core, Helen Fielding, Alison Lee, Chantal Phillips, Cecilia Preyra, Aniko Varpalotai), Toronto (Kelly Gervais, Tamara Sugunasiri, Marnie Woodrow), Montreal (Hélène Roulston, Wendy Adams, Nairne Holtz), Kingston (Catherine Dhavernas, Helen Humphreys), Vancouver (Philippe Roulston), Rochester, New York (Claire Sykes), Vermont (Sandy Reeks), Boston (Anne Habiby), Los Angeles (Dana Lawrence, Debby Leonard), Sydney (Cris Townley), Dublin (Susan Coughlan, Turlough Downes, Helen Stanton, Katherine O'Donnell, Maria Walsh), County Leitrim (Miriam Crowley, Mel Howes), County Carlow (Deborah Ballard, Carole Nelson), Cardiff (Gráinne Ní Dhúill, Debra Westgate), Cambridge (Janie Buchanan), and London (Sinéad McBrearty, Fiona McMorrough, Diane Gray-Smith). Yana Petronis and her son Josha appear in "Heavy Weather" as a little fundraiser for London, Ontario's Lesbian Film Festival (fifteen years and going strong!).

Big thanks to my friends Arja Vainio-Mattila and Ali Dover for advice on my plot; Ali also took the trouble to trawl through the manuscript for un-Canadian phrasings. My brother-in-law Jeff Miles was my source on all manly things, from cars to fist fights, and kindly critiqued an early draft. Finally, for insights into Dublin today, as well as for inspiring several strands of this story, I want to thank my beloved friend Margaret Lonergan.